MW00883431

Wailing Wood

A Yarn Woman Mystery

By Brooks Mencher

He bargain'd with two ruffians strong,
Which were of furious mood,
That they should take the children young,
And slaye them in a wood.

— Thomas Millington, 1595

A Land of restless spirits

LOCALS — Sheriff Stanton Tully held off a riotous mob assembled at the steps of the Court House and jail this 10th inst.,
preventing the lynching of Mr. Hypolite Dupree, a vagabond
accused of robbing Colbert & Switzer's Livery, and pummeling Edward Colbert nearly to Death late the 9th. The angry
crowd, which included men of prominence in Whitesboro,
disbanded by dawn. The Trial of Mr. Dupree, who is charged
with robbery, assault and attempted murder, is to begin 16
April, the Honorable Eli Trogden presiding.
— *The Whitesboro Ledger, April 12, 1906*

Whitesboro's Main Street was pitted from hooves, and
traces of carriage wheels ran straight until they drowned in
pools of brown water. From his narrow oak desk behind the
plate glass window of the Whitesboro Ledger, Robert Stanley
listened to the clopping of the horses and the creak of carriage
joints as shadows passed down the mire. Outside the warmth

of the newspaper office, gas-jet lights burrowed meekly from shop windows onto Main and Franklin streets, and they glowed in a soft yellow from the living quarters above the shops, casting flickering shadows onto the muddy streets and boardwalks. It was late evening.

Stanley took a deep breath and pushed a stack of papers away, stretching his arms in the process and almost spilling the tin ink bottle. The newspaper would go to press Wednesday evening, tomorrow, and he had barely begun the "locals." Though each item would only be a sentence or two, five or six lines at most, he had reams of them, each scribbled on foolscap and thrust onto a sharp steel hook that hung on the wall to his right near a small shelf that held a pot of mucilage glue. The printer's devils would tear them from the hook and render them in hand-set type, spelling out, backward in their composing sticks, letter by letter, Whitesboro's grand history.

Outside the polished storefront windows of the Ledger, Stanley could see three men lead a horse, half running, across Main to Franklin in the obvious direction of Switzer & Colbert's Livery and Feed, but in the darkness they looked like the shadow of a centaur. Stanley, the editor, wondered about the horses' owners — were they visiting, were they somebody's relatives? Were they *somebody*?

The light of his oil lamp seeped out onto the street as he dipped his pen carefully into the ink and scratched down the first of his locals — the arrival of the steamer Noyo at Whitesboro Harbor and the departure of the Townsend II, bound for San Francisco two hundred miles south of the thriving but isolated lumber town, laden with redwood millwork from the mills at Whitesboro and at Soldier's Point to the north. The original Townsend went down some thirty years before, making it all the way from Whitesboro to the Golden Gate before meeting its doom with all hands aboard.

The Amethyst, yet another "doghole" schooner, named for the small ports they plied, would arrive late Friday or early Saturday, and aboard it would be the visiting judge, the respected but dreaded Eli Trogden.

More shadows flitted across Stanley's field of vision, racing down Main and into the night. He knew of the judge's arrival and he looked forward to reporting the results of the court cases, especially the beating of poor Ed Colbert. Luckily, Colbert's young family had escaped without harm, but Ed would probably never walk again. He might not speak or think again. This had happened in Whitesboro; it had been a shock. It had been very bad.

Maybe such problems resulted from living so near the restless sea, thought Stanley: Violence had always been a way of life here, and Whitesboro's many unsettled spirits seemed to wring their hands on street corners rather than sleep comfortably in the old graveyard south of town. It was the sea ...

But what a time, he thought, this year of 1906, at the dawn of the new century.

Two more shadows slipped across the street, their ghostly shapes briefly and partly caught in the nimbus of Stanley's oil lamp. These night phantoms were heading to the Redmen's Hall, Stanley realized, a block beyond the livery, the new hall, three stories tall with a full auditorium and vaulted ceiling whose carved redwood moldings were gilded and glowing — a fine addition to the civic heartbeat of the community. And yet, and yet ... Stanley didn't agree with this separation of "red" men, "yellow" men, "white" men. Coloration was a strange notion, but not one he could openly discuss in Whitesboro.

The lantern was throwing coke onto the flue, so he turned the wick up. He placed his pen at arm's length near the ink bottle, glancing back at the neck-high cabinets of shallow, sectioned wood trays of cold lead and woodblock type. Someday, maybe, he'd have a Linotype back there near the stairwell. He'd heard of them, and seen an engraving of the magnificent machine at the New York Herald. He was grateful for the exodus of the older printing equipment from the East to the West, and he would wait for his Linotype just as he'd waited for the flatbed press.

He needed some fresh air before climbing the stairs to his wife and his home above the Ledger office. He stuffed some rough-cut Tennessee tobacco into his thick briar pipe, lit it and closed the door behind him.

Walking a block south, Stanley looked down Main and, turning his head up Fourth, was still amazed at the elaborate lights of the Grand Hotel, a staggering four stories tall and en-

3

compassing almost an entire city block. How fast it had all seemed to grow, the hotels and liveries, the saloons and even the brothels — still prosperous despite the city's anti-prostitution ordinance, despite the predominant Catholics and the number of small Protestant churches lining the streets, and despite the prim morals of an industrious middle class that had taken root in Whitesboro City.

Turning down Franklin to Laurel Street, he could see the brilliant lights of the Pavilion, its two amazing turrets hovering over the Victorian street on either side of the bright marquee. The first floor was brightest; the lights from the second and third floors wavered. Stanley could hear laughing and the tunes of a mandolin band carrying out into the night. People were milling around near the two brass-edged doors. Inside, scores of revelers were roller skating, laughing and whipping across the bright maple flooring, singing, skirts flying. That would be maple transported from the East by rail, Stanley thought, almost to the Pavilion's doorstep. There was so much merchandise coming in by rail, all from the East and South: bolts of cloth, and wool, and machines of every kind ...

Stanley should have brought Amelia out with him. On Friday, he would, even at this hour. They could walk hand in hand through Whitesboro.

Another dark mass raced across Laurel Street toward the Redmen's Hall. There surely had to be a meeting, Stanley thought, but he knew of every public gathering in Whitesboro — and attended most of them. He knew there was no official meeting, but he followed the shadows.

The heavy door in the front of the hall was locked. Stanley tried it only once, quietly, not wanting to disturb the occupants and feeling uncharacteristically uncomfortable about it, and then he walked around the side where he saw a light from a basement-level meeting room window. He peered in, brushing his mustache against the cold glass, coming away wet.

There must have been fifty men inside, and maybe twice that because Stanley's view was obstructed by an inside wall. One man was speaking, but his voice was muffled. It looked like Phil Crowley, a union man. Stanley began to make out the faces of the others as well: Will Perkins, the Wells Fargo agent; Dr. Brown; Will Jackson; Andy Geslaf; Eri Huggins, the postmaster and proprietor of Huggins Cash Store; Tom Gallagher of the Knights of Labor (Gallagher hated the influx of Chinese immigrants and made no effort to hide both his disdain for the people and his love of the Chinese Exclusion Act, which had passed a few years ago); and the Bucholtz brothers, John and Oscar, owners of the Pavilion. Why were the brothers away during a rousing night at the Pavilion? Although Stanley could not make out the speech, the men were obviously agitated. There was a palpable rage, felt even through the walls of the hall.

Inside, the men raised their fists to the air or spread their arms wide in expression. Stanley could hear shouts, but couldn't make out the words. As he watched, a consensus seemed to be reached. The voices stopped and the gestures grew still.

The big front door creaked open and a blade of light cut across the plank porch. Stanley raced along the side of the building and quickly crossed the street where his view was clear but he couldn't be seen. The blade widened and the mob poured silently into the street. The men milled around a few minutes before turning west to the courthouse. Stanley could clearly make out the dull glint of blued and browned steel — the barrels of rifles and shotguns — and the varnish of axe handles shimmered in the light of many lanterns. Like one massive creature, the men lumbered to the intersection of Franklin and continued on, gathering below the white marble steps of the courthouse on Main, five long blocks from the Ledger.

A lone figure waited at the top of the courthouse stairs. He'd been there for some time, expecting the crowd, waiting for it, growing impatient at its pathetic slowness. The thin shadow flicked a cigar ash onto the step beside him; the crowd assembled, mumbling. Stanley could just make out the first few men separating from the front of the mob like the antennae of a giant insect, stepping forward to address the solitary figure on the marble steps.

"Stan," growled the foremost portion of the creature.

"Time for folks to be home," was Sheriff Stanton Tully's stiff reply. He sat down on the steps, pulled another short cigar from his vest pocket and lit it from the first one, which he crushed under his boot. Stan Tully was a short, nearly emaciated man, but disproportionately strong and mean. His cheekbones were prominent and high, providing a sort of crag on which his steel-gray eyes could settle and smolder.

Tully looked down at Phil Crowley at the front of the pack. He stood up and smiled. "Now, Phil," he said, "I guess I'm standing here on these steps, looking out at the night ... dark out here, I would say, and late, and wet, and I'm thinking maybe I should be home, too. I think it is going to rain again. Is that what you all come to tell me? That we should all be home because of the rain? And if it is, then you're right, and I would wish you a fine evening."

"Stan!" shouted Crowley in a voice that carried well to the back of the mob, "You know damn well why we're here. We got business with a prisoner of yours." Then Crowley's voice rose even stronger so all could hear clearly, "... and protect our own! Have you had a good look at Ed Colbert? My God! Ed's gonna die, Stan. You know what we are here for, Stanton Tully, so you can help or hinder or just step aside." Eagerness spread through the mob, and the men closed in behind Crowley.

The sheriff's alto voice lifted above their heads. "Got an idea here, boys!" he shouted. "Listen! Got an idea there's a trial in just one week on this man you say you want so damn bad. Everything you want to do now is illegal, but it'll be official and legal in a week!" He paused for a moment, looking across the faces, judging the impact his reasoning had made on the minds of these men. "Hell, maybe less, if the judge works on a Sunday. A trial, boys! And you can put wagers on the outcome!" he said. His voice was firm but it wasn't as loud as before, as if he were speaking to each man individually.

"But that ain't why you can't touch him," Tully admitted, his voice softer, personal. He took two steps down toward the crowd, removing the stogie from his teeth. Smoke streamed from his nose. "I got me a good reason to keep the man alive," he said, and paced calmly back and forth on the marble steps as if he were deep in thought and expressing his thoughts aloud for the first time. He spoke confidentially to each of the men and they felt a certain privilege in hearing him. "... We have to keep him alive for the trial," he muttered, looking up as if awakening. Louder now, he said, "So go on out of here, go on home and warm up, and no harm comes to no one. You boys are not giving me those six days till trial, I'm giving them to you."

There was mumbling and confusion.

Tom Gallagher had been standing near the first step and to the sheriff's left. "You can't keep us out, Sheriff!" he shouted only a few feet from Tully. Yet he took a step back, leaving one foot forward.

"The hell," said Tully, almost quietly, turning only half-way in Gallagher's direction. Enough light was cast by the lanterns and especially by Crowley's big ship lantern to show the sheriff's gray eyes. It was clear to all he'd shoot the first man to touch the lowest step.

"Sheriff," said Crowley, standing to the sheriff's right, "we're here in the name of justice! You're only one man, Sheriff, only one."

Tully's voice was firm and carried well to the back of the mob. "Don't you know what I got here?" he snapped.

The men began mumbling and the voices grew stronger, more chaotic. Yet there was a hint of uncertainty among them. Their feet shuffled. They turned to one another seeking some sort of agreement or affirmation, looking for a nod or a comment, any gesture that would reassure them of their mission, their unity.

Tully could smell the change emanating from the back of the crowd. "What I got, well, I'm going to tell you," he said as he began to thread the labyrinth of their confusion. "I am, because I got a big thing here. But first, yeah, you, Phil, and you, Tom," he pointed, "first you got to consider if you can work with one leg or one arm. You boys," he said, raising his voice and pointing to the center of the men, "all you boys be thinking about the first four or five men to climb these stairs, because I'm going to cripple them for the rest of their lives."

Crowley and Gallagher had edged back toward the other men. The sheriff addressed them all. "Now, I'm not even going to try to talk you out of this because I feel like doing it myself." He wiped his nose with the side of his finger. "I'm not going to tell you all about not cold-blooded murdering that prisoner of mine," he said, "because I'm here to see he hangs anyway. Fact is, I'm telling you this sorry excuse for a prisoner'll be on his judgment day in ..." he flipped the ash from his cigar, "... six days."

"And by God, you know who the judge is?" Then he shouted, "You boys know who the judge is?!" They grew silent; the shuffling stopped and the men all faced the courthouse steps and the man who stood there alone. "Got us Judge Trogden! Now that judge is a hard man. He don't believe in prison — not a bit. Do I got to spell that out? Yeah, Phil? Well, I never was a proper speller," he said, and there was nervous laughter among the men. "But see here," he said at the edge of their laughter, "that judge hanged a man for shooting another man's dog! That's the truth, I swear." He paused again and then with a sweeping motion of his arm, said, "Now, get around here because I'm going to tell you a thing here."

The men found themselves gathering around the sheriff, waiting. "First off, I got me a crazy-headed ruffian in my jail. A cold-blooded killer and a murderer. Oh, he's a bad man, my friends. Damned if that poor bastard didn't knock his own teeth out today — on accident. You know, while we was talking." The sheriff waited.

"Hit hisself on my desk!" There was a general laughter, and men glanced knowingly at one another.

"But he had a story, boys." Tully said, his voice low. "He had a story, and I want you all to hear it ... ever one of you ... and your families. He is a crazed man, like I said. Told me right off he was robbing Ed Colbert's money when Ed come downstairs. Oh, he beat poor Ed real bad ... he went crazy and beat Ed within an inch of his life. We all know Ed's crippled for life. We all know he might not live, or might live a day or a week. We all know that. His insides ain't right.

"Crazy ... you could tell." He glared across the faces. "It's in the eyes. Then, after a bit, we was sitting in there, and he just wanted to talk, boys, wanted to tell me everthing ... you understand." He smiled and then the smile vanished.

"So he's trying to talk without his teeth ... telling this tale about hurting Ed and when he was beating on him, when down the stairs comes Ed's youngest, his two youngest, and there they was just standing in the stairwell, and Miss Colbert, you all know Annie, and she come barreling down the stair to save them, save them little ones. So what happens? What does this hardened, murderous criminal do? Huh? What does he do now?"

Tully turned slowly to survey the men. "Now, recollect, them babes was wearing their little white nighties and all, looking like little angels. What does he do? Boys, he starts screaming in fear!" He could feel the shock register among the men. "Screaming that he seen the ghosts! Scared them poor Colberts out of their wits ... the missus!

"And so I'm saying to myself," he said, looking around in a second slow semicircle, " 'What ghosts? Two little-kid ghosts?'

"Now, boys," said Tully, slow and penetrating, "I ask you, whose ghosts would they be?" The silence was deafening. Memories stirred, but could find no harbor. "You think hard on that. Think back, way back about fourteen year ago."

He turned halfway to the door of the courthouse at the top of the staircase behind him, hitching his thumbs into the waistband of his trousers. He began to walk up the steps to the door and then turned back, having abandoned the men, offering no resolution to the riddle he'd posed. Over his shoulder, he said, loud enough to carry to the back of the crowd, "And that's why I want you to wait till trial. That devil I'm holding in jail, right behind this door and down them marble stairs, has got a story to tell ... not just a story of his beating poor Ed Colbert, but a story of murder. He told me a tale of murder, boys, and I want you all to hear. He took those children, to the wood, and he killed them fourteen year ago on that cold winter of eighteen and ninety-two. You'll hear it from him, boys, while he's still alive ... hear it from him if I have to beat it out of him at trial.

"And I say good night to you." He walked to the door, entered and closed it quietly behind him. The sharp snick of the door latch could be heard, but there was no sound of the lock being thrown, which was unnerving, almost an invitation.

The men outside, like the mist from the sea, faded and vanished. Only Robert Stanley was left standing near the courthouse. He slowly walked back to the Ledger, looking up briefly at the gas lights of the Grand a few blocks west on Fourth, wondering which room would hold the traveling judge and wondering if Judge Eli Trogden was really such a terror and if he'd really hanged a man for shooting a dog.

He sat once again at his desk, his hands warming at the freshly lighted lamp, and he turned to scribble down the evening's events. He raced back through the years, as Sheriff Tully had instructed them all to do. He had to remember — he was Whitesboro's historian, after all. Back fourteen years. He looked at the shelf that held the volumes of the Ledger, every edition since 1861; forty-five years of Whitesboro City, half of it compiled by his father. He pulled down the books of 1892, and with them came the brief, fond memory of working with his father that year. He began leafing through the pages, the winter months, but then he stopped, no longer needing the book. He remembered ... so clearly. The shock penetrated even to his feet. He rose stupidly, reaching for the cabinet where he kept a small bottle of brandy. Memory was sometimes a terrible thing, and so was the death of children.

Mike Franzetta's Very Long Day

Desmond Blake III looked at the red light flashing on his phone console, then peered down through the glistening office windows at 555 California Street, overlooking the financial district of San Francisco in the hard light of the late afternoon. The shadows were defined this time of day and this time of year, deep autumn, adding layers of depth to the ecru-colored sides of buildings that fell sharply to the street fifty-five stories below. He could see a lot of traffic, as always. And construction, always. For decades, men milled around down there like insects, working on the sidewalks and streets, and working under them ... labor that was never finished. Delivery trucks squeezed through the barricades, barely.

It was quite a view. Amazing, he thought, what a BA from Harvard and an MBA from Stanford could buy — a lot of fives, actually, from the number on the building to the floor on which he stood. Lucky fives.

He looked back at the console, remembering when phones actually looked like phones, and when you spoke directly into them instead of into the empty air. But that past was thankfully long dead. "What is it, Mrs. Carlson?" he said. He stepped back from the window, his black walnut desk behind him, his wool-silk suit without wrinkles. His reflection in the window looked strong and slim, his graying hair thick and masculine.

"It's Mr. Franzetta, Mr. Blake," said Mrs. Carlson's air-voice.

"Fine," he said, the flatness of his own voice catching him by surprise. He looked away from his reflection. "Thank you, Mrs. Carlson." That was better, much better in tone, he thought.

Franzetta wouldn't call unless he absolutely had to. Friction between the two men was putting it civilly. Mike Franzetta's gravelly voice filled the room, projected by an invisible Bose multi-speaker system. How could such a gruff, crude, uneducated voice sound so full? The miracles of expensive audio technology, thought Blake.

"Hello, Mr. Blake. Franzetta here. ... Mr. Blake? Yeah, I'm afraid we have another slowdown." The voice paused briefly. "Some skeletal remains turned up when the boys were grading a roadbed in the harvest area. You asked to be informed of anything unusual. ... They say they found a kid's skull late this afternoon, apparently. Some clothes, they say. I'll go out in the morning. Well, that's the score." There was little friendliness in Franzetta's delivery, and certainly no enthusiasm in this mandatory phone call to his new master.

Blake walked over to his desk and sat down, the leather of his chair hissing under his sculpted weight. "Unfortunate," he said aloud, fighting the urge to raise his voice slightly for the hidden microphones. There was no need for that. He could whisper and his voice would be picked up. "Mike, are you saying the archaeological records check was incomplete? Mike?"

"No, that was as good as it could have been," said Franzetta. "Our RPF was thorough, always is." His defense was already prepared. These calls were always a game. "Paul Grassi found three sites on the walk-through, and everything was mitigated weeks if not months ago." Franzetta simply wasn't going to say Registered Professional Forester to Blake; it might be taken as condescension, and if it wasn't, Franzetta had no reason to be responsible for Blake's continuing education about the timber industry. For the millions Global Resources had put into its theft of 300,000 remnant acres of what used to be redwood and fir, Blake could look up RPF on Google.

"Missed something in the field survey?" said Blake, his tone irritated.

"Nothing that was physically visible. So, no. This here couldn't of been avoided."

"That was Grassi? The forester? I thought his field survey was supposed to have found anything like this. My understanding is that he's supposed to be the best — second generation forester and all that." Paul Grassi was Northern Timber's only remaining registered professional forester. At one time the company had a staff of five, but after Global Resources (Desmond Blake, Regional General Manager) acquired the historic White County timber company three years ago, the foresters' bags were packed for them and the door was shut firmly upon their exit. Any work Grassi couldn't do alone was contracted out at considerable savings.

"There wasn't the slightest indication," said Franzetta. "Anyhow, Grassi's certified for any of the archaeological work we have to do at this point. Like I said, I'll run out there in the morning and take a look." There was a silence of ten or fifteen seconds, which Blake often inserted, as if conducting an employment interview. It was an effort to have the other party offer more information.

Franzetta sighed, then said, "I don't know whether it's native remains or settler, yet."

"Okay, Mike." By now, Blake was tipping back in his chair. "Have the procedures been followed to the letter? I don't want another oversight to land us back in court, Mike, and more importantly, I don't want anything covered up. Not a mote of dust, this time. Are we clear on that? Everything aboveboard? Remember, the system was set up to facilitate the work, not impede it. You old-timers never did understand that. And I've about had it with the court system. We're talking a couple of hundred million dollars here, Mike, and we're going to feel it even if they only manage to shut it down for the winter. I don't think I need to say much more."

He paused. Franzetta waited in silence.

Blake finally picked it up again. "I want us to be seen as true stewards of the land. Let's not give Senator Pike an excuse to make another damned tree park. And Mike, he's your damned senator, you know. And it's the Honorable Hugh Pike who could do it, too. So," happily now, "let's look good and cut it cleanly, okay?"

Cleanly? Cleanly? thought Franzetta.

Hugh Pike, California's junior senator, was raised on the north end of Northern Timber's holdings in a dilapidated, depression-era town called Grayport about forty-five minutes north of Whitesboro, and part of his election platform two years ago was to expand the existing old-growth redwood park system, both national and state. He had a lot of supporters in key places, and among the people as well.

Blake quickly called up a map of the harvest site on his PC, which manifested simultaneously on a six-foot-wide high-definition screen on the wall to his right. The glass windows of the office photo-darkened to allow easier viewing.

"I want you to hire a professional archaeologist for this, Mike," he said. "Forget the Grassi guy."

Franzetta's blood pressure rose. "Mr. Blake," he said, obligated to take a stand for the sake of his soul, if he still had one, "Grassi's qualified — certified — in that area. His father was on the committee when CDF instituted the archaeological review program thirty years ago. He invented it! And Paul's done it since he's filled his father's shoes. Twenty-five years. There's no one better."

After a pause, Blake's voice returned, softly. "That's not what I said, Mike."

"Right," mumbled Franzetta. The Bose speakers picked up a sigh that should never have been heard. "No problem — good as done."

"Get the guy at Sonoma State, Mike, the one nobody likes."

"But, I can't see him working with us like the others would. He's ..."

"Mike. Look, you don't like anyone, and that's not good for the team. This is a team. Politically, it's excellent to get a guy like this involved. It creates the aura of objectivity, of concern for the land and the law. We need that."

14

Franzetta's face flushed. "Done." Franzetta thought about the old days — three short years ago — when he was general manager of Northern, and not in name only. And what was left? Not much, just Timber Harvest Plan 287, a tract that everyone had called Wailing Wood for as long as he could remember. After 287, there'd just be pole-cutting for chipboard, like shaving what was left on thousands of acres of stubble.

"What's his name, the guy no one likes?" Blake's voice broke the silence that had descended in both offices.

"Miller. Jim Miller."

"Yes. When everyone hates you, Mike, it means you're doing something right. Whatever he finds, mitigate it. Immediately. Yesterday."

"Right."

"It only means that we swap out steel-tracked dozers and remove the logs with rubber-tired vehicles in the area around your little skull. That's all it means. We finally have a 'friend' in the state Forestry Department, and he'll run it all through, priority. Anyway, so we don't drive the rigs over a hundred, hundred and fifty square feet of so-called sacred ground out of 556 solid acres of old-growth redwood and Doug fir. Is that a big deal? Hardly. So that makes something like 247 million square feet of silvicultural resource extraction. A hundred square feet, which is what we're talking about, is something like one part out of two and a half million, right? Ten feet by ten feet?"

He'd made his point, Franzetta thought.

Blake picked up the monologue again. "Who found it? Who found the bones? The road grader?"

"A guy named Bob Cooper. They live just east of the Northern ... the Global ... holdings. He's from an old family."

"What was he doing on Global land?"

"He has historic access," Franzetta said.

"An easement?"

"No, historic access is different. Cooper runs cattle, mostly north and south of the wood in the two river valleys. But he has access across the ridge between the valleys, on the extreme east end about a dozen miles inland, informally grandfathered in, you could say. But legal."

"Did he call the police, too?"

"Sheriff, and no, I don't think he's done that yet. Oh, maybe, I really don't know." Franzetta looked at his watch. "He called me about an hour ago."

"Okay. You call the police or the sheriff or whoever is the hell in charge of bones up there. You're personally going to call the tribal board to send a representative. You're going to call this Miller. And," he decided, "I want a textile man involved. No, stop. Don't even start, Mike. I don't want the sheriff's forensics people left to their own devices. Get me a textile man to look at the clothes or whatever, some academic familiar with the manner of dress ... a couple of hundred years ago to the present."

"Miller would know the clothing, or if there's baskets or whatever," said Franzetta.

"Then have Miller get the textile man. There's got to be someone, maybe from one of the big universities. But have Miller get him, that way it will have no appearance of bias. We need to log those damned groves. And if the tribe wants to hire its own expert, we'll pick up the tab. Understood?"

"Yes."

"Contact the press?"

"The press?"

"We'll just get it all over with at once. Mike, let me tell you, it's a lot easier to control the flow of information if you ask the media along. They came out and took our photograph when Global acquired Northern ... get that outfit." The Whitesboro Ledger, weekly circulation about four thousand in a town of about three thousand.

It was a day Franzetta would never forget. "Sure. The daughter has the newspaper now. Old man Stanley died a few years before the acquisition. It was his daughter that took your pictures."

He didn't remember exactly who she was. "So call her. You know," he continued, "I think I'll go ahead and have Sal and the bookkeeper fly out tonight. They can meet with you before noon tomorrow, check things out at the plant on Sunday and then go out to the site with the gang on Monday."

Franzetta's stomach lurched. He put his hand on the desktop. "You don't really need them," he said as softly as he could manage.

"Why don't you make a reservation for them at that hotel Sal likes so much, the Italian Best Western? And Monday morning — you and Grassi, the sheriff, the press, this Miller, Indians, lawyers, the cloth guy, all of them, meet either at the plant or out at the site. Take them out to the cut. Take them to the bones."

Make a reservation for them. Should he bring them coffee? "Got it," Franzetta said. His mouth was dry.

There was a slight pause; then Blake spoke again. "Mike? I have a little bad news for you here. I've gotten the quarterlies, and we've had the auditors in. The board has opted to dissolve the harvest planning department, forestry. I know this is difficult, but we're going to let your forester go."

Franzetta was speechless. He said, "Uh ... jj ... Oh, I'm ..." He sighed. "Okay."

"The bean counters say we'll save thirty-five percent of the planning budget by contracting it out to the university system. I'm not saying I agree with this ..."

Yeah, right, thought Franzetta. "About Paul. When's this coming down?"

"I want you to wait until the cut starts. Then we'll see. I may do something before that. I'm telling you now so there are no surprises between you and me. I know you'll keep it close."

Blake disconnected the line, brushing his hand along the touch plate of the console. There was a brief hum as the contact ended. He looked at his watch, a Breitling chronograph he'd had for three years, since the acquisition of Northern Timber: It was 7:30 p.m.

Mike Franzetta set the receiver down and pulled out a roll of mint-flavored Rolaids. He picked up the phone to call Paul Grassi and tell him. It would be something concise, like, "Paul, you're fired." If Paul was out the door, Franzetta knew, so was he. Maybe they could go fishing; the steelhead were running. They could get a lot of fishing in, for old times' sake. Maybe even go target shooting with Paul's big pistol, a forty-four magnum Ruger. That was always fun. Franzetta wanted to try it out because he was thinking of buying one like it.

But he put the phone down again. He couldn't do it. He'd known Paul for forty years and worked with him for twenty-five. He'd tell him after Monday. Over a beer.

The Yarn Woman

Ruth M greeted me at the twin glass doors of the Avaluxe Theater on San Francisco's chilly Pacific side, where she lives with her ancient black-and-white cat, Methuselah, a small harpsichord, a textile library that any university would covet, and a truckload of yarn, needles and knitting patterns. The scientific equipment she uses in her profession — she is a textile forensics consultant for law enforcement agencies — is spread from the kitchen, which is just off the lobby on the ground floor, to her living quarters above.

It was four in the morning. I think she had been up since two. Time is not important to Ruth. As for me, my world is upside down anyway because I work the graveyard reporting shift at the San Francisco Daily Bulletin: My days begin about six in the evening. At 2 a.m., I'm usually just leaving work.

Time, which is ignored by the Avaluxe inhabitants, had in response forgotten about the cat, who was now in his twenties. Time had forgotten about the theater as well. The small, wood-paneled lobby was just as it had been in 1925, when the theater was built, (though the ticket kiosk had been moved inside in 1931), and even the carpeting, clay green upon which maroon vines and flowers had been poetically placed, is original. The small auditorium, which seats a hundred, and the twin balconies at the top of twin sweeping staircases, which each seat another thirty souls, have the original purple velvet cushioned seats.

Her flat upstairs, accessed by the north staircase, overlooks the western part of the city — the Sunset District, which was formerly called the Parkview District. It has a view of rooftops and brick and stucco buildings, and a usually overcast sky that rubs itself demandingly against long windows of partitioned wavy glass that was rolled out about the time the place was built. The sole descent from her aerie is along the curve of the north staircase, which moans "Hollywood" at odd times, usually at night when the city is quietest. Both staircases end in oddly carved newels depicting medieval "greenmen" with beards of oak leaves and pates rubbed smooth by nearly a century of very happy, popcorn-fingered moviegoers.

A ticket kiosk is perched between the staircases on what little floor space is left. Originally, the kiosk was outside, but the blowing sand of the old Parkview District — the edge of human habitation at the time — forced a re-evaluation about 1931. It was hauled indoors.

It was the first week of November, the midpoint between autumn equinox and winter solstice, known, at least by Ruth, to be an auspicious date for dyeing wool yarn. After I arrived, we began her annual autumn dyeing ritual. I was very pleased to be included, and surprised because of the very personal nature of her world. Except for her harpsichord, fibers occupy the entirety of her being when she is not working as a forensics consultant for law enforcement. Police call her "the Yarn Woman," and for good reason.

I soon found myself immersed in something she had been doing each year at this time since the age of about eleven or twelve under the tutelage of a Mrs. Reynolds, with whom she lived and from whom she gained the first few volumes of her vast knowledge of fibers. This rite of theirs formed a foundation of knowledge that eventually led to Ruth's textile forensics expertise and her *nom de guerre* among law enforcement. The rite of dyeing wool with Ruth, the Yarn Woman, was, from both our perspectives, incredibly intimate.

The wool she was working with this year was spun at what she called a "micro-mill" in the central eastern part of the state. The fiber was from the rare Santa Cruz Island sheep, she said, a hardy, early crossbreed of merino and Rambouillet that had been on the island since the late 1800s. Santa Cruz Island is now part of the Channel Islands National Park, and its sheep, removed long ago, are now raised in Northern California. The cream wool is fine and soft.

Ruth had already washed and skeined her yarn. The dye had arrived a week ago from the same supplier of madder root that she and Mrs. Reynolds had used years before. The madder-root family farmed the traditional red rootstock in Middle Tennessee, and the madder farming had been passed down the genetic line much like Mrs. Reynolds passing her knowledge and skills on to Ruth.

The root had been chopped, dried and aged to perfection in a Tennessee drying shed that was home to various herbs, including ginseng. The family kept a separate shed for tobacco, and a new one to dry industrial hemp was already half built. All were tended by the well-trained younger members of the family.

This year, though, Ruth's ritual was bound for derailment. To her benefit, she had not begun to prepare the root.

She had, however, begun the mordanting process very early that Sunday morning in the Avaluxe Theater's small commercial kitchen. There, in ages past, delicacies had been prepared for luminaries of the silver screen who attended the premieres of their movies here, in San Francisco. Like the rest of the theater, the kitchen had neither fallen into disrepair nor experienced the melancholy of disuse. It simply lived on in a vibrancy of its own.

She hummed a bit of Mendelssohn's Violin Concerto in E Minor, Opus 64, as she hovered near a pot on the gas range. Methuselah was appropriately supervising the operation from a small rolling serving table, perched on half a dozen newspapers. They belonged to Mr. Kasparov, the building's caretaker and Ruth's longtime friend. The papers were printed in Cyrillic; I don't know if Methuselah reads Cyrillic. I doubt it. From his position, though, Methuselah monitored Ruth's every move, and every move he found satisfactory. Her performance of her duties was just as it should be, and just as it had been rehearsed over many, many years.

The pot had about five gallons of warm water, with the burner barely glowing beneath it. The vessel was large and stainless steel and the walls were thick. It was very heavy, and the steel was bright and looked like chrome. It was of Italian vintage. This had been Mrs. Reynolds' pot, and there were at least three of them, one of them being larger. It was not straight-sided, as one might imagine, but slightly bulbous, with heavy-duty handles not on two sides but on four, for convenience sake. And the water was not ordinary water, either. Ruth had strained rain water through a series of filters in an elaborate system of tubing and vessels she'd set up on rolling shelves in the kitchen, and it looked much like the work of a mad scientist. She had tested the water for iron using a brew of potassium ferrocyanide, but found it, as expected, blueless and therefore ironless and satisfactorily pure.

Using a nineteenth century brass and bronze balance, which also had been Mrs. Reynolds', she delicately placed her hundred-gram weight on the left and began sifting powdered alum onto the dish on the right until the needle registered in the middle. She sifted the alum into the warm water in the vat and stirred it with a large bamboo paddle. After the first order was dissolved, she wiped down the balance and set twenty- and ten-gram weights on the left plate. She measured out the cream of tartar and stirred that into the brew.

When everything was dissolved, she carefully added her yarn, each skein neatly tied with cotton string in four evenly placed spots. Each tie formed a figure eight, which divided the skein into two lateral parts.

She gently pushed the yarn down with the paddle and turned up the burner and floated a thermometer in the vat. Then she cleaned up her scale and put it back in a walnut box with the weights. It went onto a shelf to her left, about chest high. She navigated so smoothly around my rather useless body during the entire operation that it seemed like a dance.

At the vat, she stirred slowly, Mendelssohn still in her head, but the floating thermometer was the focus of her eyes.

So she remained for the better part of two hours as the temperature slowly increased to 175 degrees. She pushed it to 185 or 195 and there she kept it, adjusting the gas knob by millimeters. We had two hours to go, with no variation in temperature. She had done this a hundred times, but only a few dozen during the first week of November, the halfway point between equinox and solstice.

Ruth didn't madder-dye every year. In the "old days," she said, she and Mrs. Reynolds would gather chartreuse wolf fungus from forest floors west of the Central Valley, in the Sierra, and come back to the city (though not to the Avaluxe at that time) and dye their lot in brilliant yellow — once to the accompaniment of a string quartet arranged by Mrs. Reynolds. And there was often indigo; there were wood dyes, mineral dyes, green plant dyes, mushroom dyes (very delicate) and more than once, cochineal.

Ruth's world was one of ritual and memory, and I knew it was no light matter when I found myself a part of it. After we had completed the first phases of mordanting, she made tea and we went out to the quiet lobby. Saying nothing, she took out the knitting she'd stowed earlier in a basket beside one of the chairs on the north side and was soon deep in her meditative work. She aimed a small space heater at her bare toes.

Knitting is Ruth's usual pastime when she's not engaged by law enforcement, not editing an arcane historic pattern collection or not lecturing on her specialty — textile forensics — in some far-off land. Or not dyeing, as was the case that morning. In her hands and amid a symphony of double-pointed threes, was a sock, and its subtle magnificence seemed to embody the fallen autumn leaves through which I'd wandered on my way to her theater in the middle of the night. I am still astounded that a mind capable of such artistry is simultaneously capable of deducing the facts of a sinister crime, maybe a kidnapping, even a murder, from little more than the microscopic or chemical analysis of fiber. But such was the case, as I had personally witnessed, having worked with her on three cases in the last year or so. That is how long I have known her, though I had seen her magnetic green eyes several years before that, only to have lost them in the fog that is known as San Francisco.

The chandelier above the north staircase threw off rainbow-colored sparks that danced along the walls. I took a seat near her on the north side of the lobby and said nothing. I picked up one of Mr. Kasparov's neatly stacked newspapers, avoiding the ones with Russian typography — not because I can't read it, which I can't, but because the black and white cat of hers had already claimed them, curling up on them warmly. Mr. Kasparov, a Soviet dissident and refugee from eastern Ukraine before the breakup of the USSR, is quite a linguist. Russian is his native tongue, though I saw among his newspapers Ukrainian, French, Italian, Spanish, and … I'm not sure what else. Polish, I think, which he learned, he had told me once, from a Polish Olympic wrestler.

We sat in very old but comfortable chairs, the staircase to our backs, the walnut and oak seeming to warm us at the dawn of a cold, overcast autumn day. My eyes were tired but I was not. I put down his Financial Times, which relies on tiny nine-point type to jam as much news on the page as humanly possible. Ruth and I both turned when the heavy glass doors opened, though our vision was blocked by the kiosk.

"Are you there, Miss M? May I disturb you, please?" It was Mr. Kasparov. He poked his nose, as sensitive as it is large, into the lobby. "Are we dyeing this morning? You should have called."

"Second mordant," said Ruth. "I'm mordanting twice to brighten the color. It will be worth it, don't worry. The madder's arrived and it looks great, as usual. The yarn is soaking, for now." Ruth set down her needles and went over and greeted him with a hug. He seemed sad to have missed any part of her morning.

"You have grease on your hands, Mr. Kasparov?"

He looked at his hands. They were gnarled and knuckled, the fingers short and thick, wrists strangely wide-boned. On the right was a small gold watch of unknown vintage. "Some," he admitted. "Nevertheless. Did you get my message, Miss M? I left a brief entry on the cellular telephone I gave you last week." She looked at me, smiling slightly; that would be the phone she texted me on this morning, inviting me to the Avaluxe. She likes phones about as much as most people like hornets.

"No," she said. Only Mr. Kasparov with his trained English called a cell a cellular telephone. And only Miss M pays no attention whatever to cellular telephones and their unwanted and unneeded interference in her life. Fingers, she has said, are not for poking, but were designed for the realization of greater artistic potential.

"What's a milliner who works in red felt and jumps down rabbit holes called?" she asked him.

Mr. Kasparov was not taken off guard. But he stared blankly, waiting for the punch line.

And the punch line came: "A hat madder," she said, waiting for a reaction. Eventually he cracked a smile. He didn't do it obligingly, however; it was sincere. It just took him a few moments to connect all the dots in English.

"Yes, very good," he said. "Very good. A pun. A play on words."

Of course, she hadn't heard his phone message, however urgent it might have been.

"You received a telephone call from Mr. James K. Miller late last night," said Mr. Kasparov. "Saturday, shall we say, 10:33 p.m.? I checked a few sources I know, and we needn't worry about his reputation. He is a noted archaeologist with the state university system, and he was seeking your opinion on a certain matter. It sounded urgent. His center name is 'Keith.'"

She squinted. "I've never heard of him. It's called a 'middle name,' Keith. That's his middle name."

"Middle; I must have misunderstood. Thank you, I hadn't run across the word in use in all this time. Imagine. Middle name, then."

"Well, we've never met. How did he sound? Was he the nervous type or the solid?"

"He's heard of you."

"You don't say. How would he have heard of me? Do you think we frequent the same circles? I doubt it …"

"Yes. He said that he, Mr. Miller, had been hired, contracted, actually, had been contracted by a large timber company that operates several counties to the north, even though there are company personnel capable of doing the work assigned to him. I don't think I understood the distinction fully, but … it is archaeological work: Some bones have been found. Bones, yes. They have been dug up accidentally, from their place of rest."

"This is becoming interesting," she said, perking up, "though bones are not my specialty."

"Mr. Miller, who is distrustful of the timber company that contracted him, called the local sheriff to see if he, the sheriff, had been notified about the finding of these bones. It turned out that he had, for the finder of the bones, not trusting the timber company, called the sheriff first, before informing the company.

"The point is, Mr. Miller is seeking a textile expert, and your name came up."

"Which one knew who I am?"

"Apparently, all of them."

"I take it there must have been clothing in the vicinity of the skeletal remains," she said.

"Yes," said Mr. Kasparov, "cladding them."

"Enwrapping them," she said.

"Yes. Just so."

"All three knew who I am, including the bone-finder? Interesting. One or more of their wives or sisters or brothers or something knits, perhaps. So what's Mr. Keith want? Anything cool?"

"Mr. Miller," corrected Kasparov, though he knew very well that Ruth did not forget names. She forgot nothing, ever. "He left his cellular telephone number and the office number at his academy and the number of the secretary of his department, part of the state university system, and his e-mail and business and residential addresses and home phone number. As you see, he is anxious, though not, I think, the nervous type as you earlier suggested. Quite solid, I would say. He said he saw your recent article in the quarterly, the American Journal of Textile Conservation. Mr. Miller's project sounded ... very cool." Kasparov smiled and folded his arms.

"You left all this in an audio message to me? I'm glad I didn't listen; I'd still be glued to the phone. Would you like tea? Don't answer," she said, and poured his cup. He entered fully into the dim, wood-laced lobby and stood beside his cup, waiting for her to sit down first.

She smiled and sat, and Mr. Kasparov sat. And I, too, sat. She was still in a reflective mood from mordanting her yarn, and then knitting, and she thought Mr. Kasparov looked very little different now than he did when she was twelve: receding hair, very large nose and large, protruding, independent teeth like white stones set in a happy-faced cantaloupe that spoke in a mild Russian accent. Or French, depending on the day.

"Apparently," said Mr. Kasparov, interrupting her reverie, "your Detective Chu is vacationing in the town in question and is acquainted with the county sheriff, being in the same trade, and I suspect he may have dropped your name."

"William Chu?"

"The same."

"He takes vacations?" She looked at me.

"They always went up there," I said, swimming around in my boyhood memories of Billy Chu and me. "His father took them all up there for fishing or hiking once or twice a year, always about now, late fall, when the steelies run. They run twice, usually, an early run and a later one. I went with them a couple of times, seeing as I was practically living with them back then. Junior high years; his father died when we were in high school."

"So Mr. Chu and Mr. Sheriff are probably old acquaintances," she said.

"They are close enough," said Mr. Kasparov, "that Mr. Chu, to the sheriff, spoke very highly of your abilities, and the sheriff relayed the sentiment to Mr. Miller."

Mr. Kasparov sipped his tea. He glanced at the little table around which we were sitting, looking for a cookie or roll, but found nothing. He didn't mention it. He thought about The Miss, and how, really, she appeared to be the same little girl he knew when she was twelve. Of course, he said to himself, she had never been twelve intellectually.

Even had there been cookies, Ruth could see that he was sad this morning. It was in his eyes. He was always sad when she dyed or mordanted yarn because it reminded him of Mrs. Reynolds. Imagine the truth about olfactory memories — that they are the strongest — but then take into account that nose, she thought. My God. "Don't get bummed out," she said, "I can't stand it. I'll get depressed, too."

"Sorry, sorry," he said, forcing a smile. "But, then, to the point. Your Mr. Miller said the following: He is a professional archaeologist, a university professor, and has been called in on a timber harvest plan in White County near Whitesboro on the (this is true Miss M, really) White River ridge. Don't smile like that; apparently the region was settled by a ..."

"Mr. White," they said together.

Mr. Kasparov continued. "A timber harvest plan, you see, is a logging operation. He said some disruption of the soil disinterred a skull, and possibly some other bones, of an unknown age. And, I understand, accompanying the skeletal material is some remaining textile which he was told was fibrous and quite damp or wet. He hasn't seen it personally yet. The find has the potential of stopping or slowing the timber harvest, and the questions are these: Are the remains Native American or not, was it a murder or a natural demise, and when did the person die? And so on."

"It's not a timber 'harvest.' It's cutting. Whack, whack, zzzz with the chainsaws," she said. "Have you seen the blades on those things? You harvest ... corn or something. Wheat. You *cut* trees. You don't harvest them."

"It's technically called a timber harvest," said Mr. Kasparov, his voice hesitant.

"Doublespeak. Don't use the word around me."

Mr. Kasparov brushed some lint off the cuff of his sleeve. "I thought it sounded interesting. The name of the timber cutting plan is Wailing Wood. I find that ... I am not sure ... evocative."

"Wailing Wood. Really? The case does sound intriguing. Does he want me on site, I hope?"

"Yes, but by tomorrow morning. Monday."

"You're kidding. Tomorrow? He calls last night and wants us there tomorrow? What about my mordant vat? Did you tell him I was in the middle of a very important annual festivity here? That's the second mordanting and it has to rest for three days! I'm set up to dye fifteen skeins of Santa Cruz Island undercoat and I've got half of it stewing in alum at this very minute. I mean, this is very big, Mr. Kasparov, very big ... did you indicate the degree of inconvenience?"

"No, actually," noted Mr. Kasparov. "Mr. Miller said Monday morning. I'm sorry. I am only telling you what he suggested."

"I'm dyeing here," she said in her best Rodney Dangerfield manner, apparently already beginning to lighten up and accept her fate.

"It wasn't that funny, Miss M."

"It was very funny, Mr. Kasparov. I mean, I'm dyeing my yarn. It's a joke."

"I see. Actually, I told him you would be there. I have made a professional commitment ..."

She smiled.

He continued. "I hope I wasn't presumptuous. We can leave tonight. They have motels in Whitesboro. It is, I believe, rugged but civilized to some degree. But I think we should call for accommodations."

"Fine. Maybe I should take some things. I have the socks," she said, holding up her current project, "and a sweater, and there's a shawl I've been working on that I should bring. Did it sound like it would be a few days — or longer or shorter? Days or weeks? I'll need the fiber testing outfit, some chemicals ..."

"He seemed uncertain, but suggested the possibility of an extended experience."

"I should bring a robe, if there's room. Did he say why he'd been called in, and not have one of the regular company foresters check it out? They're supposed to be qualified in archaeological matters, you know."

"I didn't know that. Where did you learn?"

"They have to take classes in it to get their professional certification."

"I'm afraid I didn't ask him why he'd been hired."

"Probably because no one trusts the timber company, and they're worried about public relations or, more likely, a lawsuit. They'll expect me to clear the way for them, I'm sure. I guess we can worry about lodging when we get up there; I don't feel like calling ahead. It's off-season, anyway, isn't it?"

"It is the season of 'steelies,' I understand."

"From Detective Chu? Did you talk with him, after Mr. Miller?"

"Yes. I wished to confirm Mr. Miller's level of profession-alism."

"That's very thoughtful. But it's the season of 'Ruth always dyes yarn in the fall,' Mr. Kasparov, as you know."

"I know. I am sorry. But I am sure you would not want to miss this ..."

"You're right, Mr. Kasparov. Thank you. I'll figure something out ... probably have to start over ..."

She was just giving him a hard time, I thought.

"Perhaps you could call ..." began Mr. Kasparov.

"I'll call Julie to finish up with this batch. That way Methuselah will be mollified, too."

Mr. Kasparov hesitated for a moment, and said, "Well, you see, there are two slight complications."

She looked over at him. "You're driving me up there, right?"

"Of course I am driving. I drive," he shrugged.

"Well, then?"

"I must return by Tuesday morning to sign for some parts."

"More car parts."

"Yes."

"That's a problem? You can come back and check the yarn. And play with Methuselah. I won't have to call Julie until later, if we're up there that long."

"Apparently it is not a problem. But I have wood coming as well."

"For the puppet heads." Among Mr. Kasparov's hobbies was a fondness for carving marionette heads and bodies and stringing them as simple four- and six-string characters.

"Yes. And, well ..."

"Don't tell me. You have to go down to the Oakland port to pick up another of your car films."

Mr. Kasparov flushed slightly. Since his affiliation with the Avaluxe, he had begun collecting 35mm celluloid films, which he would watch at his leisure or on special occasions. They were moderately priced, being out of fashion in this Age of Technology, and he shopped internationally, specializing in car movies, which he called "automotive dramas." The shipping costs, due to the tremendous weight of four to eight reels of film in their protective cases, would have been prohibitive had he not received them via tramp freighter at the Port of Oakland. He tracked the vessels en route, though I'm not sure how. A film, obviously, was due Tuesday or Wednesday.

"Blah, blah, blah," she said. "What are you going to do without me?"

"Pine, Miss M. I will pine."

She smiled.

"Well, to go on," he said, "Mr. Miller had been called, he said, by the timber company and it was understood that he would lead the investigation … the digging up of bones, rather than the forester for the timber company that owns the land, Northern Timber Products, which is now known as Global Resources."

Kasparov pulled a small paper pad from his pocket to review the notes he'd taken while on the phone the evening before. He was wearing loose poplin khakis so the pockets were easily accessed, and out with his pad came a rock about two inches round.

"That's my rock," she said.

"I was cleaning. It was behind the chair in the south corner." He handed it back to her.

"Thank you. Someday it could save my life."

"Secondly, Mr. Miller told me that the bone was a skull."

"I see."

"He said it wasn't normal." He waited, letting the words soak in.

"I'm listening," she said.

"The skull, which was found deep in the redwoods, was that of a child."

She cocked her head to the side and exhaled noticeably. Mr. Kasparov had, I finally realized, done everything he could to avoid delivering this final gram of knowledge. He knew the effect it would have. In fact, as he said it, he grimaced as if inflicting a wound on himself or, worse, upon The Miss.

"How sad," she said. She thought for a few minutes in silence. "I don't think I'm really up for this. Turn them down. I really need to work on this yarn. I have almost two pounds of madder, you know."

"I'm afraid there's more," he said.

She waited.

"He was uncertain, but when this person who discovered the situation, a rancher who lives nearby, looked more carefully, it appeared there could be any number of other bones. He said he found no immediate indication of Native American habitation, though the child could be such. The rancher did not relay this information to the company, however, fearing it could spur them into action, that is, to simply cover up the site. To prevent that, he secretly telephoned the sheriff of the county, an individual that this person knows personally ..."

"Whom."

"... and only afterward called the company. In other words, Miss M, I am afraid that a very sad tale has been unearthed up north in the hinterlands, and that there is some degree of intrigue and distrust among the parties involved."

"Okay. We can do it. I've decided now. How can I say no? So it appears not to be a native cultural burial?"

"I gather, though that has to be established."

"I see." Ruth sat quietly, pulling her shawl across her midriff. She felt chilled. She was silent for some time, staring off through the room, her gaze settling on the little greenman on the newel of the magnificent north staircase whose image was reflected in the glass covering a black and white photo of the actor Edward G. Robinson. The photo had been taken there, on that very staircase, beneath the same chandelier.

She thought the greenman had to have been hand-carved, yet the two matched so perfectly. ... She wondered briefly if you could ever trace their origin. Maybe, but you'd never meet the long-dead artisan who created them and added so much life to their puckered faces.

She looked at me, as if waiting for me to speak. I noted that I'd heard of this particular timber plan because it had been in the courts for at least the last three years and intermittently before that. The company had been trying to log it for a decade. "Wailing Wood has a long history of controversy," I said. "But the bottom line is that it's the last of the ancient redwood groves on private, corporate-owned land, the last trees that are still legal to cut. Everyone has been throwing every lawsuit they can come up with to save it, but the company, Northern, which Global Resources bought out a few years ago, has deep pockets and is intent on leveling it. It's maybe six hundred acres. I have notes I keep at work."

She nodded, processing. Then she rose and started up the staircase. "Okay, so when do you want to leave? Tonight for sure?"

Mr. Kasparov replied, "I was told that Mr. Miller is to meet with the parties of interest on Monday morning in the city of Whitesboro, and then they will drive to the site at 6:30 a.m. He will travel from Sonoma State University in Rohnert Park. He is a scholar there. There is a small lodge or hotel at or near the harbor, where Detective Chu is staying. Apparently, the steelhead are running, and the detective is determined to catch one."

Ruth looked at Mr. Kasparov with those intense green eyes, and, unable to stop herself, said, "Mr. Kasparov, steelhead have no legs."

Mr. Kasparov, quickly cogitating between his native language or languages and English, caught the joke and smiled, teeth protruding, dark eyes with a bit of a flash in them. He laughed. He said nothing. Then he snickered again.

"Good," she said. "So let's do that. What about Mr. Fisher? It looks like we could use his background."

"Mr. Fisher?" he asked suggestively, looking over at me.

"Of course I'll go," I said. "Could there have been any doubt? Ever?

"I'll pack a few things," she said. "You know, I'll bet it's beautiful up there this time of year. If it hasn't started raining, anyway ... or even if it has."

Ruth went upstairs. Mr. Kasparov watched until she disappeared behind the door to the upper apartments. I walked with him back to his garage and to the car he'd rebuilt for a king: the Silver Cloud. He had a peanut butter and butter sandwich for lunch and offered me one. I accepted, but with the obvious reservations. Then I phoned my metro editor to tell him about the story and get everything approved. There was no problem — everyone loves a tale of infanticide, he said. Then I went back into the kitchen where Ruth had been simmering her vat, to see if there was anything I could do to help before we all had to leave. She said we would have to let it cool in the vat. Mr. Kasparov could take it out and let it drain in mesh sacks for a few days and then hang it to finish drip-drying. Her friend, Julie, would take it from there if need be.

The History of Wailing Wood

Before leaving for Whitesboro, I stopped at the Bulletin to gather some information on Wailing Wood. I'd covered some of the legal maneuvers and lawsuits earlier, and the rest I borrowed from the newspaper's morgue and digital library. The landowners, Northern and now Global, were so intent on logging the little tract — little in relative terms — that they'd been fighting to do so for longer than I had worked at the Bulletin. The stack of paperwork was six or eight inches thick, which I decided wasn't bad under the circumstances. I printed out the full timber harvest plan, known by its acronym, THP, and realized that I was missing the confidential pages regarding some mitigated Native American sites.

To my knowledge, there had been three such sites discovered over the last decade, and each had been "mitigated," which meant that it had been left isolated and undisturbed, or mined for its relics which would either be given back to the tribes or kept for further study by a university. The sites are mapped, but the public has no access to the maps. This is the

34

state's way of preventing looting by treasure hunters. Only the landowner, Global, or its affiliated people, plus the state Forestry Department, have access to the files. The files are stored in only ten places in the state, and Sonoma State University in Rohnert Park, is one. That's Jim Miller's university, and its archaeology program is specifically geared toward California's Native American past. Whether they knew it or not, I realized that James Miller was a perfect choice for the case at hand.

I also had an abbreviated version of a court decision that hinged on the northern spotted owl, an endangered bird whose habitat is limited to old-growth redwood. This case, also, was settled in favor of the timber company, which had to leave an old snag standing here and there after a proposed clear-cut. An isolated tree, no doubt a future victim of fierce winds, was considered habitat enough by the court at the time. Most of the owls in Wailing Wood, it was pointed out, were barred owls, a non-endangered cousin to the northern spotted.

I was curious, once again, how much that old grove was really worth monetarily, though I realized it was botanically priceless.

I carried my trove of papers out to my car, a 1981 Saab 900. It was mostly blue, or had been at one time. But it ran well. I knew of a small motel in the harbor that I liked, and I was sure that William Chu would be staying there — that's where his family always stayed. I called for a room, and yes, said Mrs. Morton, the longtime proprietor, Mr. Chu was already ensconced in No. 4. Funny; I can remember the times as a boy that Billy and I stayed in the same room, 4, with his parents and sister. It was a bright spot in my life.

I left San Francisco about noon on Sunday. I was alone and in no hurry, so I took the snaking scenic route, Highway One, also called the Coast Highway. I meandered my way north and stopped in Bodega Bay for a late lunch.

The wind was sharp at times, and whipped the rigging on the trollers in the marina. It was nice to see something besides the yachts and expensive sailboats. Not that there weren't any, but there were a lot of fishing vessels in the mix, both trollers with their big twin booms and small draggers with their nets rolled in the back.

Soon I was back on the road heading for Whitesboro. There, even more working boats would be seen in the harbor, and hardly any from the leisure class. I'd forgotten that I did really like a practical, working community; things like that are easy to forget in the city.

I turned on the old CD player, but then turned it back off, realizing it didn't really fit with the rolling headlands, the wildflowers, the old moss-covered remains of split-stave redwood fences crawling down to the cliffs for absolutely no reason at all. Below me to my left I could see the waves smack the rocky shoreline, and in places throw themselves up onto the sand.

I watched the sun set orange on my left, and hoped to see the infamous "green flash," a rare occurrence in which the setting orb's spectrum of light is diffracted by conditions of the atmosphere and all the wavelengths of light are skewed and somehow dispensed with, leaving only the emerald green wavelength. I had seen it once before. It reminded me of *her* eyes, Ruth's. But I did not see it on my journey to Whitesboro. I saw only the huge orange ball fall below the indigo green, restless sea.

I had a room at the Herring Gull Motel in the harbor and pulled in early in the evening. It didn't get many reservations, even now during the early steelhead and coho season, situated as it was between a fish processing building, which emitted the aroma of cut fish and attracted gulls as thick as politicians, and an ice house. Both old structures were painted thick in sky blue enamel, the paint peeling with age. The Gull was as rundown as the other buildings. It had once been painted gray and white, and once bluish and white, and most recently with the leftover blue enamel of the fish and ice houses, the owners of which were on good terms with the owner of the Gull.

But now, the Herring Gull was a bit of all of the paint colors with a hint of bare wood and flat, peeling white. Ah, I thought, this was comfort. It had a dozen rooms set horizontally, all facing west to the harbor. You could only see a piece of the rougher ocean, though, because the land curved around, north and south, to enclose the harbor. About all I could do was watch the fishing boats go in and out. I found it relaxing.

I was in No. 3. The room next to me, 2, which was actually the first room because there wasn't a 1, had a Ford Maverick nosed right up to the door onto the cement walkway, the hood up, the engine out and suspended on the short chains of a hydraulic stand and hoist. Mrs. Morton, who had owned and run the place as long as I could remember, said her son was rebuilding it. He lives in that room, with the engine, which she told me, unflinchingly and with a certain pride, was a 250 cubic inch, straight-six Ford. I just nodded, yup. It was no wonder they didn't get many lodgers: Car in the foyer, and Mr. Morton, dead these fifteen years, buried in back with a small marble tombstone graced with plastic roses. These bits of character don't really attract customers. However, I did note that there were occupants, surely sport fishermen, in rooms 9 and 11. Their blinds were drawn, which is very uncharacteristic of the Gull's otherwise social clientele. But there were no cars: The occupants had gone fishing and had not yet returned.

I asked about William Chu, and reminded Mrs. Morton of the times Billy and I came up with his family. I didn't need to bother; she noted how I'd grown and how "presidential" I had become. She said Billy hadn't yet returned from fishing. I asked where he'd gone, and she said north of town on the Usal, a river about fifteen miles away. It was seven-ish and dark. He could drive up any minute, and I was looking forward to seeing him here at the old motel.

"Never catches a thing," she said. "Him and that father of his, Lord rest his soul, I coulda sold 'em grunion and told 'em it was a steelie and they'd of paid good money." She laughed and coughed. She was just kidding.

Mrs. Morton has a Mexican velvet painting in the lobby, where the motel's only TV is located, and you have to watch it communally, a throwback to the 50s and 60s, the heyday of the old harbor area when the Herring Gull was the only reasonable place to stay. The painting is of Theodore Roosevelt shaking hands with Pancho Villa. A person couldn't help but smile. She got it from the owner of the Mexican restaurant, located thirty yards farther into the harbor, just a bit north, about ten years ago when the owner died and the business went to his daughter. She bought herself a painting of a female flamenco dancer in a pink dress, which is very nice, to replace the political one. The Roosevelt painting is a preposterous scene, of course, but Mrs. Morton saw in me the likeness of the former president, even when I was young (she had a photo of Theodore as a young man, boxing, which was framed and on the lobby wall) and I was always treated royally when I stayed at the Gull. But I had been away — three years since my last visit, maybe more.

"You're looking more like him, these days," she said as I was checking in. She stabbed out her Winston; this was a no-nonsense smoking motel, and her ash tray, which had a Yosemite scene in the bottom, was full. There were two or three similar commemorative ashtrays in each of the rooms.

I smiled.

"You're up on business, I take it," she said.

I said I was, and handed her the credit card I used when I put in for my expenses at the end of the month. She had one of those old card squashers that predated the magnetic-strip-swiping technology. It impressed the raised numbers in purple, in triplicate.

"Gonna be looking into that skeleton they found up to Wailing Wood, I take it," she said. At first, I wondered how she knew. But Whitesboro is a small town with many, many inter-relationships. And there was also William Chu, who'd known enough about it to advise the sheriff to advise the archaeologist to contact the Yarn Woman. That's the way it works up here; I was sure Bill Chu was quite at home.

"I'll meet with the sheriff and whoever else in the morning up there," I said. "An archaeologist."

"That'd be old Jim Miller, the ornery one. Not many friends except me, I'd say. Anyways, old Tully'll put 'em all straight, Nat. Guess Muriel Stanley'll go up there, too. What I hear."

I said I wasn't sure about the finer points of attendance. And I was not acquainted with the name Tully.

"Well, you can take it from me," she said. "But probably no good come of it anyways. That timber company's crooked, my friend. Not what they used to be. Fired all our boys two years and four months ago ... the town can't even muster a fire department these days." She shoved the receipt over for me to sign; the rooms have no amenities, like phones or video streaming that might add to your bill. "I'll just keep this. You want another night or two after, we'll tear it up and start from scratch.

38

"Anyways, can you believe that? No fire department? My Renton just helps around the Gull now, but he don't like it. He feels useless. Used to work the second shift at the mill, run the big saw, do some sortin'." But she lamented only briefly, then said, "The boy's heard them children cryin' up there, you know, Renton has."

The boy, Renton, was her younger son, now in his mid-thirties, maybe late thirties, Renton Morton, who was rebuilding the Maverick engine about fifteen yards away. His older brother, Micklen, was and apparently still is a small-time commercial fisherman operating out of the Whitesboro harbor. I asked if he, too, kept a room at the Gull; I didn't ask if he scraped the hull of his boat at his front door. She said he was up in Alaska jobbing out on a big crab and halibut trawler for the winter.

I told Mrs. Morton I'd heard of that old story about crying children in the wood when I was covering the second court hearing on the cut. I'd even gone out there, to the edges of the wood on Overland Road, but didn't hear anything. At the time, the company had posted guards at all the access points and took trespassing very seriously, and it was especially interested in keeping the press out.

"Oh, he heard it, all right. According to the story, first you see the owl. Some old owl. Then you hear the voices of those children. That's a thing I know. Boy was only seven or eight years of age. All of them used to play out there anyways, and in the river. Micklen never heard, but he's a pragmatist. That's what he says. I guess pragmatists don't hear much more than what's on fourteen hundred on the radio dial." Fourteen hundred was the local AM station.

I'd never been able to trace the origins of the old story of the sobbing voices of Wailing Wood, but assumed that's how the tract got its name, which meant that the tale was an old one dating at least to World War II.

"He seen ghosts in there, too."

"Ghosts?" I said. "I didn't know that was part of the story."

"Oh, yeah. Now that, that part is out of that old logging camp up there. Let me see here," she said, moving some papers and tourist brochures from the countertop in front of her. "This here's Wailing Wood," she said, scooting over a postcard. "This, it'll be the ridge." She put a pencil down the middle of the postcard. "This here, we'll call that the old grove where the voice come out of." She placed a pink eraser of the kind we used in grade school on the postcard on, from my angle, the left half of the postcard.

She thought for a moment.

"Need a logging camp here, Nat. Let's see." She picked up some paper clips and put them on the postcard on the right side of the pencil, the ridge, touching it. "There, that looks like a logging camp, don't it?"

I noted the similarities.

"Now, listen up. This logging camp is called Bear Breach. Everyone knows about it. There's still some old foundations and chimney stacks there. Micklen got a metal detector once and found a horseshoe. Now, old Slaughterhouse Gulch runs from Bear Breach down to Old Lake County Road. Sheer cliff, my friend, and in case you didn't know why, it's on account of clear-cutting on a slope. The land give way, that's all. You know that road, right?"

I said I did. A dozen miles south of Whitesboro, it runs all the way from the Coast Highway and through the Coast Range to all points east. It was and still is the main artery from coastal communities to the rest of the United States.

"That's where you see the ghosts. Bear Breach! Ghosts of old loggers. Some Chinamen, they say, that used to dig out the tunnels. So you never heard that?"

"No," I said.

"Dug that God-forsaken tunnel between Bear Breach just up from the South Fork, through the ridge a quarter mile to the North Fork, there on the north side of the forest."

"Are there ghosts in the tunnel, too?" I asked.

"Well, stay away from there. All the town kids used to go up there and dare each another to go into that tunnel at night. To drink beer. That kind of thing. They say there's the ghosts of Chinese laborers in there. Them that died."

I asked her how William Chu was doing.

"We all go back. He's got a real jones for steelies," said Mrs. Morton. "I tell him he should wait it out for the late season in January, but he says he likes the fall season better. Even if it's raining, he says." She walked over to an old cigarette vending machine in the corner of the lobby, probably the last one still operating in the continental states. It was so old she inserted only three quarters and pulled the knob for a new pack of Winstons. I knew it was time to get to my room: The next thing out would be the nightly glass of whiskey. With a little plastic sword stuck through a strip of lemon peel.

She looked up at me, new soft pack in hand, and said, "Be my last one, you know. Yeah, it's easy to quit. I do it every day."

I said goodnight, which took another half an hour, and walked outside through the main front door and north to my room, past Renton Morton's shop project. I was sad Billy hadn't returned yet.

I tossed my duffle on the bed in No. 3 and deposited my laptop and folders on the desk, then opened the window to catch the cold night air. I wondered if Ruth and Mr. Kasparov had left the city. What were the chances of them staying at the Gull? I hadn't talked with Mr. Kasparov about lodging arrangements. Some of the motels that catered to tourists were nicer, cleaner, and newer than the Gull. But they didn't have a Mrs. Morton.

I reviewed my notes, a few history pamphlets and the case files I'd brought. I took a few notes on Mrs. Morton's ghost stories, which might, I decided, add some tang to whatever story I'd be running into tomorrow when we all went into Wailing Wood ... this time without trespassing.

The modern tract of forest called Wailing Wood, or THP 287.2003, or 287 for short, had been controversial for more than a decade, with most of the lawsuits filed in the last four or five years. Its story boils down to money, of course. It's part of a larger surrounding forest about three miles north to south, and five miles deep — fifteen square miles or nearly ten thousand acres. It's now wholly owned by Global Resources, and is part of Global's 330,500 acres of declining timberland in northwest and north-central California. Global is a mining concern with a newfound interest in timber, despite the fact that it's a waning and, as proved in the last few years, probably a nonrenewable, resource. Some people think the company will simply clear the land and either pit-mine, frack for oil and gas, or sell to a developer. I predict the second option.

Wailing Wood itself, a grouping that includes six old-growth redwood groves, each with one to two dozen ancient behemoths, is just under a square mile at 556 acres. A mile is 640. What makes it unique is the antediluvian trees and the resulting volume and value of the lumber — the clearest, tightest redwood grain on the planet. Most of the Northwest's residual forests produce about $30,000 worth of so-called lumber from an acre — little poles of tanoak, bull pine, fir, and redwood if you're lucky. Much of it so small it's used for chipboard. The value of the trees in Wailing Wood, taking into account that Global also owns the mill and the retail outlet (it acquired a big-box lumber and hardware outlet when it bought Northern Timber three years ago), is many times the average, a total of half a billion dollars, maybe more. We might be talking a billion.

The old timber stand, as Mrs. Morton kindly pointed out, sits on a ridge between the North and South Forks of the White River starting about five miles inland, and its closest access from Whitesboro is Overland Road, six miles south of town on the North Fork. The road only runs inland a dozen miles.

On the South Fork is Old Lake County Road, the through-road to the east.

The lumberjacks took what they could from 1840 to about 1920, but the ridge was too steep — it would be at least sixty years before sophisticated yarders and steel chokers would be able to make mincemeat of those tree-covered hillsides — all but the ridge, all but Wailing Wood.

Why was Wailing Wood still around? Something has to be last, I suppose, as the industry sweeps through its inventory, taking the low-lying fruit or, in this case, wood. Perhaps it was the steepness at first, followed by years and years in court.

In general terms, the region south of the ridge was logged first. When the south sector was laid bare, a tunnel was dug under Wailing Wood, through the ridge, for logging trains. The tunnel was a quarter-mile long, piercing the ridge at its narrowest point, and owes its existence to the slavelike Chinese labor of the late 1800s, and it opened up the timber on the north side.

Nathaniel White originally owned everything on the north. He was the most famous and powerful of California's North Coast timber barons. A second baron, Peter Johnson, acquired the south part around the turn of the century. He owned Wailing Wood. His holdings eventually included Nathaniel White's north sector. The operation became Northern Timber around 1940.

My last visit to Whitesboro was just before the takeover of Northern Timber by Global. I'd stopped in at the newspaper, the Whitesboro Ledger, to see the old editor, my friend, Len Stanley. He had unfortunately died a few months earlier, and I paid my respects to his daughter, the new editor. He had passed away like so much of this old logging town. And like Bear Breach. Maybe even like Wailing Wood, after Global eventually gets its way and logs it to kingdom come.

At about three in the morning, waking, I wondered whose skull they found so deep in that old forest.

An Old Friend

I met William Chu on Monday morning before dawn in the motel lobby, well before we were to meet the sheriff and everyone at the wood, just off Overland Road. He was carrying a mug of coffee, brewed in his room on one of Mrs. Morton's old machines. She checks them out at the desk and you have to sign for them, but you have to provide your own coffee, which you can buy at the marine supply store in the harbor — if it happens to be open. It's run by one of her in-laws. Chu said it was "at least as good as the mud at headquarters, if not worse." Then he laughed and produced a second cup for me. I don't think he'd slept at all, but just stayed up, like a child ignoring sleep on Christmas Eve. He shoved a note under my door about one to meet at four. I saw the note because I, also, don't sleep much because of my work schedule.

He wasn't wearing a suit, and I hadn't seen him dress casually since he started with the San Francisco Police Department almost fifteen years ago. He took a lot of pride in looking professional, as if he represented every person of Chinese lineage

44

in his old neighborhood of North Beach/Chinatown in San Francisco. He'd made good. Very good, and he was proud of it — but without the hubris one might expect from lesser men.

Casual for Detective Chu, however, is not the same as casual for someone else, especially, for example, newspaper people like me. His wool slacks were pressed and his sport jacket steamed. They did not match, but they paired very nicely. The "casual" comes in with the sport coat pattern, which was green-and-reddish plaid. The colors were not bright, but subtle, rather like William Chu himself.

"She'll be there, the Yarn Woman," he said, smiling in anticipation. "I'm going to bring some popcorn. I picked it up yesterday at Ralph Morton's, the marine supply, along with more coffee. They sell everything. Did you know Ralph's real name is Jubilee? Seriously, seriously. Jubilee Morton. He only goes by Ralph so people, thinking they heard it wrongly the first time, won't ask him again."

"I like the name, Jubilee. It has a ring to it," I said.

"He's the late Mr. Morton's brother. He wasn't around much back when we used to come up … you and I and the rest … Mrs. Morton's a little vague on where he was back then, whether it was in prison off and on or up in Alaska on the trawlers. Not that there is much of a difference …"

"Catch anything yet?"

"Working up to it."

"Bait or lures?"

"Oh no. I'm fly fishing, Nat! Fly fishing! There's nothing like it. I'm using streamers."

"But you're going to take a little time off fishing to, you know, go on up to Wailing Wood?"

He sobered. "This is a very interesting case. Very interesting. I haven't been up to the wood there yet. But I was talking with the sheriff, John Tully, and this case has got enough dry powder in it to blow this place sky high. It's extremely political, and millions of dollars are riding on what these people have actually dug up. I mean, when Tully said that the archaeologist that the timber company hired was looking for a textile expert, I had to recommend Miss M. He seemed very interested in her vita, and the next thing, they're all making phone calls to line it up.

"No, Nat, really, this is going to be good. You've seen her. I can see it: They have their such-and-such theories, all good and proper, and they're all primed to cut down those trees, and then she comes up with something no one saw, right out of left field. I mean, believe me, it'll come so fast they'll need catchers' mitts." He joyfully slurped his coffee. "I'm telling you, one of them will be standing there and won't even know what hit him. Then, he'll catch it and, if it's a typical situation, he'll just be mad as hell. Men are like that, Nat, when women outsmart them."

"But not the sheriff?"

"No. Nope. The sense I get is that old John Tully ... I'd never met him before two days ago ... is a pretty straight shooter. In more ways than one, I might add, from what I hear. And so's this Miller guy, the archaeologist. They sound like quite a pair. We should be in for some top-tier entertainment."

That's what I liked about William Chu: his sense of excitement.

We walked out onto the porch. At four in the morning, it was cold and damp and the air was fresh, right off the sea, and laced with coarse mist that dampened our faces even under the motel's porch overhang. I had a wool jacket on, which was sufficient but certainly not overkill; I'm guessing the temperature was about forty-five to fifty. A streetlight a few yards north cast enough light to see that Chu was wearing a soft violet dress shirt and a gorgeous steel-blue Banks tie knotted in a double Windsor, under the sport coat. This was his idea of casual hiking clothes.

"You fish in that?" I asked.

His brow furrowed. "Of course. Why?"

"Just saying ..."

"It's not so much the fishing," he explained. "It's being out there on the river. It's deep, and cold. Did you know that a deep, slow river reflects darkness just like it does light? Well, it does. People don't think about that. Anyway, I cover them up with the chest waders, if that's what you're worried about." I wasn't worried, it just seemed to me that maybe an old pair of jeans at thirty dollars on sale, worn for five or six years, would be better than a pressed pair of new slacks at a couple of hundred dollars.

He hadn't caught a steelhead in ... how many years?

"Well, it's not the fishing. That's just the excuse. I don't like coming up here in the summers, though. Too many tourists. If I wanted tourists, I'd stay in the city, learn to speak German. French. We can walk up on the headlands later, you know, tomorrow or something. I'm going up with you this morning, of course, on an invite from the local sheriff."

"Sounds like he knows the backstory to whatever's happening in his town ..."

"He said something about he couldn't trust the forester from Northern, that's the timber company, and I said trust him about what, and he said they'd found the skull, you know, and some scrap of cloth or something. I said, cloth!, and he elaborated to some degree, and so I dropped her name and some of the people she'd worked with besides myself, that thing with the FBI a couple of ... that was before your time, I'm afraid ... before you made her acquaintance, and, so, there you have it. The sheriff told the archaeologist.

"So, what do you think?" Chu asked, swallowing.

"About the case, the bones in Wailing Wood? It'll be a good story."

"About her."

Here we go, I thought. Chu, my boyhood friend, had introduced me to Ruth maybe a year ago, something like that. It had come out of the blue. We both ended up at San Francisco General, following up on the case of a woman whose child had been either beaten or had an accident. The girl was found wearing a sontag, an old style of shawl that hasn't been around for about a century and a half, so Chu took the opportunity to introduce me to his textile forensics consultant, Ruth M, known by his department as "the Yarn Woman."

Now, he wanted to know about my private life, and whether, essentially, he'd done me any favors. I think he wanted to know if I even had a private life.

He had done me favors, of course. I'd be in his debt forever. But life is so nebulous.

I said, "Mrs. Morton says the wood is haunted."

Chu smiled slyly. "Okay, Teddy, okay. Let's get down to business." He calls me Teddy because he, like Mrs. Morton, believes there's a similarity between me and Mr. Roosevelt. I suggest, however, that a husky build, mustache, block head and reading glasses do not make a president. "The wood isn't haunted. I've known Marguerite Morton as long as you have, and I always come up here, at least once a year, and stay right here at the Gull. Knew her husband, know her boys. Renton's rebuilding that 250 right in his room ..."

"Does he know what he's doing?"

"Don't worry about it."

"Why don't worry about it?"

"Because Miss M is bringing Mr. Kasparov with her, I'm sure. He understands all universes applicable to car engines. Anything Renton Morton isn't sure about, Mr. Kasparov will tell him. Down to the smallest microminist scrap of nickel cadmium."

"Microminist?"

"Really, really little, Teddy."

He'd called me that since junior high, and he's convinced that I grew to look more and more like Theodore as we became adults. This is the problem with having friends that "go back." It's also one of the comforts.

"You really like her," he said.

I was stoic. What was I going to say that wouldn't compromise her? My mouth was shut on the matter. It would be like making some inference to Diana, the goddess ... what if *She* found out?

"They use roe, little eggs," I said. "To catch steelies."

"Yeah, in a microminist mesh sack. I used to buy a bunch of the stuff. But this time? Streamers. I'm fly fishing."

"Even a nibble?"

"Teddy," he said, shaking his head and leaving it at that.

He checked his watch — it was safe to do that until Miss M arrived. I think he kind of gloried in it, checking his watch. It was brownish, very stylish — it was subtle but one can't help but noticing. But it was only good for another few hours, until we met Ruth at the wood. Then it would whisper, "Hey, put me in your pocket, Bill ... now!" Then he'd have to use his cell phone, with the time posted down in the lower corner, and even that would have to be surreptitious.

The Introductions

On Overland Road, there's a pull-off at mile marker 5.2, about two miles beyond the perpetual maritime fog belt. Locals park their pickups and Volvos there to spend a hot afternoon in or on the North Fork of the White River. A sunny day is the most inviting, when the water's warm because of the inland heat. That's in the summer. But in late autumn, which was Monday, there weren't any leisure cars parked at the 5.2 marker. The whole month had been unseasonably chilly, and the onset of the winter rain seemed only hours away. Rain clouds were building invisibly in the dark, and their presence would delay the dawn itself.

The sheriff's Bronco was among five vehicles that filled the pull-off when Detective Chu and I pulled up, and the sight of the assembled cars and vans, very official looking, would discourage all but the most curious. Yet even the curious would know nothing about a skull hidden deep in the trees.

An old logging road, newly graded, oiled and graveled, began at the edge of the pull-off and led into the wood with an immediate incline. The gate was a fifteen-foot-long horizontal iron pipe that swung on a cement-secured iron post, and nearby was a small, empty trailer with a five-gallon propane tank at the front end. The tank's white enamel had chipped off almost entirely. The trailer was an old model from the sixties or seventies, originally white with a baby-blue stripe running horizontally. Rusty drips ran from screws that secured the doors and windows and the sides and top. The white was no longer white, and the baby blue was hoary.

Sitting and standing near the gate was the excavation party, consisting of Sheriff John Tully, the six-foot-eight, multigenerational arm of the law in White County; Bob Cooper, the cattleman and landowner who discovered the bones and would lead the rest of us to the site a mile or two into the wood; archaeologist Jim Miller and two of his students from Sonoma State (a thin young man named Steven, with blond hair wearing jeans and a T-shirt, and Lucy, who had long, dark hair, was not thin, wore a red plaid shirt and jeans, and was perhaps in her thirties), who would undertake the exploratory dig; two Native Americans who legally had to be notified of the find but didn't have to participate in the foray into the wood, Daniel Thom, the local tribal chairman and a Pomo Indian, and Luther Eaglejohn of the Native American Heritage Council, who was Hoopa; Global's forester, Paul Grassi, who was unhappy at having his position usurped by contract labor, namely Jim Miller (Grassi may have simply been unhappy in general); Muriel Stanley, the owner of the local weekly newspaper, the Whitesboro Ledger; and a thug named Sal Mendez, Global's all-purpose "fixer," who had arrived with Global's damp-skinned bookkeeper, the latter apparently having no name at all. Detective Chu and I had driven from the Gull in his Honda, and I'd left my Saab at the motel.

We waited. Ruth was late, but I knew she'd be here. They probably hadn't started from the city until a few hours ago.

Tully was off to the side with Grassi, and having little else to do or say, Tully asked him how his wife and the kids were.

"Oh, just pretty good," Grassi said, happy that someone, anyone, had started a conversation. "Meg's off to the church this morning. She'll be all day. I guess they're setting up a table or something for the auction. I don't know. They're making flowers or something. You going? Mark's got a science project he has to finish by Friday so we can all go on Saturday." The church auction was an annual fundraiser to support the Sunday school.

Sal Mendez, with a dark complexion, black oiled hair and deep brown eyes, moved a little closer to Grassi and Tully, just within earshot. He appeared muscular, his forearms used to either manual labor or free weights, and was a little over six feet. The bookkeeper, a pot-bellied, waxy-skinned man with a bulbous head, was never introduced. His thin arms hung at his sides, and his hands were disproportionately long and they looked sticky, if that's possible. He wore a white shirt with a button-down collar, starched, with short sleeves that made his arms look as thin as rope and as bleached as a corpse. I took an immediate dislike to the man, and it seemed to me that he had grown used to people rushing to judgment about him; he carried it on his shoulder like a wood chip. He and Mendez had arrived last night and stayed at the Italian Best Western motel in town. Both wore ties.

"Drop the kids off on the way, I guess," said Tully. His mouth seemed almost clenched, hard to talk.

"No. They're on the bus today," Grassi said. "Meg's got this thing now. She's 'power walking.' Down the Gulch Road, then onto that little path along the highway, to the church. About two miles." Tully noticed that Grassi said nothing about his younger child, the daughter, Jessie.

"Well, that makes for a nice morning," Tully said obligatorily. I don't think he ever looked at Grassi as he spoke. They really had nothing to talk about. I wondered if this was how adults handled mutual disgust in a small-town setting. But then, the disgust might not have been mutual. Tully, however, certainly was disgusted.

"She carries these two-pound weights in her hands while she walks," said Grassi. "I don't know … she's closing in on forty … I think she's worried about that."

Oh God, thought Tully.

"I don't know what gets into them," Grassi said absently. "She's taking yoga at the rec center, too, from that, well, they say he's the new guy, really knows yoga. From L.A. … don't ask me what he's doing in Whitesboro." He made a weak motion with his wrist, indicating the sexual orientation of the new rec teacher. Tully ignored it.

Tully was tired of the conversation. He looked over at the rest of us, to see where everyone was, how we'd clumped together to form small groups. Mendez was alone but within a few yards of the bookkeeper, but there was no doubt he'd been listening to Grassi go on about his married life.

"You know," said Grassi, laboriously getting to his point, "if they shut this thing down, it means jobs. Mine included, but the timber workers, you know."

"They already moved the mill," said Tully simply. The machinery had indeed all been trucked from the flat near the harbor to a scaled-down nonunionized facility forty miles inland that made mostly chipboard.

"Yeah, yeah, yeah," said Grassi, as if responding to a broken record. "Company still plays a role here, Sheriff. The ball teams, the school sports programs. Jobs. A shutdown means millions to them. Many millions, even if it's just a delay until late spring. When they hurt, we hurt. And talk about your tax revenues! That all goes to the county and the city, and it's a lot of money."

Mendez, seeing that the sheriff was eyeing him, walked over to the rest of the group, but still maintained his distance. Mostly, he thought about the location of the wood, the precise spot where they stood, even how far Paul Grassi had to drive to get here. He'd booted up his laptop at the motel the night before and put in the Best Western wireless password. And he did a little research with Google Earth, as if he had nothing better to do.

"Franzetta borrowed the old man's forty-four," Grassi said, referring to Global's general manager, who was fond of target shooting on Global's property north of town, and who was interested in buying another gun. The "old man" was Grassi's late father. "Mike wants to see if he likes it. I told him he should take the Walther." He laughed the way males do in locker rooms. The smaller gun was sort of a nagging joke to him; his father, the "old man," had given the small semi-auto to Meg, for her purse. It was a "sissy" gun. But he'd really meant it for his son, a sort of hard-to-pin-down, passive-aggressive insult. Paul Grassi had never measured up to his father's expectations.

Perched above the road on the pull-off, we watched a long gray and white automobile float up Overland Road, its engine a steady, low hum. It was Mr. Kasparov driving his Rolls Silver Cloud. The windows looked like obsidian in the morning light. Mr. Kasparov pulled off slowly, and you could tell every effort was made not to create a dust cloud. The driver's door opened and we watched the short man exit. He was wearing a Pendleton black felt zip jacket, black wool pants that were a few inches too short and old black shoes freshly polished, glowing as if to match the Pacific at dawn. His nose was prominent even from sixty feet upslope where the rest of us were waiting.

Mr. Kasparov closed his door; the sound was solid, muffled by the sheer volume of steel that was common in British luxury cars in 1957, and further drowned by the sound-absorbing nature of the wood behind us. He walked around to the passenger door and pulled it open. A foot clad in an ancient ankle-high, blunt-toed, thick-soled brown boot settled in the dirt, followed by the other foot and then the rest of her. She had a pair of rust-orange paisley tights under a thrift-store jean skirt that came down past her knees but was loose enough to allow trail hiking. Her equipment, including her microscope, books, and a Chinese thermos of green tea, was in an old red rucksack. William Chu crossed his arms: This was his doing. He's cute when he smiles, like a tall, slender Ho Tai — but with great hair and no belly.

It was cold, but Ruth M was wearing layers, including the tights and skirt, a golden yellow body shirt that plunged modestly at the chest just enough to show the thin, worn leather thong of a necklace or pendant hidden beneath her top, a tarnished gold and rose-tan upholstery vest and a corduroy jacket that pulled in nicely at the waist and descended a little past her hips. She had a finely knit, diamond-patterned multi-hued scarf, sort of peach and rose. Over that she wore a Gore-Tex shell to fend off expected rain. It was unzipped. Her hair was up, of course, with hair sticks. She swung her large, very used canvas rucksack over her shoulder and waited for Mr. Kasparov to close the door. It was better (for him) that she didn't try. He slipped out of his loafers and jammed himself into a pair of thick-soled, oil-stained auto-garage work boots and carefully folded his pant legs into them before tying the laces. Then he headed briskly and powerfully uphill behind Ruth toward the rest of us at the gate.

Miller, who, on the advice of the sheriff, who, on the advice of Detective Chu, had made the arrangements for Ruth to participate in the excavation and analyze the textile remains that were already partly exposed, began the introductions. Hands were shaken all around, but Ruth noticed a cordiality-covered stiffness in Daniel Thom and Luther Eaglejohn, and especially in Paul Grassi, the dethroned forester, who seemed to experience pain as he held his hand out to shake whatever hand he had to. The sheriff, John Tully, was probably the most amenable, even for a lawman, and, because of his height, he bent at the waist to shake Ruth's hand with affection. Bob Cooper, who was usually an easy-going man, was on edge: What he'd found in the forest had unsettled him and seemed to play on his mind continually. This trip back into the grove was uncomfortable for him, for he was well aware what they'd find, but at the same time he almost looked forward to finalizing it all, purging himself of it.

He was, however, particularly pleased to meet Ruth, as though she were an old friend of the family.

Chu was very much in his element. He is genuinely fond of people, and, being very much in shape, would have no trouble with the hike. He had a rucksack and I had the sneaking suspicion that he was carrying his dress shoes so he could wear them during the excavation. He did, in fact, have a large sack of caramel-coated popcorn, just as he'd threatened. He was truly looking forward to entertainment, cop style. And with a cop's eye, he studied each member of the party, and took umbrage only with the two Global men, Mendez and the bookkeeper. Mendez had obviously, to Chu, done prison time. The other man was a bit more difficult to peg, but something psychological was clearly awry, as Chu saw it. And the man had something in his front pocket that moved when he walked; it was heavy, like a serious folding knife. And he was a bookkeeper? Maybe it was a folding letter opener that only happened to bounce around in his trouser pocket like 440 carbon steel in a shatterproof plastic handle.

I realized that Tully and Cooper, whom Ruth had neither met nor heard of before, reacted to her much as cats do. I assumed that maybe their wives knew of her work in the knitting field, or something like that. It was as if she were a cousin or something, which she wasn't. Ruth is attractive, with a very nice figure, but this seemed to be more than just physical.

Muriel Stanley was happy to have another woman along, and she was friendly to Ruth, though standoffish to some of the rest — Grassi and the Global men, for instance — for reasons that were unknown to me. I knew her, of course, because of her father, and she greeted me warmly. Mr. Kasparov had a notebook and pencil out and might have been seen as journalistic competition of some sort, but Muriel handled it pretty well, turning from me and greeting him with a firm handshake.

Somewhere in the midst of it all, Ruth gave me a welcome hug on her toes and let it go at that.

All things considered, Ruth figured it wasn't a bad collection of bodies, except for Global's men. Mendez sent chills down her back when he introduced himself just before they started walking. If a man could smell like decayed flesh, she thought, this was the man. She could hardly wait to squeeze a blob of sanitizer into her hands and rub the hell out of them. But, "Mr. Mendez," she said pleasantly as they shook hands. A wolf stare seeped silently from his dark eyes and she felt like she needed to brush off her blouse and vest, and hold her rucksack in front of her chest. She might have chosen a different top …

Mendez was a few inches shorter than me, maybe six-two, solid, strong-looking, no gut, maybe forty-eight or fifty. To escape the man, Ruth graciously introduced him to her dear Mr. Kasparov, her "good friend," and Mr. Kasparov was extraordinarily pleasant and his greeting was extremely full of his nose and teeth. Mendez, who had cultivated the testosterone-laced habit of spreading out his hand just before gripping another man's — all the better to enwrap the unwitting victim in a crushing vice — found that the short driver was prepared, and with the slightest manual twist Mr. Kasparov unsettled the larger man's balance, forcing him to unspread his hand and enter the handshake in a submissive position. All the time, Mr. Kasparov was smiling, smiling happily and jabbering on about nothing, fading into French for a few sentences and then back into English, which obviously infuriated Mr. Mendez. Ruth watched all this from the corner of her eye, and found it immensely satisfying as Mr. Kasparov applied the pressure from his well-worked right hand, grinning and yakking about the trees or something, until Mendez somehow managed to pull ungracefully away. Everyone, she thought, should have a Mr. Kasparov. I felt a genuine appreciation for the odd Ukrainian myself.

Ruth avoided the bookkeeper entirely, much to his displeasure.

Muriel Stanley asked Mr. Kasparov who he was working for, because of the notepad. "I am with The Miss," he said. "I have taken it upon myself to scribble some notes, in case she needs them in the future. As best I can. For a lecture, for example."

Whatever that meant. She frowned. Mr. Kasparov smiled obligingly. Muriel Stanley, he decided, was a nice enough person.

He guessed her age to be middle to late thirties, but he was uncertain of his judgment. Though very good at weight, he'd never been good at judging age. Her dark blond hair, shoulder-length and stringy, kind of mousy, had suffered from unsuccessful early-morning efforts at styling. He noticed her nails. He always noted that about people, and hers were short and shaped, buffed but without nail polish. He hardly ever saw buffed nails anymore. But this told him that she was fastidious, and her eyes betrayed a native intelligence. She had lovely hands, not too thin, somewhat strong looking, her fingers somewhat short. She was, by the demanding standards that helped him survive his many years in Kiev, Kharkov and Moscow (to say nothing of Kaisk, the prison colony in west central Russia, a stone's throw from the medieval city of Nizhny Novgorod), satisfactory, and therefore worth developing a friendship with. He decided he would apply himself. He was quite aware that her glance went to Detective Chu more than once; but then, Chu was really about the only person she didn't know, other than Miss M and himself. He decided it was his responsibility to introduce Ms. Stanley to Mr. Chu, and soon.

"Do you have a deadline, Ms. Stanley?" Mr. Kasparov asked, slipping into the jargon of her profession. "I am sure Mr. Fisher does, though I don't know what it might be."

"Me?" she replied, "It's the usual, Mr. Kasparov. I'll file to myself, take my own pictures, edit my own copy, lay out my own page and take all the flak from the timber company myself afterward, all in my own time: Thursday. We print late Wednesday afternoon for morning delivery, second-class mail." She cast a fairly harsh glance in my direction, and continued. "Press day."

Had Mr. Kasparov spent time in prison, she wondered? Something made her feel that way, made her feel that he'd been a political prisoner somewhere, not a criminal prisoner. Maybe somewhere in Central Europe? She knew Mr. Kasparov had been evaluating her, and she realized that he had found her up to muster, though she was uncertain as to what his muster might be. Yet a subtle pride seemed to wash through her. She could tell he was making decisions on how he would relate to her. But she didn't see what she most expected, the typical male evaluation of the female, and it was a relief. She avoided Sal Mendez for that very reason, at least for the moment. She'd seen him before — the day Global announced the acquisition of Northern Timber three years ago, and he looked the same: like a snake.

As witness to it all, I decided that Muriel Stanley was attractive and had admirers. I was partly wrong on the second point, however. She had a history of conflict in Whitesboro that I was unaware of.

"That sounds delightful, Ms. Stanley," said Mr. Kasparov. "Mr. Fisher? Your deadline?" He was such an enthusiastic meddler, after all.

"Tomorrow morning," I said. "Write it up, e-mail it in to the paper, where they'll cut it from thirty inches to five, throw in a few errors, make a few false assumptions, write a headline that has nothing to do with the story but fits in one column, and then tell me to start the second-day follow-up." Muriel laughed, Mr. Kasparov smiled. There is much to be said for being one's own boss.

Mr. Kasparov introduced Muriel to Detective Chu, and she said, "I'm Muriel Stanley, with the Whitesboro Ledger. So, tell me, what's an out-of-town cop doing on this little excursion?"

William Chu's smile could have been at home on the cover of GQ or Esquire except for one thing: It was too sincere. I might categorize him as a little stiff, having known him for so long, but that seemed to be more like a mild case of stainless steel bones rather than personal discomfort. Formality was his comfort zone, and beneath the formality was an uncommon sentiment, something usually lacking in the male professional. I have always attributed that to his mother and perhaps his grandmothers.

He said, "Oh, no, Ms. Stanley, I'm here only unofficially! I come up once or twice a year to fish — for example, now, when the steelhead trout are running. I fell in with bad company, I'm afraid … you know, Sheriff Tully." He glanced over at John Tully, who was painfully involved in a conversation with Paul Grassi. "When the sheriff noted that some bit of cloth had been unearthed along with the bones, I suggested he contact the Yarn Woman, that is, Miss M. She's consulted for us numerous times, and serves as an expert witness."

Muriel surveyed him. "You're hiking in that?"

"I suppose I am."

"What if you tear, like, the trousers, on a wild rose?"

"I won't."

She raised an eyebrow. For some reason, she knew he was right. "Do you have a jacket?"

"My suit is at the hotel."

"Motel. Whitesboro doesn't have a hotel. I think you'll need a jacket. I have an extra one in the car."

And with that she walked down to her Toyota and back, briskly, as he watched, and handed him a black pile jacket a little on the slender side — it was hers — but he accepted it gratefully. "It'll get cold in there in the wood, especially if we're there a long time or if it starts raining. And there's never any light, not that deep in, where the trees are big."

"That's very kind of you," he said. He could leave it unzipped.

"Oh, no, it's nothing," she said.

"You'll be writing tomorrow," he suggested.

"Yes, yes," she said.

"And the newspaper, the Whitesboro Ledger, will be open?"

"Of course."

"I understand you are the owner and editor."

"Yes."

"How very excellent," he said. "Do you make your own doughnuts for the morning, Ms. Stanley, or may I take care of that tomorrow, under the circumstances?" He smiled so thoroughly that Muriel had to laugh. No one aside from her son had ever offered to bring her doughnuts. Chu had somehow managed to say just the right thing.

"Since we'll be on doughnut-intimacy, Mr. Chu, please call me Muriel."

"William, or Bill," he said, silently hoping she wouldn't call him Bill in public.

"So, what do you do, charm the criminals into giving up?" she asked.

"I have found that they rarely respond to charm." She was sensing a little more business in that comment. Upon re-evaluation, she realized that William Chu could indeed be a force to be reckoned with. What she saw, or thought she saw: straight and stiff bearing, but not military; wonderful hair, very thick, very black, very trimmed; round and pleasant face accented with eyes that were dark, steady and perceptive; an athletic build and probably, beneath the pressed clothes, a black belt in some martial art or other; strong hands …

"And you should meet his mother," I said. Both Muriel and Chu jumped slightly at the unexpected voice.

"I'm sorry?" said Muriel.

"His mother. You'd like her. Wouldn't she, Detective?" Chu appreciated it when I called him that in public. But I tried not to overdo it. He'd been quite aware that she'd been evaluating him, and he seemed relieved I'd changed the topic.

"Oh, yes," he said. "She makes very good shrimp dumplings." Then he wondered why on earth he'd said that.

"Really?" she asked, not knowing how else to respond.

I think it was his mother's shrimp dumplings that did it. I could practically feel the barriers fall, the little walls that people build and keep and tend, whose purpose is to keep things ever so slightly removed — and safe. And professional. But I realized that, in mentioning his mother, I was meddling.

With the formalities over and for the most part positive, the group headed single file into the wood. Mendez's friend, the bookkeeper, excused himself for physical reasons, and left toward a silver Acura parked below, telling Mendez he would be at the Global office "going over a few things." It didn't surprise me: He was a sickly looking man who did not seem capable of walking a few miles in a forest.

Although I'm uncertain about this, I felt later as if the bookkeeper was somehow following us at a distance, as if studying the lay of the land and the play of the people, although every time I turned to look, I saw nothing. I decided it was just the eerie feeling of the wood.

Ruth, who preferred solitude when she hiked, hung back about twenty-five yards so she could enjoy the silence of the trees. She seemed to be in an odd, pensive mood. Her introduction to Muriel Stanley was very brief; I was sure they'd catch up with that later. Ruth watched us leave, turned, and studied the waxy, bulbous head of the bookkeeper as it bobbed down the path, overjoyed that the creature would not be accompanying us. She waited to hear him start his engine down on the flat, but heard nothing and finally began following us.

Though morning light had come to the earth, it dimmed as soon as we began winding through the trunks. It was now after seven, November cold and Northwest damp.

Into the Wood

I stayed with the larger group, leaving Ruth to her solitude.

After the first fifty yards, she noticed a small creek running alongside the logging road, and fifty yards farther the troop left the graded roadbed and followed the creek on a well-worn deer and human trail through the fern-covered, canopy-shaded landscape. We trekked uphill for twenty or thirty minutes. Ruth studied the undergrowth as she walked — the shamrock-like redwood sorrel was blooming in small pink trumpet blossoms, and there were trilliums, their white and maroon three-lobed blossoms hovering above matching triplet, deep-green leaves surrounded by young emerald ferns whose ends were still curled.

The tanoak and red-skinned madrone that, along with the rhododendrons, marked the edges of the forest, eventually gave way to large, and then to truly massive redwoods and rough-barked fir. After an hour, the slope began to level off and the groundcover grew sparse. It grew silent, dull to the ears. The light was dim, thin and indigo as it seeped through the canopy. A rain a week ago had given rise to clumps of brown mushrooms and thickets of black, shiny-wet fungi that looked like crumpled satin ribbon — edible black chanterelles.

The most notable change as we walked deeper into Wailing Wood was the darkness created by the increasingly massive old trees and the green-black of the sky they supported. Gone now were the tanoak, madrone and low bushes. The big rhododendrons had vanished, and we were surrounded by the ancient silence of the forest and by its muted blue half-light. The snapping of a twig became an abbreviated crack and cry, and then the sound simply vaporized and you wondered if you'd ever even heard it. The trees, with trunks now five and ten feet in diameter, may have touched the sky and stars, but whatever was above was invisible and far removed, like an echo. And the trunks grew thicker still as we proceeded, soon measuring fifteen feet across. Did Grassi, the forester, see dollar signs? Did Sal Mendez? Perhaps it was best the bookkeeper wasn't with us.

The columns rose for forty or fifty feet before branches thrust out laterally, forming the first layers of the dark, vaulted ceiling. Then, as we walked ever farther into this world, the massive redwoods, second growth after all and only a century old or so, gave way to sporadic ancient trees easily a thousand years old and twenty to twenty-five feet across at the base. As the redwoods attained their giant proportions, so, too, did the silence grow vaster.

Bob Cooper, the rancher who led the party, stopped momentarily, pointed up into the darkness, and said, to no one in particular, "Seen, at times, little lightning storms up in there, up in the trees. Never did know how it happens, but damned if it don't." He looked at all of us behind him, and seemed surprised.

We continued east and south, and the going was slow because the trail ran along a slope and the soil and duff were slippery. The big old-growth trees became more and more visible, as if they'd hesitantly wandered into view after hiding for hundreds of years from the eyes and steel-toothed saws of men. Long spider webs hung from the distant branches, looking to Ruth as if thin strands of woven moonlight had infiltrated the canopy and attached themselves to the old trees. Yet outside, she knew, it was broad day and bright despite the cloud cover.

Ruth took a moment and sat on a downed redwood. It was small, only seven or eight feet thick, and she had to walk along the length of the horizontal trunk to find her seat, for it was about ten feet above the ground. She wasn't worried about catching up with us. I don't think it really mattered to her.

She sat because she heard small voices. This was the old folk tale of Wailing Wood. They were children's voices, but there was no laughter, as one might expect. None. The light was dim. It was difficult to see at any distance because it was still early. But she glimpsed a quick-moving form at the right edge of her vision. Then it was gone. What color had it been? she asked herself. White, with pink. And so small, the size of a two- or three-year-old.

It vanished quickly, but not behind a tree. It just vanished. She waited. She heard the voices again. She couldn't make out the words, but she perceived specific feelings. She felt they were discussing berries. There were two voices, but one was sobbing about berries. Near where the ethereal voices seemed to come from was a spindly thimbleberry bush at the base of a massive redwood.

But like the fleeting form of the child in her nightclothes, an image that Ruth realized only after piecing together the fractured visual interruption, the voices vanished and Ruth was left feeling a great emptiness in her chest. She sighed quietly and stared off again.

There was a rustling to her left. She looked up into the trees. A large barred owl swooped in front of her and then, with a rush of air, it sailed back up into the trees. She couldn't see it, but she knew it was still up there. Shortly, she heard its voice. And then that, too, was gone. There was nothing more. After a few minutes, she rose, walked the trunk of the tree and leaped the last five feet to the ground. She followed us once again.

She heard the high rush of air through the raptor's wing feathers. The owl seemed to be following as well.

We had entered the edge of the first of the old-growth groves, and the thick green groundcover of ferns and trilliums and gorse thinned and then withdrew altogether. Our vision consisted solely of the great trees, and, in their ancientness, they filled the recesses of our minds as if they'd been talking among themselves in deep, hollow voices in melodic languages long-vanished from the earth.

And as slowly and silently as these antediluvian behemoths appeared, the trunks of the great redwoods retreated again into a morning fog that had begun to settle in the ravines. Then we passed the edge of the grove and were once again amid second growth. The trees were a scant ten or fifteen feet in diameter. If she really concentrated, Ruth thought she could see the most ancient trees move slowly away, trying to hide again in the blue gloom and cotton mist.

The rest of us had stopped for a few minutes, and we waited for her in a clearing that might have been the crest of a ridge. In truth, it was only the first crest. She caught up to us when we were passing around cookies that Bob Cooper's wife had made. She took one and thanked him, and got a newspaper-wrapped thermos out of her bag and poured herself a thin tin cup of green tea.

"Keeps it warmer," she said to Cooper, who was watching. "Want some tea?"

"Naw. No thank you," Cooper said, and pulled a green steel Stanley thermos from his bag and poured what might have been a cup of coffee. It could have been asphalt, but it smelled like coffee, sort of. He offered Muriel Stanley a cup, which she declined appreciatively. Mr. Kasparov and the sheriff also declined his kind offer. The muck was not offered, however, to Paul Grassi or the Global thug.

"Careful it don't grab you by the throat," said Grassi to him.

Voices carry in the forest. It's not an echo; it probably has more to do with the pervasive lack of white noise. The two students, who were standing a dozen feet off, paid attention to the conversations around them, and cast knowing glances at each other, especially at Paul Grassi's little verbal gems.

Cooper finally held the thermos out, offering Grassi some of the tar, or daring him, but Grassi declined.

Soon we were moving again. Ruth straggled, absorbing the sylvan nature of Wailing Wood. I decided to hang back as well, and walk with her. I knew she'd tell me if she preferred solitude.

The trail began to run downhill along a gulch and switched down and back between massive trunks — a mix of the ancient and the simply old — and as we lost elevation we could hear and sometimes see another thin creek below. We were more than a mile in, by my estimate, and we'd been walking for quite some time. I wasn't sure how long. Beside the rivulet were tall, intensely green fiddlehead ferns and beyond the ferns was a single fallen giant, its trunk hollowed out after centuries of decay. This archway was fifteen or twenty feet high, and at least thirty feet of the trunk had been preserved, wrapped in thick green moss.

Ruth and I sat down on a log about fifteen yards from the massive, moss-covered old-growth arch, simply to listen to the sounds of the wood, and again she thought she heard a child's voice, in singsong recitation, say,

"A forest is where things can hide ..."

and she looked around, but she saw no one. She looked at me. I didn't hear it, but I thought the leaves rustled on thin, low willow-like plants. I heard the call of an owl. She said it had been following us. Though distracted, she offered me her tea in silence. We had once again come to an edge of the old grove. But it was the same grove as before, so I had some understanding, now, of its size. I thought, there were six such groves that made up Wailing Wood. It was no wonder everyone wanted not just a piece of it, but the whole thing.

I was sipping tea and staring into the archway. I found it oddly shadowed. I noticed that Ruth was staring right at the lower part of the arch where the shadow lurked. Suddenly, her body jumped as if she'd been electrically shocked. And she looked at me, then back at the shadow. I did, too, but saw nothing more than shadows. "It was a boy," she said. "His hair was light brown, and curled. He was so worried. He was wearing shorts. Like an old style of children's clothes. But no shoes. His feet were bare. He had a knitted vest that was blue."

"A small boy?" I asked.

"Maybe four. But barely."

Except for her voice, it had been very quiet, and except for the brief shadow, it was quite still, until I felt a soft and momentary breeze. It lasted only a moment.

Ruth slowly pointed to her left. I turned to look, and saw a mottled owl of considerable size. It was looking directly at us. Then it rotated its head, looking to both sides, spread its enormous wings and flew deeper into the trees.

Ruth rose slowly and soon we were walking again along the edge of the big trees, which were off to our right, and to our left was the little creek. There was no sky, and the canopy wasn't visible. Ruth, pulling free from her reverie, from the spirits of Wailing Wood, picked up her pace and soon we were with the rest of the walkers.

Bones Exposed

The others stopped and gathered together when Bob Cooper, in front, slowed and turned around. Ruth and I quickly covered the last ten or fifteen yards to where Cooper was standing, and waited.

Cooper is in his late fifties, just under six feet, and he wore a gray cowboy hat that he'd had so long it looked like his cropped gray hair had taken root in it. He had an old Western shirt on, so old that the back and shoulders had faded, but it was starched and clean. The sleeve creases were perfect. He'd hiked in a bolo tie, the sliding nugget of which was a chunk of turquoise with a lesser stone of orange coral enwrapped by two silver leaves and set upon a base of silver with a coiled edge, and his Wranglers were new: Robert Cooper wore his Sunday best. It appeared to me that he'd cleaned up in case Muriel Stanley happened to take his photograph for the paper. I was, as usual, only half right: His dress was a display of his respect for her, and her alone. It wasn't for the rest of us. At the time, I had no idea why.

More, Cooper had hiked from the cars in a new pair of cowboy boots, never slipping once despite the mud and frequent slopes that were covered with redwood needles and duff. His boots were still black, polished, and free of mud and needles. I had no idea how he managed it. He now stood a dozen feet from the side of a berm that rose about two feet higher than a newly cut roadbed. We stood at the crest of a rather low hill, shaped like the top of a huge skull. The roadbed was directly in front of us, with the older trees behind it and to our left. The second growth was behind us and to our right, for the most part. The spot marked the long east edge of a shallow plateau that continued east into the forest. The road grader had cut partly into its side, exposing fresh dirt and rock. A few tree roots protruded; they looked like hands grasping for support but finding only the thick air of the forest.

The scar from the earth-mover was about twenty feet from a truly massive, ancient redwood and there were another ten or fifteen thousand-year-old giants surrounding us, mostly ahead and to the left, which was north: We were at the edge of one of Wailing Wood's six remaining old-growth groves.

"So I was working my way down, just the same," Cooper said, as if picking up a conversation that had been cut off only a few moments before. The sound of his voice interrupted the stillness of the ancient forest, and there was little doubt that his words attracted the attention of whatever spirits inhabit trees. "And I'd been running five or six young steers over the ridge here, over to the south branch meadow where they could graze with another part of the herd. And I come across that road grade," he said, looking down at the cut made by the blade. We could see the hoof prints of his horse from his initial visit, and a few of his boot tracks. The big yellow grader was now off to the side. "That part there slumped straight down, and I could see some roots and whatnot sticking out, and then some of that rock that fell to the bottom. Along the side, there, was something a little whiter than the rest and that's what turned out to be the bone, there, in the side of the berm. The skull bone. Complete skull, but small.

"So then, I stooped to pick it up. Anybody would. And this old barred owl swoops out of nowhere and just near hit me. With his talons out! I jumped back, I mean, and kind of thought about it a minute. He almost got a piece of me just that fast."

They all walked closer to the cut, the sheriff in front since Cooper was mostly addressing him. "Those tracks are mine from before," he told the sheriff. "But I didn't touch much, not after I saw that the white really was head bones, and then there was some of that cloth sticking out there from the berm. You can still see it ..."

The "bone" wasn't white. Cooper, uncertain what he was actually looking at, had dug the skull out of the matrix by hand. The bone was light gray and yellow-brown and had been about three or four inches from the top, but now, having been extracted, the small skull lay at the base of the berm, whole, looking up into a canopy it hadn't seen for more than a century. What would it have been thinking?

It was indeed the head of a child.

Nothing else seemed out of place other than the broad, shallow wound where the soil had been shaved down by the grader. Ruth bent down to feel the dark earth: It was more like peat than soil. That meant it was acidic, and eventually she'd need to know its pH. Had she packed the litmus papers or had she left in too much of a hurry this morning? Sometimes it was hard to remember to bring everything when there was such a good chance of needing everything you owned, down to the smallest vial of acid or a pack of matches.

The skull wasn't much larger than a big man's fist. Sheriff Tully, who was squatting down to get low enough, brushed the remaining dirt from the bone, and the brow and nose crest became more visible. The skull was stained like a cracked eggshell that had been soaked in coffee. Amid the illusion of cracking, the dark, tannin-rich outlines of small leaves were imprinted like tattoos on the bone itself. They wreathed the little head like a fairy crown, like an elf's tiara. I felt I was looking at a drawing from a children's grotesque fairy tale.

The small bit of protruding fiber, the cloth or clothing, was hardly discernable. But Tully studied it, sighed, and mumbled, "It's murder." His voice was swallowed by the trees.

Ruth was aware of Sheriff Tully's unexpected and premature conclusion: murder. She'd heard him, though most of the others weren't near enough. But, she realized, he had enough experience in his life to make such a call with confidence. Perhaps it was the appearance of the cloth, she thought, that influenced his words.

She couldn't take her eyes off the elven head with its sylvan coronet and knelt down near Tully with her nose almost touching it. She wondered morosely what it would look like with light, curling hair, like the boy's she'd seen earlier. But she managed to break the spell and turned and looked closely at the exposed fibers just a few inches away.

Paul Grassi looked to his right where Muriel Stanley, Cooper and Mr. Kasparov had plopped on a downed fir trunk. He glanced quickly at Tully and Ruth as they stood up, leaving the skull at the base of the cut. Then he eyed Sal Mendez, who was standing away from the rest, closer to the old tree on the south side. Ruth looked over and studied Grassi's face. She detected a general animosity toward Mendez, which, she thought, was to be expected. No one likes a watchdog except its owner.

Grassi singled out Muriel Stanley. He didn't like her and she didn't like him. And it went back a long way. It was about as apparent as the big trees themselves, even if you'd never met either of them. But Grassi was intent on coming out ahead in this, and if that meant playing to the Ledger, fine. The last thing he wanted was to be portrayed as a corporate flunky while Miller and the county sheriff took center stage. This was, after all, his timber harvest from the get-go, and his territory, and he knew the land better than anyone, including Miller, Daniel Thom, Luther Eaglejohn and even Bob Cooper. Well, maybe not Cooper, whose family ranch was only a few miles east on Overland Road. But he had more knowledge about this cut than anyone, including his boss, Mike Franzetta, or Global's big-boss, Desmond Blake, to say nothing of Mendez, the grease-bag who hovered off to the side like a rabid dog.

"Above us," Grassi began, pointing south to the ridgetop, "and over on the other side of the ridge was an old timber camp called Bear Breach or, in its earliest days, say 1870s, Camp 7." His voice carried well in the otherwise silent forest. Grassi had an easy way of talking; he was a storyteller, the kind you could listen to and get lost in the trail of words. But they were laced with a hard-to-disguise irritability today. Ruth watched him closely, at times detecting the tension behind his

just-one-of-the-guys delivery. She had picked up on his atti-
tude toward Muriel Stanley and was curious about their relationship, if that was the word to use, but shrugged it off as
small-town/long-history. She was also curious about the history between Muriel and Bob Cooper, who might easily, age-
wise, have been Muriel's father. And that was exactly the feeling that Ruth got, though she knew very well, even then, that
they were not related by blood.

Grassi continued: "Camp 7 — what Bear Breach was
called in the earliest days — is about a mile from here, over the
hill, south. Mile and a half. You'll see some stonework there if
we was to walk over, and there's some rock foundations, and
those are probably a hundred, hundred and twenty, hundred
and forty years old. Late '70s, 1880s or so. They were set as the
camp became more permanent, so there's foundations for some
of the business buildings, like one, I mean, two sides of the
slaughterhouse on the edge, or a couple of private homes and
the old mercantile. Brick or stone foundations and some river-
rock chimneys. Most of the mortar's gone, of course, but, well,
that's what happens when you use sea sand in your cement."
Most of us were listening with one ear, looking around, and
waiting for him to stop. "Yeah, sea sand, it's got its edges
knocked off, sort of rounded, and weathers faster than it
should. Got no teeth left.

"Camp 7, after a few years and few hundred settlers and
timber workers, became Bear Breach."

Then Grassi looked at Ruth and over to Daniel Thom and
Luther Eaglejohn. "We've taken some precautions around the
ruins, of course, but there's nothing that's one of a kind." Although the company had found some historic artifacts at Bear
Breach, nothing was important enough to stop the planned
logging. It was, in fact, one of many, many old logging camps
that peppered the North Coast like raindrops. "We've gone
over this on foot — there was three or four of us — and there
was nothing big. Until Bob saw these bones come right up out
of the ground the other day, I mean. No one could have predicted that, believe me. We were careful; I don't need to point
out that this harvest is critical to the company. It means millions of dollars, it means jobs, tax revenue to the county. Funds
the schools. I mean, I wouldn't be surprised if that skull was

just somehow planted … I mean, something like that could happen."

He put his hands in his pockets, leaning back a little, then forward. He was back on track. "Then, underneath us, almost right where we're standing, running due south, is the old steam-train tunnel connecting the south and north valleys of the White River forks. If there wasn't any trees, you could of seen it from where we all parked, down there just off Overland Road. You all never even noticed, and I'll tell you why. That slope was logged about twenty-five years ago, and Northern replanted after the operation. That's called good forestry. We planted fir and redwood, and you were all looking at third growth silvaculture. But you couldn't see the tunnel mouth! Northern is a good operator, with ecology in mind." Grassi paused. Mendez was looking at him. Grassi realized he'd said Northern rather than Global, but he had no intention of back-tracking now. Besides, Global had nothing to do with logging a quarter-century ago.

"The tunnel holes are higher than the floors of the two val-leys, and the rails come out of both ends up on a trestle, maybe ten, fifteen foot off the ground, the valley floor, but the old tunnel floods all the time anyways, from groundwater. You couldn't see the remains of the trestle, either, from the parking pull-off, also on account of the re-growth. After the spring rains, they used to push all the slash out the north end with a steam engine, wash it down to the fork and then on out, and then they'd be set for the cutting season. The whole tunnel has flooded ever since it was dug, about 1890-something. Right now, it's jammed with slash and trash dating back to the war.

"They'd dam up the water and fill the resulting pond with logs and then open the gates and wash the whole kit and ca-boodle down to the Whitesboro mill. That's still some of the best deer hunting in the county, grown over as it has due to good logging practices."

Muriel had taken notes, though she knew the history and the lay of the land. She just needed a few quotes for the story. Grassi, having finished, having offered, he believed, Muriel Stanley's article a selection of appropriate quotes and knowl-edgeable history of "good logging practices," squatted down and looked at the cut in the road.

Sal Mendez, who had listened attentively to Grassi's little speech, walked over to acknowledge the forester, and thank him for the background.

The Dig

"You want to take it from here, Jim?" Sheriff Tully asked.
"No telling what we'll find. If those old stories are true ... well,
I don't know." Just as he was turning away to let Miller and the
students set up a string excavation grid so all the pieces could
be catalogued by position, Ruth brushed her fingertip along the
dirt where the edge of the grader blade had run, a little farther
back and to the left of where the skull had come loose. A thin
black clot tumbled out and trickled down the side of the berm.
She carefully picked it up between her thumb and forefinger
and on close examination it appeared to be a small blackened,
silt-crusted chain, the end of which remained in the side of the
berm. Carefully, she let it fall down the side. She looked up to
see Miller and Tully staring down at the find. Unscientifically,
Tully bent down and pulled lightly at the chain. A small, flat
black cross tumbled from the dirt.

Daniel Thom, still kneeling across from Ruth, frowned and
looked back at Luther Eaglejohn, who was standing silently
behind him — this site, with a newfound Christian cross, was

not Native American. Talking quietly, they turned and found
an old tree trunk to sit against and wait; it was going to be a
long and fruitless day. Thom put one of his two jackets under
him, sat down and got out a Mason jar filled with coffee and
wrapped with newspaper and string. Eaglejohn had a regular
workingman's thermos like the one that Cooper carried, but he
kept the lid on, saving it for later. Thom had a couple of plastic
cups and handed one to Eaglejohn, who shared the jacket rather than getting his jeans wet from the earth. Thom pulled out
an old pipe and jammed some tobacco into it from a leather
pouch and lit it with a kitchen match he carefully extracted
from his shirt pocket and fired up with his thumbnail.

They sat to the right of the dig, the south side. To their left,
right across from the skull, were Grassi, Ruth and Muriel Stanley. Kasparov sat on the other side of Stanley with Chu and me.
Tully and Mendez remained standing and changed their points
of view every so often, with Mendez always the farthest away,
like a weasel watching chickens. Tully handed Miller the chain
and cross, and he carefully placed it in a paper-lined metal tray
for the time being. The blackened metal was obviously silver,
and it was quite intact, though soiled. Then he and the two assistants started stringing the grid. "Could be interesting," he
mumbled, not sure if he was upset with Ruth for starting the
dig without him, or pleased with a fruitful sign of things to
come. He looked into her eyes as best he could without seeming inappropriate, and, besides finding the most unusual shade
of green he'd ever seen, he discovered he couldn't feel upset
with her even if he'd wanted to.

Soon the scraping of trowels interrupted the silence of the
forest, and buckets of dirt were carried to a screen rocker where
the rhythmic shaking served as counterpoint to the scraping
trowels. No one was in a hurry; everything was slow and
steady and meticulous. The excavators jabbered among themselves. Jim Miller's two students, Lucy and Steven, were hard
workers, especially Lucy. I understood why he chose them
both, especially her.

Grassi, quiet now, looked over at Miller and the assistants
but couldn't see what kind of progress they were making. He
walked over to the sheriff.

"This find isn't going to be too big of a deal," Grassi said. "I've seen dozens like it. Bones turn up, we remove and return them to one of the tribes; they bury them. Give them to the tribes: It's that simple. This here's probably not an Indian kid anyway. Might be a kid from Bear Breach, in which case the county'll have him buried at the Whitesboro Cemetery. Over and done."

And if the site was Native American? It would only mean that Global would let its steel-tracked dozers sit idle while the logs were removed with rubber-tired vehicles in the area around the where the skull had been found.

Grassi said, his tone conversational, "For another thing, it isn't connected to a historic event or person."

Tully tried to listen, but it was hard … he didn't like the man … but Chu had migrated from Mr. Kasparov to listen in. There was more in the comment than appeared on the surface. Tully and Grassi, as well as Thom and Eaglejohn, still within earshot, had been around logging their whole lives, and all of them could tell Grassi was running down the list of what it takes to legally stop a timber harvest. Information about a known historic event is the first on the list — General Custer's battlefield might be a blatant example, had there been trees.

"We found no sign of Native American habitat in here, so there won't be anything that's really unique or scientifically important." Keywords here: unique, scientifically important; in other words, information that must be saved in the spirit of historical inquiry because it can't be found anywhere else. So the list continued. Tully sighed. Eaglejohn and Thom shook their heads and attended to their coffee. Eaglejohn looked ready to take a nap.

Grassi raised his voice a notch and directed a comment to the two: "There's nothing here that'll further anthropological research, nothing that applies to you." The comment went over like a bird dropping from the sky, dead. Eaglejohn turned, glared briefly, and then closed his eyes again as if the proposed nap was now upon him. Thom breathed pipe smoke out of his nostrils.

"You're pretty sure it's minor stuff?" said Miller to Grassi as he filled a plastic bucket for screening, raising his voice slightly so it would carry the fifteen feet to him and the others.

"We were thorough," said Grassi, his voice formal. "Where you're digging, right there," he said, pointing loosely, "wouldn't be typical of an Indian site anyway. There's no creek anywhere near here, or even a seasonal rivulet within fifty yards. That creek we was following's a hundred, hundred-twenty yards off now. And there's no openings — caves or rock overhangs. It's not even flat. No sign of flake-spread from making stone tools, either. Like I say, no sign of habitation, none of the signs."

William Chu, knowing little or nothing about timber harvest rules, was nevertheless detective enough to know that Grassi, the forester, was reciting from a timber-harvest operations handbook. Chu was disappointed; rote memorization had never impressed him, and more than once had such a bureaucratic approach stalled investigations in their tracks. One has to remain spontaneous, he'd said, and creative ... "nothing in this world is rote."

A thought crossed Chu's mind: Did Muriel Stanley, today's assigned historian, realize that Grassi was just reciting entries from a timber harvest primer on how to avoid a work stoppage?

Grassi shrugged a little more dramatically than the situation called for. "There wasn't much need to send for a 'professional' archaeologist and whatever little experts Mr. Blake took a fancy to," he said, referring to Desmond Blake III, Global Resources' regional manager, and to Ruth, to whom he fired a quick unfriendly glance. Mendez, who was standing to the south toward the big trees but still within earshot, squinted. Grassi finally realized he was talking too freely, that Global Resources had ears in the forest. But it was impossible to know what Mendez was thinking — if, indeed, he was thinking.

Miller raised an eyebrow. "Well, you might be right," he said. "Who knows?" Then he signaled the digging team to move slightly east, back farther from the edge.

"We have the lower vertebrae now," said Miller, pointing for whoever was watching. "And that's the left femur. We have the left arm." The bones were charted and removed. But the child's neck bones were still invisible beneath the soil near their feet and very near the edge where the necklace had lain.

"I'd like to see the necklace again," Ruth said.

Miller produced the metal tray with the small, flat cross and delicate, broken chain spread on a sheet of paper covering the bottom. "I can't tell yet about the design because I don't really want to clean it here ... because of the time."

Ruth brought out a triplet and asked one of the students to shine a battery-light on the blackened sterling. "Good shape. Interesting, don't you think? This is pretty old, but it's in really good shape. I think it was poured ... it's so thick. We need to clean it. Do you think it was still around the child's neck?"

"I would say still around the neck," Miller said. "The child's neck is likely a few inches below where we are right now. An inch, even. There appears to be slight movement of the land, but only slight."

Tully moved over and looked closely at it. "Maybe we can get some more information on it from old Father Percy. He's pretty good with that kind of thing. I haven't seen one like this, I don't think." Yet, somehow the border along the edges of the cross seemed familiar. Maybe he had seen one like it once, a long time ago.

Daniel Thom and Luther Eaglejohn were quietly disappointed. They knew that the only Indian children who wore crosses at the time lived on rancherias, and they both knew there was never one in this area. The largest, Nome Cult, was three hours northeast on rough four-wheel-drive roads, and it was nowhere near old enough. Both of them had wasted their time coming for what amounted to the exhumation of a settler's child who had probably wandered away from the old logging camp on the other side of the ridge. And both of them knew their invitations were a ruse to make the company look good. What better way than to ask them along?

Ruth walked back to her bag and took a packet of paper slips from one of the inside pockets. Then she pressed one against the damp soil near the surface."

"What's the pH?" Miller asked.

"Guess."

"Five point five, or six."

She smiled. "I think I'm in love." Miller laughed. Muriel studied her.

Ruth looked at a series of small bones from which the dirt had been removed. "The hand — did you find the metacarpals or phalanges?" she asked.

"No. They were gone. It looks to me like the hand was exposed, and was taken a long time ago by scavengers … the ends of the radius and ulna were possibly chewed, but also very long ago."

"Early in the decay cycle …"

"Exactly. Shortly after death."

"I'm curious about the condition of the rest of the skeletal material."

"Hmm. A lot of decomposition has occurred in the region closer to the surface," said Miller. "But we're only down a few inches so far."

The low, hollow hoot of an owl caught our ears. It came from the older trees to the east. But we couldn't see it. A few seconds later, there was a murmur from Miller's assistant, Lucy. She had a sharp eye, and had been in the department for three years. The mumbling caught Ruth's attention. A few seconds passed.

"I have another skull here," said Lucy matter-of-factly.

Miller, swallowing his surprise, excused himself from Ruth and turned around to see what the assistant had discovered.

"That changes things," he said. "We have to expand the grid a little."

The second skull was slightly smaller than the first, and deeper. This was another child. Miller and Lucy knelt over the new find. Steven, the other assistant, left the area he was working to look at the new skull. Lucy moved the dirt away with a brush, exposing the upper two inches of the temporal and parietal bones along the side. They had none of the leaf tattoos that the first skull had, and as they removed the dirt, the bone was whiter and less decomposed — it appeared to be many years more recent. She scraped her trowel across an exposed section of soil below and to the side of the skull and touched a second bone group, then removed some of the dirt.

"That's a radius and ulna," said Miller. The new find was a foot behind and situated below the first: They, the children, were clearly nestled together. Lucy brushed the hair out of her face and continued to scrape the dirt but kept the bones exactly where they lay. She signaled Steven, who was in his first year in Sonoma State's anthropology department, to move the department's camera, shoot a series of stills, and then log the bone positions on the graph paper they'd been using.

The excavation was fully underway. Ruth went back to the area where she'd been sitting and poured herself another cup of tea and sat on a long log, thinking, silent. Daniel Thom left the grid area and leaned on a thick piece of deadfall beside Ruth. He wanted to talk to her, so he sat down and crossed his legs. "I think Luther and I'll be going back to town pretty soon, then back home," he said dryly. He waited quietly a few moments, and then added, "That silver necklace Jim Miller found is unusual." A conversational opening, Ruth thought. "But I was just curious ..." He hesitated and then said, "... about the pendant you have, yourself, on the leather strip. I wondered where you got it, you know, how you acquired it."

"You saw my necklace?" she said, her voice soft but surprised. "It's under my shirt." Ruth looked up at him, her dark eyebrows raised. To Daniel Thom's eye, they were sculpted, but not thin like most women's. They were, he decided, slightly magnetic.

Thom, whose complexion was dark, blushed deeply at what might have been an accusation. Ruth doesn't wear much jewelry, and her appreciation of it differs from most women I've been acquainted with, which is not to say that many. She wears no rings, no earrings. She has, to my knowledge, one brass bracelet and one silver and coral one, which were given to her many years ago. To my knowledge, she has never bought herself anything silver or gold. And she has that pendant, only one, which I've never seen in the full light of day. I know it's silver and turquoise; there's something white in it, but I don't know if it's bone or stone, white turquoise or shell, and it's on a thong rather than a chain. She wears it often, but not all the time, yet she has never exposed it to view. I've assumed it to be an heirloom, like the bracelets, and I've guessed it came from the Southwest, though I have no proof.

"It slipped when you leaned over."

"What? I look at you when you're stooping over?" she asked. It was impossible to tell if she was actually offended or found a little fun in poking at Daniel Thom.

"It's like," stammered Thom, "you know, when you're out on an old dirt road and you keep your eye down, looking for the glint of an old arrowhead. In the morning light or something. You get attuned to it. That's what. Really. Attuned to it. I wasn't, you know ..."

"Oh," she said, but there was no malice in her voice. She smiled. She liked him, I could tell. "An old dirt road."

"Yep," he said, and only then caught the fact that he'd compared her to an old dirt road. He blushed again, and felt even worse. Daniel Thom wanted to drop it before it became an issue. He kind of liked her, Miss M, and didn't want to leave a bad impression ... such a common male impression. But he couldn't let the idea of the pendant go. Not after what he'd seen. "You know, it's an Atsidi Sani," he said. "The necklace. You know who he was?" He waited for a reply, but didn't get one. "I've seen his work in a museum, and I know one man that has one piece that was handed down, so I've seen the real thing twice. In my life. I'm sixty-eight years of age."

"Who," she said automatically.

"Atsidi Sani ..." That's not what she meant. She let it go. "Atsidi Sani, it means 'old smith.' He was ... he was an iron worker, worked in iron. A smith. He did silver later. He was the first. Navajo. Smith, silversmith and medicine man. It's the way they look, you see, the style, of course, but, the way it is, it's the spirit of them. You can feel it.

"That was his work ... I don't even think it was made by one of his sons. But I didn't see it clear." Was that an invitation to pull it from beneath her blouse and vest? It was hard to tell. Ruth opted not to show it.

"It was a gift from a friend," she said. Finally, she smiled. "When I was very young."

"Did he marry you?"

"I was eleven or twelve, Mr. Thom."

His brow furrowed as if that didn't make sense. You could sense him thinking through the scenarios in which a young girl might acquire such an heirloom, and he realized there was more here than he would ever know. He reminded himself that she was only an acquaintance, and, he knew, hers was most probably a story meant to be heard only by a close friend. He said to himself: Her eyes were deep.

Silence. Like Thom, her appreciation of it, almost entirely, was in the way it felt. "But a very special person, nonetheless," she added.

"I expect. He was Indian?"

"He was Navajo."

"He loved you like a daughter, then."

"I don't know about that, really. Someday I'll run into him again."

"Oh, my." Daniel Thom didn't completely understand her response. It was none of his business, but there was no question about the ominous feeling it left, as if he were standing beneath thunderheads. He shook his head. Maybe it would be better to stay away from her. He had the same feeling he got from his old mother, and he remembered the time that she went to the tribal *curandera*, the medicine woman. After glimpsing his mother's past, the *curandera* just cried. That was not a good sign, the crying.

"We had other things in common," she said, which ended the discussion.

"I can hope only the best for you," he said solemnly.

The necklace was priceless. Beyond price. You couldn't possibly find one because no one would ever let one go. Daniel Thom knew that if a piece somehow hit the market, perhaps through an estate auction, an assigned and funded individual of Native American heritage would snap it up before an outsider could get his hands on it. How could this woman possibly have had a Sani? He looked carefully at the tone of her skin. It seemed slightly darker than most Caucasians he'd seen. Was that enough to indicate anything? Probably not; however, he thought, he'd seen plenty of Indians who were as white as a white man.

Meanwhile, Luther Eaglejohn had circled slowly as they were talking, and he sat beside Daniel Thom. Then, together, they turned their attention to the dig and watched its slow progress.

"You guys want part of a sandwich or something?" Ruth asked. Both nodded and she tore a cheese and avocado on nine-grain bread into three parts. Thom brought four cans of Coke from his knapsack and Eaglejohn had a sack of Keebler chocolate chip cookies. Ruth waved Chu, Mr. Kasparov and Muriel over, and they each brought something to add to the pot. Chu hauled out a huge sack of caramel popcorn from his daypack: True to his word, he'd brought popcorn and was ready to kick back and be thoroughly entertained by what he called "The Yarn Woman Show." Mr. Kasparov, always prepared, spread a square cotton cloth on the ground for all the food. He had little paper bowls, and set them out. He had little plastic spoons and forks and knives, and placed them appropriately. He did not, however, set a place for Mendez or Grassi, a habit he'd picked up in the USSR to keep the snitches away.

There were more sandwiches, a half-crushed sack of Lays potato chips, and Muriel had some really yellow potato salad and hard-boiled eggs and cheese-flavored crackers and five-inch paper plates that she'd grabbed on her way out the door that morning. In short order, Miller and his assistants set their tools down and, with Tully and Chu and me, joined the impromptu lunch.

"After lunch," Miller said, swallowing a forkful of potato salad, "I'd like you to look at the fabric, Ruth. I think we'll have most of it exposed shortly."

"Showtime?" she asked happily. She pulled the pop-top of her can and spewed Coke a few inches into the air. She leaned over toward Muriel and said, voice low, "I never drink this stuff. I don't even drink the diet stuff."

"Me neither," said Muriel, and opened hers.

Showtime

After lunch, Ruth edged over to the grid and quietly began studying the newly unearthed fabric, which was in various states of decomposition. She tried not to think about the boy in the wood. She tried not to think about the girl, who was even younger than the boy. Most of all, she tried not to think about the vest that the boy wore, but she was not successful. When she looked at the fiber protruding from the dirt, she knew she was looking at the vest.

The mass at her feet was a single color — that of dark mud — and fibrous, perhaps felted. Only half an inch of it had been originally above the surface. As I looked at it, I wouldn't say it was fabric. It reminded me of the time my father washed and dried my stocking cap at the laundromat, using too much soap and heat. The mass in Wailing Wood didn't look like fabric to me, but like filthy cotton balls.

First, she used a simple magnifier and then a Peak CIL-series pocket microscope she'd retrieved from her bag. The scope had a glass reticle for measuring, and the light source was battery-powered. At 300X, it provided enough magnification for her purposes in the field.

It was initially clear to Ruth that the fiber was wool and the individual strands, under high magnification, had reached what she called "a crystalline state," which was very brittle. She misted it with water and finished extracting it from the ground. She placed the dampened mass in one of Jim Miller's metal trays, and placed a chemical hand-warmer that she'd brought with her beneath the tray. The warmth and moisture, she said, would help preserve it by temporarily returning it to "a rubbery state, from the crystalline."

What resulted, once she'd magically restored at least some of its youth with moisture and warmth and pulled and pushed it into shape on the warmed metal tray, was a mass about nine or ten inches by about thirteen or fourteen inches, representing what was clearly (once Ruth pointed it out) the left side of a child's knitted vest, apparently with an armhole. The shoulder was intact, and the swath below the arm. The right side of the garment was nowhere to be seen.

Curiously, the ribs of the child's right side, which were deeper, were in far better shape than the left ribs and the skull, which were near the surface. The left was more decomposed, yellow brown, leaf-stained and porous, and in places outright rotting away. The piece of vest accompanied the most decayed of the bones. A portion of the vest near the neck had been above the surface, and that's what had been spotted by Bob Cooper.

Ruth spent fifteen minutes studying the filaments, adjusting the archaeologists' battery lights as well as her own to provide useful shadowing over the wet, soiled fiber mass. She said what she really needed was a powerful laboratory microscope, but she worked with what she had.

Leaving the "vest" in its tray, she searched the area around the second skull and skeleton, but found no sign of other fabric.

She knelt, transfixed by her thoughts, for several minutes. Then she spoke briefly with Miller's assistants: Had they seen other textile remains? They said they had not, but noted they'd only gotten six inches below grade.

After a few more silent minutes, Ruth realized she would not find the remains of the second, smaller child's clothes. And, working the matter like a chess game, plotting her pieces several moves ahead, she realized why.

In studying the dig, Ruth saw that the second child was perhaps five or six inches below the first. She searched again, close down to the soil, and found, again, nothing. She noticed that the smaller child's bones were less decomposed — she looked up at me and noted such, followed by that enigmatic smile, which is a little higher on the left side of her face. Clearly, she was on to something, though I didn't know what.

Ruth closely examined both skulls, from which the surrounding dirt had been mostly removed. She noted the differences: the smaller one was whiter, less porous and generally better preserved. The larger one had deteriorated significantly, was pocked with decay and certain leaf patterns had been etched on the surface — they were tannin stains, somehow preserved in the acidic forest environment.

She spoke to Mr. Kasparov, who dutifully wrote down that she found the level of decay crucial to her working theory: greater bone decay near the surface, greater preservation if you dug down past six inches. Except, of course, for the portion of the vest, which was the opposite: It was preserved near the surface and decayed below.

"Theoretically," she mumbled to herself, "her cotton nightie would have gone the way of the other half of the vest: Gone, gone, gone."

She did not indicate what that theory might be; she did not explain the "nightie." Yet there was no reason for me to ask, and no reason to break in on her thoughts. She wasn't addressing any of us at the moment.

Returning to the task at hand, Ruth also microscopically observed the soil that had covered the bones.

We were pretty quiet as she went about her work. I like watching her. I could feel her brain making connections that I would never understand — until she eventually decided to tell me. But the bones, small as they were, made her pervasively sad. She couldn't help it; melancholy seeped from her much like the sweat on her back.

The smaller child was older than two, Miller explained as Ruth handled the little white skull, because the fontanels of the skull had ossified. He pointed. "Two or three years old. The larger child is about four, based on the ossification of the elbows," he said. They stood over the site, examining the work so far. "We can try to date the bones later, and we'll also look into the silver cross and chain. As for the fabric, do you need more time?"

It had taken Ruth less than half an hour to thoroughly study the scene. "No, I'm good. I can define and date the textile," she said, but she really would have liked half an hour to ponder what she'd seen, time to put it all together.

Sheriff Tully looked over at Daniel Thom and Luther Eaglejohn. Thom looked over at Sal Mendez, who was staring off into the forest, clearly bored out of his mind. Thom had to stop himself from spitting, and instead shouldered his old canvas knapsack for the hike out. Luther Eaglejohn picked up his small nylon duffle.

"Where are you guys going?" asked Ruth, turning as they attempted to steal off. Eaglejohn was, at the moment, stashing his jacket in his duffle.

Daniel Thom shrugged. "Not much sense in staying," he said. They had been fighting the Wailing Wood timber cut for most of the ten years it had been in various courts, and Northern Timber, and later, Global, had triumphed continually. In short, they were through.

Eaglejohn nodded. "Old Mike Franzetta called us in," he said of Global's Whitesboro-based general manager. "He was following orders from his handler. Following orders. That's the problem, Miss. It's the letter of the law. Not Law, with a capital letter. Not Spirit."

Thom added, "We're just being used. And so are you. Have you thought about that? You need to think about it. About being used by this company, some company that throws away its land like it throws away its workers? You need to think about that, some of these days."

Thom asked himself why he was talking to her that way. Didn't she wear that pendant? Didn't that mean anything? But was she so blind as to allow the corporation to use her? Mitigate all that she found, and then cut, cut, cut? Why was he treating her as if she were ignorant of corporate shenanigans?

He regretted his words, but he didn't retract them.

The other members of the party had been milling quietly near the dig, watching the exchange, uncomfortable. Their voices carried well in the muffled redwoods that surrounded us, but no one but Daniel Thom and Luther Eaglejohn saw Ruth pull a twenty-dollar bill from her vest pocket and, after unfolding it, place it on a stump between her and the two men. She put a small round rock on it.

"How about a bet?" she asked softly, almost sweetly, her voice down in the alto range as if in faux seduction. Her smile was so pleasant that Daniel Thom just stopped. He stood there, waiting, Luther Eaglejohn silent beside him. Chu shoved a handful of caramel corn into this mouth and smiled, thinking, Showtime. "Twenty bucks says you'll be more than mildly interested in what I have to say." Both of them were shocked by her action and then Thom started chuckling.

"I never joke around," she said, and slipped another twenty on top of the first, this one still folded, from the pocket of her jean skirt. This time Miller and the others noticed what she was doing. But that was the end of it: She didn't have any more money with her. She didn't like to carry cash unless it was fives and ones, something you could use on a bus or train. She looked my way, and I nodded. Yes, I had a twenty. Whatever she needed or wanted, I was good for.

"Okay, okay, put it away," said Eaglejohn. "I'm sorry. We're both a little embarrassed. We'd like to hear what you have to say. Yes, we would. Things are a little off for me today, and, Miss M, I apologize. But it won't change things. I really don't think it will. Tribal sacred rights will never be a part of this, and neither will the possibility of this land becoming public land, a park. Old Hugh Pike would of got it done long ago if he could of. We've all been set up. We're the very mitigation they wanted all along, us being here. We're all suckers. Global just wants all their i's crossed so they can get this done. Then, afterwards, everyone'll figure out what to do with the mineral rights."

"I like the crossed-eyes part," Ruth said. Her smile had won them over. "But the money stays. A bet's a bet and I could use the cash." I expected her to say, "... I could use the cash, *dude*," but she didn't. The two men fumbled in their wallets; Thom was short, he had only twenty, but Eaglejohn happened to have three bills, so the bet was covered. "Mr. Chu can hold the cash; I never welch on a bet." She walked over to her bag and picked out a packet of small litmus strips and walked over to the dig. She looked directly at me, and mouthed, "Showtime." I had to smile; whatever she was up to was going to be a shock to us all. I appreciated her sense of drama: She'd seen something in that mess that no one, not even Miller, had grasped.

William Chu carefully folded the bills and put them in his breast pocket. He poured sticky popcorn onto a paper plate. He opened a can of soda. It had been wrapped in a cloth and still looked ice cold. He didn't offer it to anyone. But he did offer to share the Raisenettes with Muriel Stanley. He found a lovely, comfortable spot and sat down leaning against a rot-softened stump — but only after he'd spread a small, thin blanket. He had a grin on his face that I'd been used to since we were boys. He was saying, "Okay, roll 'em!"

Miller moved to the side and everyone prepared to listen to whatever she had to say. I wondered how long Grassi would last; not long, I was certain. As for the rest of us, our sense of expectation had naturally increased after we all became aware of the bet. Muriel Stanley got out her notebook rather happily and so did Mr. Kasparov. Muriel moved over to Chu and sat beside him, seeming a little self-conscious. Thom and Eaglejohn took a seat seven or eight feet away on a downed fir trunk. Mendez was off to the south and Grassi was dead center with the sheriff. All that was missing, for me, was the popcorn. Chu had it all.

Babes in the Wood

"Let's see if I can put some order to all this," Ruth began, "First of all, I'm here as a textile forensics consultant. I was hired by Dr. Miller and I'm funded by the county in cooperation with the state university system, which is meant to protect the objectivity of the work. This is an official inquiry, and though my opinion isn't binding, it has scientific and legal weight."

I got the feeling she was about ready to drop a bomb. From where, though? A child's vest?

"So," she said, inevitably getting to the point of it all, "when I say that this discovery of the children is significant both archaeologically and historically, which is exactly what I've determined, it will have the weight of postponing the planned timber operation at least until the research is complete."

Had she just said what she said? Grassi was shaking his head like a dog who'd just been kicked by a cow. Seconds warped into a half-minute, then a minute, and no one besides Grassi moved. His face slowly grew beet red.

"What garbage!" he finally said, loudly, breaking the spell. Sal Mendez's body had knotted during that minute, and even at a distance of fifteen yards, Ruth could see the veins in his neck and temples expand and pulse. Daniel Thom and Luther Eaglejohn looked at each other with a mix of hope and confusion. Chu just smiled, his mouth full of popcorn. He didn't giggle, but wanted to.

"That's not correct!" said Grassi. "You can't possibly be right. Look, Sheriff, get a handle on this! This could screw things up here big-time."

Ruth couldn't have said anything more damaging to Grassi's cause, and Global's. Grassi looked dramatically up at the canopy as if searching for a delivering angel. "It can't possibly be of archaeological significance. It can't possibly be of *historical* significance, either. For God's sake, we've been through all that with the Bear Breach thing, and that was adjudicated and mitigated. The birds — the owls and murrelets both — were mitigated. There was a habitat exchange! For goodness sake! And the one burial site down close to the highway? We repatriated the remains! Maybe this one's historical, fine, no argument … got a necklace, a couple of settler kids, but using the word 'significant' has legal ramifications. The *legal* definition, to the *trained* forester," his voice bitter as well as irate, "means that it holds information available absolutely nowhere else — historically, archaeologically. This here is interesting, maybe, but obviously not legally *significant*."

Grassi started calming down. Levelly, he continued: "Sheriff, I think you should take these bones to the morgue and study the heck out of them. Maybe someone got killed. Maybe it was ten years ago or a hundred, whatever. It doesn't matter." He threw his hands up dramatically.

Though furious, his face had grown less red after venting. "I just don't understand how this woman can come in here, float around on her little fairy wings with her little fairy magnifying glass and knitting needles and bat her pretty little eyes a couple of times at you guys and say we have to shut it down!"

William Chu looked over at Muriel and, smiling, whispered, "This is just the beginning, Ms. Stanley. I'm so happy I suggested her to Sheriff Tully. So happy. Tell me, you're familiar with Mr. Grassi? Later, later," he said, putting his hand up.

Ruth calmly sat down on a five-gallon bucket that the excavation crew had been using to ferry the dirt to the screen rocker. She was glad to have the bombing over, and prepared to discuss the reasons behind her position. "Thanks for your opinion," she said to Grassi, "but I'm being paid to stick to the facts. May I continue? Mr. Grassi? Mr. Miller? Sheriff?"

Grassi actually bit his lower lip. He began mumbling that he'd been a registered professional forester for Northern Timber for seventeen years and an RPF for twenty of his forty-five years. And his father was the head forester at Northern for forty years before that. Then he raised his voice more audibly: "This is worse than the environmentalists, the tree-hugging hippies, the marijuana smoking, owl-calling, tree-sitting slobbering jerks that drive their oil-swilling, exhaust-smoking VW buses to their environmental sissy rallies and hand out their virulent anti-job newspapers like the filthy Ledger and fliers that were printed on *paper* made from *trees!*"

Ruth thought: cumulative impact. The tension inherent in his profession was finally getting to him. She was sure it had been building up for years. She'd seen it before; she sat quietly.

Mendez, upslope, had been poking the number keys on his cell, and, frustrated at the lack of even a roaming signal, he slammed the contraption back into his pocket. He hadn't brought a daypack, and he started on the trail back to the vehicles. "You stay and listen," he told Grassi gruffly. "I gotta know what she says. Report to me after."

This only made Grassi redder. He could have shredded Mendez for a comment like that ... and in public! But Mendez had a phone call to make to Desmond Blake in San Francisco, and he'd make it from the landline at the Global offices on Main Street if he had to. Ruth watched him stomp off in the direction they'd come.

Tully, who was the obvious mediating force under the circumstances, motioned for Paul Grassi to sit down. Mendez vanished into the trees in the direction of Overland Road; he had a mile and a half, maybe two miles, of winding trail ahead of him. After a moment, Tully nodded for Ruth to continue. The sheriff was genuinely interested. Muriel, who had turned on her mini-cassette recorder during Grassi's tirade, flicked it off and decided once again to rely on her pen and paper. She found it interesting — and quite dramatic — that Miss M, whoever she was, had started her presentation with the most sensational, shocking facts first. It was like writing a news story, pyramid style. It didn't occur to her until later that Ruth was indeed writing the story for her.

The Yarn Woman's Reasoning

Once everyone had settled back down, Ruth began her presentation again, talking about what was left of the child's vest, the object for which she was originally called in. "Looking closely," she said, hardly exaggerating because she'd been using her portable microscope, "several things are apparent in the surviving remnant. It has, over time, felted somewhat, which means the fibers have connected together, matted. But not as much as might be expected, and that's quite interesting. I wondered, actually, how time could have stopped. I've dampened the mass and pulled at it, something that wouldn't be done if it were on its way to a museum. But this is a forensics inquiry, which is different.

"The wool fibers are very fine, between seventeen and twenty-three microns. Wool is what's called a complex protein polymer, and every kind of wool has a natural crimp, or wave. When wool is spun to produce yarn, or knitted, the crimp is decreased by about 10 percent. It's still between fourteen and twenty-two crimps per inch, which is very fine. This helps me identify it as merino, which is known for its softness and loft — fineness and crimp. And this has now been exposed to air long enough to get fairly accurate measurements after I washed some of the soil away. I can tell, even after a hundred years, or in this case, a hundred and ten, give or take ten, that the vest was hand-knitted but not hand-spun. The yarn was spun in a mill, a factory. I can tell that by sight. I have dated it by observing the depth to which pollen and other microscopic dusts have entered the twisted strands, as well as by noting the effects of dyeing, in which the dye particles embed themselves in the fiber body with the aid of chemical mordants available at the time … though I wouldn't mind a bit more magnification regarding the fibers.

"The filament length also indicates that it's merino. This has always been expensive stuff. Merino sheep came to America from Portugal in 1802. The uprooted sheep landed in Vermont, and there they stayed for quite a while. I'm making an educated guess that the children here died within ten years of the target date I mentioned, based on the overall condition of the wool, taking into account this very unique environment. This was when merino sheep were still on the east side of the Continental Divide.

"But the children's mama liked very good yarn and she had the money to buy it, to order commercially dyed and spun yarn from Back East, probably from someone she used to know or trade with. Therefore: We're dealing with a family of some means, not laborers."

Ruth said she was able to discern a specific pattern of three raised rows of stitches at the bottom edge of the vest, followed by a finely knit diamond pattern in what she called "moss" stitches.

"… Here," she said, pointing, "is an alternating pattern called 'ridges and furrows.' This is a traditional design from Norfolk, England. The raised rows are purled, and the furrows between them are plain. Above that is a finely knit diamond pattern accomplished in a moss stitch. The knitting is so fine, in fact — perhaps twelve or thirteen stitches per inch — that it's a challenge to differentiate the stitching under our current circumstances."

Under extra light, with the wool pulled and loosened, I thought I could see what she was saying, but with difficulty due to the matted nature of filaments — and an untrained eye.

She paused and drank a sip from her can of Coke.

"The children are wrapped in each other's arms. What do you think, Mr. Miller? Wouldn't you say?"

"That appears to be the positioning," he admitted. "One over the other."

"But the real question for us is: Why are we even able to study these bones, or this bit of wool after all that time? It'll take me a few minutes to explain."

Ruth settled in and told us how decomposition generally occurs. Muriel was scribbling quickly, and Mr. Kasparov was jotting a note here and there, depending for the most part on his very accurate memory. I'd flipped on my recorder and, with Detective Chu, had settled back for what I knew would be a very interesting presentation.

"In the natural environment, when temperatures and humidity fluctuate," she said, "dissolved salts move in and out of objects underground — like breathing — and that accelerates decomposition. Ammonias and nitrates from the decay of flesh accelerate the decay of an animal's fur — or cloth or wool — especially when it's moving in and out as it gets hot and cold during a day or the changing of the seasons. But here, according to the records," she pointed with her eyes to a thick NOAA (National Oceanic and Atmospheric Administration) climate printout partly out of her rucksack, "we have a persistent relative humidity level of sixty-eight percent and a temperature of fifty-five degrees Fahrenheit, so there's little movement and less decay, over all. It's as if the earth's breathing is very shallow, as if it's meditating through the days and seasons of the year.

"Secondly, and thirdly, oxygen and light also accelerate decay. Light helps break down complex polymers; and microbial growth, like bacteria, need oxygen and warmth to flourish and consume tissue.

"Here, however, the layer of leaves, duff, and moisture have reduced light and created a nearly anaerobic or reduced-oxygen environment. Already, then, we've cut down the breathing, the oxygen and the light ... in doing so, we've slowed the aging process and the process of decay dramatically.

"And then, fourth, we have to address chemical aging. This is the good part. There are conditions here that kept that in check as well: The surface area is mildly acidic because of the tannins … ours measures five-point-five, and seven is considered neutral. Acid promotes the survival of wool and silk, that is, protein polymers.

"And that's why we can discuss the wool vest. Wailing Wood has, by its very nature, stopped time in four different ways."

I was with her so far, but had to keep myself from staring into the green intensity of her eyes. It seemed to me that the dim blue light of the forest just made her freckles more adorable, her hair more chestnut, her eyebrows more intense. But I had to think about the bones, and I finally did.

"Something similar but more extreme happened in Scotland, you know," she said casually, standing and looking over the grid, but still addressing the rest of us. "They found what became known as the Orkney Hood in 1857, but it dated to the Iron Age and was perfectly preserved in peat. It was between fourteen hundred and seventeen hundred years old! It was wool, and was in perfect condition! Why? Same reasons as here, essentially, but magnified. They could even tell that the wool came from a Shetland fleece. Of course, the acid totally wiped out the soft tissue and bone of whoever was wearing it, which illustrates a couple of general rules about preservation: waterlogged acidic soil is good for wool or even that little silver necklace, but very bad for bones, shell, and textiles like cotton or linen. That's why the larger child's skeleton is partly decomposed … the acid near the surface.

"Alkalinity, logically, is better for bone, way better. But it's hard on carbohydrate polymers, like cotton or linen. That's why the smaller child's bones are less decayed: She's farther from the forest duff, down deeper in the ground.

"So at this point, we're coming upon the anomaly that makes this site archaeologically significant, in the legal sense. The smaller child is buried deeper than the other, and the deeper soil is neutral and has perhaps begun a journey toward alkalinity. I suggest that she, I'll call her 'she,' wore cotton clothing, perhaps a nightie, because there are no buttons or buckles on that kind of garment. Where are her clothes? They're gone, decomposed completely.

"The four-year-old's remains have decomposed more than the other child's. I'm going to say 'boy' for the older child, because of the vest. So his bones are browned, his skull porous and stained by leaves. The portion of his wool vest closest to the surface is very intact. Conversely, 'her' bones are unstained; she has no clothing left.

"Therefore, we have two environments here: acid above and base below."

She waited for what she'd said to register with Miller. She wasn't sure he was following.

"This isn't normal," she added.

She waited longer. Grassi wasn't picking up on what she was saying, either.

Not yet, anyway.

"You see, what lies below," she said, "will postpone and perhaps curtail the proposed timber plan."

Again, she waited as though she were a teacher giving her class one hint after another, but still, no one raised their hand. Chu, however, was already putting two and two together, and elbowed me in the ribs. "Holy cow," he whispered. He'd gotten the point, whatever it was. He pushed some popcorn my way. I expected a high-five, but Chu was more reserved than that.

Grassi, however, couldn't even speak. What lies below? Nothing! The woman was nuts. Another tree-hugger. His face was getting red again, his blood pressure high. He rose, turned, breathed deeply, and sat back down on a nearby log. He'd be damned if he was going to participate in this circus.

"The site is archaeologically significant because of the two environments. The alkali below dissolved the entire right side of the vest, which was buried deeper, as it did the suspected cotton nightie."

Finally, almost exasperated with us, she put her hand in her pocket and drew out a thin strip of blue litmus paper. Grassi was aware now of what she was about to do; he took a deep breath and swallowed. The red went out of his face, and he paled to a deathly white. She had to be right. Of all the unfortunate things, this horrible, condescending woman was right. There was no other possible conclusion.

She went over and rubbed the paper strip on the peat that had surrounded the bones. It turned red, indicating acid. She bent over the excavated area under the cotton-string grid, and dug down into the mulch and soil with a trowel and then with her hand pulled up the dirt. Then she pushed the trowel down another five or six inches, digging up another clump of soil. The student aids were noticeably upset at the wanton maneuver. She pulled out a second handful of earth and tossed it aside. The soil was dark, almost black. Miller, seeing this, stood up and moved closer, as did Grassi. She stuck the damp piece of red litmus paper down deep, waited a few moments, and withdrew it. It had returned to blue, indicating alkalinity.

Miller nearly choked. One of the assistants had to pound him on the back to get some air back in his lungs. He came up shaking his head and laughing so hard he could barely catch his breath. Grassi shook his head uselessly. Daniel Thom looked like he was ready to dance a jig. He had a little Irish in him anyway, just enough to dance a jig on Northern Timber's collective heads. Then he corrected himself: Global's collective heads.

"The only possibility is that under the acidic layer of peat is an alkaline layer of soil," Ruth said. "Like layers of a cake ... complete opposites, with a thin area of neutrality in between."

"Such soil," she said, "in this environment isn't natural. It could only be produced by a midden beneath the acidic layer of mulch — a Native American kitchen dump of charcoal and shellfish. Alkali. The two children curled up on, or in, an old midden.

"It had been abandoned before they lay down to die. Beneath their bodies, beginning about ten inches down, is the black soil typical of a midden — charcoal from the fires. I just pulled up a handful. There will be rocks cracked by the campfires. There'll be lithic scatter from making knives, scrapers and arrowheads. But most importantly, as far as we're concerned, there is the alkaline soil that came in contact with the acidic soil, creating a neutral zone. We have a scientifically unique situation here. There will undoubtedly be organic artifacts. There is a chance of finding reed or pine needle baskets. The northwest tribes are noted for this. Perhaps leather clothing, or furs. The dual environment, in this unique instance, may give us wooden implements or other perishable products for which we have no specimens currently, and open up a lens on a culture that passed away centuries ago — because of the unique preservative quality of the dual environment in concert with the lack of light, lack of temperature and humidity fluctuation and all that. I don't believe there is a record of anything like this being found before. This is unique."

Grassi stood dumbly. He hardly blinked.

"Information gained from this site," she continued, "will answer a multitude of research questions; it will produce the best, perhaps the oldest, examples of an otherwise extinct cultural life; and it may be directly associated with what I am convinced is an historic event — the deaths of two children, two children who were kidnapped or ran away only to die in each other's arms, in a researchable historic period, and only further inquiry will shed light on the crime that led to their deaths. Because the children were from a prosperous family, there is, in my opinion, a good chance of an historic record of their lives, and hopefully their deaths. We have a site both archaeologically and historically significant in the legal sense."

Miller was astounded. He looked at Ruth, then over at Muriel Stanley who was checking her cassette recorder, making sure it was working.

Chu, standing now, looked pretty good in his slacks and designer jacket. He'd changed into his dress shoes, as I predicted. And he was enormously satisfied.

Sheriff Tully, whose slow demeanor disguised a quick mind and steel-trap memory, rubbed his chin and removed his hat. He sat up a little straighter when he spoke.

"Well that was worth the hike," he said to Ruth, almost chuckling, but not quite. "I guess I owe you a steak dinner. Can't help but wonder about one point, though."

"The leaf marks on the boy's skull? I looked at them very closely," said Ruth.

"Yep."

"They're there because Wailing Wood is in a time lock; there's no passage of time. The little crown is like looking at a daguerreotype from a century ago; I mean, you feel that if you get a magnifying glass, you can look deeper and deeper and you end up looking back into the past. That's how it feels. And that picture is one of tanoak, which has a serration to the edge; live oak, which is lightly lobed; and strawberry leaves, which to me are unmistakable because I stole strawberries incessantly as a child. What they have in common is ..."

"... that they have no business this deep in an old-growth forest," Tully said, finishing her point for her. "Someone killed those two children and then buried them."

The afternoon was well upon us. We'd been in Wailing Wood for at least nine hours, and in that time we'd found a tragedy dating back a century and more. We found a midden. Somewhere beneath us were, I hoped, baskets and tools.

We packed up. Miller spread a tarp over the dig. He'd return later to further secure the site while he organized a full team to extract the hoped-for relics of a vanished culture.

Muriel was taking notes on the last of her questions to Miller, and Miller was graciously answering with as much detail as he could. Grassi had already started down the trail and was out of sight. The two archaeology students went next, and then Tully.

"I think I'm going to hang back a while," Ruth said to the sheriff, in passing. "Mr. Fisher will stay here with me. I'll get Mr. Kasparov to stick with me, too. We'll come back into town in his car. You have my numbers, sheriff?"

Thom and Eaglejohn were standing nearby when she said she'd amble back down to the parking area in her own time. We were the last few at the site. Chu, always the professional, was walking with the sheriff, the volume of their conversation a little lower than normal as they walked the trail together, wrapped in a discussion of murder scenarios.

Thom hefted his knapsack onto his shoulders to get it situated. "Well, thank you, then," he said to Ruth. "I guess I'm starting to understand how that pendant ended up around your neck. If you don't mind, we may be in touch on a couple of points. Me and Luther have some calls to make. I should of bought that long-distance phone card I seen the other day. State Forestry will probably become part of the complete dig, once Mr. Jim informs them. Do you think there could really be baskets, or wooden tools? I mean, all drama aside."

"Yes," she said. "There's a neutral band of soil between the acid and base regions; something will survive. They might be digging a very wide area, but they'll turn something up, I'm sure, as the pH varies."

Luther Eaglejohn scribbled some digits on a scrap of cardboard from the empty Keebler box and handed it to her. "Well then," he said, pausing. "Anytime, anywhere, day or night. If I'm dead and buried and you need to call, my son will pick up, and the same rules apply. His name's Lester. Lester Eaglejohn."

"That's a nice name," she said, and carefully placed the cardboard in a small box in her bag. They left her standing at the now-covered dig. Mr. Kasparov was seated beneath one of the big trees, preparing for a long wait. He knew what would happen next. The Miss would have to take some time getting herself back together. Despite the science of it, she was dealing with the deaths of two children, and she was only scientific on the outside. The scientific part of her was spent.

Ruth walked off toward the grove of big trees to the south, turned, and with her eyes asked me to follow. The ancient trees began only yards away. I heard the call of an owl in the distance, and I was sure it was the same owl we'd been seeing and hearing all day. Ruth tried to smile. Once facing the other direction, she wiped off the tears. It was very difficult for her, feeling the fear and loss that those children felt so long ago, and, of course, catching their images in the shadows of Wailing Wood. It would probably take her days to finally shut it off.

A Certain Amount of Prying

Muriel Stanley, who'd been hovering to the side after saying goodbye to Jim Miller, lingered behind as well. She went over and sat beside Mr. Kasparov, who moved over slightly for her. There was no reason; the fallen tree on which he sat was twenty feet long. It was just a way for him to acknowledge her presence, like pulling out a chair for her at a table.

"Where'd she go off to?" Muriel asked.

"It's not every day one finds oneself in an ancient redwood forest, Ms. Stanley."

"Yeah, I guess. So, that was quite a show. Did you get it all down on that notepad?"

Mr. Kasparov looked at his watch. He figured they should leave the forest before it got dark. An hour? Two? He had a flashlight, of course, but that's no way to hike. Yet, there was time. There was time. "I suppose I recorded the salient points," he said happily, seriously.

"Do you write it up for her, too?"

"This, I don't know. You never know what the needs of the day will bring."

"I saw your notes; you must have written ten pages."

"Oh, really?" He smiled, his enormous teeth protruding into the air. "I hope you couldn't copy my very excellent reportage," he said, giggling. He pulled out his notebook and started fanning through the pages. Everything was written in Russian, the script was Cyrillic. She laughed, and he handed her the notebook.

She leafed through the pages. "I never had this happen before," she said, squinting.

"Well," said Mr. Kasparov, trying to hide the last vestiges of his accent, speaking precisely and slowly, "I must tell you, Ms. Stanley, I am not really a journalist, like yourself. No, I'm really not. Do not let the nose fool you. I offered to take excruciatingly detailed notes for my friend, as she lived fully in the moment. She, personally, has no need of my notes; The Miss has a very good memory, you might say."

"Oh." They waited in silence for a while. There was something touching about his statement. Something sentimental. Then she said, "You guys are going back to San Francisco tonight?"

"I will be leaving. I have other engagements, unfortunately. But it appears that The Miss will want to remain. There is work to be done, I am sure."

"'The Miss?'" she said, her voice laced with the thinnest trace of the sardonic.

"Yes, she can hardly let the matter lie. There are still questions to be answered."

"I mean, you called her 'The Miss.'"

"That's very perceptive, Ms. Stanley," he said. "You are a very good news person. Newspaperwoman."

"Oh. Well, anyway, I guess you two have, like, a long relationship?"

"Years. Decades. Moments. My notes?"

"Oh, of course." She handed back the notebook. "So, um, what do you do besides drive 'The Miss' and take notes for her?"

"Please don't think you're prying." His voice was friendly. He was used to this sort of thing.

"Oh, I'm sorry. Really. I can't help it. I guess that's why I do what I do. My father was worse, believe me. She seems rather fond of Mr. Fisher, don't you think? My father would have suggested that."

"Mr. Fisher?" asked Mr. Kasparov. "Now, there is a true journalist."

She could see he wasn't going to venture any information. Period.

"He has passed on, then? Your father?"

"What?"

"Your father," said Mr. Kasparov. "He is deceased?"

"Oh. Yes. Three years ago. He was eighty-five."

"You were a late-in-life-child, as the saying goes."

The statement stopped her short. Then she said, "That's the best of it, Mr. Kasparov, I assure you."

"Myself, I was an early-in-life child. My dear mother was barely fifteen. I arrived during difficult times, but those are all over."

"My son, Arnold, Arney, is an early child," Muriel said, unsure if she really wanted to get into it.

They sat for a few minutes before Kasparov spoke again. "Do I want to know more?"

"No," she said. "I don't think so, right now. It's just too nice here in the forest. It's so quiet."

"Excellent. Sometimes I don't know what I want, and it works out well when others can tell me. But I wouldn't mind a cookie. Would you like to share a cookie? I made them myself. This one is the cookie czar, very large, with very many chocolate chips. Ivan the Terrible! I have been saving it all day so as not to starve and grow weak as The Miss goes about her business deep in an apparently haunted forest."

Muriel smiled broadly and put her hand out for half of the large cookie. "You bake a lot?"

"Is your recorder on?" he asked. "I am not good in interrogations. They always end badly for me."

"I don't know what to talk about."

"Well. I have curiosities as well," he said, putting one hand in his lap. He was studying the half-cookie in his other hand as if to determine the artistic position of the chocolate chips, which he found to be properly placed. He noted the golden brown tone of the surface walnut pieces, also finding them satisfactory. "The position of the chips is important to many people. I try my best. It is paramount, visually. And the walnuts, well, Ms. Stanley, they must first be roasted, to bring out the flavor. And then baked."

"I think you could call me Muriel."

"Muriel." He took a small bite and changed the topic. "And this Mr. Paul Grassi, then, is this, shall we say, is he a homey? A home boy?" Mr. Kasparov loves colloquialisms, especially when they're misplaced geographically — like an urban term in rural environs.

"Oh, yeah. Way homey," she said. "Paul's like ten or more years older than me, but we went to the same high school — because there's only one school, you see. He's married and has two kids. They're like ten and eight, a boy and a girl. His wife's name is Meg and she's five years younger than him. She went to Whitesboro High, too. His dad was a forester with Northern Timber for a really long time. Then he died from cancer that he got from the defoliants they used to spray with. It was eight years ago that Old Man Grassi died. Mario. I think everyone in town went to the funeral. My father and I brought a ham loaf to the house after the service, but Meg ... hey, this story just got too long. Sorry. Anyway, Paul went to Humboldt State to get his forestry degree and got a certificate from the state, and then got hired by a timber company up there before coming back here when there was an opening. And his mother's still alive."

"He has an unpleasant side."

"Oh, he's okay. Marginally. Your typical misogynist logger type. But usually he won't call you what he thinks you are to your face. That counts as a gentlemen if you're from around here. But he *does* think it. Everyone does. I don't like his wife much, but that's ancient history. I don't think either of them has been out of the state, like, ever." She stopped herself. A little gossip goes a long way and always seems to bounce back on the gossiper; it makes one look small. Muriel was afraid she'd start looking trashy if she kept talking. "How was I?" she asked. "I didn't see you taking notes. That's a good thing."

Mr. Kasparov made a closed-mouth smile. "Who is Mr. Grassi's boss?"

106

"Oh, that. I have a tendency to talk too much. You're all business, Mr. Kasparov. Taking notes in your head, huh?"

"I have been accused of worse."

"Not bad enough to get arrested and put in jail after an interrogation, I hope."

He smiled. A slick little chill went up his spine but he managed to seize and throttle it. Were all women so perceptive, or just the ones he knew?

"Old Man Franzetta," she said. "He was the general manager of Northern before Global acquired it. Michael Franzetta is Paul's boss. His kids are my age, but one of them was killed in 'friendly fire' in Iraq. He's really old school, but he's maybe only like, mid or late sixties. Everybody at Northern liked him a lot back in the day, but then after the acquisition — Global Resources bought Northern three years ago — he's like a ghost or something. He used to raise the flag every day under Northern, but when it wore out, Global decided they didn't need the American flag anymore. They got a company flag and he was supposed run it up every morning with the state flag. It really hurt Mike, more than anything else. ... I think they cut his stuff off, if you'll excuse me." She blushed. Why had she said that, of all things? She could have kicked herself. "I mean, he thinks they did it to him on purpose. He's a vet ... the Korean War. Anyway, he used to come into the newspaper a lot, but not anymore. He and Dad used to have lunch occasionally. His wife makes killer peach pie."

"Oh, really?" Mr. Kasparov perked up for a second. "Peach pie, then. Interesting. Killer? I see. Oh, I understand. It is a slangism. Who is Mr. Franzetta's boss?"

"Who's his boss? Boss of the bosses? He flew up on a Lear jet when the sale was announced. The municipal airport is just long enough for that kind of plane. I mean, who's going to take a jet from San Francisco to Whitesboro? It's stupid. But those poor guys at the mill. They never knew what was coming. Global closed the mill about a year after the acquisition and let everyone go. Then they moved all the machinery inland. I mean, we barely had a volunteer fire department left. And then, with the fishing the way it's been ... like, basically gone. ... We had to organize a whole new system and have a mill levy to fund the fire equipment upkeep. My God, the cost of repairing a fire engine. … It's been downhill, economically, ever since. So anyway, the big boss flew in for a grip-and-grin."

"My friend uses that term. I find it amusing."

"Your friend Mr. Fisher? I met him a few years ago, about a year before Daddy died. Dad used to say he looked like Roosevelt. I never really thought so. I wonder if *she* does …" Muriel caught herself thinking out loud, running off at the mouth. She was embarrassed yet again. "Well, anyway, his name's Desmond Blake, Global's regional general manager. I'd guess he's about fifty. I mean, really young for that kind of position. He's handsome, if that matters, and very photogenic. It was like he had artificial tanning lotion on or something, his complexion was so perfect. Great contrast to his silver hair. Women would die for it — I mean, if they went in for the natural silver look, which most don't. The main regional office is in San Francisco, but they have other offices in L.A., Atlanta, and some in Germany or Sweden, and somewhere else. Brazil, maybe. He's not the overall honcho. That would be the guy in Brazil, where most of the mining is, or like in Denmark or something. The San Francisco office is in one of the old skyscrapers in the Financial District. If you write that it's in this historic skyscraper, and put it in the Ledger, they think you're a company hack. Bet your friend doesn't know anything about small-town newspapers, so you should tell him.

"But Blake's got no friends here, I'll tell you that. The guy's creepy. You might think he's just eye candy, Mr. Kasparov, but when you look at him you kind of get a queasy feeling like you need to get to the bathroom quick. And no one here likes out-of-town ownership, anyway. And, plus, no one likes a timber company being owned by an international mining and oil company. It's weird.

"Old Franzetta still has a lot of friends, but it's all kind of changing. It's like the old warhorse was sent to pasture." She blushed again when she realized she was blabbering a mile a minute and saying stuff she usually saved for friends. Or no one. For a moment she forgot she could count her close friends on less than one hand. She shut up long enough for them to eat the cookie.

"Talk about being a homeboy. So, tell me about *her*."

Mr. Kasparov tore out the pages of his notebook that he'd so carefully inscribed and handed her the remainder, still a few dozen blank pages, to take notes in.

"You really are all business. You're not going to give me a break today. That's okay," she said.

Mr. Kasparov smiled and laughed and then folded his notes and placed them in his shirt pocket beneath his jacket and zipped it back up. "Miss M's doctorate is in textiles, both the history and scientific aspects," he said succinctly. "We should consider ourselves lucky that she kept her presentation short and avoided the Latin nomenclature. I think she's very kind, you see, to do that."

Muriel nodded.

Mr. Kasparov continued. "Miss M is a noted consultant in textile forensics, and has worked with the FBI, NSA, ICE, Homeland and a number of local police agencies in recent years. She is not fond of ICE and has indicated she may not work with them in the future. I don't know why, exactly, though I have my suspicions.

"Miss M was involved in a recent serial murder case in Los Angeles. It upset her for weeks and she had to purchase much yarn to get over it. I drove. She was distraught. But that is the way with sensitive artists, I dare say. Did you know that there are more than thirty yarn stores in the central portion of the state? Well, there are.

"She often serves as an expert witness in criminal or court proceedings. In those circles, she is known commonly as the Yarn Woman ..."

"They call her what?" interrupted Muriel.

"They call her the Yarn Woman. The police do."

"Why?"

"It's nothing she wanted."

"Yeah. But, I mean, why?"

"It is a term of endearment. I think they know that she also knits. I suspect as much."

"She had half-knitted socks in that red knapsack of hers," said Muriel.

"Practicality is important, you see," said Mr. Kasparov.

"Right."

Mr. Kasparov continued. "She often serves as a research, adjunct or visiting professor of textile history and is regularly engaged in various university lecture circuits and in museum acquisitions.

"But most important, Ms. Stanley, or, Muriel, is … her cat. She has a cat. Need I say more? Cat, yarn, harpsichord. Therefore, the 'Yarn Woman,' I suppose." He shrugged.

"A harpsichord? She's a musician, too?"

He nodded. Muriel suddenly felt a little overwhelmed.

Mr. Kasparov, realizing the situation, noted, "I am fond of Detective Chu. Are you?"

The abrupt turn left Muriel trying to land back on her feet. Mr. Kasparov continued, "He is an enjoyable person and quite intelligent. He does not play chess, however." He shrugged.

"So, he's a San Francisco cop? Mr. Fisher said something about his mother?"

"Mrs. Chu. An excellent cook. So now I will tell you, Mr. Chu has a mother, whom you know about, and a sister and a brother as well. His father is deceased. He is well-loved by the officers, oh, it's true, he is, and, confidentially, this being from Mr. Fisher, he was known early in his career for his speed afoot, and used to run down various criminals on his beat, Chinatown, as they were no match for his lightning speed. He is quite athletic. Some might consider him good looking."

"Yep," she said. She might have asked more questions about Detective Chu, but no one likes to be obvious.

She was looking at her notes, wondering where the conversation would veer. "When you're writing a story," she said, "usually you just want to know what a person does for a living. You put that in the article when you mention the person the first time. It helps the reader identify the character. If you had to say, in a phrase or a sentence, what she does, what would you say? Police consultant?"

Kasparov cleared his throat. "She knits, Ms. Stanley."

She just sighed. There was a long pause. "Maybe that's why they call her the Yarn Woman," she ventured. "What do you think?"

"I never considered it."

"I could say, 'criminal textile expert.' "

"That would be fine, I am sure. But she is not a criminal. Perhaps textile forensics consultant would be better?"

That embarrassed Muriel. She'd never have written it that way; why had she verbally placed the adjectives as she had? She was beginning to feel like a hayseed and she didn't even know "The Miss" yet. She scribbled a little on the notepad and set it in her lap, looking at Mr. Kasparov. "She's from San Francisco, they said. Jim said. Miller. Was she born there?"

Mr. Kasparov looked over at her. "So I understand. She was just an infant at the time."

Funny. Was he joking around? It was so hard to tell. "She's acquainted with Detective Chu?"

"Some half-dozen cases. Yes."

"Does she know his mother?"

He forced a nonsmile and feigned ignorance. "Ms. Stanley, everyone knows Detective Chu's mother. Let us not read too much into that. I learned to make jiaozi from her, though not nearly as well. My dear friend, Mr. Fisher, practically grew up in the Chu household. He has jiaozi in his blood, though one can't tell that by looking at him. That is what he has said, has mentioned to me, personally, saying, 'Mr. Kasparov, I practically grew up with Billy.' "

"Jiaozi?"

"They are dumplings of Chinese cuisine. They are stuffed with wonderful things, perhaps shrimp on a very good day, and perhaps green onion and, for example, there may be an exceptional dipping sauce ... mustard with soy and vinegar."

"You're making me hungry," she said.

"Yes," said Mr. Kasparov. "It is not the best time of the day to discuss jiaozi."

"Okay then," she said, ready to stop talking and listen to the silence of the old forest.

"Please don't call Mr. Chu 'Billy.' He is unfond of the name," said Mr. Kasparov before silence could settle in and take hold.

"'Unfond.' I see. I won't call him Billy. I'm sure Detective Chu will do. And thanks for the cookie, by the way. Mr. Kasparov, do you mind if I excuse myself and wander after her? I don't mean to be rude." She looked at her watch, then at the canopy above them, forgetting momentarily that the sky was out of reach. There wasn't much light left in the outside world, however. "And so, where's she staying, anyway? In town?"

"She will let me know in good time."

"Whew. Talk about wearing the pants." She rose and left her bag near Mr. Kasparov, who was smiling at her comment, and walked quietly south. Mr. Kasparov watched her walk away. He liked her. He did not consider her quaint. She was a woman, and they are never to be underestimated or considered quaint. As creatures and as intellects, they are anything but quaint.

Muriel found Ruth and me seated on a long piece of deadfall near the foot of one of the giants. Ruth didn't look up as Muriel approached, though I know she heard her. Muriel sat down beside her and silence reigned for several minutes. I greeted her, excused myself and went to find Mr. Kasparov, allowing Muriel to talk with Ruth privately.

Finally, Muriel broke the silence, saying, "It's almost dark. We probably ought to go."

"Yep," Ruth said, standing. "But I'm not finished here, Miss Stanley."

"Muriel. What do you mean?"

"I have to find out who they are. And how they died. … I don't feel there's any choice in the matter. I may very well need your help. Actually, I will certainly need your help."

Muriel nodded. She thought she understood what Ruth was saying when she said there was no choice, and maybe she knew what Ruth was feeling.

They walked back to me and Mr. Kasparov, who was still sitting, pondering the magnitude of Wailing Wood. I was ready to walk back. He stood when he saw them approach, and shouldered his bag and picked up Ruth's. We walked back in the settling eve.

For a moment, Mr. Kasparov thought he heard the sobbing of children, but when he tried hard to listen, it faded like the forest mist. I didn't hear it. It took us more than an hour to make the road because of the dim light. The Silver Cloud was still there, of course, its polished paint reflecting a foggy moon. He walked around it; everything was fine. He'd been only slightly worried. He banished the thought of Paul Grassi scratching the paint with a quarter. Why would he even think it?

Parked about fifteen feet away was Muriel Stanley's Camry. It was once brown, but had faded and rusted. It was coated with dust and the driver's door had noticeable grease spots at the creaking hinges where the lubricant had been over-sprayed.

"So, you might have some trouble getting a room," Muriel said to Ruth. "It's not that they don't have rooms, the motels I mean, it's just that the night crews all hide out and watch foot-ball and don't answer the bells, especially in the off-season like this. I mean, it's Monday night, after all. I have room at the house, if you want to crash there tonight."

"I wouldn't want to put you out," said Ruth.

"No, it's easy, it's just Arney and me. That's my son. You'll like him. We live in town, above the newspaper. Daddy had it structurally restored and we've lived up there since Mom died. I did the recent cosmetic restoration … it took me six years. It's a cool building."

"Well, yes, okay, that's very hospitable. I should have made hotel reservations before we drove up to the wood, from the city by phone. It's just hard to make yourself do that, some-times. You know how that is?"

"Hard to spend the money, you mean."

"Well, yes, but I meant it was hard to use the phone."

Muriel asked Mr. Kasparov and me about staying, but he said he had to leave on business, something about shipments arriving, much to her chagrin, and I said I was staying at the Herring Gull down in the harbor, where Detective Chu also had a room, to which she said, "Mrs. Morton's one of the good ones."

Ruth drove into town with Muriel. Mr. Kasparov followed them like a gangster tailing a victim. We waited as they parked and watched them walk to the front doorway of the old news-paper building, and they waved at the door before walking around to the staircase at the side. Mr. Kasparov returned the wave and slowly pulled back onto Main Street, cruising through town. He drove down to the harbor and dropped me off at the Gull. I went to the lobby to watch the TV news with Mrs. Morton and leaf through a few of the magazines she kept in the lobby for guests: Atlantic, New Yorker, NYRB, a few punk zines — an odd selection, I thought, but nice.

"That Stanley girl," said Mrs. Morton, "she's okay. But they don't treat her right." She held out her pack of Winstons and shook one up for me. I declined, graciously.

Paul Grassi

Paul Grassi slid most of the way down the last stretch of the trail back to the cars and walked to his blue Ford pickup, passing the long Silver Cloud. He looked into the Rolls' windows at his reflection. He thought, not bad, but wasn't sure if he was referring to his own reflection or the leather upholstery inside. Yes, his reflection, though the upholstery was probably nice — it was too dark to really see. Even in the near-dusk, the reflection of his lightly grayed hair looked distinguished and somehow youthful, his face was tan from being outside and still clean-shaven because his beard didn't grow that fast. Take that peculiar Kasparov, for instance, he thought. The man could have shaved twice a day. He should have some of that beard moved to the top of his head.

Grassi had a momentary urge to take a quarter out of his green polyester work pants and scratch it across the driver's side of the Rolls, and though the thought caught in his head for a few seconds, like a fly in a web, he subdued the urge. It wasn't Kasparov that made him think twice about it, it was the magnificent car itself. He just couldn't do it. It was inspiring. He had his father's old 1972 GTO in the garage at the back of the property, and he'd been meaning to restore it for at least the last ten years. Seeing the Cloud gave him new hope — maybe even new energy, just knowing that such things were possible.

He bashed his right knee on the steering column getting into the pickup, winced and slammed the door. He was tired. He pulled onto Overland Road and headed west and then north through town. Grassi lived on a ten-acre spread about three miles north of Whitesboro in a rambling 1960s ranch-style house. His father had it built, and Paul grew up there with his two sisters, both now living in other states. The cedar shake roof was nearly new, and he'd carefully kept the exterior in fine shape. The lower half of the outside was pink sandstone and the rest was oiled cedar. The big chimney on the end was sandstone, too.

Grassi was forty-two, had been married to Meg for fifteen pretty good years, and they had Mark, ten, and Jessie, eight. In two words, he was modestly happy; in one, satisfied. The only time he'd left town was to attend Humboldt State, which he'd finished a semester early, and to work a stint with a Humboldt County logging outfit. When he got back at age twenty-three, Meg was a senior at Whitesboro High. They waited.

The kids were watching TV in the living room when he got home. Meg was still in the kitchen. She and the kids had been home about an hour. "There's casserole in the oven," she said. "You could have called. Your mother wants to know if you'll come by this weekend. And there was a message from the office — Mike called, wants you to call him back, at home." She gave him a kiss and hug. "It sounded important." He grabbed some stick pretzels from a bowl on the counter and got a beer from the refrigerator.

"How'd it go?" she asked.

He shrugged. "This harvest plan ... it's like the plan from hell, the curse that keeps on taking. It makes me wonder why I ever got into this business."

"That bad?" They walked out to the living room. Mark and Jessie took the cue and went to the den and turned on the

TV there. Grassi flipped the channel to a football game, turned the sound down and put the remote on the coffee table.

"It wasn't bad enough when they called Jim Miller in from the university to do my job," he started, "Miller was told to hire a fiber expert to look at the site. Really … I don't know … nasty."

"I'm sorry it was so bad, Paul."

"I mean her. This so-called scholar was one of those women who can't wait to make you look like a fool. And that's just what she did."

"How could you look like a fool when they took the project out of your hands a long time ago?"

He shrugged. "I was the one who did the initial walkthrough. I was the one who didn't see the skeletal remains … "

"But they were underground, Paul. That's what you said."

"They were. But still. Between this woman and Miller, they managed to unearth a second skeleton and an entire midden, an Indian site, and there's probably baskets and objects like that, preserved under the surface. The whole thing'll be shut down in a matter of hours."

"Shut the whole harvest down? For how long? Oh my, the jobs …"

"Well, we won't be able to get the roads cut. No roads, no logging. It'll be May before Northern, before Global, can get started again because of the rains, and because of the mitigations, whatever they'll be. So it really doesn't matter if they take two weeks or six months digging out their May baskets.

"I mean, you should have seen her, Meg. She's decked out in this … these rags. She has a skirt on and pants, too. At the same time. Like a tree-hugger, but it's like she's never seen a tree in her life. I made some comments and she replied with … such sarcasm. I get enough of that at the office these days; goodness knows I don't need it from a stranger."

Grassi seemed to settle down. He stared at the game on TV. "Mike tipped off the Ledger about the site review, too."

"Oh, great. I think he's getting senile. Why ask *her* along? The Stanley girl?"

"No, Mike said they told him to do it. For PR. Anyway, Stanley was there taking down all her notes, so I'm going to look like a three-ring fool to everyone in Whitesboro, come Thursday."

"I don't like her, Paul, but let's leave it alone. I feel sorry for the boy. They say he's a good kid, anyway."

"Arney? All he can do is hit a ball and take care of Mommy."

"Hit a ball all the way to the majors."

"Maybe the father was a big-leaguer. He'll never go. Apron strings."

After a few minutes, Meg said, "You probably should listen to the message from Mike. It sounded important."

"What time did it come in?"

"I don't know, maybe five this afternoon. Or after. The kids and I were out until six."

They both went to the kitchen and Grassi hit the playback button on the phone. He leaned over it, trying to catch the words from the tinny speaker.

"Yeah, Paul, this is Franzetta. Give me a call at home soonest. Thanks." Buzz.

He looked at Meg; she shrugged. He picked up the phone and called Mike Franzetta at home. Franzetta picked it up on the second ring.

"What?" Franzetta said. It didn't matter who was on the other end.

"Mike, Paul. You left a message. Anyone else would think it was overly brief. What's up?"

"Yeah, Paul, where are you? You back?"

"Just got here. Been a bad day."

"So I heard. That mutant Mendez stomped into Northern like he owned the place . . ."

"Global. Probably does . . ."

"And told me mostly what happened. There must have been eight of our people that watched me get kicked out of my own office so he could call Blake — you know how visible my door is to the rest of the desks.

"Anyway, the point of my call: Blake said they're killing the forestry department and not to tell you yet."

Grassi was silent.

The Whitesboro Ledger

Ruth waved as Mr. Kasparov and I drove off, the engine of the old Rolls purring down the night-blackened street. The overcast sky made it darker still, and puddles from an earlier drizzle reflected the lights of the stores across Main Street. She could smell the wet asphalt and dirt, mixed with the scent of the sea.

The Whitesboro Ledger building looks like something out of the nineteenth century. That's appropriate, because it is. It's a two-story box with a square storefront. Behind the façade is a gabled roof you can't see from the street, and there are twin draperied windows upstairs in living quarters that look down on the north end of Main. The building is long and narrow, and the cement sidewalk and two cement steps at the front entrance seem out of place: The building cries out for wooden steps and a boardwalk ... and townsfolk toting six-guns and leading horses to street-side watering troughs.

Behind the building is an alley followed by fifty yards of sandy soil punctuated by sea oats and wandering, low-lying fat-leafed sand-dune succulents that blossom in yellow and pink in the dead of winter. At fifty yards is the elevated trestle once used by old logging trains that carried redwood south to the mill. It hovers about thirty feet above the sand, its twin rails secured by a latticework of huge redwood timbers, grayed by age. Three hundred yards long, it once connected higher grounds on the north and south and even now has been rehabilitated by the city into an elevated walkway along the beach.

After a hundred and twenty yards of sand is the Pacific surf, which carries the wind and an incessant spray over the west end of Whitesboro most of the winter and spring.

The Ledger's storefront windows are wide and night-black, with gold lettering on the glass:

The Whitesboro Ledger
Voice of the Northwest Coast
Established 1861
C. Lawrence Stanley, Founder

Ruth looked in. There was a desk light on inside toward the back and she could see most of the way through the building. It looked like something from the age of letterpress printing, with devils' tables and strange-looking presses behind the thick oak chairs and desks near the front and down the north side of the long room.

"That's the office," said Muriel. "I'll show you later, or tomorrow. I'm starved, so let's go upstairs and get something to eat."

"Oh yeah." Ruth had forgotten how hungry she was. "We could go somewhere, maybe …"

"Too tired. Can't eat hamburgers this late, and that's all you can get on a Monday night. I mean, without reservations. Anyway, I like being at home after dark unless there's a meeting. I'm out a lot for meetings. Have you ever been to a sewer board meeting? That's where all the really good stuff happens."

"I hadn't thought about that," said Ruth.

They walked around the side of the Ledger where an outside staircase ascended. About ten feet away was an adjacent building, a store of some sort. Sensible, Ruth thought, since this was the downtown. Probably.

Under the stair frame was a chicken coop. Ruth peeked around the steps. There was a low-watt bulb above the coop.

"We have three," said Muriel. "Edward R. Morrow, David Brinkley and Horace Greeley. Horace is the black and white one, Eddy's white and Dave's the brown one. They're all good layers, but Horace is the best. Print media, after all."

"I like them. Maybe I can meet them tomorrow."

"Sure. They'd like that. Especially if you have some bread."

The siding was tongue-in-groove, with about a half-inch gap between the boards where only the tongue was visible. It made the building look older, but it wasn't decrepit. The paint job, visible in the dim glow of neighboring lights and a bulb above the upstairs door, was new and the color tones were tan and soft sage green with orange accents — colors you might choose in a restoration project to bring back the turn-of-the-century feel of a place that somehow found itself in the twenty-first century. They both paused for a long minute at the top of the stairs and looked west over the ocean, peering beyond the silhouetted framework of the train trestle. They could see the waves roll in, moonlight hitting the crests. The sky had cleared, at least for the moment. "Yeah," Muriel said, "I can't tell you how many times I've been out here at five in the morning to see what the ocean's washed up. Mostly kelp, I have to say," she laughed and opened the unlocked door. Ruth noticed the lack of security, but said nothing. After all, Whitesboro wasn't the city.

Inside was a modest, well-lived-in three-bedroom flat. There was a small mudroom and foyer as they entered. To the far right was the sitting room, which overlooked Main Street with two broad windows and thick curtains. The near right: the living room with a small thin-screen TV and an older stereo system, a couch and a couple of worn but matching chairs. Along the far wall: an upright piano of uncertain lineage. Left of the living room was the kitchen, followed by two bedrooms and bath and finally the "granny room," which had been set up for her father. It was an independent apartment with its own bathroom, kitchenette, entry door and staircase facing the sea. The end. If the furnishings were any indication, Muriel Stanley was not a wealthy woman.

"We moved back in here after Mom died," she said as they walked through the living room and around to the kitchen. "Daddy had the work done while we were still living on Grant Street. We had a two-bedroom bungalow. But he didn't want to stay there anymore after Mom died. I mean, he asked me what I thought, but ... was I going to put the kibosh on it? No way.

"So Daddy and Arney and I lived here, and then Dad died. I took care of him. I'm still tired and that was three years ago."

"I think it's lovely," Ruth said. "It's even warm. ... took care of your father ..." she eyed Muriel thoroughly.

"We insulated when he had it redone, and that little fireplace burns coal, hot and dirty. Sometimes we buy hardwood because it burns so much hotter than pine. There was a lot of structural work done — I mean, it's an old building. We found calendars in the walls. I have them on the wall in Dad's old room and one in mine. They're from 1889 to 1907. Very Victorian." She started plowing through the cabinets and refrigerator, rounding up whatever was handy.

"What can I do to help?"

"Can you chop? How's a salad sound? We could have a salad with steamed zucchini or green beans on it. I have feta. You like feta? I mean, are you vegan or something?"

"Nope. Great. Will your son be home for dinner? He might want more than a salad. I don't know."

"What's today, Monday? God, Monday all day. ... I'm really tired, Ruth. He might be back late or not at all. I'll make sure there's extra and leave it in the fridge."

Ruth shrugged. At least he wasn't running around in some city like San Francisco or Oakland. Whitesboro — the town that crime forgot. It must be nice having that kind of peace of mind when you have a family, kids, she thought.

Muriel got out a big wood cutting board, a strainer for washing the lettuce and other greens and an old chef's knife that had been sharpened so many times over the decades that the edge was concave. "I need to have that blade reground. That was Daddy's knife ... . I just have to keep using it. You know how it is." She wondered if Ruth M, the Yarn Woman, harpsichord consultant, did know how it was, really. "Anyway, I have to go pick up a few things around the house, then I'll set the table if you're into taking care of this part."

"I'm in. Mind if we turn on some music on the stereo?"

"No. Some nights nothing comes in. The DJ's are all old hippies. Gray hair. So beware. Daddy had an antenna set up on the roof for the shortwave — he was a ham operator — so I have this hooked up to that. But it's still not perfect."

"He could get news from all over the world, I bet."

"Mostly gossip."

Ruth flipped on the stereo and then walked back to the kitchen and started washing and cutting. She could hear the stereo in the other room, vaguely at first, but then she went back and cranked it up so the sound would carry into the kitchen. It was a console stereo circa 1970 by Magnavox, with light oak cabinets and a turntable and analog radio in the top, AM and FM stations displayed in a backlit strip like a ruler. Muriel was still cleaning up some part of the house — no one's ever really prepared for guests. She returned about ten minutes later, just as Warren Zevon's "Werewolves of London" started creeping out of the old speakers and into the kitchen. Ruth went out and solidly cranked up the volume and started dancing around the kitchen as she finished the salad and tried to set the table.

> "I saw a werewolf with a Chinese menu in his hands,
> "Walking through the streets of Soho in the rain
> " … Lee Ho Fook's
> "… get a big dish of beef chow mein …"

Following Ruth's lead, Muriel started bobbing from cabinet to table with plates in her hands, shuffling over to the drawer to get napkins. Ruth shook the lettuce in the drainer and danced the bowl over to the table. Green beans steamed in a colander.

> "Well, I saw Lon Chaney walking with the Queen
> "Doing the Werewolves of London …"

Chairs were out, places were set, water was poured in glasses, a lemon slice in each, and the two were dancing around the kitchen.

"... *drinking a pina colada at Trader Vic's*
"*His hair was perfect ...*"

The song faded and Ruth ran into the living room, diving for the stereo. She switched it off.

She said, "How on earth can you follow 'Werewolves of London'? I couldn't stand to hear anything else after that. Let's eat, I'm dying."

They sat across from each other at the small round table, a bowl of salad between them and the feta, dressings, and steaming beans to the side. "Makes it easier to get dinner ready," Ruth said. "I would only do that for Warren Zevon."

"Mr. Kasparov said you had a harpsichord. You must have broad musical interests."

"Mr. Kasparov said I had a harpsichord?"

Muriel caught the unsettled feeling in the question.

"I was prying," she said. "That's about all he said." Muriel decided that Ruth might be overly private, maybe reclusive despite her profession.

"He talks a lot."

"I bet werewolves are good dancers," said Muriel.

"I bet they have mites and roll in dead fish."

Muriel looked strangely at Ruth. "I never thought about that. You want some crackers or something with this?"

"Yeah, but not now. Later, second course."

There was no salad left after twenty minutes. "What do we do about Arney?" asked Ruth. "Should we fix him something? Pour some cereal into a bowl?"

"He can cook. Look, let me show you your room — this is a big deal, you get your own room — and where to wash up. I can get these later," meaning the dishes. "If you're as tired as I am, this is must-know stuff. And the dishes can wait until morning, anyway."

"Yeah, great. I left my bag at the door, I'll get it."

They walked back through the house, Muriel flipping lights on as they went. The bedroom "suite" on the end overlooked the headlands and, during the day, had a picturesque view of the landmark trestle and the ocean beyond. To the north about half a mile was an old gravel-crushing outfit, with big industrial silos and stacks jutting up into the night's backlit blackness; they were shadows against shadows and seemed ominous, like metal rock-chewing beasts grazing on sand. To the south were lights from sporadic beach houses, not many, just enough to seem like fireflies at a salty watering hole. And directly west was the Pacific, its moon-white waves rolling in, and the sound of the surf on rock and sand. The window was open and the curtain on the right was fluttering.

"This is the guest room, and the little bathroom is there," Muriel said, pointing. "It just has a shower. But the larger bathroom with a tub is out there off the hall. It's clean, you can shower or use the bath first. Or whatever. The linens are clean, so just make yourself at home. Do you have everything you need, I mean, did you get packed in time or did you have to leave half-together? I think this deal was on pretty short notice."

Ruth put her bag on the bed and rifled through it. Then she poured it out. There was nothing but microscopes, sample vials, books and knitting projects: the back and front of a sweater, a Russian shawl on circular needles, some socks. Litmus papers, a bottle of solvent. Pattern books: yes. Toiletries: some. A few extra clothes. Nothing to sleep in. Muriel studied the items as they exited the bag, then watched as they re-entered. Ruth went over to the window. "A million-dollar view. It's beautiful. I don't think I'd ever go back to wherever it was I came from. Where was it I drove in from this morning?"

"Well, things are that way here," said Muriel. "You'd never find anything like this now. I mean, unless it was millions. But forty or fifty years ago, this was just normal. Rundown and cheap. But it's been in the family since 1861. It's kind of average, and, I mean, who'd want to live right in town, really? Every other building in Whitesboro used to be a tavern, and they were all open and full by nine in the morning. They ran three full shifts at the mill until Northern sold out, and the bars would be the workers' first stop on the way home. We used to watch them from the sitting room windows and drop juniper seeds down on their heads."

"We?"

"Me. Arney. Daddy, fifteen, eighteen years ago, before we lived here full-time."

Ruth sat on the bed. It was a double with three pillows and a down comforter. A thick chill went up her back. She sneezed. "If you don't mind, I can sleep out in the living room on the couch." She wasn't sure quite how to say it, but it was out before she could run through it mentally too many times. She was pretty tired.

Muriel looked confused. It was a nice room. Then she said, "Sure. Well, actually, I don't know. Do you have allergies? If that's it, I mean, everything's really clean. I even vacuumed under the bed last week. Week before last. I dusted. Is it the lemon dusting stuff? We're low on cats right now, so you don't have to worry about that."

Ruth sighed to herself. Why did it always have to be like this? She looked up at Muriel from where she sat on the bed. "Well, hmm, your father was into short wave radio, right? So you probably know what a cat's whisker is?"

"Sure. But it's not for transmitting, just receiving. It's part of an old crystal radio set. It doesn't have much to do with shortwave, just early radio in general. Daddy and I used to build them out of razor blades and pencil lead. I don't remember how, now."

"Exactly. My mother used to call me one. And this was your father's room."

"Yes."

"This is where you took care of him."

"Sure."

"Well, if I tried to sleep in here, Muriel, I'd end up knowing more about your father than I need to."

Muriel thought about that for a moment and then it became a little clearer. "Oh. Well, that would be a little weird, huh? So, like, can you see ghosts?"

"I just feel things sometimes, is all."

"You could practice. Maybe you could get really good."

"I guess."

"Sure. You could be a natural."

"There are a lot of yeah-buts to that idea. For one thing, you end up on the frying end of everyone else's obsessions."

Muriel thought about that and then nodded. "Right. Okay, so, you could sleep in my bed? I guarantee you won't get much there." Actually, the thought concerned her more than a little, when it came down to it. "Come on, let's go change the sheets. I'll sleep in here."

"Really? I don't mind sleeping on the couch. Look, I'm really sorry. I make a terrible house guest. I should have gotten a hotel room."

"It's not a big deal, Ruth. Besides, there're no hotels in Whitesboro. Just motels. Like the Gull in the harbor, out on the flat. Where your friend is staying. Mrs. Morton's place. Car headlights go right in the front door of every room. (It was built when the renters all had skiffs, not cars.) Or there're the chain motels in town. Right on the Coast Highway. Man, when the logging trucks downshift on the way south, it'll send you into the ceiling."

"You must have a lot of sheets."

"I'm good on sheets, low on guests. The mercantile in town went out of business last year — ripple effect of the mill closure — and I stocked up. Eighty-five percent off."

"You should have called." Ruth stood up and walked to the doorway with Muriel.

"I lost your number or I would have," Muriel quipped. "Hey, I have to bring the radio with me, though. I listen to talk radio. You can keep the clock."

"Nice. I know, take the clock, too."

"Clocks give you the heebies, too? Like dead daddies?"

"Yep. Where there's a clock, there can be no soul, is the old saying."

"Works for me; I'll take the clock too. Sheets in the hall closet. Come on." They walked down the hall to the bedroom nearest the living room, stopping to pull out sheets and pillow cases. "Besides," she continued as they stripped the bed, "you can't sleep in the living room tonight. I only have one TV and there's a show on that I want to see. It's a pretty good bet that I'll fall asleep watching it, and I have to get up early tomorrow."

"What show?"

"Yeah. There's this thing at the Salmon Hall. Big meeting tomorrow. The fishermen are getting screwed again this year.

An early Tuesday is okay, though — free doughnuts and coffee."

"Yum. But I meant, what's on TV tonight, a cooking show or something?"

She looked up. "Yeah. Secrets of Udon. I've been waiting all week."

Ruth stared and half-smiled. "Okay then. Do you mind company?"

"Sure. I mean, no. It's on in about thirty minutes. I always make popcorn. You want popcorn?"

"What kind?"

"What do you mean, what kind?"

"In a way, I mean, what kind of popcorn is it?"

"It's not the cheap stuff, if that's what you mean."

"I only eat expensive popcorn," said Ruth.

"Good. I'll get the Sunday best out, but you'll have to pop it. Put on lots of salt. I have to see the opening."

"Fine."

"If you miss anything, I'll tell you. Should I record it?" asked Muriel.

"No, I can take the verbal," said Ruth.

Muriel: "This is great. Get me a Coke, too, with ice? Not diet. Want one?"

"What the heck."

Ruth went into the kitchen; Muriel set up pillows and blankets on both ends of the sofa. The blue light from the TV filled the room.

Secrets of Udon. Ruth wondered if this was the Iron Cook thing out of Japan.

Muriel's son still wasn't home when Ruth finally meandered off to the bedroom not long after the cooking show was over. Muriel had fallen asleep on the sofa as predicted; it was 1 a.m. There was a pair of flannel pajamas waiting for Ruth on the bed. Apparently, Muriel had noticed the lack when Ruth unloaded her bag earlier. Ruth took a quick shower and slid into them. The arms were long and the legs longer so she rolled both and crawled under the blankets. Thank God this one was over. She felt like she could sleep till noon. The distant wail of the buoy to the south, offshore from the harbor, wooed her to sleep.

About two, a semi-conscious Muriel shuffled off to her father's old room. She'd already gotten into bed when she realized the dirt of Wailing Wood was still stuck to her, sweat having become the glue of the day. She got up, showered somnambulistically and zombie-walked back to bed.

At three, Ruth heard the door to the outside staircase slowly, carefully open. The lower hinge needed a drop of oil. She could tell. Shoes came off and stocking feet crossed the mudroom. She couldn't tell how many feet were sliding across the linoleum. She thought she heard a whisper. After a few minutes, her bedroom door opened silently, and a shaft of dull, sixty-watt light from the hallway slipped in. She was looking at the wall opposite the door, sleeping on her side, her back to the door. Someone pulled her blanket up over her shoulder, and the interloper, registering surprise at the unexpectedly thick, dark head of hair, slowly retreated in absolute silence, pulling the door closed. Ruth sucked in the cold sea air that came in through the window and watched the curtain wave slightly with the breeze. It had been forever since she'd been tucked in at night. She went back to sleep.

Arney Stanley, Muriel's Son

The first light of dawn was trying to illuminate the surface of the Pacific when Ruth awoke. The light wasn't having much luck. The sky was overcast, although yesterday's brief rain wasn't yet staging an encore. It would spend the day building up its strength for later.

She unwrapped the pajamas from around her legs and arms and re-rolled the cuffs. Ruth is so used to people being taller than she is that it didn't register with her anymore; so she didn't really pay attention to the fact that Muriel Stanley stood a good four inches above her.

She had slept fairly well, but a dream troubled her. In the dream, there was a man of medium height and slight build with a wide handlebar mustache. He was seated in her room, Muriel's room, where Ruth was sleeping. In her dream, Ruth woke up and saw him, and together they went downstairs to the newspaper offices. They walked to the back and there was a small room that had very large books that held newspapers from long ago. The man pulled one down and showed it to

Ruth, and he rambled on about something she couldn't remember. On that page was an advertisement for gingham cloth at Bear Breach Mercantile. She nodded. And that's all she could remember of the dream.

Awake now, in the morning, in Muriel's room, Ruth wandered barefoot out to the kitchen to find some tea or coffee, the misbuttoned pajama top covered by a peach alpaca shawl she'd pulled from her bag. She'd pinned her hair, and though it was out of the way, it was still a mess. The hallway was dark but when she got to the kitchen she had to squint until her eyes got used to the overhead light. She held her arm across her eyes. After a few seconds, she could see. There was a young man of about twenty sitting at the table with a cup of coffee and a half-finished plate of scrambled eggs and toast, reading yesterday's New York Times. He looked up and out through a shock of dark blond hair.

"Whoa, you have your mother's eyes, dude," said Ruth. She navigated to the table and sat down. "And her hair."

"Hi. I'm Arney. Who are you, dude?"

"I'm Ruth. We were up at the dig yesterday. Thanks for tucking me in last night."

Arney flushed. His complexion was light like his mother's. He was a tall young man with an athletic build like a baseball player, and quite handsome beneath a scrappy, weeks-old beard that was strawberry blond.

"Imagine my surprise," he said. "I'm sorry. I hope it didn't scare you. I always check on her when I come home. The last one up always checks on the other. That's our general rule of survival. That and phoning about forty times a day. We don't buy minutes, we buy months."

"Is that, like, coffee from a pot, I hope?"

"No. But I'll make some more. It's from a press. It'll just take a second." He was up and setting water to boil before Ruth could say much more. "You want some eggs or toast?" He looked at his watch. "I've got to get some stuff started anyway. Mom'll be back in about twenty minutes, something like that. She's down at the Trollers' Hall. The fishermen are getting shafted again this year — no commercial salmon season to speak of … maybe three weeks open, then a month-long closure and maybe an open week after that; no one knows. There aren't many fishermen left anyway, but it still hurts. They're a bunch of anarchists. … I think that's why Mom likes them. She'll come back zeroed out after a couple of jelly doughnuts and coffee. She's a sugar freak. Toast?"

"Sure."

"I do her toast about one-third to one half and then leave it. That way, when she comes in, it only takes a minute to get the toast toasted. It's a good system, because double-toasting it makes it crispier, the way she likes it. So, like, how are you doing? Are those eyes natural?"

"Oh, great, thanks. You're really awake, huh, Arnold."

"I get up early. In about an hour, you'll notice a hair creature sliding out into the kitchen. That's Lou. She's a real sack rat."

"I thought I heard more than one last night."

"I thought you were asleep."

"Faking it."

"Why weren't you in Grandpa's room?"

"That's a long story, Arney. Look, I have to go brush my hair and teeth. I wasn't expecting breakfast service. Not that I'm complaining. I'll be right back."

"Don't get them mixed up. Do you always wear your hair up?"

"Yep."

"Too bad."

"Too bad, you." She walked down the hall and turned left. He watched her. She had on his mom's pajamas. He'd never seen eyes that green, but wished he hadn't mentioned it.

Ruth came back out to the kitchen after fifteen minutes, having dressed and splashed water to wake up. She threw the bed together and put on some thick socks. It was cold in the house. When she got back out to the kitchen, there was a full plate of steaming eggs, toast, coffee, and the inside sections of the Times. Arney was still engrossed in Section A.

"Wow," was all she could say.

"So how'd it go yesterday? What'd they find?"

Ruth talked between forkfuls. "The skeletal remains of two children. It was sad, Arney. I mean, it's very interesting, of course, but I have a hard time with loss. But scientifically, this place turned out to be one of a kind. There's a layer of acidic duff and soil over the top, but beneath is the alkaline presence of an old midden. And it's down far enough to be really old, more than just a few hundred years. I mean, you can't see the dark soil common to middens until you're down quite a way. Totally hidden. That forester, Mr. Grassi, couldn't have seen it if he'd tried. I think the company was upset with him for not catching it. But anyway, the juxtaposition of the acid and base matrices sets up a truly unique condition, with the pH neutrality capable of preserving even cellulose — carbohydrate polymers, I mean, if they're in the right place, which they weren't, at least for my purposes. That didn't happen because the cotton was placed just right to be wrong."

"Whoa. Cellulose: You mean like baskets or wooden fishing implements? That's what you mean, right?"

"Exactly. It's going to be really interesting if anything emerges fully intact. I mean, in some places the pH levels are so defined that, for example, the left portion of the boy's wool vest remained because of the acid; but the rest was consumed because of the alkalinity. The girl's cotton gown was completely gone. Some of the bones had substantial deterioration, but, depending on their position, other bones were excellently preserved even after a century."

"I missed it. I can't believe it. Mom called, but I couldn't get back. I always, I mean almost always, get in late on Friday and leave Sunday night so I'm almost never here on Mondays. I try to get back midweek sometimes, like today or Wednesday, but I couldn't earlier because of tests. I left after the exams, but didn't get here until, like, two in the morning."

"Probably around three."

"Yeah, but I'm good for like three days now, so I'll go back Friday really early, and come back here Friday night."

"Where are you so-called going to school?"

"Humboldt. This is my third year. I was admitted to a lot of schools, but I didn't think it would work out. This way, I can come back and do the books. Mom can keep up with most of the rest. She has a full-time reporter and a part-time person for sports, and Charlotte, of course, and an ad designer and a pressman. The ad designer's a belly dancer; she gives lessons at the rec center. That's Sally. She basically comes in three days a week. And she trades classes with the new guy from L.A., who teaches yoga. But Mom ends up working her butt off every day of the week unless I buy her a ticket to something. Then she'll stop." He poured himself another cup of coffee from the press. "I sell a few ads, and Mom does. Almost all the accounts are standing, so, I mean, how much more could be brought in? Whitesboro's population is only three thousand. We have only so many stores."

Ruth swallowed some coffee. "So, Arney, who's this guy with the handlebar mustache? Do you or your mom know him? He's regular height, like five-ten, maybe one-fifty, one-sixty, dresses like something out of the nineteenth century."

"Sounds to me like old Robert Stanley ... that would be my great-great-grandfather. We have a picture of him up on the wall in my room. Why?"

"Just wondered. I wasn't in your room, though."

"So how'd they get there, the two children?" Arney asked.

"That's the thing," said Ruth, her voice betraying her sense of the strange. "I'm trying to figure out how to begin looking into it. Muriel says there are some old local scary stories about the wood, and I'm thinking that the bones and the tales could be related. Meaning, I need to find someone who knows any of the old stories about Wailing Wood, stories in their purest form."

"Oh sure, the intrepid folklorist. Did you ever see 'Song-catcher?' That's a ticket example. Buy her a movie ticket, and Mom takes an hour or two off. But, the stories, that would be Gran ... Mrs. Cooper. Bob Cooper was the one who found the bones, Mom said. You must have met him, right? It's his mom. You must have met him yesterday. And Grandma Cooper is like in her eighties and she's lived there north of the wood all her life. She'd know."

Ruth raised an eyebrow. "Insider information. Great, thanks."

"That classifies me as an informant, technically. Did you like Bob Cooper?"

"I think Mr. Cooper's skin has somehow attached itself to his hat and boots."

"No, he's got new boots. I think he went to Fresno last month to get them."

"Bob Cooper strikes me as a man who'd stand with you, you know? Thick or thin?" she said.

"Yeah, I think so. That's good, a good way to put it."

"We didn't talk much because there wasn't much of a chance. He seemed, you know, pretty together. Like, decent. I thought maybe he lived with his mother, or vice versa."

"Yeah? How'd you know?"

"Cookies and cookie vibes."

"Oh. That makes sense. Are you staying for a while?"

"A few days, at least. I have to find a motel room this morning or afternoon. I have a friend staying in town; I'll probably stay at that place. Your mom was really thoughtful in asking me to stay last night, but it'll be really easy to get a room."

"No, you should stay. I have to work all day today, and then study here the rest of the week, but Sunday is the day we go out and do something. That's why Lou comes, for Sunday. Well, other things, too." He smiled, but he didn't mean it the way it came out. "She doesn't have to go back with me on Friday … she could take you out fishing." Arney had his mother's loose tongue, Ruth thought, but it was nice to be around people who didn't filter everything that came out of their mouths.

"And you work all day today on the accounting?" she asked.

"Right. It takes eight or nine hours, but what's cool is that Mom brings lunch and snacks. It's like having room service. Usually I do the subscriptions first because it's quick. We lose subscribers only if they move or die. We gain a few every once in a while, but it's basically stable at forty-three fifty, paid. Then I catch up on the classified billing, which is fairly light since the Internet took over the universe. Then display billing — we usually do pay-as-you-go, but a few of the accounts are thirty to sixty. National advertising is up front, so I don't have to bill for that. We settle for 'check's in the mail' on all our local accounts. I don't do the payroll; Mom uses an accounting firm in town for that. But I plan on it after next year. While I work, she uses the time to write up most of the news she's gathered since Friday, she's on the phone for ads, and Lou goes fishing or paints or sketches. She prints. Lou's a printer, her specialty."

"And she is …"

"She's very good."

"I expected," said Ruth. "Maybe I can see her work at some point ... unless I already have seen it and didn't know at the time? Does Lou fish in the ocean or the river?" Ruth asked.

"Ocean. She likes being outside. She keeps a set of oils here."

"She's at Humboldt, too?"

"She's studying art."

"And you're in business or journalism?"

"Business. I have a business acumen. I just got a day-trading program to start experimenting with."

"Okay then."

"Just no money yet. I already knew journalism from the College of Human Osmosis. I mean, between Mom and Granddad, you absorb more than just the basics. What do you do? Dig up bones?"

"I'm into textiles. The sheriff asked the archaeologist who planned the dig to ask me to come up."

"Jim Miller. He's a really nice guy. The nicest guy that everyone hates. This town doesn't forgive easily. He's put a stop to more than a few logging plans over the years. Things have settled out now, since there're basically no trees left to cut, but all the litigation used to fuel raging battles in town. You could say. Once Mr. Miller was up here and had to buy four new tires because someone drove steel spikes into the sides of his. Along with his radiator, down through the top. He said he was just happy they weren't between his ribs. He actually said that. If you pound, like a spike or a nail, into the tread surface of a tire, you can use tubeless patching glue, but when you do it on the side, the tire wall, you have to buy a whole new tire. He had to buy four new tires. He teaches at Sonoma State. Do you teach somewhere?"

"Here and there sometimes. I like to be a little freer than some, so I've avoided tenure track."

"Where'd you go to school? I mean for the doctorate. You do have a doctorate?"

"Vancouver."

"That's a really beautiful area. Great school, too. Mom went to Columbia."

Ruth raised an eyebrow. "New York or Missouri?"

"New York. The Ivies — does the Columbia School of Journalism count as Ivy League? Anyway, they always have a few social experiments running, if you know what I mean. Like Harvard, when they admit a brilliant but homeless rag-person, or some of the other universities inviting really brilliant but challenged people from, like, Somalia. Or from difficult, isolated rural regions in the U.S., like the coal country of Virginia, or Maine, or, you know, Whitesboro.

"Anyway, they must have seen Mom as a gold mine of social challenge. She got a free ride and books, room and board for two, everything. I think, perhaps, they considered her a possible journalist from the deep, dark underside, you know, which doesn't happen that often. The year before, they opened the doors to this dumpster diver, who turned out to be a really fabulous reporter on poverty. I mean really, he spent like five years living off glass bottles at a nickel each ... before he was nineteen, so that would be, like, he was fourteen years old, alone on the street. And he won a Pulitzer. You ever see those street guys with black toenails ... really bad? That's him. But he could write. Journalism's Bukowski. Well, I mean, there was a difference, you know ... he didn't have the psychological problems that so many of them have to deal with, or not deal with ..."

Ruth didn't understand the room-and-board-for-two comment, but didn't bring it up. Instead, she calculated the ages of Muriel and Arney and figured it out.

"That's what they considered my mother to be the equal of, except maybe like she was from Arkansas and not the Bronx like the bottle-picker was, if you know what I mean. Northern Maine, that kind of thing."

It was a strange way to talk about his mother, but Ruth just listened. This wasn't exactly the time to pry. With Arney talking, who needed to pry, anyway? So Ruth simply smiled and took a big bite of toast with butter and jam perfectly applied for her.

"She went when she was eighteen. The grands took care of me for like a few months at a time. She worked it out pretty well — I'd go with her for like the first three months of her school year, go to the classes with her, go home to her room at night. Study with her in the library. I must have been almost three when I started. Then when the studies got rough, we'd fly back here, spend a little time, Christmas, then she'd fly back out and I'd stay here for a few months. It worked out that we wouldn't see each other for only about three or four months of the year for four years. Well, three and a half because she finished a semester early."

The room for two was now clarified.

Arney picked up the dirty dishes and carried them to the sink, an action he'd done a million times — it was effortless and thoughtless. "I talk too much. Was the sheriff there at the site? Mr. Tully?"

"Yes. I don't know yet how he's going to handle the investigation. I mean, it'll have to be investigated because even though it's something like a hundred and ten years past ... that's just a guess ... there are too many questions."

"Like?"

"The bodies had been purposefully buried in leaves that aren't available in that part of the forest. Live oak, tanoak and strawberry leaves, in an ancient redwood grove. They'll have to get a palynologist to test the samples, but I know what kind of pollen they'll find in the soil and peat: oak and strawberry. It was deep into the weave of the extant textile."

"Wow. Sounds like a good story. Sheriff Tully's a good guy. A lot of people don't like him ... the new people ... probably just scared of him. You know, his father and grandfather and so on were sheriffs here. Five generations. His uncle was. People're all a little afraid of him, but, you know, apparently they trust him to take care of their county."

"Things seem to run in families in Whitesboro."

"You can say that again. Anyway, I was like four or five years old and we were walking on Van Buren down by the grade school." Arney was now washing up the dishes. "I wasn't in school yet. We were back from Columbia for a while. This guy walked by and spit in front of my mother. This happened a lot because she had me so young and she wasn't married." The delivery was matter-of-fact, just like the stacking of the dishes. "I had new shoes that Grandpa bought me that week, brown things with really hard heels. I was really happy with them. I practically clicked going down the sidewalk. So I kicked this guy in the shin as hard as I could. I mean, I whacked that guy so hard I lost my balance and fell down on the sidewalk." He started laughing, his ratty morning hair shaking. "So the man ran into the school, limping and whimpering, and tried to call the cops. Whitesboro doesn't have cops. So he called the sheriff and so John Tully rolls up in this old four-wheel-drive white and green sheriff's Chevy with his lights flashing. Well, it turned out that Mr. Tully had a little talk with me, and then him, the spitter, and the guy let the whole thing drop, thinking I'd be punished later. Like at home."

"Sheriff get you straightened out?"

"I'll say. He said next time I felt it necessary to kick someone for an insult, go for the side of the knee!" Arney started laughing, his eyes getting bright. "I mean, he actually said that to a four-year-old! Mr. Tully's great. He doesn't take crap from anyone. Everyone around here knows he'll shoot first and regret later. He's done it. No really, don't look at me like that. Wow, has anyone ever told you that you have incredible eyes? Anyway, he shot a guy, face to face; it's practically a legend around here. There was a big inquiry. I mean it was huge. All the big papers from Oakland and Los Angeles and San Francisco were up here for it. He'd chased down this man who had committed a rape that morning. It was a terrible thing … Whitesboro's really pretty safe. But it was a horrible situation. I was really little, maybe six by the time this happened. I think Mom was gone that part of the year. And the girl was really hurt. Tully had the man cornered and, I mean — Grandpa wrote the story — this rapist just started laughing at the sheriff because it was like, 'Okay, I give up, take me in, ha ha, I'll be out in three days, jerk.' So Mr. Tully shot him. The end. The guy died immediately, but Tully got off, of course. All the Tullys have had leverage with the local judicial system, even the state system. It was determined to be an accidental discharge. They couldn't do self-defense because some witnesses had heard the guy say, you know, 'take me in.' But it made the sheriff a local hero.

"Anyway, this guy I kicked got pulled over six times in the next week or two for speeding and lost his license. That's what the law in Whitesboro is like. I'm glad you hit it off with the sheriff. You will be, too, believe me."

The light of day was pushing its way into the kitchen, and it looked like Tuesday would be a beautiful though overcast day. Arney looked at his watch. "Time to get going. I'll be downstairs. My desk is along the wall. Lou better get up pretty soon or she'll miss breakfast. I'm very happy to meet you, Ruth."

A shuffling sound emanated from the back. The bathroom door opened and the creature known as Lou crawled out to the kitchen. Her hair was all over her head, her robe in disarray, one foot was bare and the other with a white sock half on. Her toenails were polished several shades of red. She was two or three inches taller than Ruth, six shorter than Arney. She walked up to Arney and leaned against him, squinting from the rising light.

"This is Lou," he said. "Lou, this is Ruth, Mom's friend."

Her voice was thick. "We thought you were Muriel," she said. "We didn't mean to scare you. Freaked Arney out for a sec." She tried to hold her hand out to shake Ruth's. "Do I smell coffee?"

About Muriel Stanley

Muriel Stanley returned home just after ten that morning. Arney was downstairs in the Ledger office, Lou was fishing about a quarter mile north just past the end of the train trestle, and Ruth was on the phone with Mr. Kasparov. She pulled the phone from her face and said, "I had to use the landline, Muriel. But I dialed into an Internet service for long distance, so there's no charge. I have like two thousand and something minutes left because, frankly, I don't talk much on the phone. The cell service doesn't work this far north. Arney has your breakfast half-cooked … and remind me to ask you how you got an angel like that …"

She was back on the line with Mr. Kasparov, but hung up after a few more minutes.

Ruth told Muriel that she wanted to follow up on the silver necklace that had been around the child's neck, and also the old stories about Wailing Wood. She said the cable pattern she'd discovered in the remains of the boy's wool vest was also very high on her list, but her new first order of business was to visit Bob Cooper's mother to talk about the wood, as suggested by Arney.

"Was that your friend, Mr. Kasparov?"

"Yes. He's on his way from the city to the Port of Oakland to pick up a package. He thinks if things are shipped by freighter, they're cheaper."

"So you met Arney? Lou?"

"Yes. They're both sweet. He cooked me breakfast. You want to go to the grocery with me later?"

"Why not. How'd you sleep?"

"Really great, thanks. Except for a brief visit by Arney's great-great-grandfather, but that's another story."

"God. I don't know what to say …"

"Look, I'll find a motel room today — I think I'll be staying a few more days." She decided not to dwell on the troubling dream. Maybe it didn't relate to Muriel, but seemed rather to be the residual effect of spending a day in Wailing Wood. She shouldn't have mentioned it, but it just popped out. She put it out of her mind for the moment.

"Oh, you might as well stay here, especially if you're buying the groceries."

"My friend's here, but he'll be busy, I'm guessing." Muriel caught a wistful look on her face, but didn't know how to interpret it. Jumping to conclusions, she said, her voice soft, "Mrs. Morton blabs everything that happens under her roof. I mean, if you were thinking you might have some privacy here in Whitesboro."

Ruth looked up, but her face registered no thought or emotion. Then she smiled. Muriel realized that this poker-faced "Miss M," as Mr. Kasparov had called her so obediently, was really quite pretty in a plain sort of way. But her eyes were so magnetic, even to another woman, and so distinctive that she probably made a lot of female enemies.

"Take my advice, Ruth. Don't wait around. That's all I have to say. It never works out if you do. And Mrs. Morton sleeps like the dead, anyway."

"Thanks. Will do," said Ruth. She tried to sound as serious as Muriel.

Muriel said, "There's still room here. Just leave your stuff in my room for now. And I'll stay in Daddy's and listen to the surf."

"That's very thoughtful. Thank you. I don't want to be an imposition."

"You're not. You want to see the rest of this old place? Great. Give me a minute, I've got to soak up some of this coffee. You want some cereal? I have Quisp or Lucky Charms; that's what Lou eats. No, really. She's a sugar freak."

The thought wasn't pleasant. Ruth wondered if they still made that stuff. They sat down at the table just as they had the evening before, and Muriel had breakfast as Ruth sipped her second coffee.

"Well?" said Muriel, the last of her toast in her hand.

"Well what?"

"Well, aren't you going to ask the question?"

"Sure. How was the fishermen's meeting? How many fishermen does it take to bait a hook?"

Muriel looked straight into her eyes. "That's not what I meant."

Ruth sobered. "Like, your hair? No questions — I know it's natural. I'm very good with color perception. Was your father's hair red? Maybe white later in life? Muriel, I don't know which question you expect me to ask."

"It's the one everybody asks the first time. It goes like this: 'How is it that your son's so mature?' Or, 'Oh, Miss Stanley, you look so young!' I *am* young. I just feel old on Wednesdays about midnight, after the paper's finally put to bed. Or it goes: 'And where is his father?' People expect me to have a five-year-old. They expect Arney to have a dad."

Ruth shrugged. "Okay. But …" Not knowing what to say, she shrugged. For Ruth, Muriel's question was completely out of the blue. Muriel Stanley studied Ruth's face for quite some time, trying to detect the slightest degree of insincerity, a hint of superiority or condescension, the kind that nibbles rather than bites, or hidden meanness, bias, anything at all that might indicate what was going on in her brain, but the only thing she got was the impression of a simple, biological radio receiver with a lot of amplitude. For some reason, Muriel flashed on her great-grandfather, Robert Stanley, but only briefly, as if a photo of her mustachioed forebear had been blown in front of her by a nonexistent wind. She blinked, and then held her eyes on Ruth, trying to melt through, and when she finally did, she found a strange, soft core where judgment has no place, where even the word can't land because there are too many birds and sonatas and things in there and all the branches are occupied. That's what it felt like to Muriel.

Muriel sighed. "I was really young when I had Arney. He's the best thing that ever happened to me."

"Yeah, I can tell. Has he always been so thoughtful?"

"Yeah. Even when he was little." She paused. "It's a really small town, Ruth. The influence of religion is very strong here. Most of the churches have a strong fundamentalist contingent, if you know what I mean."

"But you're still here. You own the newspaper ..."

"This is where I live," Muriel said simply. "Sometimes I don't know why I didn't leave. But I didn't. A lot of people don't like me or my family because of that. People like winning. Whitesboro is very unforgiving. They still call me names, but not to my face anymore. Our birthdays are a week apart, Arney and me, and man, do we have a party. We make ice cream, I bake a cake (Arney does it, now). We go out to the beach behind the Ledger and dance till sunrise. I have Daddy's old ghetto blaster that plays eight-tracks, and I play old music like Ray Price or Deep Purple, that I got from Bob Cooper's brother, Blain. I mean, it's not even from my own generation! They're from my mother's!" She paused. "It's just if someone says something, you know, or does something ... since you'll be in town a few days, and some of that you'll be with me. Somebody'll say something or do something and you wouldn't have known why."

"I would have figured it out."

"I worry. Anyway, life here was indescribable. Then Daddy makes it all worse when he starts writing editorials about how Northern is cutting the redwood too fast, using poor logging practices. In a logging town! Between the two of us, good lord. I thought we'd both be stoned. Like I said, it's a small town ... and everyone worked for the timber industry in some fashion, and every one of them attends one of the churches and every darn one of them had a white-dress marriage with clumps of flowers to throw. Except for the fishermen, some of them.

"But my father … he was older, Ruth … he was so good to us. I mean, not because he was older. He just fell in love with Arney, and he refused to ask about, you know, all that. Mom was good about it, but Daddy was the reason we're okay. He was in his fifties when I was born, and Mom was my age now. You know? He started teaching me about the newspaper. I was his ten-year-old apprentice … followed him everywhere, and when I had Arney, I'd be hauling the kid along on my back working with Daddy. I don't think it was that easy for him, I mean, outside the house. Did we ever lose business. The church groups worked on most of the merchants, and he lost so much advertising from the double boycott that we almost went under. Paul Grassi, you met him yesterday, well his wife, Meg, was on the ecumenical council that made everything so bad for us. We were apparently all for free love and no logging. Terrible combination in Whitesboro. I think she was, like, nineteen or something at the time, Meg. The real estate ads and the grocery store specials became ancient history — gone and forgotten. That's how newspapers make their money. But you know what they couldn't take away from us?" She smiled and downed the last of her lukewarm coffee. Ruth studied her smile, her lips: Muriel was so sincere in what she was thinking, and it materialized in that smile.

"What?" Was she supposed to say something like 'pride,' maybe?

"The legal advertising and paid obits!" Muriel laughed as she delivered the punch line.

Ruth raised an eyebrow. Then she laughed, too.

"Legals are the mandatory announcements from local governments, basically," Muriel said lightly. "Public hearing announcements, city and county development plans, estate settlements when people die. Only a newspaper of general circulation — that's a legal description — can print them, and it takes like five years of audited paid circulation to qualify. Between the legals and the obits, we managed to limp through the worst years. We didn't lose the classifieds until later, but that was because of the Internet, not me or Daddy. In this neck of the woods, that would be the early '90s, maybe three or four years after we lost the other ads. I've managed to get most of the regular advertisers back, but it's taken years. People don't forget, and they don't forgive. Not that I want either.

"They helped a lot with Arney when I went to school. My parents. I'll go back at some point, and focus on weekly newspapers, get my master's. I'd like to teach part-time nearby, maybe at Humboldt, while I work at the paper. Nobody understands weeklies, especially these days with all the chain ownership. We get a buyout offer about every two years. I tell them to get lost. They just want the legal advertising base, and they'll gut the rest. They always do. I've seen it happen to four other papers in this part of the county. I employ four and a half people, besides Arney and me. In this town, that's not bad. It's a lot."

"Arney must have had a hard time in school."

"You wouldn't believe it."

"I probably would."

"He got beat up every week until he got his growth. The teachers slapped him around, too. But he's a really good baseball player. He was recruited by a lot of schools from the Midwest when he was a senior. He plays third base. We talked a lot about that, but Arney's, like, really, really pragmatic. And objective. He decided he didn't have what it would take to make it all the way to the big leagues, to MLB, and didn't want to waste his time in college pursuing what he believed would only be a four-year baseball career that wouldn't get him beyond the farm teams. He's really smart, Ruth. Like, genius level. Don't tell him I said that. But he ended up going to Humboldt."

"Because it's close enough for him to come back and help at the newspaper."

"Exactly. I mean, would you feel guilty? I do, but he does what he wants. I tried to kick his little butt out, but it keeps coming back like a boomerang." She started picking up her dishes and putting them in the sink. "Thank God." She rinsed them off. "So I just thought you should know."

Ruth sat for a minute with her chin in her hands, her elbows on the table. "Yeah, I was lacking an adjudicated father, too," she said as if speaking only to the air around her.

"What?" asked Muriel, turning quickly to look at her.

That woke Ruth up. She said, "I mean, Arney's not the only one in this building is all I said." She shrugged. Ruth wondered why she'd said anything, and wished she hadn't. She'd been around Muriel and her son too long for her own good. Muriel's story was exhausting enough, and Ruth definitely wasn't into saying more. It was Tuesday, for God's sake, and there were things to do. "I was stuck in a church school — very unpleasant under the circumstances — and then when my mother died, good lord."

Muriel didn't know what to say. There was no question in Muriel's mind that Ruth, in perhaps the world's most succinct, emotionless admission, had turned upside down everything Muriel had surmised about the woman. She stood there for about two minutes. Muriel wanted to know more about her, just to hear it coming from someone else. But not now, not for either of them. Then she gave Ruth a big hug, and was surprised at the strength in the smaller woman's well-disguised muscles. "I'm sorry. I had no idea."

Muriel sat back down in an awkward silence for a while.

Breaking the silence, Ruth said, "I lived with my grandfather from when I was two until he died when I was seven. My mother went to India, but came back after Grandpa died. He kept chickens in the side yard — we lived in a small, and I mean small, cottage in the South Richmond.

"He was in his late eighties when he passed, so old he'd been in vaudeville. He's mentioned in the pages of the old newspapers, in the ads and reviews around 1923. He was in vaudeville and the Jewish theater when it passed through. He always said he was their token Scot," she laughed.

She was Scottish, at least in part, Muriel thought. That was her first and only clue about Ruth's ethnicity. She was convinced, however, that there was more in her blood than a single strain.

"He taught me to juggle."

"Juggle?"

"He said if you could juggle, you could do anything. I believed him."

"How long did it take you to learn?" asked Muriel.

"A few weeks. I'd just turned four. At four I knew I could do anything," she said, laughing lightly. "We used to walk up to Folsom and stand on the southwest corner where people were leaving Golden Gate Park and juggle balls back and forth to each other for money, with the hat out and all."

Ruth stopped talking for no apparent reason — just as she had started. They sat in silence again. Muriel looked at Ruth and wondered, deeply. Finally, not knowing what else to do, she said, "Anyway, you want to see the Ledger downstairs?"

"I'd be very interested."

"Great." They left the kitchen to walk down the back interior staircase, which led from Muriel's father's room to the press area behind the street level front office. "Just one thing."

"Oh?"

"Where's Mr. Kasparov come in?"

"Who's the man with the mustache?" asked Ruth.

"What do you mean?" asked Muriel, surprised by the sudden change of topic.

"Man with a mustache. He has something to do with the Ledger. Arnie said it was his great-great."

Muriel wasn't sure how to react. Her great-grandfather, Robert Stanley, had a mustache, but that was the only one in her line, that she knew of. "My great-grandfather, Robert Stanley, had a handlebar …" They detoured into Arney's room to look at the photograph on the wall. The man was indeed Robert Stanley.

"That's him," said Ruth. "I had a dream about him. We went downstairs together to a room where there were all these large books of full-sized newspapers. He was rather insistent."

Many thoughts coursed through Muriel's head. She didn't like it. After a few moments, though, she relaxed. It started to make sense that Ruth hadn't wanted to sleep in her father's old room. The room Ruth was in now, Muriel's room, had been Robert and Amelia Stanley's bedroom more than a hundred years ago. A chill went up Muriel's spine. She tried to shrug it off.

They left the bedroom and went to the staircase at the back of the building. Ruth waited until they'd descended the stairs, then picked up the conversation at the point where Muriel had asked about Mr. Kasparov. "Grandfather passed when I was seven," she said. "I still miss him. My mother came back from India and took over, but then died when I was ten. I had a few bad years after that. I was kind of adopted by Mrs. Reynolds, a musician, just before I turned twelve. Mrs. Reynolds was classically beautiful, like a soft-featured Sophia Loren. She andMr. Kasparov fell in love at the '76 Olympics in Montreal, Mr. Kasparov being a minor Soviet athlete in the games, and Mrs. Reynolds playing a harpsichord tour in Canada at the time. She was playing with the city symphonies as a featured soloist. Kind of funny, in a way, because her main instrument was the piano. Anyway, it sounds like a movie plot from the forties or something, a big melodrama with dance numbers. It took Mr. Kasparov another five years to escape from the USSR after the games that year — please don't ask him about it. About the gulag. He escaped through some kind of Jewish railroad through Yugoslavia, to France. He speaks like six or eight languages. It took him a few years to get to the states; he was in France for quite a while. And they met again, Mr. Kasparov and Mrs. Reynolds. And Bob's your uncle."

Muriel nearly choked at Ruth's last comment.

"Or great-grandfather," said Ruth, cracking a smile. "Or something."

Muriel wasn't used to the old saying, and hadn't heard it until she began covering news down at the Salmon Trollers' Hall. But she knew it meant, essentially, something like "And there you have it." But the literal words tugged at her: The only Bob of any importance to Muriel was Bob Cooper ... and Ruth was closer to the pin than she should have been.

She recomposed herself and said, "But you haven't told me why Mr. Kasparov is your apparent driver."

"You're good, you know."

"You think?"

"Sure. You could go somewhere. You could become a journalist."

"Yeah, that's what they all say."

Ruth shrugged and smiled, but left the question somewhere on the staircase.

Arney waved at them from his desk. "Hi, Ruth. Have you seen Lou?"

Ruth said, "She walked out to the beach. Kind of meandered, like a top that's slowing down."

"To draw?"

149

"She had a big fishing pole and a thermos and some bread and cheese."

"The bamboo one or the fly rod?"

"Not a fly rod."

"That's what I thought. She's going to poke-pole on the rocks. The tide must be way out.

"So Mom, we had a good month," he said, turning to Muriel.

"That's good news."

"Where are you guys going?"

"Don't know yet," said Muriel. "Ruth wants to find Grandma Cooper and talk to her. Might not be today, though. Definitely not tomorrow."

Ruth didn't ignore the word "grandma," finding its use strange for the second time.

"We need some groceries. And I'm ordering some more office supplies," he said. "Once I finish this, I'll work on the website and then call it a day at about three. I think I'll go fishing, too. You feel like rockfish tonight? I could make something really cool for dinner if Lou's had any luck. Oh, and Mark is down at the middle school and Lori's doing a feature out at the high school." Mark and Lori were the Ledger's two non-Stanley reporters.

"Sure," said Muriel happily, "like what?"

"I don't know yet. Let me think. We haven't had fish chowder in a while. You could get some cream at the store while you're there. Get beer, in case we make a batter, instead. In fact, let me work. I'll see you later." He turned them off like a radio and put his head back down into the books.

"We could go talk with Mrs. Cooper this afternoon," Ruth said, pushing the issue. "That would leave tomorrow open for you to work."

Muriel Stanley thought about it. It was always great seeing Grandma Cooper, but the undercurrent, the history, was sometimes a little much. It all depended on Muriel's mood at the time, nothing else. "Well, okay." She looked at her watch. "We need to give her two hours. And we can't eat, because she always fixes something and if you're full she takes it personally. Like you don't like what she's prepared. I'll call her."

"Tell her hello from me," said Arney. "I'll drive by tomorrow morning."

"I'll tell her." Muriel went over to the phone on the desk nearest the plate glass window. The shadow of the word "Ledger" fell across the receiver. "This one's my second desk," she shouted to Ruth, who was still standing near Arney. "I usually sit in the back at the other one. But I guess we'll wait on the famous pioneer newspaper tour until later. Maybe we can get the groceries and bring them back before we drive out to the Cooper ranch. Does that sound okay to you? It's a lot of running around, but the timing's good."

"Yeah, great," said Ruth. Then she turned to Arney and said, "What are you guys going to do tomorrow, anyway?"

"I don't know yet, but get something to barbecue outside while you're at the grocery store in case we don't catch any fish. And get some salad stuff." He put his pencil down, looked squarely at Ruth and said, "You're going to get veggie burgers aren't you? I know I'm right. Have Mom pick out something for the rest of us."

Mrs. Cooper

The Coopers live on the back half of about twenty acres of mostly rough pastureland, and the southwest side of their land abuts Wailing Wood. It's surrounded on the other sides by national forest and BLM land, which forms a patchwork across the Coast Range. Mrs. Isabel Cooper, the matriarch, still lives in the main house, one story plus attic, a rust-red, low-roofed structure that hunkers like a Dungeness crab in a flat meadow accessed by a curving half-mile dirt and gravel drive. Fir trees grow to the east and north, but not for a hundred yards. Behind the house is a goat pen with three whitish, long-haired beasts of medium height, and woven into the wire of the fencing are freshly cut blackberry vines to keep them entertained … like potato chips for goats. Three big redwoods interrupt the "pasture" behind the house, and a double-trunked redwood not far from the house is over fifteen feet across at the base.

Bob Cooper and his wife, Sheila, used to live in a second similar but smaller home on the same tract fifty yards east, but they returned to the big house five years ago when it became clear, finally, that Isabel could no longer keep up with the house. She was eighty-two then, eighty-seven now. There's a third house, a cottage, almost touching Wailing Wood on the southeast end of the property — it's small, but the woodwork is profound. Samuel Cooper, Isabel's husband, had spent years working on the place. The interior is a case study in built-ins and joinery, as if carpentry were therapy for Samuel's life in general.

Bob Cooper has a brother in Pescadero and a sister in L.A. Each of the three children was given one of the houses, and the sister and her family visit several times a year, bringing the grandchildren to romp in the outback of the Pacific Northwest. The little woodworked cottage went to Bob's brother, Blain, who visits when the spirit moves, the spirit being influenced, according to Muriel, by the parole board.

"God, enough about Mrs. Cooper and the Cooper clan," said Muriel impatiently. "Can I go on about nothing, or what? And on."

Ruth's face said, "What? Me?"

They drove past the Wailing Wood pull-off they'd parked at the day before and after a few more miles pulled off Overland Road, making a hard right onto the long driveway to the house. The windows of the old brown-turned-bronze Camry were down and Ruth could hear the pounding of old rock music coming from the house as they drove up.

"I haven't heard 'Rainbow Demon' in … weeks," Muriel said. "Sometimes I feel that Whitesboro is like walking into the Land that Time Forgot. I feel like I'm in Oz or something."

"Yep," said Ruth. She hoped it didn't come across as a slight.

"You are, believe me … in Oz, I mean," said Muriel. "Like last night on the radio. By the way, that's Grandma Cooper herself who has the thing cranked up like that."

"You're kidding."

"No, really. She had two boys and a girl. One's Bob, the one you met, the other's Blain, the one with the cottage. Bob and Blain, get it? Blain had a really good music collection on vinyl, all rock, and a bunch of eight-track tapes that he left at the big house. Mrs. Cooper plays his old records a lot; I think it's because she's a little senile. Maybe she misses Blain a little, too. But she's eighty-seven, so I figure she can listen to anything she wants, and, out here, as loud as she wants. She really likes Bob, but she thinks Blain was a troublemaker. But Blain is, like, really interesting. I mean, Blain's in his sixties … how much of a bad boy can he be anymore, right? Now that she doesn't have much filtering left, it's pretty clear who's been the favorite, i.e. Bob. Blain and the sister, Abigail, just come up part-time. She says Bob was the angel and Blain was the devil himself. The thing is, she's not kidding. But Blain's not that bad, really. He's not in jail right now. I think. And that says something."

Ruth listened. "Okay."

They knocked on the door but there was no response. "She can't hear us knocking," Muriel said. She opened the door and the raging music leaped out like an ogre, bellowing. She tried to shout over it, but couldn't get her decibels high enough. Then she went and turned down the old "quadraphonic" sound system in the wide living room. Ruth peeked in the door and then entered. Mrs. Cooper came out of the kitchen wiping her hands on her apron, and smiling. She had been, in her time, of substantial frame. Even now, she was about five-nine, and though her weight was featherlike, her bone structure was solid and her joints were large and strong.

A full-size dachshund, gray in the muzzle, followed her from the kitchen and tried to bark, but, having no luck with his aged vocal chords, managed only a squeak and sat down on his right hip and waited, panting at the effort.

Mrs. Cooper's white hair had been thoroughly brushed and curled, and there was a blue cellophane tint you could see when the light caught it just right. She wore a mid-length skirt under her apron and a freshly ironed white blouse with a white needlework collar. She wore nylons and low-heeled ivory shoes. A deep blue lace wool shawl was folded in half to form a triangle, with the midpoint at her lower back and the fold spread over her shoulders and pinned in front with a rather formal opalescent, deep blue-green beetle broach that looked Egyptian. It wasn't gaudy. Small silver earrings, each with a brightly enameled scarab, matched the broach. Her lipstick was subtle but apparent.

She gave Muriel a very warm hug that lasted longer than Ruth expected. It was clear that the newspaper owner had a very special place in the older woman's heart. "And how is my Arnold? I haven't seen him for weeks. Is he keeping up with his schoolwork and the newspaper both?"

She knew he was, and she'd seen him not more than a week ago.

"Just had a round of tests. He said he'd be by tomorrow morning, Belle, but don't you dare keep him. ... Oh, God, I'm sorry ... Belle, this is my friend, Ruth. She's up for a few days." There were hugs, not handshakes: Muriel was the golden girl for Isabel. "Ruth is here because of the bones that Bob found in Wailing Wood. She's the fiber expert that Jim Miller recruited."

"Ruth. I'm so pleased. Please sit, sit. I have to go finish up in the kitchen and I'll be right out. I am sorry to have such a tragedy bring you here. We don't get that many visitors to the ranch, you know. Muriel, please make Ruth comfortable, dear." And she returned to the kitchen.

Muriel motioned Ruth to the sofa in front of the fireplace. "Bathroom's down the hall," she said, and left in that direction.

Ruth was immediately attracted to the photos that covered the fireplace mantle and the wall on either side of the chimney stack. Had there been any more, it would have seemed funerary. The facial features in the many framed photographs were distinctive, and she could tell with a degree of certainty who was related to whom. On the left side of the chimney were four of Muriel Stanley and her son, Arney. One showed Arney at about four years old playing in the snow with his mother. She was so young; it was in her cold-reddened face beneath a knit cap. Ruth thought it might have been taken at Yosemite. A second showed the boy in his early teens on a pitcher's mound, gangly and pre-handsome at that transitional age, and a third was his high school graduation photo, in cap and gown, leaning over with his arm around Muriel; he was very handsome by now. The final picture of the Stanley clan was a recent portrait taken at a studio in Sacramento, complete with gold-leaf script in the lower corner.

There were a number of photos of Bob Cooper at various ages, with and without his wife and children, and also Bob's brother and sister (the three of them were shown in one photo around a Christmas tree at about ages ten to sixteen, Abigail being the youngest). There were several photos of a tall, plain man with various members of the family, and the more Ruth studied the photos, the more familiar the other face seemed to be. Finally, it dawned on her that it was Hugh Pike, California's junior U.S. senator. He had clearly been as homely in his younger years as he was today. But even in the older photos, Hugh Pike seemed to exude a sense of leadership, and of destiny.

The last photos to catch her interest were one of Bob Cooper and his son, Orrin, on a hike along a wooded trail, and one of the same boy (Orrin, again, his name written below the image) as a lance corporal in the Marines, about the age of eighteen, she guessed. His face was still boylike and it didn't look like a beard would materialize for years. One of the boy's military medals was in a glass case on the mantelpiece. The story of Orrin Cooper was already clear to Ruth. She sighed, wondered briefly about the why's of war, and then other things about the family began to fall into place.

There was enough information on that wall to answer a lot of questions that had built up quietly since she'd met Muriel Stanley. She was still staring blankly at the wall when Muriel re-entered the big room.

"You've got to like knotty pine to like this room, don't you think?" Muriel said casually as she stepped into Ruth's thoughts.

"And shiny varnish. One has to be very appreciative of marine varnish," said Ruth.

"Abigail — Bob Cooper's sister — had a collection of paperweights with objects like, I don't know, like a scorpion, one with bright coins, set in Lucite. You wonder where she got it, huh? They're pretty much into deer racks, too," she said, glancing up at a pair of trophies on the wall.

Ruth said nothing, but they made her uncomfortable. "These are nice photos, though. Bob Cooper and Senator Pike were, what, good friends?"

Muriel didn't look. "Oh yeah, Belle's a photo hound. It's like a funeral parlor in here, don't you think? Yeah, Bob still has Old Hugh's private number. He can call anytime. And he does. Hugh Pike, senator. Can you believe it? Kid from Grayport, California? But Bob was always closer to Cailin, Hugh's little brother. They used to play together, and they fished a lot up north at the little harbor there at Grayport."

"I didn't know about the little brother thing, about Cailin." Ruth was aware of her own senator, of course, but wasn't enough of a politics wonk to be interested in political families. At least, until now.

"Yeah, we always compared them to Moses and Aaron, from the Bible. Not that I'm the expert. Belle Cooper did that. She said Hugh was like Moses, the lawgiver, and Cailin was like Aaron, the mouthpiece. Cailin's the reason Hugh ever got elected to anything … I mean, as far back as City Council. And Cailin still handles everything for Hugh: chief of staff and all that. Election chair. If I ever need a quote for a story, I call Cailin first and he gets his brother on the line. Sometimes he makes up a quote that you can just hear coming from Hugh's mouth." Muriel jabbered on a few minutes about the brothers, and said that they would both be coming home soon to visit. "They come up and resubscribe to the Ledger every year about this time, always in person, always just for one year. I think it's an excuse to visit mom."

Behind the chatter, though, Muriel seemed nervous to Ruth.

"Hugh's been trying to get Wailing Wood into the national park system for years. Before that, when he was the district congressman, it was the state park system," Muriel continued. "But it's just too valuable. The counties can't afford to take land like that out of production — they get a heck of a lot of timber taxes — and the state or, like, the federal government, can't afford to buy that much standing timber. Lots of money, way lots. He's getting closer, though, at least that's what they say. He's real country, you know, Senator Pike, and he's got senators from some rural states on his side now because of that. Even Texas. That's what I've heard. Virginia and Arkansas, too, if you can believe it."

Muriel sat down. She looked up at Ruth, who was still standing near the photos. Ruth could sense a wall descending slowly between them, probably made of knotty pine. Then without a word, Muriel got up and went into the kitchen to check on Mrs. Cooper, leaving Ruth standing alone in the silence of the big room again, with all the old faces on the wall trying to stare her down.

It was too drafty, she thought, and she placed a small log on the embers in the fireplace. Ten minutes later, after the fire was rekindled, Mrs. Cooper and Muriel brought several plates of cookies and a tray with tea and coffee to the heavy round dining table on the north side of the room. The sliding glass doors on that end looked out onto the rolling pastureland and the big redwoods in the back, the view finally ending in a rim of fir and redwood, about half a mile away.

"You have a lovely house, Mrs. Cooper, thank you for having me," Ruth said. The older woman, appreciative of the formality, pushed a plate toward her, and Ruth took a lemony creation, a butter cookie and a peanut butter sandy with a decorative fork print on the top and put them on her small plate.

"Thank you, dear. Ruth, I've never been one for yakking. You didn't drive all the way out here to see the house or, for instance, the photographs on my wall. This is a business trip, I'm sure. Muriel said you had something of special interest that I might be able to help with, and I'm at your disposal. What can I possibly do to help? I assume it relates to the children." She looked up wistfully to the wall of photos, as if the reanimated skeletons might appear beside the chimney, full of life and color. "You've met our Arney, I take it."

"Yes," said Ruth, "we just left him at the Ledger."

"And?"

"We should all be so lucky."

Mrs. Cooper smiled softly. "Then you know about our Arney?" Muriel paled but said nothing. It was too late now.

"Of course," said Ruth, trying to diffuse the mysterious issue after seeing Muriel's distress.

"Well, thank goodness for that," said Mrs. Cooper, "It's hard being so secretive. For years. Not so much, now, of course. Years heal social ills, they say, and I think the old saying is fairly true. It will be so good to see Arney tomorrow. Now Ruth, what do you think I know that you need to know," said Mrs. Cooper in her best business voice.

"Well, in light of the children's remains, Mrs. Cooper, I specifically wanted to know if you remember any stories about the wood. I mean, I'm aware of the tale that some people have heard children's voices in the forest, but that's the end of my knowledge. I don't know where the idea comes from, or if there's anything more to the story. I'd really like to know if you've ever heard any other tales at all about the wood ... perhaps when you were young."

Mrs. Cooper sipped her tea. She preferred coffee, but it was too late in the morning and her stomach disagreed with it. "It wasn't unusual," she said. "The wood, I mean. When I was a youngster, a squirrel could have jumped from Oakland to Eureka by treetop, never setting foot on the ground. The forest was everywhere." She barely paused. "But today, the old wood is quite an anachronism, isn't it? That's why everyone wants a piece of it, I suppose.

"I don't know where I first heard that name, Wailing Wood, but it was around that time; I was eight or ten or twelve ... I really don't know." Her pale blue eyes, flat and moist, appeared to look into the distant past. "After the war," she continued, "they began logging extensively, and with the land cleared like that, Samuel, my husband, invested what we had in cattle. I was twenty-two when the war ended, and Sam was twenty-five. He was one of the lucky ones ... he came back.

"The land surrounding us is national forest, almost all of it, but some is BLM. Sam bought grazing permits through the government. He had a long-term access agreement with the timber company to move the cattle over the ridge or round up the strays. It was never put down on paper, like an easement, so Bob's had a little trouble with that new owner of the wood, the mining company that bought Northern out a few years ago. But we've had the federal permits renewed every so often, and paid the fees, often since then ... Bob takes care of all that.

"I'm afraid I can only come up with one story about the wood, and I've been trying to think about it since Muriel called. I've heard it several times, but the version I remember best was when I was young, and it was Jenny McConnell who told me the story," she said. "I don't know how old it is, but it's true, at least some of it. I hope I don't forget how it ends." She settled into her chair and nestled her cup in her lap. Ruth leaned onto the table and Muriel slouched back into her chair.

"Jenny taught at the grammar school. We were very good friends ... lifelong friends. There weren't many young ladies in

Whitesboro in those days. It was before the war, so we must have been in our late teens. I'd heard the story before, of course, but this is the version I remember, being more complete — at least in my memory!

"The little school was about half a mile from the sea and up a long steep slope from the White River, south side of the North Fork. There were homes on that hillside at the time, salt-block style; simple, really. Most were made from milling scraps that were given to the millwrights at that time — the chunks not thrown into the furnace at the mill for steam power. The mill was down on the flat. I think Jenny's parents' had no stick of wood longer than four feet in the whole house; it was built from scrap. Her father ran the big saw, not the band saw but the other one with the circular blade. Then the mill shut down and he had to get a job at the mill down at Caspar Point, and then he had to go farther north, up to Grayport. They re-established the Whitesboro mill some years later, but then just a few years ago toted the whole thing inland. Twice devastated, as they say. I think Mr. McConnell ran the molding planers at Grayport. My father owned the mercantile in Whitesboro, and we lived above it. We didn't own the building, though.

"It was a lovely little school with a small bell tower. Jenny taught both our boys, Robert and Blain. Did you see their pictures?"

"They look very much alike," said Ruth.

"Oh. Yes. You met Bob. Blain was trouble. Everywhere he went. Nothing serious, just always into mischief.

"Jenny taught Robert and Blain, but not their sister because she was so much younger and by then Jenny was teaching down in the Valley, that town near Sacramento, with the university. But Jenny and I had tea twice a week in those days, which was an extravagance at the time. She told me the story of Blackie Peterson, and I didn't believe her, of course, thinking it was one of those campfire tales meant to scare the daylights out of a person."

Ruth looked out the big windows at the sky. It was clouding over. It was a good day for a story, she thought. She warmed up their tea and sat down again, and Mrs. Cooper, though she did lose her train of thought here and there, related

the old folktale as completely as she could. Muriel took notes;
Ruth did not. Mrs. Cooper spoke for a little more than an hour.

Mrs. Cooper's Tale

Like many good, solidly scary stories, the tale of Blackie Peterson began on a night that was cold with rain, and twice as dark as normal because of the low-lying clouds. It was probably November, when the rains, which start in October, had reached a runner's pace, never slowing or letting up, just continually seeping from the sky, interrupted only by heavier rain and an occasional gale rising from the northeast like a banshee.

Amid the night and rain, lantern lights of the White House Tavern bled out onto the east-west road that ran through the makeshift logging town of Bear Breach. It was little more than a dirt and mud track on which carriages ran, and it was short-lived, soon to be replaced by Old Lake County Road, which was mostly parallel but about a mile south.

The tavern was full and bustling on that particular night. They had a ragtime boy on the piano — a young, red-haired Irishman. The inside was well lit by the lanterns, and warm because of the number of revelers and the heat from a coal burner near the center of the broad room. Loggers and fishermen were drinking with the seriousness of the common working man, and most of them were from Bear Breach Camp or Whitesboro or one of the smaller, temporary logging camps that peppered the region to the east, inland. But no matter where they were from, all were familiar with the faces and habits of one another.

There were, however, two traveling men among them, and these strangers were sharing a table toward the back of the ratty, board-and-bat tavern. They were ruffians and were avoided even by the very drunkest and meanest of the local workers. The area around their table was empty. No one sat with them or near them, and they were left to themselves to drink as they swam in their own miseries.

Late in the evening, after most of the squall had passed and nature had calmed herself and settled down for the rest of the cold, wet night, a tall man dressed in black silently entered the tavern. His slicker was glistening and dripping, and a wide hood had been thrown up in protection against the rain and wind. He looked to be the image of Death, though he had no scythe. The huge hood still covered his head and hat when he entered, and no one could see his face. A few of the men sitting near the door noticed the third stranger enter, but he seemed more like a ghost than a man and they simply cleared away, hardly looking at him. They didn't really notice why they moved aside for him, but had they thought about it, the realization would have struck them that they had responded bodily to the entry of a dark and evil force. And had they looked, they might have seen the glowing red eyes of the Grim Reaper himself.

The music grew louder, and some of the men began singing. The hands of the ragtime boy flew over the ivory keys almost too quickly to see.

The dark stranger's riding cape seemed to disguise a body that may not have actually been there, and even when he pulled back his hood, the face, grim as it must have been, remained hidden by the shadow of a wide-brimmed black or dark hat that was pulled down along the front and side as if to hide the glowing coals of his eyes.

He moved slowly across the empty wood-slat floor from the bar in the front to the rough tables in the rear. As he passed, he first rustled the "crying" towels, which hung from brass rings on the front of the long bar, and then the table linens, like a foul wind that had blown in through a door inadvertently left ajar, or through a window, abandoned and gaping. As if their meeting were preordained, he found his way to the two traveling ruffians, and the three slinked silently to the darkest corner of the tavern where the din of the working men was muffled and the ringing of the ragtime piano and the singing of the off-key drunkards dared not go. There, they took their seats at a small, round creaking table.

Their conversation was short, and in whispers. The two men, the ruffians who were there first, looked every so often at the crowd in the direction of the bar, but then they returned their gaze to the taller man. After a certain number of minutes, the man in the dark cloak stood up, his body towering over the two at the table, for he was tall and gaunt, and he tossed a small sack of coins in a stained leather pouch onto the table in front of the ruffians. It made a heavy, smacking sound when it landed because the coins were silver and gold. The two men, still seated, looked up at him and smiled wickedly. The bolder of the two reached for the sack, but no sooner was his hand on the table than the tall man slammed his own fist down on it, and the tremendous bang was heard across the tavern. A brief and absolute silence followed, but then the revelers from town turned back to their nightly business, leaving the three to their private and evil dealings.

"If you betray me," rasped the tall man, "you will die before four years are out, for you have been richly paid. You have an errand to do, a promise to keep. If you fail, if you falter, your lives and souls are forfeit. Together, we are the hand of murder. We are forever one, through all time. We will prosper together, or we will suffer as one. If our endeavor is unsuccessful, punishment cannot be avoided, though you may run, and run, and run. You must complete the task."

According to the agreement that night, for which the payment was rendered, the two ruffians would steal a certain child from his crib, the child of a judge, and slay it in the wood, and bury the unlucky soul so he would never be found. They were quick to agree to this revenge killing. How much easier could it be to earn so much gold so quickly? And what murder is safer than the killing of a child? What better conditions than under the cloak of night and the veil of seeping rain?

Who would be their unhappy victim? they asked. And they were told the name, and the place, and they were given instructions on how best to proceed.

"Unlucky is the child who is heir to wealth and power," said the grim man to the pair.

The names of the two hired ruffians were known before the night was out, for they took some of that money and bought drinks and caroused and danced and sang; they talked the talk of fools because the liquor had gone to their heads. They shouted to the rafters. Yes, they had wealth now, more than they could earn in many, many years. More than they could steal.

Black Peterson was the name of one of the pair, but the other name, though known at the time, was lost with the passing of the years. The tall, dark traveler's name was never uttered and he was never seen to leave the tavern that night. Yet he vanished, and his departure was realized only when the crowd heard the maddened footfalls of his horse on the muddy road that led east from Bear Breach.

Next morning, shortly after dawn when the sea mist cloaks the headlands, they found the body of Black Peterson, knife-slit from end to end and lying face-down at the edge of the forest, about twenty yards north of the White House Tavern and the lights of Bear Breach. They found him dead beside the road, the fingers of one hand gouged deeply into the thick mud like a raptor's talons. He had pulled himself along several yards by the strength of one arm, away from the light and into the darkness that he loved, and he had left a trail of blood in the water and mud of the road. The blood had gone black and the body had gone white with the lack of it.

The surviving ruffian vanished and was never seen again. But after four years, his evil caught up with him, they say, for he alone wielded the hand of murder, and he was found hanging from a large oak tree very near where the other man's body, Black Peterson's, had been discovered. His own belt was wrapped and strung from tree limb to neck, suspending the body twenty feet above the ground — far higher than if he'd been lynched by anything natural, and his bootless feet were bloody, as though gnawed by wide jaws. Two silver coins had been jammed into his sightless eyes.

Cypress Trees

Mrs. Cooper leaned back in her chair. "How's that for a story, dear?" she asked coyly.

Ruth was elated. Muriel smiled. She'd heard the story before, but that was a long time ago and not nearly as good. Now, she remembered why she had loved "Old Mrs. Cooper" so much as a child. She looked at Ruth, whose brain seemed to be calculating something.

"Now, that's a good story," Ruth said. She wondered if Muriel had flicked on her tape recorder. "But there's more, isn't there?"

"I suppose," said Mrs. Cooper, sitting up again. "But the child was never found. We never learn for sure if he was slain, because his body was never discovered, never mentioned in the tale. His little spirit remains in the wood, Jenny told me. That's who we hear, those of us who have been fortunate or unfortunate enough to hear it, the soft crying. Let me tell you, that old story frightened the devil out of me at the time. And people today say they hear the crying of a child in the wood.

Blain heard it; he used to come running home when he was little, seven or eight, telling me about it. The wood is not far from
here, you know.

"How much of it is true, I don't know. But there is a Black
or Blackie Peterson buried in an indigent's grave at the
Whitesboro Cemetery, and the grave is still there, I'm sure. It's
my deepest fear," she said, "that more than a little of this story
could be true."

"The grave's there?" asked Ruth in disbelief, eyebrows
raised, green eyes nearly glowing.

Mrs. Cooper, noticing the unusual hue of her eyes, mentioned it, but only in passing so as not to embarrass Ruth. "Oh,
yes," she said, "I've seen it myself. Well, let me be clear about
that: I saw it back then, before I was twenty. That's a very long
time ago; I am eight-seven years of age. But I told Jenny Mac I
didn't believe her, so she took me to the cemetery and we
found Black Peterson's gravestone. We walked to the graveyard from her home just up the estuary at the edge of the big
meadow there. The daisies were out all over, and pennyroyal
was blooming and the bees were in a frenzy over the pennyroyal. There are blackberries all along the edge of that meadow
where it butts up against the ridge, the trees. The berries are the
size of a child's fist, for goodness sake, and the smell of blackberries wanders from the meadow's edge down to the river.
The meadow, thick and wet, was hot, the air muggy but scent-
ed lightly with the minty essence of the pennyroyal and blackberries. They say our strongest memories involve scent, and I
think it's probably true. It's a lovely meadow; I think you
should go see it while you're here. There are fragrant azaleas
along the riverbank. It's about a mile inland. Bob and Muriel
could take you on horseback and I think you'd like that. I'm so
sorry you missed blackberry picking. Perhaps you'll come up
next year earlier in the autumn?

"But. I don't want to lose my train of thought, dear. Jenny
and I wandered to the ocean and south to the graveyard. After
such a frightening story, then seeing that gravestone ... it was
right beside a huge old cypress tree. Many of the cypress trees
have been removed, or they've fallen, but, of course, others
have grown back since. I love the cypress, and always have,

leaning inland from the sea wind like they do, great branches always pointing inland.

"That big old cypress is still there, or it was the last time I visited on Decoration Day some years ago. I couldn't get to it because of the weeds in the old section of the cemetery. I haven't been there for … perhaps … twenty years. I don't get out. I just stay around here.

"Well, I will tell you, we ran off screaming when we found that gravestone! You know young girls." She laughed quietly, her eyes wide, soft blue, tired with age.

Ruth sat and thought quietly among herself. Mrs. Cooper and Muriel Stanley were a world away until Muriel came to and began picking up the few dishes and bringing them to the kitchen. Knocked from her reverie, Ruth looked over at Mrs. Cooper, who was staring at her.

"May I ask a few questions, Mrs. Cooper?"

"Call me Isabel or just Belle. Of course you can."

"Okay. Well, do you remember ever hearing any different versions of the story? For instance, maybe one with two children?"

"I remember once hearing that there were two children, but that would have been from my childhood and the memory is vague. The one child became the campfire version, Jenny's tale."

"How about the socioeconomic class of the child? You mentioned that he was a judge's child."

"Always from a wealthy family, at least every time I heard it. I assume that was the reason for the killing … as the story goes. Perhaps a ransom, perhaps a vendetta. Revenge."

"Were there always two ruffians and the dark figure, or were there sometimes more or fewer individuals?"

"Once I heard there were only two ruffians who hatched the plan, and the dark figure wasn't in the story. I seem to remember hearing that a bit later. But again, that was so long ago. My earlier memory is the three of them. Before my teens."

"Do you know if anyone ever wrote this down?"

"We've never had the story in the paper," Muriel said. "I mean, I guess we could look in the morgue; I've never looked. The Ledger has all kinds of things in it, especially long ago, poems and like that."

169

"Oh, the paper, good point," said Ruth. Her memory, jarred, conjured up an image of the man with a mustache who, in her dream, showed her the old books that held newspapers. "You've never run across a similar historic incident in the pages of the old editions? You have all the old papers, right?"

"We have them all," said Muriel. "I've researched just certain items, but usually don't go back farther than, like, the 1940s. We have history clubs visit, and they go through everything, and a lot of visitors are trying to find parts of their genealogies. But I haven't seen anything like this, even when I'm helping them. But that means nothing, Ruth, because you have to launch a concerted effort. It's easy to get distracted and miss the very thing you're looking for. I mean, it's nine-point type … and I always end up reading the old ads, for instance; it's deadly. Like a loaf of fresh-baked bread for a few pennies."

"Well, this is a good one. Who wants to go to the cemetery?" Ruth asked brightly.

Her suggestion seemed to hit the floor with a flop, though Mrs. Cooper's dachshund seemed to perk up at the thought that someone was going outside for a walk.

"Hm. I guess I'll just ponder things for a while longer and then try to round up some help," said Ruth. "I don't do cemeteries alone."

"I'll bet you don't," said Muriel.

A Few Last Pieces

The drive back to Whitesboro was slow. It seemed that Muriel was purposefully dragging, as if she didn't want to go back. That wasn't the case, however. She had something on her mind and she finally pulled off and cut the engine, swiveling her hips to the right so she could face Ruth. The keys swayed in the ignition, and her lucky penny in an aluminum horseshoe key fob spun one direction, then the other.

"Mrs. Cooper is almost ninety, Ruth," she said, restraining the emotions she'd been feeling most of the afternoon. "She has no ability to shut up. No filtering. She can't be suspicious of anything. She doesn't know, you know, how much ... I mean how close we are. You and me. She thinks you ... I don't know. She thinks you know about *everything*." She was distraught, and there was nothing Ruth could do to allay whatever discomfort Muriel was feeling because she didn't know where Muriel was going with this. She thought about chancing a comment, but, on reflection, people usually weren't prepared for what came from her lips. She decided to sit quietly and wait, but then said, "You want to know how much I know about everything. About you and Arney."

"Yes."

"Muriel, you were kind enough to tell me a lot about your life. Mrs. Cooper's selection of pictures filled in the blanks. I wasn't trying to go where I wasn't welcome, but I can't help but see the obvious, that's all. You can't hide family resemblances, especially when the photographs are good. What the pictures told me is that Orrin, Bob Cooper's son, is Arney's father, that he must have been pretty young at the time, that you said nothing to anyone for at least the first four years — you told no one, not the Coopers and not your parents, not your father, not the sheriff — I'll bet one of the Sheriff Tullys was asked *not* to look into it, whoever was sheriff then. You did that for Orrin. And then you told Mrs. Cooper or Bob after Orrin was killed in the military. That's why she doesn't have any of her own photos of Arney until he was four, when you told her. Or when you told Bob Cooper. He must have liked you even before; he sure loves you now, Bob does. But there were no pictures of Arney with his father, Orrin, on that wall. I'm sorry. I didn't pry, it was just there. And I'm so sorry that Arney never knew his father."

Muriel was silent. She told herself this was not a big deal. The charade was only important at first, and, really, who knows now how many of Whitesboro's overly inquisitive, overly imaginative citizens had put it together anyway? Who knows what the gossip has been these many years, the whispered voices, the silent, searing glances. It just wasn't talked about to her face, that's all. It didn't matter; it wasn't really a secret any more. It just ached, that's all, and for no real reason. She had tears behind her eyes, and that ached, too.

"I just don't get it," she said. "I could just cry and I don't even know why. I asked Belle years ago to keep her photographs in her bedroom. I mean, what if there were visitors? And then, I thought it was safe. I mean, what can you tell from old pictures? And who cares anymore?"

"It's ancient history, Muriel. Right? Arney's in really good shape. He's just so … Arney. I don't know. What else matters?"

"It's never over, Ruth. Not in Whitesboro. What upsets me is that you figured out twenty years of history in about two minutes. It's just not normal. God, I wish you could pull that off with the skeletons in Wailing Wood. I sat there taking all these notes during Belle's entire story, and you just sat there and I know damn well that you have a more complete memory of the story than I do even with notes. Did you ever get shit for being so smart? Sometimes I wonder what the hell I'm doing. I'm not stupid. The least you could do is play me something on Daddy's piano ... why? ... because I can't play worth a dime and never could."

Cumulative impact. Ruth had no idea what to do. "That's why I knit," was all that passed her lips. Then, "Yarn therapy."

Muriel paused, reoriented her thoughts, and said, "Wow, am I ever sorry. Geez. You'd think a person would get over all the stuff. It's just stuff. And anyway, there was a reason I kept my mouth shut. I mean, at the time. Even then, the state had a legal age of consent. We couldn't risk it."

"I know."

"We were making plans for when he got out of the Marines. Instead, he was killed by a roadside bomb."

"And you shouldered the entire burden for the rest of your life. Muriel, let's talk about something else. Like this murder, Muriel. The children in the wood."

"Just a minute." She opened the driver's door and stuck her head out, breathing in the cold air of the afternoon. She twisted the key and the engine coughed and started, then she closed the door and sat with both hands on the wheel. "Sorry. I can't really express how lonely it's been. Just me and Arney ... it's been so unfair, and I mean unfair to Arney. He's propped both of us up his whole life."

"Don't worry about him."

Muriel looked closely at the woman beside her. Strange. She couldn't put her finger on anything about Miss M. Not even her ethnicity, other than her Scottish grandfather. And did anyone ever wear freckles as wonderfully as her? What she did know was that this stranger was right about Arney — there was nothing to worry about. She was overwhelmingly sure of that now, and shook her head.

They both stared out the front window of the Camry. The windshield wipers needed new rubber, so it wasn't easy to see when they pulled out.

"I told Daddy first. I think he already knew about Orrin, but he never said a thing. Other than, now that I think about it, that he liked Orrin a lot and was very sad when the news came from Iraq. Anyway, he told Mom. Daddy and I went to Bob Cooper's that same night I told him. You won't believe this. Bob and Sheila just started crying. They were so happy ... now they had Arney. Ruth, it was so agonizing and so wonderful at the same time." She sighed and flipped on the windshield wipers. Then she shrugged. "I think I'm glad I don't have visitors that often."

They drove into town in silence, but it was comfortable. Muriel turned on the radio. It was AM and the speaker was tinny. The night DJ had excavated "96 Tears" by Question Mark and the Mysterians, and played it three times through. It was still playing when Muriel pulled in behind the Ledger.

"Sean's the DJ tonight," said Muriel. "He's always stoned."

Ruth nodded.

"Sean's almost Daddy's age. He's still on the fire department, working as a mechanic. No one else understands the big truck they have. He works one night a week at the radio ... says he never sleeps anymore, anyway."

Muriel was finally getting used to Ruth. She liked being around her. She enjoyed sharing her Whitesboro, or talking about the people, like Sean, whom she'd known her whole life. She liked being with another woman — a small pleasure that was most often denied her, Whitesboro being what it was. She didn't look forward to Ruth's return to the city, whenever that would be. The only difficulty was figuring out how to get her usual amount of work at the newspaper done.

They got out of the car. The door hinges creaked. "What did you learn from Mrs. Cooper — anything besides that we need to go to the cemetery?" asked Muriel.

"We'll search for a stone with the name Peterson on it. It's somewhere near a large cypress, or the stump of a formerly large cypress, but hopefully the tree's still there," said Ruth. "Where's the 'old section,' anyway? Or a hole where the tree used to be. Once we get the date from the stone, we can look through the old Ledgers; you said you had the complete set from the beginning, right? And you know what I bet? I bet there's a mercantile ad right next to what we're looking for."

Muriel had no idea where the mercantile ad idea came from, but she'd been through enough old Ledgers to know that there was probably a fifty-fifty chance of that happening no matter what: the Whitesboro Mercantile was a major advertiser until it closed down a few years ago.

"We have them all," said Muriel. "Everything. But we can't do the cemetery tomorrow. I have to work. We'll have to figure it all out later. You tired?"

"I am totally exhausted. I'll probably just go into your room and crash, if that's okay with you."

"Me too. Arney'll have to cook us something for dinner. We could rest for a couple of hours and then have something to eat. Are you going to see your friend? Ever?"

"I think. It's a newspaper thing, you know? I'm sure you know. How are you going to get all your usual work done, anyway? There could have been a last-minute story, like a big murder in town or something."

"It's always something. Like a really important ad hoc subcommittee meeting. It doesn't get any better than that, unless it's a sewer department meeting."

"But I think my friend is probably out fishing with Mr. Chu anyway, is what I think."

"You did say that Detective Chu was staying down at the Gull, too?"

"Wasn't me," said Ruth. "But I think he is."

The Whitesboro Cemetery

The graveyard at Whitesboro Cove is four miles south of town and it stares with a thousand pairs of subterranean eyes over a sheer cliff to the sea. At one time all the plots had been a safe distance from the surf far below, but a hundred and fifty years of wind and rain had sunk its teeth into the headlands, and some of the graves are now practically perched at the edge, where a fine spray sails up the cliff side and over the land, keeping them moist like young plant seeds. The whole cemetery might slide into the Pacific if the prevailing wind were to stop.

The graveyard retreats from the cliffs and crawls east a hundred yards to the Coast Highway, and you can see the stones in the groomed north half poking up like the rising dead when you drive by. An old rock wall cuts the cemetery in half, separating the older overgrown south section from the new area. A ditch runs along the old wall, and it fills with a foot or two of water after heavy rains. Tree frogs live there and sing incessantly, their single voice loud enough to wake the proverbial dead — especially at night, when the dead don't sleep anyway.

The two sections are bookended by cypress trees, whose twisted trunks and limbs bend sharply inland, pushed and formed by the same sea wind that keeps the graves from sliding into the Pacific.

The newer section looks like any graveyard. The grass is properly green and short, and the stones are orderly and white and facing east so that when the dead, reclining on their backs, awaken, they can catch the first post-apocalypse sunrise. Almost every grave is graced with a bouquet, though close examination shows that many of the bundles of colorful flowers are made of immortal plastic and varnished silk.

The south half is overgrown and nearly impenetrable. It is thoroughly and thickly hidden by brush and trees and tall grass. It is a forest of wood and stone and strands of red-leafed poison oak. With a little imagination, one might see the gargoyles of Notre Dame crouching on the few mold-blackened obelisks that are visible above the clinging weeds. With just a little more imagination, one might see those granite and marble gremlins leap from their pocked pinnacles back into the protective caress of saw grass and thorns, where they have their nests.

The rock wall at its edge once stood six feet high, but the rocks dislodged over time, and people made off with them and used them for building projects. But thin slabs of cement mortar that had held the stones together were left behind, piled against the low remains of the wall. The brush that grows up along its edge is so thick you can see rabbit trails boring into the gnarled mess, and these rabbit routes are the sole means of communication between the ghosts of the old section and the spirits of the new. The tunnels appear to be used by the ancient dead to gather and gossip with their more recently deceased descendants. It's a small town, after all, and the surnames are the same, generation after generation.

Ruth talked Muriel into exploring the old necropolis the day after they'd spoken with Mrs. Cooper, leaving Arney to "slap the stories around until they fit," in Muriel's words. How could Muriel resist?

177

There was a white-painted, rose-entwined wooden Victorian arbor opening onto the new area, which itself dated to about the First World War. But the old section was beyond reach. They stood at the edge of the highway, but Ruth could see no entrance to the older section.

Muriel headed through the arch, but Ruth hesitated. The superstitious Scot in her was rising to the surface: You just didn't walk through a passageway like that rose-covered arbor without doing something to protect yourself from the forces on the other side — uttering a spontaneous incantation at the very least. She didn't know one. So instead, she fished out the pendant that she wore under her blouse, the so-called "Atsidi Sani," and fisted it as she passed quickly under the whitewashed wood and thorns. It had to be good for something; she'd had it for years and was, with it, still alive, after all.

The newer graves went back a hundred yards, and at the far end near the cliffs on the left, the south, was a decaying iron arch that was still attached to the remains of the rock wall by huge rusted bolts. The remaining igneous stones were red and black. Two heavy iron gates that had once swung in the arch, and that had protected the dead from the living, were visible just past the wall, off in the brambles, thrusting up at odd angles as if thrown there by enraged trolls many, many years ago.

You had to pass through the iron arch to get to the older graves, and the ocean bluff was about fifteen yards west. Ruth and Muriel peered in. The old cemetery seemed to have spawned a forest of stunted, beaten trees, tall grass, dry, twisted, broken, and small-leafed bushes that probably fed off old bones. Wild roses ran along the ground and climbed all that they touched. The sporadic ruin of fences made from irregular lengths of gray, split redwood and capped with viridian moss surrounded some of the graves, and smaller, tighter, older fences marked the resting places of children. There were many of these.

They ducked through the iron gateway and began pushing aside the overgrowth, trying to forge a path to the interior. After the first fifteen yards, their way opened slightly, as if the long crabgrass and sea oats had become starved for air and light, turned brown and joined the dead.

Ruth and Muriel emerged into a roughly cleared area a third the size of a football field but whose edges were hidden by madrone and oak and huckleberry bushes and small wild brambles with thorns. Throughout this section of the cemetery, the headstones, their edges gnawed by sand and salt and time, stood like the plaque-blackened ribs of prehistoric beasts. There were many small headstones that had been placed flat, but they were hidden, lurking under the twisted roots of saw-toothed grass and vines of glossy poison oak. Every upright stone was ajar, as if a swirling gale had tried to fell the lot but succeeded only in tussling with them.

Marble angels a foot or two tall stood forlornly beneath a close canopy of leaves that still clung to branches. They looked skyward, as if for salvation. The rain had washed blackened mildew and soot from the crowns of their heads down below their eyes, and to Ruth it seemed as if they'd been weeping, their tears running their angelic mascara. Sap-seeping bull pines grew behind and beside the cherubs, whose chubby-toed, moss-covered feet were hidden by layers of pine needles and patches of black and sage-green lichen. Emaciated gray-granite saints, their features softened by years of weathering, listened mutely to the surf below and watched in unblinking penance the quiet passage of time.

It was silent. A few larger marble tombs, once no doubt magnificent, now lay in ruin, cracked by the prying roots of trees and overgrown by poison oak. And somewhere in all this was the gravestone of Black Peterson, hopefully still bearing his name in some sort of age-drunk immortality. Maybe the stone stood upright, visible to the living. Maybe it was a flat one and had buried itself in the sand and clinging grass, hiding like a burrowing crab, afraid of the light.

So they began to look for the name: Assuming they were somewhere about the middle of the City of the Dead, they began to spiral out, Muriel clockwise and Ruth anti-clockwise, and they met as they approached the east and west perihelia of their orbits, smiling at each other briefly every time they passed as they continued their revolutions. Muriel wondered, but only briefly, if the planets did the same — smiled at one another or nodded when their paths crossed. But then she remembered that they all orbit in the same direction, and she wondered why.

Every so often, Muriel said aloud a name on a headstone, and Ruth wondered if, perhaps, Muriel knew the name. Such familiarity caused Ruth no discomfort, but the recitation of any name in that forest of stone and branch sent chills up her spine. Finally, she asked Muriel not to say the names.

"What's the big deal?" asked Muriel.

"One doesn't call the names of the dead, where I come from."

"So, they don't do that in San Francisco?" she said, slightly irritated.

"Muriel, this is your town, your cemetery. I just don't want any of your friends following me back to your place. You've got enough ghosts of your own, believe me."

Muriel thought for a moment and came to two conclusions, which were not mutually exclusive. One, Ruth appeared to harbor superstitions. Two, when she thought about it, Muriel saw no reason to tempt fate. After all, maybe Ruth was more enigmatic than eccentric.

"Fine," said Muriel, and they continued the search.

The influenza epidemics of 1873 and 1884 were well-represented on this knob of turf above the cove. The furious pandemics had been brought to Whitesboro by globe-sailing Russians and Scandinavians, and by the many travelers and sickened immigrants arriving on trade schooners from Europe. There were innumerable graves of children, and even more of infants who were a week or a month old. There were generations of Swedes and Finns — remnants of what was called the Scandinavian Navy — and Portuguese, Russians, Scots and Irish: the legacy of the European invasion of the redwood country.

After two hours of circling, Ruth spotted a smattering of light gray surrounded by its own small forest of red-skinned madrone trees, which rose eight to twelve twisting feet above the ground. A large cypress rose to her left. Virtually hidden among the spindly trunks below the cypress, amid clinging vines and saw grass, was a simple stone. As she worked her way through the mess, she stubbed her foot on a short, upright headstone she hadn't seen. It was beside, and in this light nearly obscured by, a small madrone whose gnarled trunk seemed to choke it. The position was either a protective enwrapment or a passionate stranglehold. Everything in the little forest seemed to shout that it was the latter.

The stone was two inches thick — by now Ruth had determined that thin meant poverty because even the simple stones of Whitesboro's working people were four or five inches thick. This one was gray marble, not white. The stone was pocked on top like a salt block left out in the rain. Its height was sixteen inches, green and black where it met the ground, and on the lee side was multicolored lichen as if the artistic dead had painted it by numbers. Essentially, it had been camouflaged. The eroded surface made the inscription difficult to read. To the touch, however, the inset letters were well enough defined, though the years of erosion had made their surfaces sugary. Ruth, with her nose right up next to it and crouching down and peering from below in an effort to get the light's angle correct, read aloud the name, "Black Peterson," and the date, 1892.

"I have it!" she called softly to Muriel, afraid to raise her voice. "I have it, I have the date. It's 1892. I have the date!"

Muriel started wading through the center of their concentric circles and came up along Ruth's side. Both women were sweating, not from work but from the dampness caused by the sea and the warmth caused by the crippled forest composting itself. "It's always muggy before it rains like hell," Muriel said. "And it gets really still, except for the frogs. The frogs go nuts." And they were; Ruth hadn't noticed and then wondered how on earth she couldn't have. Their voices rang in her ears.

The base of the stone was partly hidden by moss and grass, but when they pulled the vegetation away they discovered an inscription in a different lettering, as if it had been chiseled into the stone as an afterthought. The lettering was smaller so the whole phrase could fit on the stone. By kneeling and adjusting their positions to use as much of the light as possible, they could both read, "Those Who Trespass Against Us."

They looked at each other. "Wow. Creepy," said Muriel. "What do you think that means?"

"I hope we find out. What's even weirder is that Black Peterson's is perfectly straight. Every other stone that's not set flat

181

is off-kilter. Maybe we'll be able to make something of that later, too. And I haven't seen one stone dating earlier than 1859 or later than 1911 in this older part. Whatever that means. How are we doing for time? Do you have to get back?"

"Pretty good. I'm hungry. I think it's about noon. We ought to leave pretty soon."

"You're the one with the watch," Ruth said.

"Yeah, right." She looked at her wrist. "It's like 12:33."

"Arney gave me some sandwiches."

"He gave *you* the sandwiches?" Muriel said.

"Isn't he sweet? Want one?"

They sat carefully on the grass, avoiding poison oak, twigs … everything they could. Ruth wouldn't sit on the stones.

A Tour of the Old Ledger

After their cemetery foray, Ruth and Muriel walked into the Ledger through the front door. Ruth was struck by the welcoming nature of the single, wide office. Across the front was a broad counter with a cash register from the 1930s, an elaborate bronze machine that stood two feet tall. Seated at a desk behind it and to the left was the office manager, Charlotte, with her hair curled neatly on the top and sides of her head, dressed in a floral blouse and antique-white polyester slacks. She wore house slippers on the refinished oak floor and her shoes were placed neatly beneath a coat tree in the corner.

Ruth looked down. "I love the bunny slippers," she said to Charlotte.

"A half-inch of foam, dear, makes a significant difference in my public demeanor," said Charlotte. Ruth liked her immediately.

"Where's Arney?" asked Muriel.

"He's at City Hall getting something or other. He said he'd be back by two."

"Ruth, this is Charlotte. She keeps it all running. Charlotte worked with my father for years."

"Great, hi, I'm Ruth." They shook hands.

"She's the fiber consultant they sent to the Wailing Wood excavation. She's got papers ..."

They chatted amiably for a few minutes, and then Ruth said, "We're going back to the morgue to start digging up some of Whitesboro's history." She turned to Muriel and said, "Is there anything I need to know about the 1892 folio?"

"No, it's right there on the shelf. I made sure everything was in order after that genealogy club visited from Tahoe. They made quite a mess, but they came out rather happy."

As they walked to the back where the old newspapers were kept, Ruth carefully looked at the place. The ceiling was high, about twelve feet, and consisted of tin-plate squares molded into relief patterns with *fleurs-de-lys*. They'd been painted at one time, but Muriel and Arney had stripped them to bring back their period feel. The floor was refinished oak in the front and unfinished oak toward the back. The raw wood in the back was dark, almost black, from decades of ink being tracked into it, and from ink dust, paper dust and mineral spirits that had been used to clean generations of printing presses. The wood would have been soft to bare feet, and splinterless from decades of scuffling, but the soles that touched that wood would look like coal forever.

There were four desks — three on the right and one on the left (Charlotte's), and there was a glassed-in room in the back with a fifth desk — the editor's chamber where an interview or discussion could be conducted with a sense of privacy. That was Muriel's office and her father's before her, and so on back through the generations, and from there she could see everyone else in the building, including patrons at the front counter and door. And everyone could see her, a necessary ingredient to a successful local newspaper. Yet, like her grandfathers before her, that was her second desk, for her primary residence was right behind the big plate glass window in the front, where the generations of Stanley's watched over Whitesboro's Main Street.

Between Charlotte's desk and Muriel's office was a complicated-looking machine about seven feet tall and five across with a keyboard. A lead weight like a baguette was hanging by a chain and hook at the top, as if being fed into the enormously complicated contraption.

"That's the old Linotype machine," Muriel said. "We don't use it anymore, but it still works. Old Papa Robert bought it ... great-grandpa. It made slugs of type that were set into galleys, justified. It's one of the greatest inventions of the industrial revolution ... ranks right up there with the sewing machine and cotton gin. And those benches there," she said pointing, "are where they used to hand-set type before we got the Linotype, which is called hot type, you know, from the molten lead. Anyway, we still have drawers and drawers of type, like lead and copper and wood, and three letterpresses. There's an old flatbed here, too. It doesn't work, but the letterpresses do. Lou really likes the letterpresses. We had the rollers on two of them resurfaced, I mean, the cores and trucks were good, we just needed new rubber, and she's printed a few things, really good ... posters, I guess you'd call them. She draws and stuff, but her specialty is printmaking, so you can understand her enthusiasm."

"My friend would love to see this."

"Oh, yeah ... so when's Mr. Kasparov coming back?"

"I thought he would have been back by now, but I guess he had to do some errands. I mean, like look after my cat. Since he had to drive back to S.F., I asked him to check on my cat before he came back up here. He should be back by now. He's getting old."

"Your friend? How old?"

"The cat. The cat's getting old, but don't tell him I said that. Methuselah doesn't like being abandoned. He won't eat. After three days, he freaks."

"Oh. I like cats." They continued back. "That's the darkroom." The smell of chemicals, mostly fixer, wafted half-heartedly from the blackened room through a narrow, hollow-core door. "We don't use that anymore, either, because all our cameras are digital. I mean commercially. This is like a museum of technological change, Ruth, and I doubt there are too many places like this left, where you can see the progress of the last hundred and fifty years, and still use most of it. I really like it, though. Somehow, it's reassuring, like a sense of belonging. It's like having old recipes or Black Jack gum."

Ruth silently wished she could understand what it was like to live, to work, generation after generation, in the same place. "Does anyone at all use it?" she asked. She could smell the tang of sodium thiosulfate, the fixer for both paper and film.

"Lou. She's really into black and white photography. She has an old twin-lens Rolleiflex that uses two-and-a-quarter roll film that I gave her; it was Dad's. Anyway, I think Lou just likes to duck in the darkroom with Arney, truth be known," she said, raising an eyebrow and making half a smile. "I think they're cute together. Anyway, one of these old Chandler and Prices will make a nice gift for her sometime," she said of the nineteenth century handfed letterpresses. "I mean, right?

"Lou's really cool, but she's poor as a pea-picker," Muriel said. "Like who's not, huh? Her parents are really nice, maybe in their fifties, but they're always stoned. They love my music collection — it was my mother's and Blain Cooper's. It's probably worth something by now. They should see Belle's collection! Lou's grandparents were always stoned, too. But Lou won't touch it." She shrugged.

"Okay, here we are at the morgue. Back past this is a four-unit Goss offset press. We have a pressman who comes twice a week: once to run the thing, once to wipe it down and work on it. He lives north a little past Grayport and drives down and back in a blue Chevy Luv pickup, which he's had since about the dawn of time. He keeps it running like he does the press. Very smoothly. But the body's rusted out completely.

"The morgue is what a newspaper's library is called." It was a large room on the north side of the building, about two hundred square feet with the same high ceiling as the rest of the lower floor. They ducked into the guts of the strange time machine known popularly as the Whitesboro Ledger.

There were scores, maybe hundreds, of small cabinet drawers on the left, at the very back, each drawer about nine inches wide and six high. Ruth pulled one out — it was a foot long. They were striking in their excellent workmanship. "So, those were made by my uncle, Arnold, Daddy's younger brother by three years. They were partners until Arnold died in

1969. He was hit by a logging truck going seventy miles an hour into town. The logging truck, not Uncle Arnold. I never knew him, but he was quite a cabinetmaker and Daddy talked about him all the time. He ran the presses; that was when the pressman was as important as the editor. The old days."

The edges of the drawers were rounded and reminded Ruth of something from the 1940s, which they were. She pulled open a second drawer. The joints were dovetailed and the drawer moved easily but seemed nearly airtight. The back and bottom of every drawer were made of milled cedar, which kept the papers inside from being savaged by moths and worms.

There was a free-standing cabinet at the far wall with long, thin drawers like the drawers for hand-set type out in the press area. But rather than type, the drawers were filled with old maps that Arnold and Len had collected over the course of decades. Some were timber harvests, others were residential plots, and many were topographic. There were harbor charts as well.

Ruth pushed the drawer back in and pulled out another and found small, hinged doors facing upward. She opened a miniature door and found buttons and other items, each with a stringed label and some sort of number that indexed it to, from what she could tell, nothing. There was a Woodrow Wilson campaign button in one slot in a P drawer: Presidents or pins, probably, she thought.

The opposite wall, which separated the morgue from the rest of the office, held about a third of the bound volumes of the newspaper, with the other two-thirds on the back wall. "There's a heater in that corner," Muriel said, "if you get cold. The floor in here's cement, and so's the back because of the press. It makes it as cold as a refrigerator, especially being on the north side. I have to go out front while you're doing this; the work doesn't seem to do itself, even with Arney's help. It depends on how long you're in here, whether you start getting cold or not. You might bring some of the volumes out front after a while, could be the best."

There was a chipped enamel table on which to set the large volumes, and beside the table was a tall typesetting booth with a slanted top that was perfect for poring over the newspaper-size books. In front of the booth was a tall stool with a swiveling clay-blue Naugahyde seat.

"What's that?" Ruth asked, pointing to a two-foot-square rusty iron door just off the floor on the side wall. It was originally chromed, but the shiny layer had mostly worn off. It was wrought iron beneath. Volumes were stacked against the wall on either side of it.

"That's the 'hell hole.' It's a furnace. We used it for melting lead into pigs for the Linotype, and before that, for casting stereotypes — flat text and images from molds that the agencies used to send out. That was the wire service of its time, like the late nineteenth century up to mid-twentieth. But sometimes it's good to put food in if you're going to be in here for a while."

"Nice."

Muriel gave her a quick hug and left for the front. Ruth stood alone in the very silent room. There was an old transistor radio at the top of the reading booth, but she didn't turn it on. Yet. She slowly rotated on the stool, looking at the century of history that hid in the yellowed pages of the pioneer newspaper. Strangely, she felt very alone, very isolated. It was no wonder, she thought, that someone like Muriel Stanley would stay in a town that essentially hated her. This was Muriel's life, her blood. The girl had no choice but to stay if she wanted to be true to her DNA. Too bad it couldn't have been easier on her. And Arney ... Arnold Stanley II, apparently.

Ruth tried to shake off the feeling of isolation; there was no time for nonsense — she had work to do. The skeletons in the wood were, in her mind, more than just two children who lived briefly more than a century ago and died, forgotten. There was something more mysterious about it, something that cried out like the voices in the wood, something she couldn't put her finger on. There was a feeling that was hugely immediate about them, as if they even heralded the rain that would surely come in the next day or two. And there was something sinister, not *in* the bones, but *around* them. She felt as if bad ghosts, unsettled, would again walk the earth anytime now.

Soon she had two or three books stacked on the low table to her right, and she lifted the first one to the reading bench, which had just enough room to spread it open. The spine said, in gold lettering, "The Whitesboro Ledger and Journal, 1892, Jan — Apr." The Stanleys must have bought out a competitor, probably the Whitesboro Journal, about that time, she thought, absorbed it, added its name for a while, and then dispensed with it. She dusted it clean with a rag she'd seen on the table and opened it. Then she skootched her butt sideways to get a little more comfortable on the round stool and settled in.

The Ledger's Records

The format of the older newspaper was straightforward, and each of the editions was either six or eight pages. Of each edition, the first page was a mix of local items and canned news — stories gleaned from other publications or sent from the news and features services that existed nearly 120 years ago. The second, third and fourth pages were local, with a large collection of small local ads. The fifth and eighth were full-page ads from the local mercantile or White Timber Co., which were, of course, one and the same (this was the dawn of the age of the "company store"). Smaller mercantile ads were peppered throughout the paper. The rest of the paper was canned, mostly magazine features, and had smaller local ads.

The local news was of two types: One consisted of longer stories of six to thirty inches. Each shorter story had a small bold headline set in movable lead type, and the heads and all the text had been hand-spiked by printer's devils, meaning every backward letter was put in a rack so it read backward but printed left to right. Thousands of tiny letters were hand-spiked for each edition. The longer, more important stories covered the front page and had larger headlines set in wood-block type that had been polished by use, cured by the oils in the ink and were as hard as rocks: Ruth had looked in some of the drawers as they walked back through the shop.

Most of the minor information, like the historic items sought by genealogical researchers, were to be found in the "locals." These consisted of four to eight lines of text, some-times a few more, with no headline, separated by horizontal lines called rules. There were inches and inches of these under the single common headline, "Locals."

Ruth got some reading glasses from her bag and settled them on her nose. This was going to be a long process; she wished the tombstone had given her the month of Black Peter-son's death or burial. But it hadn't. She had the entire year of 1892 ahead of her in two volumes and she couldn't just gloss over the text or she'd miss something. She could be scanning and reading the locals for hours, possibly days. If mummifica-tion didn't occur, and she survived, she wouldn't simply know *of* the comings and goings of Whitesboro's cast of characters for 1892 and beyond; because of Miss M's iron memory, she'd know *all* about them, know them intimately, and she'd retain her memory of the smallest fact for many years to come.

It was, however, mostly gossip, presented as breaking, important news, and although the timber baron's ads paid the newspaper's bills, the locals were the reason that residents spent a penny for the Ledger.

Eventually, Ruth rose from the land of the newspaper's dead and left the spirits of Whitesboro a few yards behind as she walked dizzily out into the front office. She'd been digging around for hours. Her reading glasses were coated with a layer of dust and she was too bleary-eyed to remember to take them off. Her hands were cold and dry, but she felt as if she'd just left the nineteenth century with its carriages, nobby coats and bowler hats, rather than the dusty little morgue of the twenty-first century Ledger. After a few minutes, she realized the sun-shine she thought she would see didn't exist. Outside, it was dark and no one was in the office because it was after six. The front door was locked and the lights were out except for two desk lamps that burned all the time. She knew Muriel was upstairs and so was Arney, unless he'd gone back to Arcata to the college.

But Ruth had indeed found the horrible death of Black Peterson in those first few hours. She thought herself lucky, considering the sheer volume of text she might have had to cover had she not stumbled onto the late Mr. Peterson in print, much as she had literally stumbled onto his gravestone in the cemetery.

The paper of Thursday, April 21, 1892, was yellowed only slightly. There was a quarter-page ad from White's Mercantile on the third page. As she lifted the front page, exposing the locals of Page 3, she could tell by feel that the paper had a high cotton rag content, and briefly indulged her primary interest by getting out her pocket microscope to analyze the fiber. Wood pulp, which was used later, may have spawned the yellow tint of yellow journalism, but the older cotton or linen rag was better, lasted longer and stayed whiter. And it didn't crack when you turned the pages. It didn't disintegrate.

There was still a slight indent on the page from the pressure of the hand-spiked type against the press's platen. She wasn't sure exactly how many generations of Stanleys had operated the Ledger, but it was Robert Stanley, editor and publisher, whose words described Black Peterson, face down and soaked in blood. Peterson had been found on the outskirts of Bear Breach Camp on Monday morning, April 18. He'd been stabbed to death. There were signs of a struggle, Stanley wrote, on the nearby east-west wagon road that ran through the Coast Range.

Everyone was probably having dinner upstairs. Ruth had already missed it. Too bad, she was hungry. But rather than giving up for the day, she poured herself a cup of lukewarm coffee from the urn and turned away from the dim light of the office, shuffling back into the morgue with her cup to reread the long columns of type and find what she'd missed the first time. She turned on the heater and wished for a pair of bunny slippers like Charlotte's. Then she went out to the coat rack and found the woman's slippers neatly set beneath it. She slid into them. It was a matter of survival, she decided. Besides, she had socks on. They were still too large.

The big book remained open. She found that her reading glasses were still attached to her face. She turned up the lamp and parked herself on the stool again, this time with a pillow she'd found near one of the desks, and discovered how stiff she'd become, sitting like that. She'd have to stretch for a while before she went to bed after this kind of day.

Black Peterson had been the apparent victim of a barroom brawl. He'd been beaten. He'd been stabbed many times. His hands were bruised, even in death, from pummeling his unknown adversary. But the body was several leagues from the nearest tavern or brothel, and the fight took place outdoors. Ruth wondered if Robert Stanley used the word "leagues" because it seemed dramatic, of if they really measured distance in leagues at the time. She'd have to find out some other time. Stanley reported that several men in the taverns of Bear Breach had seen the man drinking the night before.

There were fresh carriage tracks on the road.

From her vantage point above the broadsheet pages, Bear Breach didn't appear to be the simple timber camp that Paul Grassi had said it was. According to the historic record in front of her, it was a full-fledged town with its own mercantile, post office, hotels and taverns. There were homes with fireplaces and chimneys and families. Maybe the children had, after all, been from Bear Breach. But it didn't have a newspaper, which accounted for why the mercantile ads were in the pages of the Ledger.

Finally, Robert Stanley described the identification of Black Peterson by several rogues who had been drinking with Peterson two or three days before. As Stanley's account drew to a close, he wrote:

> Mr. Black Peterson, a large man known to no permanent resident of repute in all of Whitesboro and Bear Breach, will be buried at Whitesboro Cove without formal service but with a Head stone donated by the Church Women of St. Bartholomew's. Other churches will have nothing to do with the man, dead or not. May we all remain safe from such a gruesome and mysterious Death, and refrain from so vulgar a way of life that, in the end, would foster such a cruel passing.

"Whoa," she said involuntarily. The notice in the briefs was followed by a short mention of an arrest. It was one of a dozen little locals that followed the account of Black Peterson, but it caught her eye because the incident occurred on the day Peterson was discovered, and she found it peculiar that an arrested vagabond, careening madly through Whitesboro in a horse-drawn carriage, had so much cash on him, as mentioned in the brief account. Ruth realized that Robert Stanley was smart; he wouldn't have mentioned the excessive bail, a hundred dollars, unless it struck him as odd.

The pages of 1892 and 1893 flipped back and forth for Ruth like a scene from a black-and-white movie. Fanning forward, then backward, she ended up in the edition one week before the death of Black Peterson, landing on April 11. She'd visited that edition three times by now, but this time she noticed a local she hadn't seen before. Below her now was a mention of children, which seemed out of character for the newspaper's coverage because the pages were filled mostly with items on commerce, civic activities and visits of relatives to the residents of the town or the travels of residents to visit their relatives — always adult relatives. But this item concerned children:

> Mr. Peter Johnson has sent his very young niece and nephew, Benjamin and Emma Johnson, to live with intimate friends in New York. Mr. Johnson, of course, assumed guardianship of his young wards barely one year ago, upon the deaths of his brother, Daniel Johnson, and sister-in-law, Mary Johnson, both of whom are well-remembered by all of Whitesboro. According to Mr. Peter Johnson, who was at the time of their deaths named executor of the Daniel Johnson estate, and trustee of all holdings, the children may now be raised with greater opportunity in education and the arts. It must, however, be noted that the community of Whitesboro is stung by the surviving Mr. Johnson's decision, and the children of Mary and Daniel will be sorely missed, surely more than their guardian would have been.

She looked up from the page and tried to focus her eyes on the wall. She was starting to like Robert Stanley — she appreciated his little comments at the end of a local, which told you exactly where he stood on the matter, and where the town stood or, perhaps, should stand.

Was the connection she was seeing between the Johnson children and the children in the wood just wishful thinking? She looked back down at the page. Beside the entry, there was a three-column ad for Bear Breach Mercantile. It was the same ad that the mustached Robert Stanley had pointed to in her dream. It was an ad for gingham cloth. A slick chill ran down her back and caused her to shiver.

Ruth couldn't help but wonder if Ben and Emma Johnson had ever arrived in New York. Could Blackie Peterson of Mrs. Cooper's story have been their killer or one of their killers? And the other man? What was Stanley's etheric dream presence trying to say to her? That if Mrs. Cooper's story even partly reflected a real case of infanticide in early Whitesboro, Ruth might possibly find the second murderer in the pages of the Ledger four years after 1892 because of Mrs. Cooper's purported four-year curse? That was a long shot, she realized, but Belle said the second killer was found hanged from a tree four years later. But she'd also said there was only one child.

Long shot, yes. But so was finding the entry about the death of Black Peterson. So was finding the "local" about the Johnson children. So was finding Black Peterson's gravestone in the first place.

Ruth tried to straighten her back. She sighed, knowing she'd been perched there for hours with at least four years of weekly editions still in front of her. She had enough puzzle pieces now to get hooked into trying to figure out what was going on — but knowing there weren't enough pieces to draw firm conclusions. Yet she had to consider the day a raging success: She'd not only found Black Peterson's gravestone, but the story of his death and possibly the children they'd discovered in the wood. That was not a bad day. The old story was already half true, and what she really needed now was the date of the hanging of the second man. Yet by the time she'd worked her way through November, 1896, she hadn't found even the vaguest reference to the second mysterious death, which Ruth believed would be the hanging of the companion, the killer of Black Peterson. Neither did she find any further item on the Johnson children.

But she did learn more about Mr. Peter Johnson, uncle and caregiver to the young children: One of the man's sons died in 1895, although the report wasn't published until early in 1896. He had perished on a voyage by ship.

That same year, 1895, Ruth found a short reference to a barn fire at the Peter Johnson property in which several sheep and horses died. Finally, in 1899, she found the obituary of Mr. Peter Johnson himself, and it felt strange peering down onto his death notice as she hovered more than a century above the pages. Peter Johnson died in the county jail the night of October 23:

> Finally, we note this week of 26 October, in the waning of a difficult year in Whitesboro, the passing of Mr. Peter Tobias Johnson. Mr. Johnson, long time a prominent figure in this community, departed the Life in disrepute.
>
> We can only say, let this man be a lesson to us all, and to our Children, not for the way he lived, neither for his accomplishments as a citizen, but for the way he chose Not to Live and for those things within easy grasp which he chose Not to Accomplish, for himself and for others. Though he needs no man in Whitesboro to judge him now, no man here should envy his final accounting before that larger Judge.
>
> An apparent attempt to contact his sole survivors, the children of his late brother and sister-in-law, Daniel and Mary Johnson, in New York, was unsuccessful and chances of future contact are dim.

So what the heck was that? Theories rushed through her head, each one battered by the next as they scrambled for prominence. Ruth realized she might have most of the elements necessary to know what had happened if she could get everything in the right place. Black Peterson or the second man had killed the Johnson children: Yet they seemed to have simply disappeared in the vastness of New York. She was sure, now, that the skeletons were Ben and Emma Johnson. One of them wore a silver cross. Maybe they both had crosses at some point. Peter Johnson was the shadowed man from Mrs. Cooper's story, the man who'd paid Black Peterson and the other man to kill the child; Ben and Emma were, together, the child in the cradle. Black Peterson was the rogue who had been left dead by the second killer, yet to be found.

She started to close the book, but several of the pages were raised as if something had been stuck between them. She flipped forward to find an old photograph, creased, cracked and brown. Beneath it was the same Bear Breach Mercantile ad for gingham cloth that Robert Stanley had pointed out to Ruth in the dream. The photo was a child about four years old. She turned it over. "My Howard, 1887, Mary," was written in elegant cursive on the back. She turned it over again and pulled her glasses back off the top of her head, squinting at the photo. Little Howard, it appeared, was wearing a knitted vest. She brought it closer to the light. She caught her breath when she saw it was the same pattern as the vest she had found on the child in Wailing Wood: ridges and furrows followed by moss diamonds. How very strange. She kept the photo and, for the night, closed up the book.

Ruth's eyes were burning. It was well past midnight. But she may have found most of what she sought, and a photograph that would have sent chills down her back had she had any feeling left after sitting for so long. She didn't believe in coincidence, and all things considered, she had to take the photograph into account.

Right now, Ruth just needed to get upstairs, wash the dust off and go to bed. Maybe eat something.

She got upstairs to find that Arney had left her a sandwich in a plastic wrapper on a plate. She'd eaten it before she even tasted it. The note was written by Lou. It had very rounded letters, and the dots for the i's were circles. Muriel was asleep in the bedroom that wasn't hers. Submitting to the Stanley tradition, she pulled the blankets up over Muriel's shoulder. It was raining outside. Ruth gazed through the window toward the ocean, and looked downward nearer the building. Clearly it had been raining for hours. The thought surfaced in her typography-fuddled mind that the Johnson children were, as Mrs. Cooper had said, children of privilege. And the same was true of the children in the wood. She could tell by the wool that had been bought for the vest. She could still see the pattern in her mind, the raised ridges and diamonds. She went to Muriel's room, where she'd spent the previous nights, and fell asleep with the window open, listening to the surf but seeing the little skeletons, partly clad in decaying wool, their heads crowned in leaves like elven royalty, dancing among the ancient, silent trees.

Robert Stanley, or the shape of him, visited her late in the night, and talked at length. Yet Ruth remembered nothing of what he'd said, only that he'd been there, in his old room above the Ledger. She woke an hour after she dozed off, and couldn't go back to sleep. She'd have to go back to the cemetery tomorrow. Maybe old Robert Stanley had said something to that effect. Or not. Tomorrow was actually today already, early though it might have been. She knew she had to find the second ruffian, and maybe his headstone looked similar to Black Peterson's. Would she have any better luck sticking with the old Ledgers? It was hard to say. The old folk story placed the death of the second ruffian four years after the murder of the first, making it 1896, but she'd found nothing. She got up and sat on the side of the bed, wrapping the comforter around her shoulders as she stared out the window at the black sky. Raindrops were hitting the outside of the sill and splashing back on the glass.

Why a second ruffian? she thought. Because of the lower inscription. She could see it plainly: "Those Who Trespass Against Us." Us being the people of Whitesboro, of course. But it was in a different style and size of lettering. It was added later. According to the mention in the locals, Black Peterson was just a bar rat. But he'd been murdered in a gruesome fashion, at least according to Victorian standards. Robert Stanley, the editor, had no knowledge of any crimes perpetrated by Black Peterson. Surely, the lower inscription was added when Black Peterson's partner — and murderer — had been captured or found out, and their story finally became known to all of Whitesboro. That's when they went back and inscribed the words. She lacked the name of Blackie's partner in crime, but she was certain his gravestone would have the trespassing inscription as well.

All things considered, she preferred to be outside tomorrow anyway (today, she corrected herself again), even if that meant the cemetery, and even in the rain, rather than stay inside another whole day flipping through the pages of who could tell how many volumes. She'd be looking for an inscription this time. But she'd have to go without Muriel Stanley. As the editor said, the work didn't do itself.

Hypolite Dupree's Grave

I met Ruth at the cemetery. I was a second-fiddle searcher because Muriel had to get her newspaper out. Of course, Ruth had phrased it more delicately, asking if I were busy.

Under such circumstances, I'm never busy. She hugged me on tiptoe when I met her at the broken iron gate that led to the old, unused part of the graveyard. Second fiddle was just fine.

We began her second careful and tedious search of the Whitesboro Cemetery in a light rain near the headstone of Black Peterson. I looked at it carefully, and marveled how the madrones had enwrapped the old stone as if strangling it. I puzzled over the inscription about trespassing, trying to engrave the font style in my mind's eye so I could recognize it on any other stone. In a way, it was like looking for agates on the seashore by tuning in to the peculiar luster. It gives you something to focus on.

Ruth had borrowed a yellow rubber rain suit that she tried to leave unbuttoned to keep the air flowing — rubber, she decided, was great in a slow, thick rain like this, but it didn't breathe. Though her hands were cold and her nose kept running, the temperature was only cool, maybe fifty degrees. There was hardly a breeze, so the misty rain fell straight down. The light was thin. It was gray.

The graveyard looked exactly the same as when she'd left it the day before: muted, with all the colors tending into gray and brown. Ruth had walked the half-mile through town and four miles south to the cove and it was just past six in the morning. I drove. We met at the edge of the old section in the half-light of dawn just past the gate, and she leaned back and parked herself against part of the old rock wall. She pulled an apple out of her pocket and bit into it, watching the gulls glide up from the surf below. They flew over and circled back to the sea, calling. She offered me the other half.

A robin flew out from the older section. His breast was bright orange. First he landed on the rock wall about ten feet from Ruth, toward the ocean. He had an oak leaf in his beak, probably for nesting material. I'd always wondered where robins went during the winter, and now I knew: White County. As she studied our visitor, Ruth became aware that there were at least a dozen robins milling around at the edge of the old section, rustling through the tall grass in search of bugs and worms. She pointed. I've always liked birds, I said. Her attention returned to the first robin. He still had the little oak leaf in his beak, and he looked at her out of his left eye, turning his head slightly. Then he fluttered about ten feet to the north and landed on one of the newer headstones. There, he dropped his leaf and darted for a tree in the old part whose branches overhung the wall and ditch. He seemed to be waiting for us to enter, luring us into a forgotten land.

I threw the apple core twenty feet over the edge of the cliff. It probably didn't make it to the water. I didn't look. Then we plunged into the wet world of Victorian Whitesboro. I wondered, briefly, if ghosts ate apple cores, or if they even liked them.

It was difficult to see. She used the same spiraling strategy, and marked her path by tying the tall grass in a knot every six or eight feet. I did the same: It seemed reasonable. What would the ghosts make of that? It took us hours because we continually had to push the grass away at our feet and on the left and right so we didn't miss the stones that had been set flat to the ground. Yesterday, she'd torn a nail on a stone from 1883 and cut her hands on blackberry vines, but this time she decided to put on a pair of leather work gloves once she'd entered the old section. The gloves, like the raincoat, were Muriel's.

It was about 9:30 when she found it. I'd been closing in on it, and maybe would have eventually seen it or at least walked into it. She stood thirty feet from Black Peterson's headstone. She'd practically weeded the whole lot, which really needed it anyway. Amid the brush and saw grass was a forest habitat in miniature — four-inch-thick madrone trunks, four or five sizeable oak saplings, blackberry vines and tall seeded grass, little roses, many species of fresh mushrooms, and, of course, the cypress. There were thick huckleberry bushes bearing small, rotten blue fruit, and branches from the oak saplings hung low, obscuring the day's mild light. White molds lay close to the earth under the grass blades and crabgrass stems, and above it all were the taller madrone, oak and bull pine.

Hordes of tilted tombstones with dates ranging mostly around 1904 surrounded her. She gave a shout but realized that except for me she was lacking corporeal company — the overgrown landscape swallowed the sound of her voice quicker than she could stifle the yell.

The dark, stained granite headstone was pushed tightly up against a foot-thick oak trunk, and cowered in its shadow.

At first glance, it was more shadow than stone. It bore the name of Hypolite Dupree, and the name was wrapped at the H in the leaves of poison oak. Small patches of lichen and moss filled the hollow corners of the letters. She had to bend down to within a foot of the stone to decipher the rest of the inscription:

"Shot for Hanging, 1906, For Crimes Against The People Of Whitesboro."

And beneath that, it had the same epitaph as Black Peterson: "Those Who Trespass Against Us." The link was complete, despite the fourteen-year span between their deaths. Fourteen years! Ruth was elated and her enthusiasm was contagious. She was practically spinning, leaping … inside, anyway. But fourteen years? It should have been four, according to the old story. But that was the trouble with lore and legend. She thought for a moment how long it would have taken her to pore over that many years of locals in nine-point type.

"Shot for hanging? Geez. Western justice, I guess. Must have been one of the Tullys," she said, laughing.

"Tully justice."

"Don't mess with the Tullys," she said.

"Don't mess with their town."

Unlike Black Peterson, the lettering on this stone was the same style as the trespass phrase: very square with, at one time, sharp corners. Everything on Hypolite Dupree's stone had been inscribed at the same time. And like Black Peterson's, Dupree's stone stood bolt upright, not tilted like the rest. It was obvious they'd been implicated in the same crime; it was obvious that Hypolite Dupree was the second killer. And it seemed likely that after Dupree's death, the message was inscribed into Peterson's stone, which had probably slumped like the rest of the stones, only to be righted in 1906 when Dupree was shot, hanged, and buried, and his stone was set.

"Maybe H. Dupree killed Peterson early on, outside the tavern, possibly after a drunken argument, then was found out, somehow, fourteen years later," I said.

She just looked at me. Was it that obvious? I may have blushed.

"But his punishment wasn't for killing Black Peterson," she said. "He trespassed. Much worse than killing a fellow ruffian."

The old story from Mrs. Cooper, though not exact, was ominously close. She said the crime was killing a child. Ruth was sure the Ledger, from 1906, would confirm this, except that there would be two children. And she would find, she hoped, the remainder of the tale.

My Howard

That afternoon saw Ruth, in Muriel's slippers and with her hair still wet from a hot shower after our rainy excursion to the cemetery, skip down the steps that come out at the back of the Ledger office from the upstairs living area. They weren't bunnies like Charlotte's, but they did look like fake bunny fur. Muriel watched her come down, the second time the women had seen each other that day, because Ruth had told her about the Ledger articles before leaving for the cemetery.

"I found it," Ruth said.

"Why do I believe that?" Muriel had decided Ruth could find anything she decided to find. "So, what's his name?"

"Hypolite Dupree. He died in 1906. I mean, he was 'shot for hanging,' whatever that means, exactly, 'for crimes against the people of Whitesboro.' It doesn't get much better than that. And like Blackie Peterson, he trespassed against us. Now we just need to use your Wayback Machine here and set the dial for 1906."

"The big quake."

"But besides that, the double execution of Hypolite Dupree."

Muriel furrowed her brow. "Shot and hanged, both?"

"Not sure. I don't know what it means, exactly."

Muriel nodded, however odd it sounded. She said, "I have news, too. Jim Miller called me this morning. Guess what he found yesterday between eight and fourteen inches down?"

"Baskets."

Muriel sighed, frowned, but the frown worked its way into a soft smile. She realized she really liked Ruth M ... even if she was omniscient. "God. You take all the fun out of surprises, Ruth. But you're right — he went out yesterday with something like five assistants to finish up the preliminary and take deeper samples, and came back with a clutch of little baskets ... and one was eight or nine inches in diameter — apparently the size is a really big deal. I mean really big. Museum stuff."

"I wonder how unique that soil really is ..."

Muriel paused. "You mean you don't really know?"

"An educated guess. Bluffing, but the odds were in my favor."

"He wants to talk to you about it, Jim, about the site or the baskets, I wasn't really sure. One was almost complete, he said. And he found wooden tools. And the stuff's really old. He said it wasn't just couple of hundred years, either, but maybe five or six hundred for some of the things. He was so excited he was practically shouting over the phone. It'll be a regular excavation next summer, he said. I called Daniel Thom to let him know (he said to say 'hello'), and I was going to call Luther Eaglejohn but Jim had already let them both know. He expects it to be such a big find, Jim does, that he'll have visiting scholars. I was working on the story when you came down, and Jim's going to e-mail some photos any time. He was so impressed, I had to listen to the whole story of acid-over-alkaline twice."

"That's good. He should be," Ruth said with a smile.

Muriel pushed some papers back on her desk. "You know, we had a fire in the mill, from the 1906 quake."

"Did it burn down?"

"Most of the town did. But only part of the mill. They hooked up a water line from an old steam train and saved the mill, most of it."

"It's a weird year to get shot and hanged, if you ask me," said Ruth.

"No kidding. Anyway, Arney left and he'll be back tomorrow, and I talked to Belle. Cooper. She reminded me that Hugh Pike is flying in from Washington. The senator. He comes every year to see his mom the week of her birthday. I mean, he comes other times too, but he always comes for her birthday ... it's this Sunday. There'll be about a million people up at Grayport. We all go, all the Coopers and Stanleys and all the Pikes and Tullys ... it's kind of a big deal. The whole county, really, for Betty Pike's birthday." She paused. "I want you to stay, Ruth."

"I'd love to, thanks. Could I miss the Clans of Whitesboro County ... the gathering of the clans?"

"Yeah, Clan Stanley ... Clan Miller'll be there, too. He might bring one of the baskets ..."

"All the better. Does he go back as far as the rest of you guys?"

"Oh yeah. His family name was Gitaine, French, but they weren't ethnically French, just the name — I think they were Roma — and they transplanted to Grayport like the Pikes. They go back to about, oh, I'm not really sure. Jim says they were all workers, farriers and stuff. The way he talks, I'd guess at maybe 1870s or '80s, around there."

"Mr. Kasparov might be back by Sunday, maybe."

"Your driver. I wouldn't mind one of him. He'll have to come, too."

"If we're putting in orders, I'll take an Arney."

Muriel smiled. "What about your Detective Chu?"

"Maybe as long as he's not catching fish," said Ruth.

"It's supposed to rain."

"All the better."

"Hugh Pike'll probably stop at the Ledger sometime during the week. He always does. It's nothing official, just stops by with his mom and brother, usually his sister. They were all close to my dad."

Ruth frowned. "Just don't let him play chess with Mr. Kasparov. I mean it."

"Really?"

"Not checkers, either," said Ruth. "Mr. Kasparov has a proclivity to fleece unwary competitors when it comes to chess or checkers. Political office means nothing to him. I think he bankrolled that car of his with his winnings. He refuses to tell me, of course … thinks he can keep it secret. But I know for a fact it had something to do with a five dollar bet. Go figure."

"Geez, Ruth. I guess it must get exciting at times."

"If you like that sort of thing," said Ruth, feigning a sigh. "He plays chess with the rabble on Market Street, or used to, and half the time he'd get back to the theater totally spent … from running for his life, hopping buses or taxis. He's in his seventies, Muriel …"

"Theater?"

"He care-takes the old Avaluxe Theater in the Sunset. I live in a flat there, above. But I don't know what I'd do without him, really."

"You'd pine," said Muriel. "You want some coffee?"

"Not that stuff, thanks. I tried it once."

Muriel looked at the big percolator. "It's not that bad, really. At the Trollers' Hall, they percolate it along with the sugar. Now, that's bad. This is good. And it's only the second day for that pot. Three days is fine. It's the fifth that you have to take pills or something. Calcium tabs at least."

"I think I'll go out and get a double capp or something."

"Oh. Get me one, too."

"I found a photo in one of the Ledger volumes last night."

"Yeah?" Muriel said, her interest piqued.

"Here," said Ruth, handing it to her. "Any idea?"

"That boy's a Pike," Muriel said flatly. "My Howard, so … Howard Pike. That would be Hugh and Cailin's great-great-great-grandfather. Maybe four greats."

"I thought I saw a resemblance, I mean, from the pictures on Mrs. Cooper's wall." Her statement wasn't honest: The resemblance was blatant.

"All those Pikes look alike. Ugly as a mud fence," Muriel said, but then stopped herself. She smiled and laughed. "Well, they are, you know."

"What about the name Mary? Mary Pike?"

"Well, I didn't think there were any Marys in the Pike line. But maybe I'm not remembering perfectly. But, no, I can't think of even one Mary Pike."

"Hm. Ben — I think the boy in the wood was Ben Johnson — died, I would guess, the same general time as Black Peterson, 1892, meaning he would have been born about 1888 … Jim Miller said the boy's skeletal remains indicated an age of about four. Of course, he might not have confirmed that the child was a boy yet."

"But *you're* sure? That he's a boy?"

"Yes. So Ben was born a year after this photo of Howard was taken. Something like that. And this child in the photo, Howard No-Last-Name Pike, looks like he's about four years old in 1887. He might be five. But it doesn't explain how Ben Johnson and My Howard Pike ended up wearing a vest made by the same person ..."

Muriel didn't respond. She thought.

"It's the same pattern in that photo as the partly felted vest we found in Wailing Wood," said Ruth. "They're potentially identical, right down to the size." Could they be, she wondered, the same sweater, handed down?

"You've got to be kidding? But that could be a coincidence, right?" suggested Muriel.

"Impossible. I've got some more stuff to look into — if I'm not out of the Wayback in three or four hours, call someone with a defibrillator."

"Right," Muriel said, and turned back around in her chair. "Are you going to get the coffee first?"

The morgue hadn't changed in the few hours Ruth was away. Maybe it had been waiting for her.

Arrival in Victorian Whitesboro

LOCALS: Judge Eli Trogden will arrive tomorrow on the schooner Amethyst and will be residing during his Whitesboro stay at the Grand Hotel on Fourth Street. Mayor Bailey indicated that Judge Trogden may be in the city for up to one week.

— *The Whitesboro Ledger, April 12, 1906*

Judge Eli Trogden awoke slumped in his chair beside the untouched bed, his cigar snuffed out and lifeless in a brass ash dish beside him. The early morning light could be seen through the sheer silk curtains of his third-floor room at the Grand Hotel. His back was stiff. A sharp rap at his door pulled him back to the world of the living, and a bellman with a bright silver tray of tea and steaming biscuits entered the room. Trogden's suit had been pressed during the night and was delivered by a second servant. He excused both bellmen and then swallowed what he could before making his way down the stairway to the reception hall. He was late.

Trogden was greeted anxiously by several dozen men who had been waiting at least an hour for his appearance. "What is all this?" asked the judge of the closest man.

"Yes," replied Alfred Bailey, the newly elected mayor of Whitesboro. "Your Honor, it seems that everyone in Whitesboro has an overriding interest in the case of Mr. Colbert. It has been on everyone's mind ... and of furious interest this morning especially ... of great importance to us all. The street, you see," and he cast his arm in the direction of the etched glass doors that looked out onto the city, "Fourth Street, Main Street, and there, Laurel, and even Franklin — they were full an hour ago, before it was light," he said, pulling out his watch and glancing at it quickly as if to verify the impossible. The streets were wet and muddy. The rain had stopped during the night, and the wet season was nearly over for the year. In another month, logging would resume.

"Sheriff Tully has had the center of the streets cleared all the way to the courthouse ... you can see as far as the corner of Main from here. He has made a path for you."

The walkways were thick with peering eyes and the bodies attached to them. Trogden looked through the doors of the Grand, and indeed, people had jammed the boardwalks, where boardwalks existed, and they were huddled, overflowing, several feet into the streets.

"Mercy," said the judge. "Surely, the beating of one man (as I understand it) would never foster such interest. Who is this Mr. Colbert? Is he a well-loved pastor? The head of a powerful family? A timber baron, or father of industry? Certainly this multitude cannot fit into the courthouse."

"No, Your Honor."

"Send word to the sheriff, if that is possible considering the thickness of the streets, to meet us here, and among the three of us, Mr. Mayor, we must arrive at suitable accommodations for the trial."

At that, one of the men went off to fetch the sheriff.

After discussion, it was decided that the Pavilion had the largest single room in town — the skating rink and its adjoining bleachers, stage and auditorium, as well as the removable boxing ring near the stage.

Pews were moved from nearby churches on Franklin Street, and some of the families carried their own chairs as body after body streamed toward the Pavilion. Oscar Bucholtz, who owned the Pavilion with his brother, tried to orchestrate the mayhem but soon gave up. The crowd flooded through the big doors. In one area, men had set up an impromptu arm-wrestling tournament. Card games were under way beneath the carnival-like atmosphere of the rink, and the morning began more festive than somber.

An accordionist played polkas at one end of the Pavilion's wide skating floor, and a mandolin band rang out from the other. As the chaos hit a steady pace, Judge Trogden quickly leafed through the case folders that made up the three-day docket. The judge delayed each case one day to make room for the peculiar trial of a vagrant named Hypolite Dupree. "We will have the entire day for Misters Colbert and Dupree," the judge said, "but that is all."

"All we need," said Sheriff Stanton Tully. "He don't talk much, Judge, this Dupree, but when he does, it is worth listening. He will be done today. And I got to say, Judge, when he is done, hold onto your hat. Things could get pretty rocky out here on the skating floor."

"Alright, Sheriff," said Trogden, "I will. Let's talk about this Colbert case before the proceedings begin."

The Pavilion was arranged to resemble a huge courtroom. The judge's bench was at one end of a stage used by bands and vaudeville troupes. Closer to the audience, but still on stage, was a long table where the mayor, the sheriff, a deputy of the court and the prosecutor sat. To the side was a long table for seven jurors who had drawn lots. Dupree, thin, mustached and bald with a bulbous head, would sit below and to the side of the judge throughout the trial. All the key participants, being on stage, would be easily seen by the multitude on the skating floor below.

The city prosecutor, Howard Pike, sat nearest Dupree with the judge before and between them. Below and facing the judge and Dupree were pew after pew of townsfolk. A thousand had squeezed into seats in the Pavilion and a second thousand —

practically the entire population of Whitesboro and the surrounding logging camps and every last soul of nearby Bear
Breach — filled the aisles, lined the walls, hung from the balco-
ny or stood outside in the street where the events would be
broadcast by trumpet-voiced barkers.

Shortly, everyone who had a seat was seated. The walls
were lined with leaning bodies and there were many standing
near the exits and windows.

The competitions ended, playing cards were stilled and finally the conversations waned.

Judge Trogden and Sheriff Tully entered from a side door
usually used by the performers, and without pause Tully announced the case, Whitesboro against Hypolite Dupree,
charged with robbery, assault and attempted murder. Trogden
slammed the gavel twice and silence filled the room.

"Mr. Pike," said the judge, "get started."

Howard Pike was about twenty-three. He was well-liked,
a Whitesboro orphan raised by his aunt. He was of a studious
nature and largely self-educated. Pike had been elected district
lawyer, essentially a county prosecutor, a year before, but had
little practical training. There was a round of applause, which
made him blush. "Sheriff Tully," he said, "please tell the court
your official version of the robbery and the beating of Edward
C. Colbert the night of April 9."

Tully succinctly laid out the order of events and pointed
out for the court Edward Colbert's young wife and their three
children. They, too, received a round of applause. Colbert himself clung to life in the town's small hospital, located on north
Main a few blocks past the Ledger.

Judge Trogden looked over the crowd and then focused
on the prosecutor, the sheriff and finally the defendant,
Dupree. "Mr. Dupree, do you agree with the sheriff's version of
the events of the night of 9 April, or do you see it different?"

"Seen it the same," said Dupree, his high voice terse and
clipped. His recent lack of front teeth made speech difficult. He
pushed his left mustache to the side. He stared straight ahead
into the crowd, not turning toward Trogden, hardly blinking.

"I see," said the judge. He again surveyed the extremities
of the room and then his eyes returned to the few men before
him.

"Anything more, Mr. Pike?"

"Yes, Your Honor."

"Bring it forward, then."

Dupree shifted his weight in the hard oak chair.

"You have something to tell the court?" Trogden said to Dupree, more a statement than question.

But Dupree was silent. Several minutes passed. Then, as if reaching a decision only he was aware of, the vagabond started to speak.

He began by retelling the sheriff's story: He had been traveling north to the Alaskan gold fields, he said. He'd taken the schooner Allyn Briar from the Port of Oakland to Fort Ross, and then traveled overland from that point. His money had run out, but he continued to make his way north, sometimes in the company of other travelers and sometimes alone.

Dupree came upon Whitesboro at night. He was tired from a day on foot. The town seemed abandoned. Colbert's livery was the first shop that presented itself; the downstairs lights had been snuffed out. Dupree was hungry and out of money. The door was ajar, "not that I could not of leant into it and pushed it open."

All was quiet as he entered the building. A man came down the staircase. Dupree began his assault; he told the judge he only wanted to escape without being caught — if he could have just a handful of coins to get him on his way. His hand fell on an iron poker and he began striking Edward Colbert. Colbert, with his wife and children obviously endangered, was forced to fight back, no matter the odds.

"Once I get started, I can't stop," Dupree said. "But it was the spirits that saved that man."

Sheriff Tully popped to attention. Pike, unaware of what would follow, also turned to the defendant. The judge raised an eyebrow. But only Tully knew what was coming.

That night, as Dupree looked up from the battered and bloody body of Edward Colbert on the floor below him and peered through the darkness of the shabby livery office, he saw the whitish images of two children standing in the stairwell, crying: a boy of four and a girl of three, white and ghostlike.

They had followed him, Dupree told the judge. "They never left me! They never have!" Dupree had screamed and run from the livery, sprinting down the night-black streets of Whitesboro until he was tackled by two men who had come running from a saloon only a few doors away. "But it was the spirits as caught me," he said, falling back heavily into the chair.

Pike stood up slowly. "Your Honor," he said, "those 'spirits' were Ed Colbert's two youngest children ... in their night-clothes and all. Is that correct, Miss Colbert?" he asked, and from the front rows of the vast gathering, Mrs. Colbert nervously said, "Yes." Applause followed and, red-faced, she sat back down in her chair. She was sobbing.

The sheriff stood and spoke to Dupree loudly enough for the rest of the court and much of the audience. "Let's see here," Tully began. "What was those spirits you seen?" Pike should not have redirected the testimony, and Tully was noticeably irritated at him for calling on Mrs. Colbert. He could sense a battle going on inside Dupree and knew it would be a delicate matter keeping the balance in his, the sheriff's, favor. It was a stupid move, allowing Dupree another line of thought at a time when any distraction could be fatal to Tully's case. He had a man to hang, here, and nothing was going to get in his way. "What's these spirits?" he said again, sternly.

"Ghosts," said Dupree. He was back on track. Tully sighed quietly with relief. "They was ghosts of children."

Father Percy

Ruth carefully navigated her way up the aisle of Whitesboro's Catholic church, Our Lady of the Sea, pew after pew, looked briefly at the white glass bowls of holy water that were held atop pedestals at the ends of each, and sat down on the incredibly hard oak seat beside an old, round-shouldered, shoulder-bladed priest whose lightly stained black shirt and white collar were hidden by a lovely knitted scarf of small, tight stitches. His black slacks were pressed, and the cat hair on them was also pressed. Exaggerated by sitting, the pant cuffs rose high above his white athletic socks, bought six to a pack at the local drugstore. His shoes were black. They were old but highly polished, the laces very thin, nylon and not long enough to tie a decent bow. They often came untied. There were marks and sticky patches across the top from strips of duct tape, which he used when the shoelaces became too much for his arthritic fingers.

Beside him was an Electrolux canister vacuum circa 1963, a bucket of rags and a can of lemon-scented wood preserver for the oak pews and holy water stands. Ruth was struck by the apparent newness of the church, much in contrast to the separate, older rectory behind the main building and the grounds in general whose age was betrayed by the thickness of the rose trunks.

There was no one in the church except the old priest, who was cleaning near the front.

"Must be warm," she said to him, pointing with her eyes to the scarf around his neck.

Father Percy looked up and smiled, his yellowed teeth showing only briefly, as if he were embarrassed by their discoloration. It was only age. "Do you like it?" he asked.

She took the opportunity to touch the scarf, make judgment of it, and softly pulled it away from him just a few inches to observe the needlework. "Oh, yes," she said. "You are so lucky."

He smiled, closed-mouth, and said, "Ah, they learn early, the Dutch. Take their skills very seriously. She passed a few years back, five, but her art lives on. Proof of God, you know. His immortality, His love of man."

"Catching up, then?" she said, nodding toward the vacuum. It was gray, patterned enamel over steel, and probably weighed fifty pounds. The hose was made of cloth.

He looked at her, studied her hands until she pulled them closer to her, though his old eyes seemed unfocused, rather like her ancient cat, Methuselah. "I've been expecting you," he said. His eyes were gray, like his skin, and like the wisps of hair that still clung to the back of his head. Father Percy was of one color, gray, and was wrapped in black and white, the antecedents of gray.

"I'm afraid I didn't call," she said.

"You don't like phones," he said. "I can tell. I have an iPhone. Really, you should try it sometime. I can text the Vatican. I can play that chicken game. I really like that." He extracted his cell from a pocket and showed her, and took her photograph without asking. She said nothing, and even tried to smile when he did it. The device was in a hard shell case with golden crosses on it. He quickly, adeptly, took her photograph again and smiled.

"Right, for six hundred bucks," she said. "Do you know how much alpaca that would buy?"

"Ha ha!" he said, standing. "And Bob's your uncle! Tell me, my dear, what can an old priest do for you today? Don't be shy; even a mouse is bold of heart."

"I'm looking for names and dates, Mr. Percy."

He hadn't been called Mr. Percy for seventy years, and that was only once, in high school when the teacher was quite upset with him for reading during a lecture. Mr. Percy, of course, was his father's name. His eyes flashed at her feet, then focused above her shoulders, left and right, and Ruth tried to catch where those gray eyes were focusing in order to determine just what they were seeing.

But he was quick about it. Her face, sweet as it may seem, was not important to him. Her eyes were of interest, but only in that they mirrored her soul. Her hair, abundant: nothing. It was the color patterns around her head and shoulders that mattered. It was the pulse in her heart.

Father Percy knew that Ruth would never refer to him as "Father." He hadn't spent a lifetime as a priest not to see that. And it would have been inappropriate for him to suggest it — that much he could see even without the colors.

"Please, call me Thomas. Thomas, the twin of our Lord: Didymus Thomas. Said to have brought the Word to the vast realms of China, you see."

"I'm Ruth."

"You're telling me, kiddo." He laughed; it was a wheezy laugh, as if his vocal cords, feeling their age, would not cooperate. "I know you are. It's a small town, you might say. Tell me, Ruth, do you like cats?"

"Of course."

"I have two. Cats. Did you see them outside?"

"The orange one who has no tail."

"That would be Mooncat. I'm sure Leopold the Great is around here somewhere. He's a gray tabby. He has a tail!"

"A tail between them."

"Indeed." He looked around at his cleaning supplies. "I suppose I should leave this for a while. I'm sure it will be waiting for me later. The work won't do itself. There are few guarantees in life, but that much I can guarantee. I don't need to be a prophet to see that! Ruth, would you like some tea, then? Yes? In the community room or the office?"

"Whichever is easier. The community room would be fine."

"Dandy. So tell me," he said as they both rose to go for tea, "what names you seek and what dates, and whatever else you wish. I am at your service, and the more we can work together, the less I will have to work amid the pews. Have you ever noticed how wood preserver makes your hands feel so dry and funny?"

"Some use rubber gloves."

"Capital! I will make a note of that."

"Names and dates for certain, but there is a matter of a little silver cross, too," said Ruth. "May we start there?"

"Excellent," said Father Percy. "I am quite the expert on the history of religious relics, as you can see by my library." They passed a room filled with books. They were not just on shelves, but piled on the tables, a desk, piled on the floor more than a foot deep, stuck in window sills and under papers. "Homey," he said.

"Very."

"I find it comforting."

"You can never have enough books."

"Most of them are library books, you know," he said. "From libraries all over the state, the nation. Some from Spain, I dare say. I would suggest that almost all of them are overdue anywhere up to, perhaps, seven or eight years. I hope and pray that my debts will be forgiven, as I forgive the debts of others, for I simply do not want to give them back!"

She entered the room, stooped, and examined a few of the books. "These are rare books, Thomas. You might consider returning them. Some are quite valuable."

"Done!" he said. "Beginning tomorrow, I'll have our secretaries begin to sort and send. You have had a very good effect on me, and so quickly. But let us make the coffee. Did I say tea? I meant coffee."

After the coffee had been brewed and poured, the cats paraded in. Mooncat sat in Father Percy's lap; Leopold sat in the window on the sunny south side.

Ruth handed Father Percy the cross. She'd cleaned it, rubbing away the grime, and soaked it in Mr. Clean until it fairly glowed. There was some degradation of the metal, some corrosion, but it was largely intact and in reasonably good shape considering what it had been through during the last century. She handed the priest her triplet magnifier, and then opened her bag and removed the little microscope she often carried. She handed that to him as well.

"You are well-equipped," he said, removing a small book from his back pocket so he could sit comfortably at their table. It was a small, leather-bound volume. But Father Percy was thin, and a book or wallet made him sit at an angle, which made his hip ache.

"As are you," she said.

After a few minutes of examination, he said, "This is a mission cross. Very nice. And old. A century and a score, if it's a day. I have a book, I have a book," and with that he was up and on his way to the office they'd passed on their way to the community room, the one filled with books. Mooncat followed, tailless.

He left the cross on the table. Ruth picked it up, but before she could get to the library room she heard a tremendous crash. She ran down to the book room and looked in the door. The old priest was on his back toward the side of the room.

"Avalanche!" he said. "System failure! No damage. All intact." He got to his knees and started rummaging through the pile on all fours. "It's in here, over on this side I'm sure. Has a little gold cross on the cover, otherwise black or dark brown leather. Four by five inches, three-quarters thick, but, Ruth, quite heavy because of the old glossy paper they printed it on, for the photos."

So she helped him find it. She picked up what seemed to be the appropriate volume, "Mission Relics," with dimensions as listed by Father Percy. And it was heavy, the paper white and smooth with many images, both drawings and black and white photographs. It had been published in 1944, a first edition.

"Perfect," he said, and they returned to the community room. Once again she handed him the cross.

He flipped through the pages and magically produced a photo of the exact item. "Not a doubt. Minted at La Purisima in 1793. That's the mission down by Lompoc, in case you're not familiar. It's cast from a two-sided mold, you can tell that by the slight ridge along the edge … that's the seam. Many were cast, you see, poured flat like pancake batter into a single-sided mold, being flat on the back. But those are cheaper. They don't have a backside! This one was poured into a hinged mold, much like they used to pour lead bullets in a bullet mold. Or like a waffle! Oh, very nice."

She smiled. How easy. "The date's old enough."

"I don't doubt it," he said. "… whatever it is you mean by that. It indicates here that twelve hundred were minted, three hundred in gold. I would say that was a limited edition. I'm sure most went Back East — the Church made good money off special trinkets like this — and a fair share were sent to Europe, mostly Spain, I am sure. A mission cross was quite exotic in Portugal, you see. I would suggest that because the edition was minted long before these northern settlements, it came here over a period of time, probably carried north with the general push of civilization. We have no records here of buying or importing such icons, though the missions did mint many of them."

"Might such a cross be mentioned, say, in baptismal records?" she asked.

"There is a dearth of such records, I'm afraid."

"Because of the fire at the church?"

That surprised him, but only for a moment. Anyone might have known that the church burned in 1986. He reached for the small volume he'd taken from his pocket earlier, and pushed it toward her.

She recoiled slightly, involuntarily. He was up to something. This was some sort of test.

"If you would, please open that old thing to any page, any page at all."

She hesitated. He looked at her, weighing his options. To Ruth, his eyes seemed to be set just to her left, maybe just above her eyes or the top of her head.

"Don't mess with me," she said sweetly, and her smile tempered her direct order.

His face seemed to fall as if he'd lost a carnival mask he'd been holding up on a stick. "There are secrets, Ruth. Whitesboro has secrets. They say, you know, that there are unsettled spirits here. Well, I have been here at Our Lady for, let me see, forty-odd years. That's a chunk of time!" Then he grew a bit more serious. "But I will tell you that many of the unsettled are not necessarily deceased."

It was hard to say who was studying the other more thoroughly. Finally, Ruth opened the book. She decided that though she had no reason to do it, neither did she have a reason to let it lie. She opened it and pushed it over to Father Percy.

"My mother saw in colors, too," he said. The reference was vague; she wasn't sure what he was talking about. He looked at the open page and smiled. Ruth saw black type on aged, formerly white paper. There was no color. It appeared to be a book of psalms.

His mood swung. Father Percy was very happy now, as if he'd seen a sign in the pages on the table. "Oh, joy, Ruth, oh, come with me! Let us peruse what is left of the old church records!" Whatever hesitation he'd felt had vanished. Ruth would never know why, never know what he'd seen in the book. She wasn't even sure what book it was, because she never saw the title. But whatever the strange man's test, she'd passed it. Whatever purported colors his mother used to allegedly see, that, too, was in Ruth's favor.

She decided the old priest was eccentric. But in a way, she found him sort of fun, unpredictable and so far inoffensive.

A half-century of age fell from Father Percy as he hopped up from the table and led Ruth and Mooncat back through the labyrinth of the church. They finally came to his personal sanctum, his place of study, far removed from the activity of the congregation and up on the third floor overlooking an old rose garden. It was a simple room, sparsely furnished, books placed but not strewn, and there were about a dozen pair of reading glasses set strategically throughout.

They entered, and he solemnly closed the door and unobtrusively made the sign of the cross.

"Do you give me your vow of silence, my dear? What we are about to discuss and see should not go past that door."

Ruth took a seat. There were several. "You'll just have to trust me, and trust my judgment, Thomas."

There was something about this woman that Father Percy liked. He thought she was kind of fun, and unpredictable, at least when compared to the parishioners he was used to. She was a strong one. Not one to compromise. Compromise what? Her power? Her integrity? It was hard to put his finger on it, exactly.

"I trust you, Ruth. As I trust all the great Ruths."

He sat on an old leather couch, clearly his seat of choice, based on the indelible, butt-sized pothole in the center.

"You see," he began, "we burned to the ground in 1986. No, no, no one was hurt. Even my cats, at the time, escaped the blaze. Old Puddy and Nick, an old tom, none the worse. Survivors. January, you see." He reflected further. "January 24th, 5:15 p.m., only four minutes after the courthouse was set afire. The church and courthouse are on opposite sides of Whitesboro, and the fire department was sore pressed between the two. Neither was saved, but our brave boys kept the flames from spreading."

Pause. "Arson," she ventured.

"No question," said Father Percy.

"And you believe one of Whitesboro's unsettled souls, living, was trying to destroy, what? Records? Some records? Yes? So what was stored at the courthouse?"

"Oh, land grants, I suppose, court proceedings, old cases. Property listings, for tax purposes."

"And the church records?"

"Well, my dear, there you have it. It has always been my suspicion that something of great value to someone was recorded in both locations — the church and the courthouse — and so both were burned. Yet I don't know what. I have only my suspicions and they are, I fear, feeble.

"But I was so convinced of my conclusions that I made quite a big deal about saying the church records burned to ash. I was surprised, I must admit, that the old newspaper didn't burn down as well, as it might also have had a record of 'it,' whatever 'it' was. But it didn't, apparently. I appealed to dear old Len Stanley to run a story of the loss of our dear church records, more than a century of births and baptisms and deaths, even some inheritances, in hopes that whoever set the blazes would be satisfied with its permanent loss."

"I see."

"But it really didn't burn. No one knows this but Mooncat and dear Leopold and me. And now you. Len knew, of course, but he's passed on. Old Len Stanley." He looked at her, his gray eyes somewhere between kind and burning. "But I trust you. No one else, I dare say.

"In fact, Ruth (he was walking over to some wood cabinets), I had urged the other denominations in town to make copies of their records for safekeeping, and each has given me a copy for my repository. So, besides Our Lady's records, long thought destroyed, I have bound copies from the Lutherans, Baptists and Episcopalians. We may need them. I have a book from the synagogue, though it only dates back to about 1951. I can't read Hebrew, though I may begin lessons sometime. Now, may I ask, what exactly are we looking for?"

"To start with, I'm looking for Mary and Daniel Johnson, and their children, Benjamin and Emma, somewhere around 1892," said Ruth.

"You certainly are directed."

"You've got to be kidding."

"No, really."

"I seem to always end up juggling too many things at once and everything falls."

"Falls? Surely not. Tell me, are you an acquaintance of Muriel Stanley? A friend?" he asked, going to the cabinet and removing a leather-bound tome about eight inches thick, two feet tall and a foot and a half wide. It had bronze or tarnished brass corner pieces. He turned and smiled: "The missing church ledger!" She thought he might strain his tired back moving it to a nearby desktop. "The leather does still smell like smoke, after all."

"A new friend, I suppose."

"You know, I would have introduced you personally, to Muriel I mean, had you not already met," said Father Percy. "She has been ill-treated in this little village, as you might know, but she has a scholar's respect for history and her memory is worth its weight. I have no doubt you got the name and dates from her."

"I've been through a lot of the old papers."

"Indeed." He started carefully turning the pages. Everything was handwritten, and in some places the script was almost calligraphic in its artistic precision. In other places the words were scrawled and almost illegible. But in all cases, it was written with a dip or fountain pen, the letters thick, and small to preserve space. Father Percy hummed as he searched. Finally, he called Ruth over to look closely, not over his shoulder, but beside him.

"What do you see when you see a page such as this?" he asked congenially.

"Writing. It takes some effort to read it, because of the penmanship."

"I mean," he said, "when you look deeply, through the eyes of your heart, through the heart of your eyes, what is it that you see?"

She worried that he was, perhaps, past the midpoint of eccentricity. "Mostly writing, Thomas," she said dryly. Father Percy decided she was purposefully being evasive, but he accepted that as a character trait and decided to find it appropriate.

"Ah. When I look at said page, my dear Ruth, I see coloration. Each letter and word carries a very dim, yet somehow distinct color or combination of colors and patterns. Less so here than in the Bible, true, but it is there nonetheless. My mother saw such elements of vision. I suppose it's inherited. Dare I liken it to the flashes seen before the onset of a debilitating migraine headache? Because of that, because of my many years of experience, I can quickly find what I might be looking for.

"Do you see anything other than the black-brown ink, then?"

But Ruth did not. "No," she said.

"You could. Now that you know it is possible, you can begin to cultivate it. But let us return to the work at hand. I have found the Johnsons for you."

And he had indeed. Mary and Daniel were married in 1887; Ben was born the following year and Emma in 1889.

"The children were baptized together in early 1890, at which celebration they were given … two minted silver crosses!" He looked at Ruth. "Can there be any doubt that these were crosses from La Purisima? No doubt! No doubt! Such in-trigue! We can gleefully jump to that conclusion, even without absolute proof!" He sobered. "The parents died in 1891, their children aged three and two. Oh, how sad, their passing ..."

"The influenza," suggested Ruth.

"Clearly," said Father Percy. "Further, all the worldly goods of Mary and Daniel Johnson were bequeathed to the children of Mary, to be held in trust and execution, to quote, by Peter T. Johnson, Esq., elder brother of said Daniel. The uncle! And there you have it! The wealth to the children of Mary, but the power to the paternal uncle."

Ruth pondered the notation about the "children of Mary." She pointed out the oddity: "Why not the children of Mary and Daniel?"

"Indeed. So I see. Quite purposeful, I would guess. Ruth, you are quite perceptive," said Father Percy.

"Can you explain what it means, the wording?"

"I'm sorry, not a clue." He smiled, mouth closed.

"No colors?"

"They come and go."

"Well, what do you make of this?" asked Ruth, bringing out the old photograph of Howard Pike and placing it near the book.

"That boy's a Pike," said Father Percy. He turned it over, read the passage and the date.

"I think Howard's about four years old in that picture," Ruth said.

"Then let us begin in 1883," he said, pulling an inch-thick chunk of pages to the right. And he quickly found that Howard Pike was born that year to Holden Pike, twenty-four, of Gray-port, and Mary Wayland, nineteen, of Whitesboro, and, further, he was born out of wedlock.

"There was, of course, no baptism," said Father Percy sad-ly. "The rules are the rules, as they say. Ruthie, there's nothing more on dear Mary Wayland in my ledger, I'm sad to say. But these days, all the Pikes are Lutheran, don't you see. But, but," he said, scurrying back over to the cabinet, "I have a copy of their old records, as I said earlier. Shall we? Interested in Lu-therans?"

225

He returned with three, thick-bound volumes of Xeroxed pages which, like the Catholic book, were arranged chronologically.

The well-kept records of Trinity Lutheran Church of White County showed that young Howard Pike, the child in the Ruth's photo, was baptized in 1886 in the company of his father, Holden Pike, and aunt, Lucy Amelia Pike. A few pages later, the father, Holden, was noted to have died that year. "Perhaps," noted Father Percy, "allowing dear Mary Wayland to marry now that the father of her child had passed on."

It explained why Daniel Johnson's worldly possessions were willed, not to *his* children, but to Mary's, for Mary had another child: Howard, whose father was Holden Pike. "Yes," said Ruth quietly, as if thinking aloud, "Daniel might have known, but his brother did not."

"Did not?" asked Father Percy, trying to follow.

"Did not. My theory is that the uncle had Daniel's children murdered, and if he'd known that Holden Pike was Mary's child, he would have done him in as well."

"I see."

"Difficult little world, back then," said Ruth. "But it does explain why Howard, in this photo, and the remains of the child we discovered in Wailing Wood, wore the same knitted pattern. Both were knitted by their mother, Mary Wayland. It was her pattern, and probably her mother's before her. It may even be a hand-me-down, brother to brother."

"Astounding! Really!" he said. "But it is hardly any easier today on those who do not or cannot follow moral convention," said Father Percy.

"That's the truth."

He looked at her. "You speak, you know." He shrugged.

Cryptic, again, thought Ruth. She would have preferred that the old man turn his gaze away from her; she felt stripped — not naked or indecent, her flaws exhibited for him to see, but something deeper still, catching the edges of her soul, her life experience, and she didn't like it.

"I can't help it," said Father Percy apologetically. "Love me, love my cat, as they say in the cat business."

"St. Bernard," said Ruth offhandedly.

"Brilliant, my dear! I could talk with you all day! St. Bernard, indeed, with a little freelance effort from old Padre Tomas! It was St. Bernard who had said, "Love me, love my dog," referring, of course, to his own foibles."

"I want to know more about Mary Wayland, Thomas."

"I see. Then let us explore the book further! Back to our leather-bound ledger." He pushed aside the Lutheran white paper volume and, with great effort, pulled the old Catholic book toward him across the desktop.

They opened it again, and again Ruth marveled at the yellow pages of history.

"I want to know what wealth Mary Wayland had that led to the deaths of two of her children — yes, I think they were killed — and, that same motive may have led to the torching of the city's records both here at the church and at the county building. Let's find when she was born. She was nineteen in 1883. Birth year would have been 1864-ish."

"Right. Were you always good at math?"

"No."

"Because you didn't go to school."

"I did on occasion."

"Hardly ever."

"Enough."

"They gave you a hard time." He looked at her intently.

"Yes. You want to give it a rest, Nostradamus?"

He giggled. "Ruth, don't worry. You are as tough as they come. You and Muriel both. Would that all men could be so strong. Now, back to work, as you wish!

"Here," he said, pointing in the book, "we find that our Mary was born in 1865 to Col. Patrick Wayland and Mabel Wayland nee White, who were married the year before. We have found what you are looking for, you see ..."

"The motive?"

"Certainly," he said brightly, "because Mabel White would be the daughter of Nathaniel White, the timber baron for which White County is named! And Whitesboro City. And the White River. Etc., etc., etc."

"Timberland. Thousands of acres of redwood. Does that mean, possibly, that Wailing Wood, still a primal forest, was basically stolen by the brother, Peter Johnson, after he had Ben and Emma killed, when it should have gone to the surviving child of Mary Wayland, as the will decreed? I mean, Howard Pike, her firstborn? Are those the records that someone wanted burned in 1986? Had to be. Is there some descendant of Peter Johnson who still has some interest in the land? Or who, perhaps, is simply avoiding history's scandal?"

Father Percy was silent.

"Now I know why they were killed. But not how."

"You *have* heard there are unsettled spirits in Whitesboro? It's an old saying."

"No kidding."

"They're not like cats, you know."

"I know."

"Mr. Puddy was never the same after the fire. That's why I got Mooncat. To be his friend. Everyone needs a friend, Ruth. Even you." He blinked, his old eyes moist and somewhat reddened from the close work on the churches' dusty ledgers. He smiled, his yellowed teeth showing only briefly.

Her mind returned to the task at hand. "I need to know what happened regarding the heirs of Peter Johnson. What do the books show after the deaths of Ben and Emma?"

"Peter Johnson," said Father Percy. He ran his finger down the Catholic ledger. "Stayed with the church, apparently. A son, Lambert Johnson is noted to have died at sea in 1895. A second son, Lawrence ..." he said, scanning the pages, flipping them carefully, "married in 1920, aged forty-seven, a certain Iona Paulson, aged twenty-three, of Sacramento. Mm hmm. Child born in 1922, Catherine. Catherine Iona Johnson, born 1922, baptized shortly thereafter." He turned the next few pages, then a few more. "Nothing more on the Johnson clan, I'm afraid." He looked up at Ruth. "Perhaps they had misgivings about their religion. More likely, they left the area, though that would not be common. I see nothing more on them. But Catherine is your key to current, living descendants of Mr. Peter." A perusal of the other books, the Lutheran, the Baptist, showed nothing more about the Johnsons.

"Just one other item," said Ruth. The old priest smiled and waited. "Where did old Nathaniel White emigrate from? The timber baron."

"Common knowledge, I suppose. They say Norfolk, England. We can check?"

"That's fine. No need," she said. It seemed only reasonable that Mary Wayland's pattern would derive directly from Norfolk, homeland of her father. But she said nothing. There was no need.

Father Percy shrugged. "I suppose you'll have to take it from here," he said apologetically.

"I will. And thank you, Thomas," she said, and kissed him on the cheek. "I've got to get back to the morgue. I'm starting to miss it."

"Morgue?"

"The Ledger's newspaper library. In the back."

"I will pray for you, Ruth," he said, chuckling.

A Map and Old Photos

After her discussion with Father Percy that morning, Ruth re-entered the Ledger's morgue. The trial of Hypolite Dupree was much on her mind.

Muriel arrived at the newspaper from a chamber of commerce meeting just as Ruth walked in the front door. Muriel pulled a narrow reporter's notebook from her back jeans pocket, slipped off her camera and plopped down in her desk in the back, wishing she'd poured a cup of coffee before she sat down.

Muriel's legs ached. She'd been to the chamber meeting, the high school and the elementary school.

"I should have stuck with you after all, Ruth," she said, thick with resignation.

"Thomas Percy said to say hello."

Muriel smiled. "He's a character. Was he helpful?"

"He's got some books he shared with me. They were very helpful."

"What do you mean, books?"

"Oh, you know, books. Some record books that were supposed to have been destroyed and that I'm supposed to keep mum about because they're top secret and the reason that someone burned down the church and the courthouse in 1986. You know, that book."

Muriel said, "He's got that old volume of marriages and baptisms, you mean. The old Whitesboro Catholic record; it goes back a hell of a long time, pardon my blasphemy."

"So you know about it. Is Mr. Percy the only one who thinks he's got a big secret?"

"No. Not really. I know about it because Daddy told me. The fires were arson and he and Father Tom decided it would be best not to say anything; between the two fires, it was pretty obvious that someone was out to destroy some sort of records. They didn't know what and we still don't. But us Stanleys don't keep secrets from ourselves. Family first, you know."

"That's reasonable."

"I notice," said Muriel, "that you told me about the book before you knew that I knew …"

"Yeah, true. I don't believe in secrets either. They've just never worked for me."

"I think the world could use more Ruths." Muriel paused, and then said, "Do you want to look through Uncle Arney's cabinets and take a look at the maps?"

Ruth smiled. The big folios and the mystery of Hypolite Dupree would have to wait. "Great. Perfect. I need something warm to drink, first, just a minute." Ruth stuck a stained mug under the coffee urn's spout and pulled the lever. "Does this stuff ever crawl back out of your cup once it's in there?" she said as she watched the cup fill up. She looked up at Muriel, and realized she'd begun to adapt to Whitesboro; she sounded like Paul Grassi talking to Bob Cooper.

"Out of the cup? Hardly ever. You sound like Paul Grassi talking to Bob Cooper. I'd hate to see you in a month," said Muriel. "But there's a stick over there in the corner if it does … give it a good whack, or have Arney do it. There're calcium pills in the desk drawer there," she said, pointing. "The so-called fruit-flavored ones."

"I think as long as it's not panting or showing its teeth, I'll be fine."

They walked back to the morgue. Charlotte got up and poured out the coffee and made new. In all the years she'd been at the Ledger, she'd never seen any reason they had to use the same batch for two, even three days, anyway. Enough was enough. Len the Miser had been dead three years already, bless him, and it was time for things to change. He used to percolate it with sugar, a nasty habit he'd picked up from those anarchist fishermen down in the harbor; after three or four days, it was like coffee syrup, and he used to joke about carbonating and bottling it.

Once in the morgue, Muriel flicked on the heater and gave it a kick. The old coils started heating up and the fan turned with a monotonous click-snick, click-snick. It was good for a couple more years, Muriel said, but then it would have to be replaced.

"I don't know if there's anything related to the children in the wood in here, Ruth, but if there is, we kind of have to figure out Uncle Arnold's code system first."

"Like what?"

"Well, like, we know enough from the old papers and the grave stones, well, we have to think in terms of names. He filed lots of stuff under names. Sometimes he used dates, but you'd have to find a drawer with a date on the outside and there aren't that many. I don't know, 1906 was a big year because of the quake, and since that was the hanging or shooting of the Hypolite guy, too, maybe we should go through it. This is going to take forever. After that, after names, it's kind of like using keywords."

"Like Wailing Wood."

"Yeah, except if there's anything on that, it'll be later because I don't think it was called that way long ago. Called something else ..." She'd found an old Milky Way bar in a corner of a reading desk, left there by her son or one of the genealogy enthusiasts weeks or months ago. But it hadn't been opened. Muriel gnawed into half before she pushed the remainder of the hardened old thing across the desk in Ruth's direction. Neither was being too picky that afternoon.

"Can we order Chinese takeout?" Ruth asked, mouth full.

"Sure. Except there's no Chinese this week. They're out of town. Pizza?"

"What kind?"

"After eating that candy bar, you care?"

"No."

"It's good pizza, this Italian family's been making it since Adam, south on Franklin. They'll deliver or we can save five bucks and ask, kindly and with all the lovey stuff, Arney to pick it up. As long as we order enough for everyone, anyway."

Ruth pulled out two of the twenties she'd won betting Daniel Thom and Luther Eaglejohn. "Here's my cut."

"All right. But we'll split it. Let's get two big ones. You like pepperoni?" She pushed one of the twenties back to Ruth and pulled a matching bill from her pocketbook.

"No."

Pause. "Okay, then. Half of one has pepperoni."

"Half of one with artichokes."

"Half of one with chicken."

"Half of one with pesto and dried tomatoes."

"Done." Muriel raised her voice: "Hey, Arney, we're ordering pizza!"

A thin voice trailed into the back: "Half of one with dried tomatoes."

"Out with the pesto, keep the tomatoes," Ruth said. "Arney's back from Humboldt."

"Yep, back."

"Charlotte wants one with Canadian bacon." Arney's voice.

"He must drive a lot," said Ruth.

"Out with the chicken," said Muriel. "I could get used to this. He gets good gas mileage and won't drive when he's tired, so I feel okay about it. So where do you want to start?" She picked up the phone and ordered.

"Let's do it the easy way. First, let's go through all the Stanley family's map collection in that cabinet there," said Ruth, eyeing the wide, thin oak drawers.

"Lots of maps," cautioned Muriel. "What are we looking for?"

"Wailing Wood, maybe with some notations about something that we can't even imagine at this point."

"Okay. Well, just get your eyes focused on, for example, we know what the forks of the White River look like, pretty much. They part a few miles east of the wood. Just start looking for old maps that show the V, the two forks, running to the sea. Right?"

"Good point. Okay, I'll start with the top drawer," and Ruth pulled it out and lifted its contents onto one of the study desks. Muriel did the same, starting at the bottom.

"How long until pizza?" Ruth asked.

"Forty minutes. We should be able to do two or three drawers apiece by then, if we work fast. But don't miss any-thing ..."

They had finished before the pizza arrived. Between them, they had found a single map, about four feet by three feet, fold-ed in half but otherwise barely creased despite its age, dating to 1890. It showed the White River from the Pacific, inland to Lake County, a hundred miles. Despite the scale, the river fork was discernable. Many numerical positions were noted, longitude and latitude, indicating it had probably been a survey map. It could have been used by the railroad, or White Timber's private hauling line. It might have been used for property designation, and had been squared off in ranges and townships. But most importantly, it displayed some of the topography of the area, specifically around the coastal redwood tracts. The harbor, es-tuaries and general coastline were quite accurate, Muriel thought, though parts of the shore had eroded, over time.

"It says Wayland's Wood," said Ruth with finality. "It says Wayland's Wood. With Col. Patrick C. Wayland, written small-er, right under." It was Mary Wayland's land or, more correct-ly, her father's.

Muriel stared.

"That's Mary Wayland's father," said Ruth. She quickly re-lated what she'd found with Father Percy. Then they both looked closely at the map. "It's like an island there, just that ridge part, like they were keeping it separate from the rest of the family's land holdings, surrounded by the rest of their property. I don't know, but if you asked me, I'd say Wailing Wood is a derivative of Wayland's Wood. Even then, it must have been older, denser, somehow special."

"Which means," said Muriel, "that it belongs to the Pike family, from what you just told me that Father Tom told you about My Howard Pike."

"This is getting interesting, don't you think?"

"Way interesting. We could stay in here for a few more hours and try to find out how long it was called Wayland's Wood. 1920? 1930? Who knows?"

"Veto," said Ruth.

"Motion fails," said Muriel, relieved. She started rolling the map to take upstairs.

After Arney returned with the pizzas, the Ledger's doors were locked; it was past closing time anyway. It was pizza time. They went upstairs with the flat boxes of two-toned discs with raised crusts. No chicken, no pesto. But Muriel had a two-liter bottle of Royal Crown Cola upstairs.

Charlotte, who had accepted their pizza invitation, joined the impromptu dinner, and left an hour later. Ruth and Muriel went back downstairs in slippers to plow through a few more drawers. Arney and Lou cleaned up.

Muriel flipped on the overhead lights of the back shop and then they entered the morgue again, ready to get to work. Leaving the map drawers now, they took on Uncle Arnold's cabinet drawers. Muriel chose J for Johnson. Ruth, M for murderers. Their luck continued. Because of the broader category, Ruth scored. But what she found wasn't at all what she expected. Or what Muriel expected. In fact, they didn't quite know how to take what they'd discovered.

They had old black-and-white contact prints, dating from the late 1890s to the early 1900s, cracked and brown, of Black Peterson, Hypolite Dupree and Peter T. Johnson, the main players in one of Whitesboro's supreme tragedies, packaged together in an age-yellowed envelope. The writing on the envelope was illegible. Peter Johnson's photo was about four inches by five inches, and the ruffians' were about two by three.

"Those are prints made directly from the negatives," said Muriel. "I don't think we have the negatives, though."

"I'll settle for the prints," said Ruth.

The degeneration of the photographic paper from age was apparent, but the images remained sharp and clear, for they had been kept from the light. The faces of the men were very unsettling. Muriel and Ruth stood in silence, staring at the photos and then at each other for several minutes. Muriel shrugged. Ruth shrugged, and smiled, not knowing what else to do.

"Strange," said Muriel.

"Whew."

They put the photos back in the envelope. "I'll need these," said Ruth. She put the envelope on a clipboard she found, careful to catch only the paper of the envelope and not the photos within.

It was ten before Muriel trundled up to bed. She waited for Ruth. Ruth said she was going for a walk. Muriel gave her an umbrella to go along with a borrowed raincoat. "It's raining like hell already. Wear my boots, Ruth," she said. "It's going to pour all night. And what time are you going to be back?"

"When I know what I want to know, I guess."

Muriel didn't know where Ruth would go this time of night. Nothing was open. She decided Ruth was going for a walk in the pouring rain, really smart. "The upstairs door'll be unlocked, so just come in. Leave the coat and stuff in the mudroom, just on the floor … we'll wring it all out in the morning. Don't catch a chill, Ruth. Arney might still be up. Not me. I've got a lot of writing to do tomorrow anyway."

"Thanks, Muriel. Night. I'll be quiet. Thanks for the pizza."

"Yeah, yeah. Don't get too wet, you'll catch a chill."

"Right, Mom."

The Silver Cross

FROM THE TRIAL OF HYPOLITE DUPREE:
The vagrant's trial gained such a vast audience on 16 April
that the proceedings were moved, at the request of the
Honorable Judge Eli Trogden, to the newly finished skat-
ing floor and auditorium of the Pavilion, owned by the
Brothers Bucholtz. Tarps were laid across the wide floor.
— *The Whitesboro Ledger Extra, Tuesday, April 17, 1906*

"Judge," said the sheriff, "is that sack of possibles back
there or does Howard have that thing?"

"I have it, Sheriff," said Howard Pike, the district lawyer.
The trial of Hypolite Dupree, charged with the beating of Ed
Colbert, was well underway, and the immense crowd was very
quiet, like a brewing storm.

"Could you put that little sack on the table there, Mr.
Pike? Thank you. Judge, is that list of Mr. Dupree's possibles,

which I have had put on this table, back there or does Howard have that, too?"

"I have it, Sheriff," Pike said, gaining his second round of applause that day.

"Yer Honor," said Tully, stepping in on the clapping, "I ask that you have the district lawyer read that list of items that was in the pockets of Mr. Dupree when he was jailed on account of throttling Mr. Ed Colbert."

The judge looked over to Pike and nodded.

"One spool of thread, red," said Pike, "one small folding knife with a broken blade; one holy cross on a chain, silver; a leather pocketbook with two dollars in coin despite the defendant's testimony that he was out of money; one kerchief; one rollins tobacco; small box of matches; one piece of leather thong."

"Them yours, Hypolite Dupree?" asked the sheriff.

"They are mine. I signed. And I could use that rollins, Judge."

Trogden shook his head in disbelief that the prisoner would say such a thing. Dupree sighed.

"That little pocket blade yours, Mr. Dupree?" asked the sheriff. He had turned, addressing the defendant from the side in such a manner that he also addressed the spectators. There was a collective inhalation at the mention of the knife. "How come that blade is snapped?" The question brought a low rattle from the crowd, intrigued now by this new evidence — though they were still uncertain where it might point.

"Prying open a bottle," was Dupree's reply, but with it came a general moan from the crowd beyond the stage. Dupree looked around behind him for the first time.

"That money yours?"

"Mm. Forgot. Sure," said Dupree, turning from the crowd and looking down at his feet. They were tied together with a thick rope. Tully, his face sharp, angular, almost sinister in the light that seeped in from the high windows of the Pavilion, went through each item in the bag as if it were the secret to the life or death of the man in front of him. Dupree, confused at the charade, simply answered the questions.

"That little cross …" Tully said, coming to the final item. Dupree's head slowly rose again and he looked at the sheriff.

"That yours too, I suppose, seeing you're a man of God and all?"

"Yes," said Dupree. His voice wavered. He broke eye contact with the sheriff. Tully knew he'd guessed correctly about the cross, and a shiver of excitement, of confirmation, zipped up his spine.

"Judge," Tully said, "I am having a little trouble hearing …"

Judge Trogden slammed the mallet once and called for silence. And silence fell. "Repeat your answer, Mr. Dupree."

"I said yes on it."

A murmur spread through the crowd, as though some hidden fact were being brought out, and although they didn't know what it was, there was a general understanding that they were very close to the truth, and that in the revealing of that truth they might all finally say, "Of course, of course, I remember. We all remember."

Tully picked up the cross, holding it high above him so all might see. It glinted slightly as it spun on the chain. He had polished it before the trial, just for the occasion. Yet the very sight of it made him uncomfortable; somewhere, he knew he'd seen that very cross before. It was the same feeling of unconsummated recognition he'd had when he first saw it among Dupree's possessions. But he thrust the feeling aside, crushed the chain into his fist and let the cross dangle, glimmering, high above his head.

"I got some people here in town that might know this here crucifix, Mr. Hypolite Dupree," Tully said loudly. Then he raised his voice further, shouting, "Because sure as I am standing here, I am declaring that this cross belonged to *young Emma Johnson!*"

Utter chaos erupted in the Pavilion. Nearly a half-hour passed before Judge Trogden could restore order.

When the human thunder finally quelled, order was restored. Finally, silence reigned. Tully walked over to Dupree and said, in a low voice, "Talk on."

"Judge," said Dupree, "I want to speak to the court."

"Go on then," said Trogden. He leaned back in his chair. Quiet had finally settled over the rink.

Dupree began his story from a point nearly fifteen years before. He spoke in spurts at first, but eventually gained a sort of momentum or rhythm as he sat before the utterly quiet City of Whitesboro.

He had come from Clovis with a man named Blackie Peterson, and they moved west to pick over the remains of the gold fields of California, prospecting and panning for what was left. It was "eighteen and ninety-one." They had ended up, after a year, in Bear Breach where money was flowing like sap in the forests. The big trees were falling and being shipped to San Francisco, already rich from the gold rush. He and Black Peterson were drinking at the White House Tavern. It was full, it was overflowing. They were sitting in the back, far from the mahogany bar where spittoons lined the floor every three or four feet. The wall mirror behind the bar made it all the brighter inside — and all the darker outside — for a storm was brewing.

"A man come up to us," Dupree said, his voice echoing over the crowd, which strained to hear every word. "A tall man dressed out in a long black rider coat, for it was cold and it was pourin' rain. I mean, it was a cold night out there. Rainin'. It must always rain here. He gets us a drink of boughten whiskey." He fell silent for a few seconds. Dupree looked at the crowd, then to the court officials.

"He, this tall man, he explained things to us, to Blackie and me, the way things was, you know, in the world. How every man has got to take what's his. Very wise, he seemed to me. And very golden of voice. Here I was drinkin' pretty good. It was cold. He had us a task, he says, I could, you know, a task if we was to do it, and he would pay us very much, Black and me."

The tall man was Peter Johnson, a man known to most of those present at the trial, and a man who embodied a tragic story. He took charge of his young niece and nephew after the deaths of his younger brother, Daniel Johnson, and Daniel's wife, Mary.

This Daniel and his young family were prosperous, largely on account of the wife's fortune, and they were good people. They left their children, Ben and Emma, in the care of Peter

Johnson, whom their will and testament named trustee of the estate.

"And the will did run like this," said Dupree.

He had a habit of holding his hand over his mouth when he spoke, and Judge Trogden reminded him to remove it.

Dupree, his voice more audible, continued. "I learnt this later, about the will. But not from Mr. Peter Johnson, for that was his name. Heard it in the saloon, later, afterwards. He was thin-lipped, but I learnt later this: The boy to receive a thousand dollars in gold each year when he come of age; the girlie three thousand in gold coin to be paid down on her wedding day. There was something about land, I don't know what, though. He didn't tell me and Black any bit of that. I learnt what I learnt in Ukiah, inland, over the range. Just bar talk.

"But if they died, those children there, if they was to die, then all the wealth and land went to Peter Johnson, they uncle," Dupree said, his voice rising noticeably in its condemnation. He scanned the audience, searching for the man he was accusing. He saw only the wide eyes of Whitesboro — a people hearing now for the first time what many had long suspected and feared. The judge tapped the gavel, then slammed it down until the din abated.

Dupree went on with his story. He and Black Peterson were paid handsomely to steal the children away from the Peter Johnson home in Whitesboro, under the guise of traveling to New York, and to slay them in a wood. No one would suspect; the babes had lived with Peter Johnson for nearly a year and he had made much of them. To secure their futures, he had said, they would live among friends in New York where their education would be more fitting to their station in life. That was to be their story.

"Oh," said Dupree, "oh, we took those sweet little childrens, Black and me, to do them in, take them in a carriage give to us by Mr. Johnson. Took the eastbound road but stopped to Bear Breach for drink. They was so happy," he mused, "the childrens, to be in a carriage with horses and all, just laughing and all … playing.

"We was talking just outside of Bear Breach, there just off the road. But I told Blackie that I wanted to welch on the deal, and didn't want to do it no more, and Black, he says we been paid, and paid very large, and we got to do it. Kill them. And we didn't need to know no reason why. I learnt that later, like I said, the inheritance of 'em. But we had got to do it, he tells me. And I'm trying to say, telling him, you know, I mean we already got the money and, why, we could just take them somewhere. Blackie, he got more angry and more, and ripped that crucifix right off poor girlie and she got so scared — and oh God how that little thing whimpered — and bolted out of the reach of old Black. And Child Benjamin, he pulled her away by the hand from him.

"Oh," Dupree continued, nearly in tears, feigned or not, "we fell to fighting ... after them kids run off some ways, kind of in the middle of all that, see, I was just off to the side and couldn't stop old Black from grabbing at the girl, and I come up and caught Black and we fell to shouting and that scared them even worse, and we was shouting threats and Black, him being the bigger, starts in on me. Big Black and me, and I had me a knife, God knows, and it was a deliverance because that man would kill me as I stood, him being the bigger.

"I just did not want to go through with it. The kids and all. I killed him, Judge. I killed Black Peterson right there near the road. In self-defense. In self-defense!" His voice trailed, "There wasn't nobody around ..."

The skating hall remained devastatingly quiet. Moments passed. Dupree pulled at his jacket sleeves, picked at them.

"They seen me kill Blackie with my knife. Yeah, and, uh, I led them some ways into the wood so we could not be seen. And told them I'm coming back with some food or bread ... left them off some ways, see, away, and went back to Blackie's body and took that little cross out of his hand. That cross. He's still holding onto it, see," he said, pointing at the sheriff. "That one.

"Child Benjamin, he had a cross just like it around his own neck. I seen it on him. Blackie, he just got the other one, not both. But I couldn't leave him have it ..."

Then Dupree sighed. "Got to Ukiah by way of the haul road off from Bear Breach going east below the ridge, and put on a drunk, you can see why. I had the money ... mine and Blackie's both. From that devil Peter Johnson. Took the carriage and sold it off. Drank for four or five days.

"Then it was too late to go back. When I got up and sober ... all those days. It was too late. I knew. I knew they was passed to the other land." There was sincerity in his voice, though it may have been only voice deep.

"I carried the cross and that ever since. Then, robbing that livery office, I seen their spirit, there on the stair ... Child Ben and Emma Johnson. I run. That is all ... I got no more statement on this but one," he said, and standing, turning to the audience, with the judge and sheriff and prosecutor behind him, he yelled, "I say let hell fall on Peter Johnson!!"

Dupree searched frantically for the face he couldn't find, searching for that long, grim scowl of fourteen years past. It was nowhere to be seen, but every soul in Whitesboro remembered Peter Johnson.

"Sheriff," said Judge Trogden, standing and surveying the wide-eyed audience, "by the order of this court, I demand the arrest of Peter Johnson for murder and conspiracy to commit murder!"

Stanton Tully moved closer to the bench. "Judge," he said, "Peter Johnson has been dead these seven year, last March."

Trogden sat back heavily in his chair. "For fourteen years, no one knew?" asked the judge. "No man knew they were lost and dying? That they lay down in that wood somewhere and died? My God, man!"

He turned to the jury and instructed them to retire and return with a verdict.

To Hypolite Dupree, he said, "This jury will announce your miserable fate after reasonable consideration. Then we'll hang you." He stepped down from the stage.

A Night at the Gull

I saw Mr. Kasparov quite a bit after he returned from Oakland; he was back on Thursday. On Friday afternoon, we played chess on a little pine board with holes drilled into it for the peg pieces — his traveling chess game. One of the pawns had been lost and he'd made a new one from tissue paper and plaster of Paris. Actually, it was a good sculpture; he's skilled with his hands. It had a little face with a mustache and goatee, painted with a tiny brush in enamel and then varnished; the whole piece was about half an inch tall.

"We made those, such as you see, when I was in prison, a political prisoner. But without paint. No plaster. Toothpaste. I was confined for love, a prisoner of love," he said wistfully, then raised a thick eyebrow for dramatic effect. I wanted to ask him what he meant, but he changed the subject. He's like that: He doesn't want to talk about his past but can't resist getting started.

I realized I was closer to this peculiar Soviet refugee than the people with whom I'd worked at the Bulletin for the last ten years. I felt like I could trust him, which is a strange feeling in that I can't imagine what I might trust him with.

As we finished the game, Detective Chu stopped by, having had no luck with the steelhead. Mrs. Morton, checking her rooms, also stopped in. It was late afternoon. With Mr. Kasparov, they made an unsavory trifecta, plus me. Mrs. Morton had a Scrabble game under her arm (such a coincidence) and a pack of Winstons in her blouse pocket. So we played a round, if that's what it's called in Scrabble. Mrs. Morton cheated. I was fairly certain that Mr. Kasparov was aware of it and, not to be outdone, had a few sleights of hand of his own, impossible to discover but certainly not within the rules. In brief, the two of them wiped William Chu and me, law-abiding citizens, off the Scrabble map.

"The two-fifty has roughly a trillion parts," Mr. Kasparov said of the Maverick engine next door. He drew a few wood tiles, having spelled *quell*. "The object of which is to move collectively and with a precision measured in thousands of an inch. Microns. Yet you are telling me that man can understand the movements and interrelationships in something as vast as the planet Earth?" Mrs. Morton clicked down four scrabble letters, including the Z. I noticed that this was the second Z on the board, but said nothing. She and Mr. Kasparov seemed to be getting all the letters with a value of four or more. I found it odd. "Or as comprehensive as a solar system? I think not." She added up her points, turned, smiled broadly at Mr. Kasparov. He held out his cigarette lighter. It was a cylindrical stainless steel thing that looked left over from Russia's industrial revolution, maybe about World War II vintage, sort of like a miniature iron lung or industrial blowtorch that you might use to destroy a small German Panzer if it had the audacity to approach Moscow. He lit her cigarette. She blew smoke out of the side of her mouth, upward.

I had never suggested anything remotely similar to what Mr. Kasparov was talking about. Actually, I didn't know what he was talking about. No one did.

"Yet," he continued, "the internal combustion engine I can understand," he continued, doing something untoward with the letters in his rack. "Or, perhaps, a game of chess. But, for example, The Miss? Hardly, my dear friends, hardly. The Cosmos, The Miss, don't you see the connection?"

Mrs. Morton moved some of her tiles around, squinting, looking at something that might have been in her lap.

Mr. Kasparov had more to say. "And here, in this oasis of cultural tradition, Whitesboro City, a land of times past, half the time she is talking about something that occurred one hundred years ago, and the other quarter of the time she is referring to modern characters. They have the same names, Mr. Fisher! What, they live in a shtetl? Some ghetto in Kiev?" where families might also be interrelated and multigenerational.

There was, of course, a missing quarter in his arithmetical figuring, which he didn't explain. For some reason, I knew he'd done that on purpose, but, like so much of what the man said in moments of reflection, I would never know the ultimate meaning.

So it went. Eventually Friday's games were over. Had we been playing for money, William Chu and I would have been fleeced.

Mr. Kasparov, Chu and Mrs. Morton all left. It was dark, and it had been raining profusely. Buckets of water were streaming outside above the door, where the rain gutter had broken.

I cleaned up the room and arranged my clothing neatly on the otherwise unused dresser and placed my bag in the corner near the bed. I would visit the Ledger in the morning, and see how things were going. I lit a candle that I'd brought with me and placed it on the table near the window for no other reason than to feel a little warmer while the rain was so omnipresent. The window near the door was open because of Mrs. Morton's cigarette.

I had a pulp paperback crime novel I'd been saving for such an isolated occasion — a proverbially rainy night — and started it. The bedside lamp was dim, not more than forty watts, and I'd covered the LED numerals on the clock radio with a dry washcloth. I looked underneath: It was 11 p.m.

It was quiet: Even Renton Morton had put down his wrenches and ratchets for the day, thank God, and there was no sound in the harbor that was not the surf or the steady rain, the latter of which was a combination of large drops popping on the roof of the shell-like Herring Gull Motel, and the steady trill of smaller drops that descended in slow moving sheets like hissing gauze. The glooming skies had finally decided to open. Four hours of rain had flooded the parking area in front of the motel.

The Gull had retired; it had turned midnight while I was reading. The only lights in the harbor were the lights outside the doors of the rooms, and these were as dull as the reading lights inside, and one of them flickered like a yellow butterfly.

Then, strangely, there was a knock at the door. I was still up, reading, tired but unable to sleep because my normal work shift wouldn't end for two more hours, and I am a creature of habit, especially when it comes to sleep. I raised the cloth from the clock to check the time, and, reoriented, covered it up again, snuffing out the red glow. Because I was socially presentable in a full department-store wardrobe of patterned flannel pajamas and a linen-cotton robe and slippers (the latter, a must for motel rooms in harbor districts that still have an active fishing fleet), I had no reason not to answer the door. It was most likely Mr. Kasparov or Mrs. Morton anyway, on errands of their own. Maybe they wanted to apologize for cheating.

I opened the door. Ruth was standing outside, rubber raincoat flowing wet, umbrella inside out and collapsed from the northeastern wind, and she was soaked from head to foot despite them.

"Got a minute?" she asked, shaking from the chill she'd taken during the two-mile walk from the Ledger at the north end of Whitesboro to the harbor at the south. "I just left the Ledger after digging some pictures and maps out of the morgue with Muriel Stanley."

I stood aside and took her coat and so-called umbrella as she came inside. In the candlelight and the dim reading light, she appeared soaked and tired. I wrapped her coat around a hanger and hung it from a chrome towel shelf in the bathroom that held one fresh bath towel, two hand towels and one washcloth (the other was on the clock). The towel I had used earlier was hanging neatly over the shower curtain rod.

I asked how she'd gotten so wet under the rubber raincoat, and she said, "I haven't seen you for hours." I couldn't tell if she was kidding around. "We need to talk, but do you mind if I towel off first?"

I don't know whether I felt relief or elation knowing that everything in the modest-to-shabby motel room was clean and in place. "Please," I said, and she vanished into the bathroom. A few minutes later, I could hear the bath water and a minute after that I realized she was taking a shower to warm up and that she had nothing dry to change into.

The best I could do was a clean crew-neck T-shirt, unused gray sweat pants with the sales tag still on them, and a new gray hoodie — all of them many times too large for her because I'm easily a foot taller and a hundred and twenty pounds heavier. She'd have to tuck it in and roll it up, but at least she'd be dry and warm. I set them just inside the bathroom door and then turned on the water boiler for some tea I thought I had brought with me.

But I had only three bags of Lipton, compliments of the room. I was crushed.

She came out red from the heat in a gust of steam, wrapped in far too many layers and folds of gray and with a towel enwrapping her hair, looking like a cold-cream ad you might find in a 1950s edition of Look magazine. Except for the sweats. They were too big.

I felt badly about the cheap motel shampoo, but it would take more than one dose of it to harm that kind of hair, so thick you want to touch it even if she's a stranger to you.

She said, sitting on the corner of the bed as I sat down in the chair beside the small table at the window, "Here I am stuck in 1922 with a certain Catherine Iona Johnson, two generations removed from the infamous child killer, Peter Johnson."

She had my attention.

She said, "I talked with Father Percy and then went back to the Ledger files to see if I could get anywhere with the new information. I couldn't." She explained the backgrounds of the Pikes and Johnsons. It took her an hour. I wasn't tired.

"How can we find out about the Johnson line?" she asked. "Catherine Iona. The situation here is that there's a huge tract of valuable land, probably Wailing Wood itself, which should have gone to young Howard Pike, the son of Mary Wayland before she married Daniel Johnson. ... Mary Wayland, whose other children were killed and buried in the wood. But the land was taken by Peter Johnson, trustee of the children. He and his heirs supposedly inherited the land due to the disappearance of the children, the Daniel Johnson line, so to speak — and no one knew about Howard Pike, Mary's child before Ben and Emma were born. I can't get past 1922 and the birth of Catherine in the Johnson line."

It was all kind of a whirlwind. I said, "Mr. Kasparov talks incessantly when he plays Scrabble."

She looked up at me, not missing a beat, and said, "He does that when he's cheating. It's a subterfuge."

"How does that help?"

"It's an old technique. My grandfather used to use it when he performed magic. Did I ever tell you about him?"

"Just a little. That he had chickens, that he juggled and taught you how …"

"And he used to perform at one of the bars on Grant Avenue, a little magic show. He'd been in vaudeville. You get a story line going, and the audience, or your victims, pay attention to that and not what you're doing with your hands."

"I see now."

"Did he do the math thing?" she asked.

"He did fractions," I said. "Half the time for this, a quarter of the time for that …"

"Oh, that's to distract you. I bet you started trying to work out the fractions, right?"

"Yes."

"Well, that's when he got you." That said, she added: "Next step in the Catherine situation, please."

I decided that her Catherine Johnson story was getting good, but, trace the Johnson line? I had to think. "Okay," I said, booting up my laptop, "we can start here. People like to trace their genealogies, and a lot of their work is public, and maybe we can find her on a couple of websites. Even if Catherine is someone's distant cousin, we might be able to find her and wander up and around the genetic line. It's lucky you have her birth year. Do you have the parents' names?" We sat on the bed, pillows behind our backs and the laptop on my lap but pointed between us so we could both see the fourteen-inch screen. I put in the password for the Gull's Wi-Fi, "flat6ford."

This was the only amenity at the motel, and it was there largely because Mrs. Morton found the online weather forecasts more accurate than broadcast television.

The parents: "Iona Paulson and Lawrence Johnson, married," said Ruth.

Succinct.

I tried several genealogy websites, one of which I subscribed to for general reporting purposes, the other being free and public. No luck. I resorted to a name search on Google, and said, "Maybe she's famous."

We ended up on the Wikipedia entry for U.S. Senator Pritchard Clay, California's senior senator and archenemy of the state's junior senator, Hugh Pike. Ruth was surprised; I was shocked. This online encyclopedia is written by volunteers and funded by donations. You can't take their data as gospel, but then, you can't take the Gospel as gospel. It's a good starting point, is my point. And on the right side under the Honorable Pritchard Clay's photo, which was a fairly recent, was the listing of his personal data: birthplace and date, when he assumed office, spouse, children, residence, religion, website, parents. His mother? Catherine Iona Clay nee Johnson. A little drilling confirmed Catherine's birth year and parents, so we had the correct Catherine Iona Clay.

Our immediate question was answered. Ruth looked quietly at me. She seemed more exhausted than ever. Because her complexion is soft with a hint of a subdermal tan, when she gets tired all the darkness of her skin tone gathers under her eyes and the rest of her face goes that much paler. You end up looking at brilliant green irises floating in shallow, dark saucers. Surrounded by freckles.

"Nat, I found some photos in the Ledger files." She crawled over me and went to her bag, which she'd kept zipped and under the plastic coat on her way down to the harbor. The bag was the only thing that was dry. She shuffled around for a small clipboard to which an old envelope was attached, and reclaimed her spot. "Does this look like anyone you know?" she asked, pulling a photograph from envelope.

It was a photo of U.S. Senator Pritchard Clay, I said, gussied up in a high collar and suit coat circa, maybe, the turn of the century. I suggested it had been taken at one of those Old

West tourist photo services. But then she turned it over in my hand and on the back were the date and the name.

"Peter Johnson, 1902," said Ruth. "I would call that a family resemblance."

I flipped it over a couple of times, not knowing what to say. It was indeed more than a family resemblance, and she knew it. It gave me the creeps.

"Well," she said, and handed me another. There was no question in my mind that "My Howard, 1887," was a childhood photo of California's other senator, the Honorable Hugh Pike. I was wrong, of course. I was apparently silent for too long.

"Another family resemblance or what?" she said.

I said, "Yes." A chill crossed my skin, but I ignored it.

"Look, if it makes you feel any better, keep in mind that the senators, today, are the direct descendants of the men in the photos. Don't you feel better now?" She pursed her lips in a faux kiss.

"Much," I said.

"I understand that Senator Clay has been fighting Senator Pike over turning Wailing Wood into parkland," she said.

"Yes. There hasn't been much on that for the last few years, but there was a point where California's two senators were basically dueling it out."

"Well," she said, "if Senator Clay wants to keep the timberland in production, as they say … and he was an heir to the Johnson land and fortune …"

"Clay's on the Global board of directors," I said, having read about his role there when Global swallowed Northern Timber. He'd been on Northern's board of directors as well.

She nodded, knowingly. "Look, I'm really tired," she admitted, taking back the photos and replacing them in the protective envelope. A buoy a few hundred yards offshore at the harbor, moaned in the dark. She blinked slowly, which matched her breathing. She slid deeper into the sweat shirt and pants, then rolled to the side, pulled up the blanket and said, "Move over."

I did. I closed the laptop and set it softly on the floor near my crime novel and snapped off the light.

"The candle's a nice touch, Nat." She scooted up next to me.

The Escape of Hypolite Dupree

WHITESBORO IN FLAMES: ... Even as Whitesboro emerges from the rubble and flames of the Great Earth Quake, word has reached us that all of San Francisco is still burning, and that little remains of that once-great City.
— *The Whitesboro Ledger, April 19, 1906*

The day of the trial, April 16, finally arrived. Young Rene Gitaine burst through the door of the Ledger, gasping for breath, Mr. Stanley's latest rolled sheet of paper crumpled in his fist. It was Monday and it was late. The message was smudged and torn at the edge and spattered with mud from the gutters and backyards of Whitesboro. The rosebush on Franklin Street that ripped the paper had also sliced across the seven-year-old's hand. He'd quickly wrapped his kerchief around the gash, and the bloodied cloth that spread across his palm and over the top of his hand reminded him of the famous boxers — Gentleman Jim Corbett and James Jeffries — that he'd seen in the pages of the Ledger. Mr. Stanley had even given him the lead stereotype picture of Corbett, which Rene kept on a bottle crate with a candle. He had made several postal cards by rolling ink as thick as tar onto the die and carefully laying a strip of newsprint on it, rolling it again with a dry roller, and pulling his print.

He had no one to mail them to.

If you got the light just right on that block of lead, you could see the boxer, Corbett, plainly, dramatically ready to strike; but it took one of the boy's prints to really capture the look on his face.

Rene snatched the tweed paperboy cap off his head as he pushed his way through the door, whacking the bronze bell at the top of the jamb so hard he sent it flying across the wood plank floor. It came to a stop at the feet of Mrs. Stanley. Rene, the boxer, the hero, the messenger, proudly handed her the paper. Written in small cursive letters, it was Robert Stanley's latest dispatch from the trial. It was three in the afternoon and Rene had already run from the Pavilion to the newspaper and back six times since the trial began early that morning, and each time he had toured the pressroom to see his effort changed miraculously into galleys of type for tomorrow's Extra edition of the newspaper.

Amelia Stanley unwadded and unrolled the paper and spread it out on the blotter on the desk. She reached over and tested the iron that had been warming on the coal stove near the north wall of the office across from the stairwell, and pressed the letter flat again. The printer ran up and grabbed it, still warm, before she could begin to read the words, and he hurried back to the type desks with it, barking commands at his two printer's devils, so-named for the black smudges of ink that fairly tinted their skin, identifying their trade.

Mrs. Stanley calmly set the iron back down on the stove, walked back to the pressroom and removed the paper from the hook above the type desks. The printer turned from his helpers, the devils, and watched as Mrs. Stanley carried the paper back to the front office. They stood where the paper had been hanging above the desks, their hands limp at their sides. Mrs. Stanley would first edit her husband's work, and the printers could simply wait until she was done.

Twenty minutes later, she handed the perfected version to the printer and he hung it back up and assigned paragraphs to the two printer's devils who, with eyes squinting and elbows cranking, slowly filled their composing sticks with tiny backward letters, transforming Robert Stanley's hastily scribbled and newly corrected account into glorious rows and columns of cold lead ... they changed it into the Whitesboro Ledger.

It was only then that Amelia noticed the rag on Rene's hand. She tended to it with great care. Luckily, the cut was shallow. Cleaned and freshly bandaged, she allowed Rene to wrap his rag over the new gauze and tape, as he wished.

Robert Stanley had already filled four full columns of type with the proceedings of the Hypolite Dupree trial, and the events grew more exciting by the hour. Rene pulled his cap down nearly to his eyes, and began jogging back to the Pavilion, his back hunched over like a tired boxer, his eyes on the ground, his breathing rhythmic.

* * *

Robert Stanley barely had room to move his arm to write. Sheriff Tully had set up a small schoolhouse desk just below the stage where Dupree, the judge and jury, and Howard Pike were seated. He had a good view and he could even hear — when the enormous crowd was quiet.

He sent his last dispatch at 6 p.m. Guilty: the violent and murderous vagrant to be hanged.

Rene took off at a sprint. Stanley followed, exhausted with the day but feeling that rare elation that accompanies such a dramatic example of "newspapering." He arrived at the Ledger a half-hour after Rene.

The old press's rhythmic clacking continued through the night; it was the only sound in all of exhausted Whitesboro. Stanley pulled a sheet off the press, then waited as the next few pages flew by with a metallic whack-whack-whack, and pulled another. The printer frowned. It was seldom that his work was checked or challenged. The printer's helpers pulled the rest of the hundreds of printed pages from the machine, folded, rolled and stacked them, and by dawn Rene and a dozen other boys shoved them into big hemp bags and headed for the neighborhoods, street corners, and shops of Whitesboro. Three big flat bundles were taken to the post office at Huggins Cash Store.

Rene planned to hawk the Ledger at the railroad station, but sold out before he got there. He sprinted back, jammed an armload of Extras into his bag and headed to the mercantile. He didn't even make it to the door. He jogged back to the Ledger and unloaded two pockets full of coins with Mrs. Stanley, asking her to keep his share until the end of the day — it was slowing him down.

He quickly sipped a cup of tea, stuffed a few biscuits that Mrs. Stanley had made for the pressman and devils into his pockets, and went back into the streets of the wakening town. He pushed his way to the Grand Hotel, and had he not saved one special copy deep in his bag, he would have had none for Judge Eli Trogden himself. He actually touched the judge, the man who held power over life and death. He put the dime — a dime for a penny paper! — deep into his pocket after memorizing the date. He'd keep that dime forever.

Then, exhausted, the whole town slept. Tuesday became a day in history, though the notoriety of the soon-to-hang Dupree would vanish in but a few hours, because, after those few hours passed, it would be Wednesday, April 18, 1906.

* * *

Yet even as Wednesday dawned, before the light could creep in from the east, the air over the ocean seemed wrong, and it blew in strangely warm over the land. Dogs had wailed at the setting of the sun the evening before, and they wailed now, again, as they awaited the dawn. The goats, the pigs, and the cows all pitched nervously around their runs, grunting voices in the dark. Chickens seemed to become loons, running in circles. Amelia, during the night, had contracted a shattering headache. In the blackness, she sensed a nervous, electric quality exuded by the town itself, and she found it very uncomfortable. This was what it must be like, she thought, to have a murderer of infants in their midst.

The Great Quake, groaning for hours in the depths of the earth, finally struck at 5:12 in the morning, leveling and burning the great metropolis of San Francisco. But two hundred miles north, the Victorian city of Whitesboro suffered proportionally equal damage — the town burned, it crumbled and it gasped.

Whitesboro was in chaos. People, barely clothed, surrounded the ruins of their homes, crying as the sour, smoke-laden dawn approached. Men wept along with the women. Children sat dazed amid their crumpled houses and along the sides of broken streets.

Hours after the earth had shuddered, Whitesboro was still smoldering, reduced to ash, and some city blocks were still in flames. Half the marble and granite of the courthouse had fallen to the ground while the other half remained defiantly upright, its white walls scorched as if a single great ball of flame had roared through the streets of the city like a blast furnace.

Rene approached the rubble of the courthouse slowly, cautiously, and thought he could hear a voice bleeding up from below the street.

He drew closer, unable to ignore what could be a call for help. Someone was shouting up from beneath the broken blocks of the building. It could have been Judge Trogden. It could have been Sheriff Tully. Rene listened hard, with his hand to his ear. He could hear a voice calling. He inched farther into the broken remains of the building, stumbling and falling, pulling himself back up.

He ducked inside a section of the building that was still standing. He could hear the voice more clearly now. He crept across what was once a glowing marble floor but was now a pocked and battered series of jostled puzzle pieces. Even as he walked, nodules of stone fell sporadically, followed by dripping dust and sputtering gravel. A portion of the floor had fallen in, and Rene could hear the voice clearly through a hole a few feet across. It came from the basement below, but he couldn't see more than a few feet into the hole. Directly below the opening was a precarious pile of rubble, a mound that sloped back into the maw. Rene shouted down into that dark mouth, and a voice drifted back up.

The voice needed help; it couldn't climb through the pile of debris without risking total collapse. It needed the end of a rope to pull itself up into the light of day.

"What is your name?" Rene shouted into the hole, his hands cupped along the sides of his mouth.

"Sheriff's deputy," returned the voice.

Of course, the jail cells were below the courthouse. He cupped his hands and shouted again, "Sheriff down there?!"

After a brief pause, the voice shouted back, "Hurt but alive. Get a rope!"

Rene ran from the building. He wandered north, farther into town, looking quickly left and right for a rope or a chain or a wood ladder, anything that could be lowered into the hole to save the deputy.

The townsfolk ignored him as he jogged along Main Street; they had massive worries of their own. Entire blocks had burned or collapsed, and men were going back and forth into buildings, searching for survivors, removing possessions, setting up chairs and beds outdoors for their exhausted families. Dozens of search parties looked desperately for hundreds of the missing. The smell of smoke jammed Rene's nostrils and clawed at his eyes.

Sadly, Rene could not have known that Sheriff Tully was assisting the wounded at the north end of town, near what remained of the small hospital.

Rene found a long rope wound up and hanging from the wall of the Cash Store. The window was broken and he crawled in, halfway hoping not to get caught for looting and halfway hoping someone would see him and help. He lifted the rope off the wall, threw it over his head and one shoulder, and ran heavily back south along Main to the courthouse.

He shouted down the hole again, but got no answer. Rene tied one end of the rope around a large square of cut granite. He thought it was one of the big corner stones, and it was heavy enough to support the weight of many men.

Visit From a Senator

It had rained heavily all night long. The clouds broke up about dawn. There was little doubt that both forks of the White River had flooded and that Whitesboro's sewers were backing up; drainage was a constant problem during the rainy season.

The telephone woke Muriel at about nine. The conversation was brief; she smiled and hung up the receiver. She looked out the window and knew the streets would be like shallow rivers, and knew she'd have to work a little today, make a few phone calls and take a few photos of the flooding.

Already arranging the events of the day in her mind, she tossed back the down comforter. She always found it funny that "Old Hugh" would come in and personally renew his subscription to the Ledger, and strange that he'd do it every year when he visited for his mother's birthday instead of paying for a couple of years at a time. She found it odd that he wouldn't do it by mail or by phone or on the paper's website. But that was Hugh, and the Stanleys had known the Pikes for a heck of a long time. A visit was always a good thing.

Muriel threw on an old robe she'd pulled off the chair in her father's bedroom, where she'd been sleeping all week, and meandered down the hall to her own room, which she expected to be as empty as it had been the night before. Ruth had gone out, which raised Muriel's eyebrows.

But Ruth was there in bed. "When did you get back?" Muriel asked, surprised. She looked at her watch. This was her morning to sleep in.

Ruth turned over groggily and said, "The rain broke a little after the sun came up. I think I've been back all of five minutes." She pushed her hair up and tried to twist it into submission.

"I didn't hear you. How is your friend?"

"Pretty good." There was no extra information, which Muriel really wouldn't have minded hearing. "We managed to clarify the link between Peter Johnson and his descendants." She told Muriel about Senator Pritchard Clay, whom Muriel had never met, Clay being from Southern California.

"Old Hugh Pike'll be over pretty soon, Ruth," Muriel said, not able to disguise the anticipation in her voice. "Cailin called to warn me. That's his brother. Arney's probably got the front door unlocked already for when he swings by. They usually come about eleven to pay for Hugh's subscription, and always on the weekend so we can chat."

"You guys are all like an extended family. Stanleys and Pikes and Coopers. I feel a bit like Dorothy in Oz," said Ruth.

"Lions and tigers ... Oh no... Seems like it. We're still close, even when one of us is a U.S. senator."

"Did he go to Whitesboro High, too?"

"Yeah, but he's, like, ten years older than me and he's a Grayport boy ... had to take the school bus. He remembers me from grade school, and my father was one of his great promoters when he ran for city council, and then when he entered the county supervisor race. Hugh and Bob Cooper are still pretty close. All the Coopers, really, and he's pretty fond of Arney ... he's known Arney since he was little."

"I wonder what Senator Pike thinks of all the Wailing Wood hoopla," said Ruth.

"I heard he's already set a raft of lawyers onto the issue. I talked to Father Percy yesterday evening, after you did. Father

Percy called me, and he said the old church record book was being copied as we spoke, with all kinds of legal observers involved."

"I bet Thomas is in his glory."

"He's so happy. That's how fast it all moved. Hugh Pike only seems slow because he talks slow."

"There's a priest, too, who gathers no moss," said Ruth.

"No kidding. You want some breakfast yet?"

"Only if Arney'll fix it. I'm spoiled."

"I'll see what I can do. See you at the table."

Hugh Pike arrived early, at 10:30. He drove into town from Grayport with Cailin, and they paid Arney for the family's four renewals — theirs (two); one for their mother, Betty; and one for their sister, Amy, who lives in Arizona most of the year.

Cailin went back to the car to run some errands for their mom, but Hugh followed Arney Stanley up the back staircase to the apartment above, chatting as they climbed. Muriel and Ruth were sitting at the table, hovering over cups of coffee and still in their pajamas.

They clomped in, Pike's size-twenty feet slapping the linoleum. "Oh great," mumbled Muriel, trying to flick her hand through her hair without appearing obvious. She rubbed the milk from the Quisp cereal off the side of her mouth and swallowed some orange juice. Hugh Pike greeted them with a laugh and walked over to Muriel's old steel percolator and poured himself a cup of coffee. His head almost hit the ceiling. Then he went to the refrigerator for a quart of milk and splashed some into his cup and sat down across from them at the table, for which he was way too tall. He was perfectly at home, and he would never have taken such liberties had not many generations of hospitality preceded his visit. Ruth studied the familiarity from an anthropological perspective, which was the only way she could try to explain it.

"You want some, like, toast, Hugh?" Muriel asked, rising.

"Please, don't get up, Muriel. Really. Arney can make it … no, I'm just kidding. I'd love some toast, but according to the Post, I'm the kind of guy who makes his own toast. I actually read that. They might as well have said I churn the butter out on the old wood porch. Can you believe those guys?"

"No silver spoon for you, Abe."

"Oh, I have silver spoons, they just come in the form of old friends." Turning to Ruth, he said, "You're Ruth M." He stood up awkwardly to introduce himself, and encompassed her hand and part of her wrist in a warm, perfectly firm grip. Then he sat back down, his knees at acute angles due to shortness of the chair.

"I thought you might be interested in what my mother dug up at the old ranch house a couple of days ago." He handed Ruth a small black binder — it might have been brown but had been oiled into blackness in relatively ancient times — and she placed it on the table after he unfurled a dishcloth to lay it on. It was tied with hard old string, hemp, Ruth decided, crossing it with a bow, off-center. Bends in the string indicated it had been opened recently and retied. Ruth untied it only after testing the fragility of the string by sliding her finger under it and gently lifting. It wasn't a binder after all, but two pages of hard leather, very old, which sandwiched a couple of browned, nearly deteriorated butcher papers. Inside the butcher papers was a hand-scribbled recipe of sorts. It didn't take Ruth more than thirty seconds to know it was Mary Wayland's knitting pattern for the Norfolk vest with its ridges, furrows and diamonds, all so tightly knit the garment would have been nearly waterproof. The vest pattern took two pages; a third page produced the arms for a full sweater.

"This has to date from before 1887," she said, looking up at the tall man. "It's got to be Norfolk ... that's a region along the English coast. There are probably nine or ten traditional patterns from a single harbor, but they're quite recognizable. ... You ever think of growing a beard?"

Pike followed the non sequitur. He rubbed his chin and laughed quietly. "I think it would be too much for the pundits."

"Yeah, I think you're right," said Ruth.

"I understand your area of interest is textiles, and maybe even old knitting patterns."

"A nasty habit," she said.

"Mom wanted you to have this." He motioned with his hand. "She dug it up in the attic. She said she found a little silver cross with it ... I assume it's like the one you found in the wood. I haven't seen either of the crosses yet ..."

Ruth trapped the words about the cross and filed them in her mind. "There are few knitting pattern notations of this age, Mr. Pike. It could, if sold to the right person or institute, bring a significant price." She began to study the pages closely, and found a date up along the side of the second sheet, 1885, older than the photo of Howard Pike. She was, she realized, reading the scribblings of Mary Wayland Johnson, who had died of the influenza, languishing beside her husband who would also die, as they worried about the fate of their young children — and the children, too, would soon depart the living. To Ruth, it was overwhelming.

"Significant in the sense of, for instance, an archaeological find in an old forest?" asked Pike.

Ruth smiled. Had someone told him about her presentation in Wailing Wood? Obviously.

"Senator," said Ruth, "I understand you've created significant momentum in turning the old growth groves, Wailing Wood, into a park. Significant, in the sense of do-able?"

But Pike didn't immediately respond. He seemed to pale slightly, as if something were wrong. Ruth caught a strange look in the senator's eyes, as if a cloud of doubt, or more accurately, fear, had drifted across his field of vision. In a few seconds, though, he seemed to inhale the winds of stability and smiled. He forced the smile.

"Yes," he said, "I'm fairly certain I'll have thirty co-sponsors for the bill … just calling around. Very unofficial. This is staggering, though, Ruth. Three years ago, I could manage only three, and they backed out before I could muster the legislation. I've been working on it slowly. Some people, you see, do not like that momentum. There's an awful lot of redwood in Wailing Wood, to say nothing of the mineral rights once the trees are gone. But the bill will be introduced in a few months, despite the opposition."

Ruth, still dwelling on the change that briefly came over Pike, said, "So it's no secret, the likelihood of approval?"

"On the Hill? Nothing's secret."

"Ah," she said, smiling. The smile evaporated. Her brow arched. "If someone wanted to put a stop to it, for example, stop the park from happening for economic reasons, they'd have to get moving ..." She waited, urging him with her eyes to comment.

But Senator Pike did not comment. He didn't sigh. His face grew stone-like, but then he smiled. He shook his head. What he really wanted to know was how much Ruth M knew ... about everything. About the bill. About the forces opposing the creation of his park, about the threats—and one threat in particular. Unable to do anything else, he looked deeply into her eyes. He'd never seen that particular color of green. It was arresting.

Then Ruth just nodded her head and let it drop. She had all the information she needed, and she realized Hugh Pike was aware of that. He accepted it. The shared knowledge seemed to dissolve barriers between them.

Turning his attention to Muriel, Pike said, "Mom wanted me to personally make sure you're coming to her birthday party tomorrow. Even though it's on a Sunday. Yes?" He turned to Ruth, including her in the invitation. "Don't think about declining," he said, as if joking.

"Of course. I'd like to bring someone?" said Muriel.

"Always. Just show up."

"William Chu'd love to come," said Muriel. Ruth looked over at her, but found nothing visible in Muriel's eyes. "He was up at the dig with us," Muriel explained. "He's a police detective from San Francisco."

"More than welcome," said Pike. "Is Arney bringing his friend? Lou?"

"She'll be there."

"Then everybody'll be there," said Pike. "Even Blain's coming up from L.A., is what Bob said."

"Nobody's seen Blain for an age," said Muriel. "That will be nice."

"Bob said he's out of prison." He looked at Ruth, and in an attempt to explain family matters, he said, "Blain's the bad boy of the Cooper line."

"I didn't know he was even in," said Muriel. "I think that might be a surprise to Belle."

"You don't think Bob told her?" said Pike.

"Well, she didn't know a couple of days ago when Ruth and I went and talked with her, or she would have said something then."

"I'm sure Bob's told her by now," said Pike. "Parole boards can be that way, kind of spontaneous."

"Hey, look," said Muriel, "I'm going to run off for a few … mind?" She wanted to get into the bathroom and do something with the hair, splash some water on her face or something. Brush her teeth.

"Please," said Pike.

That left Ruth because Arney was doing something either downstairs or cleaning up Grandpa's room while his mother talked. Or he was trying to get Lou up.

"You have a friend named Uri," said Pike pleasantly.

"You must have Secret Service birds chirping in your ear," said Ruth. She analyzed his tone of voice, the quality of his hazel-eyed gaze. Her sensors were up — Pike was, after all, a politician — but all she was picking up on was a simple presentation. She felt no ulterior motives and she dispensed with her worries of where this conversation might lead.

He laughed. "No, no. Only the president gets Secret Service. Lowly senators have to pay for government protection or hire their own security people. A lot of them have, but, I mean, ask Cailin, it wouldn't be good for my public image. Ear-whispering is the responsibility of one's staff."

"A man of the people and all that."

"Cailin's very particular. But really, who wants to live like that? Everyone in sunglasses all the time?"

"Right. So?"

"I just asked around." Pause. "Actually, I called John Tully the other day to see how things went up in the trees. He told me all about your work up there — it must have been quite a show! — and he filled me in on all your friends. You have no secrets here in Whitesboro, Ms. M."

"Ah. I pretty much like Mr. Tully."

"Well, John thinks the world of you! He told a great story about your trip up to the wood, and John can really tell a story. He was intrigued by your friend, Mr. …."

"Kasparov."

"Yes. I never forget a name, but that's not true of John. Please don't say anything. But he remembered Mr. Kasparov's given name."

"He thinks of it has his center name."

"I see." Pike thought for a moment. "Native language thing. His middle name?"

"Yep. It's Kasparov Uri Kasparov."

"Unusual."

"Yes. He says his mother named him that because there weren't enough Kasparovs left in the world."

Pike smiled, but the smile grew distraught when he realized what he'd just heard. "That would be either the Russian pogroms or World War II."

"Apparently pogroms. That and the Kobzar exterminations."

Pike looked at her quietly for a moment as he tried to dredge up the remnants of a university class in Russian history. "Oh, yes, the minstrels. I see. How interesting. In any case, I would like to invite Mr. Kasparov. Do you think he'll come?"

"Of course."

"You'll call him?"

"Good lord no," she said. "But I'll walk down to the Herring Gull where he's staying if I have to. Do *not* play chess with Mr. Kasparov, Mr. Pike. Is that clear?"

"I'm sure it won't come to that." Pike raised both eyebrows.

"Who all comes to your mother's birthday? What should Muriel and I bring?"

"Just yourselves. Mom likes to do the cooking, and my sister Amy's all involved, and you know how that can be." She didn't. "Peach or blackberry pie maybe. Don't bring anything, just your friends. Who's going? Oh, nothing too big, just the Stanleys, Tullys, Coopers and, I'm sad to say ..."

She waited.

"Please don't be deterred, but the press always turns out for this. Every year. Don't be surprised to see three or four TV vans; it's just inevitable. But Cailin handles that ... he invites everyone inside early and they get their clips and brief interviews, that sort of thing. Sometimes they hang around outside later, but it's been pretty unobtrusive over the years, once you get used to having cameras follow you around everywhere."

"I'll wear a mask."

Pike straightened, smiled. "Now that's an idea. That could catch on. Maybe I can get some for the kids."

"Your children?"

"We have two, Elmore B., or Ebee, we call him, and Nina. Ebee's named after a great uncle, Nina was chosen by Aisha, my wife. Four and three." He paused, trying to catch what seemed to be a peculiar reaction by Ruth. "What's wrong, Ms. M? Are you okay?"

"No, no," she said. "Fine, just a cold chill ... I was out in the rain earlier. Tell me about your wife."

"Aisha. We were married in 2004. There was a lot of press at the time; I'd just been elected to the Senate."

"I remember."

Aisha Pike was a U.S. citizen who emigrated from Ethiopia at the age of five with her parents. A refugee, she attended Brown and then Harvard for her law degree. "You have to meet her."

"I'd love to."

"Do you think you could give me the dates of the newspapers from your research? The Ledgers? I'd like to request copies. You know, family history."

"Uh huh," said Ruth.

"Yes, of course, and for the lawyers. Do you see through everyone so quickly?"

"Sure."

All he could do was smile.

Ruth put her chin in her hands. "It's my well-considered theory that the children in the wood were the brother and sister of your ancestor, Senator."

"I know. Please call me Hugh, Ruth. The phone's been crazy. I've talked about the children in the wood with Father Tom, Muriel, Belle ... everyone's talking about it. Mom's been digging through everything to find out more. We just don't have any of the Wayland records, except that old pattern. Nothing more. Believe me, I read through it, front and back, found nothing ... but that's probably not saying much because the formulas there are all Greek to me."

266

Ruth began to scribble down the dates, the pages, and the columns of every brief that related to her inquiry.

Pike knew what she was doing but didn't quite believe what he was seeing. By the time she'd logged more than twenty-five specific articles and "locals," their page numbers and in which columns they appeared, though, he'd managed to accept the matter and didn't mention it.

"Could you sign it?"

"What?" she asked, looking up.

"Could you sign it, just something like, 'For Hugh Pike, from Ruth,' something like that."

"Whatever for?"

"Just a reality check, Ruth."

"Oh. Give me a second, I'll be done quickly. I'll put a little star by the really good ones. Too bad Muriel doesn't have extra copies of the originals."

Hugh Pike smiled. Muriel, refreshed, came back to the kitchen. Pike rose and gave her a hug, smothering because of his size, and said, "So we'll see you all tomorrow. Thanks so much for coming. Mom'll be so happy."

"What's that?" she asked of Ruth.

"List of citations for Senator Pike."

"Hugh," he said.

Muriel said, "I guess I'd better make a copy of it to take downstairs. That looks like a lot of copying. You could send someone in to do it, Hugh — I might not have that kind of time."

But Ruth said, "It won't take long, between the two of us. So, Mr. Pike, how does one dress for Mrs. Pike's birthday party?" She looked down at herself. "I mean, I can wear Muriel's jammies, but that probably won't make a great first impression."

When Hugh Pike smiles, he looks like a bloodhound, smiling. "Just casual," he said. "Something you won't mind getting barbecue sauce on."

Carried to Safety

*

WHITESBORO IN FLAMES: ... The hospital is gone. The mill, heart of the city and its survival, was saved, though the homes and business of most of Whitesboro must be, with help and prayers, rebuilt. To our credit, according to Sheriff Stanton Tully, there has been no looting.
— *The Whitesboro Ledger, April 19, 1906*

Rene Gitaine pulled the rope over to the hole in the marble floor and tried once again to peer down into the darkness. He could only see the first few feet of crushed stone. Throwing the thick hemp coil in front of him, Rene held it and lowered himself down the steep slope of rock, down into the dark realm where the voice had come from.

He finally reached the bottom. It was dark but not pitch black. He could see a man standing a few yards away. The voice was still alive! But it was not a deputy. Standing in the doorway of the first cell, its iron door askew and broken off at the upper hinge, was the convicted murderer, Hypolite Dupree. In one hand was the detached arm of an oak chair.

Rene shrunk back against the pile of rock. He reached for the rope, but Dupree took one swing with the heavy club, tossing Rene limply against the rubble of the wall. The boy was barely conscious as Dupree pulled himself up the rope, turning at the top to look back down into the ruins of the prison. A grim, high-pitched laugh escaped his lips, and he wiped ashes and sweat from the side of his head. Then, Rene saw the end of the rope being drawn up the pile until it vanished.

Rene couldn't get back up. Tears began to roll down his soot-blackened face. He reached up and pulled down the brim of his cap. It hurt. His head hurt. His arm hurt — he'd tried to block the blow. He touched the side of his face but couldn't feel anything. He was alone, his energy spent and his spirit gone like the vapor from a cup of tea that Amelia Stanley might have brewed for him, once. He thought of the boxers, Jim Corbett and James Jeffries. Some said he looked like Jeffries, the champion of heavyweights. James Jeffries would have to go into town to find out the fate of Mrs. Stanley; Rene couldn't do it.

As the day drifted into evening, what remained of Whitesboro grew still and quiet. The fires were out. City officials had begun to organize to serve the immediate needs of the people: water, food and shelter. The churches and buildings that had survived became camps for the homeless. Most of the work was quietly orchestrated by Sheriff Tully, who offered advice and action to the mayor and the lesser city officials. Even on that first day of the great earthquake, word was sent south out of Whitesboro, seeking help as well as informing other communities of its survival.

By dawn on Thursday, Sheriff Tully stood on what were once the steps of the courthouse, but were now a deposit of powdered and crushed stone and charred, splintered wood. Below him, he knew, was the jail and the prisoner it housed. Dupree should have been hanged yesterday.

Dust and ash had settled over Whitesboro and the long process of rebuilding had already begun. Loads of debris had been piled up and men were moving it out by cart and barrow, dumping it north of town over the headlands and into the sea. Workers brought a steam donkey to the downtown, and big sliding carts of refuse were winched up the broken streets and hauled to the ocean in the same manner that logs were donkeyed along forest trails to either rail or river on their way to the mill. They would all start again, like ants, slowly rebuilding the town and their lives. Tully grinned harshly. It could have been worse.

He squinted and looked into the courthouse. He could see a rope tied to a large granite cornerstone that had been kicked out from the wall by the fury of the earthquake. The length of thick hemp snaked along what used to be the glowing marble floor and came to an end above a hole in the marble that obviously led to the jail cells below. Tully looked around. The stairways to the lower level had collapsed and been buried, and there was no other route down.

He'd heard no stories about the courthouse and knew of no rescue efforts. No one, it seemed, could have left that rope. He picked it up and pulled its length through his hands, coming to a price tag attached by a wire. Tully dropped the rope and promptly turned and left the building. He shouted at two men across the street, demanding their help. Both hurried over to the sheriff. He deputized them without pomp, and instructed them to stand at the edge of the hole, ready to pull him up, or even to defend him in case the prisoner, Dupree, was still down there and alive.

He grabbed onto the rope and began walking backward down the steep slope that led to the basement. He paused when his shoulders were at floor level while one of the men went to retrieve a small lantern, then ran one arm through the handle and let it dangle from the bend of his elbow as he inched the rest of the way down. He hurried before the lamp's heat could singe his shirt sleeve.

Once standing on the cement floor below, his feet between blocks of broken stone, he held the lantern at arm's length, looking, listening intently. The light fell on the slumped body of a boy, his cap pulled down onto his forehead, his face swollen and his leg propped up awkwardly on several blocks of stone.

Tully went over to the form and carefully hoisted it up onto his back. He extinguished the lantern and pulled himself up the rope. The two men above lifted Rene's body from the sheriff's shoulder and the men carried him out into the light and air of day. He was badly beaten, Tully could see, but he was breathing.

History Repeats Itself

Ruth spent Saturday evening with Muriel and me. Every few minutes, a rush of rain would whip against the north side of the building, sounding like the loud hiss of radio static. After about eight, it was raining even harder than the night before.

Ruth had carefully spread the very old papers that held Mary Wayland's Norfolk pattern in front of her, as if absorbing their very essence. Muriel looked, often, to see what she was doing and to ask a question about the notations or knitting in general. I think everyone avoided the topic of the moment, which was Wailing Wood.

The three papers that made up Mary Wayland's pattern were, I thought, in very good shape considering the weight of their years. I couldn't decipher them, of course, but on the surface they appeared to be a sort of freehand grid of x's and o's and other symbols including a dot and perhaps a slash, followed by the woman's very precise verbal instructions. I was astounded that something that old could have survived so thoroughly intact. Mary Wayland had also written little notes in

272

the corners, and in places between the lines of text, and Ruth studied every pen scratch. I was sure that, where I could see only scribblings, she saw in her mind a Norfolk village pattern of lines (ridges and furrows) that, as one worked one's way up the sweater, became a delicate system of edge-linked diamonds.

So the evening passed. But its seeming coziness belied an evil of which we were unaware.

By 2 a.m., that sinister upwelling woke Ruth in the dark. She was in Muriel's room. She sat up in bed.

She was damp with sweat from a nightmare from which she could only remember small visual patches. She woke worried, and looked out the window as if seeking an answer to her feeling of trepidation. There was a flurry outside the window that was large and fast, but it was gone before she could even focus.

Ruth walked into the room adopted by Muriel during Ruth's rather extended visit, and she sat on the corner of Muriel's bed, trying to wake her gently. "Get up," she whispered. "Something's wrong."

Muriel sat up, her eyes heavy with sleep. "What's wrong," she said.

"I don't know."

Muriel hesitated. "Then, Ruth, why are you waking me up? I just got to sleep ..."

"We need to get dressed. I don't know. But you might as well get up."

"But it's only two in the morning ..."

Ruth stared at her until Muriel got up, climbed out of her nightgown and began throwing on clothes. "What should I wear?" Muriel asked. By now she realized that Ruth was fully clothed and had a fleece jacket topped with a rubber raincoat she'd found in the mudroom.

"Warm stuff and a rain coat," said Ruth.

Muriel had tossed her caution away with the bed sheets, and they both were soon in the kitchen, dressed, drinking hot fresh coffee and eating toast. Neither knew why, yet.

A few minutes later, Muriel's house phone rang. It was Sheriff Tully.

* * *

Betty Pike didn't celebrate her seventy-fifth birthday.

At three on Sunday morning, Cailin Pike, soaked and chilled, took it upon himself to wake his mother on that fateful birthday. Aisha was downstairs in tears, and the senator was already outside with a high-powered rechargeable flashlight, shining it again and again across the surface of the swollen, raging creek that ran along the north part of the property within a stone's throw of the house. Every curve of its new banks shined briefly in the glow of Hugh Pike's light.

Sheriff Tully was on his way to the Pike home, shaking off the last dust of sleep as he tried to sip coffee while hitting the corners too hard in the Bronco. He had called in a dozen members of the town's remnant search and rescue volunteers, most having drifted away when they'd lost their day jobs at the mill. He was not calling Muriel Stanley as a courtesy; they needed her down on the creek by the Pike property in Grayport with the rest of the volunteers as soon as she could get dressed. Senator Pike's children had gone missing.

The first six hours were mayhem, and the rain just made it worse. After her call from the sheriff, Muriel called Detective Chu's room at the Gull, and he in turn woke Mr. Kasparov and me and we followed her in Chu's gray Honda out of town to the Pikes'. Chu was well-equipped, and his experience in emergency matters was much appreciated under the circumstances. Unfortunately, he didn't have enough flashlights for the rest of us. I had light shoes but Mr. Kasparov had boots. Chu had waders and really good rain gear. Kasparov had a rubber-nylon poncho. I had a nylon jacket.

Within three hours, two dozen searchers had made the initial pass along the creek down to the sea and most of them had returned, ready to start again, this time with more light. That was when Sheriff Tully, satisfied that the emergency dispersion of personnel had completed the first, most important canvassing, began to wander around the big old Pike house, hoping that if there was anything to be seen, it hadn't been walked over or otherwise tampered with. Did four-year-old Ebee and three-year-old Nina just take off in the middle of the night? Why would they do something like that? Had they done this before?

How often? He had questions for Hugh, but he knew the answers already and feared the worst.

Cailin told Tully that the back door had been ajar when he first came downstairs. Why had he come downstairs? Because he could hear the wind-blown door slapping against the jamb in the middle of the night.

And so Tully stood at the door as dawn broke. The floor was soaked from dozens of people, rain-drenched, going in and out. He stood outside and looked in. There were some nicks along the door jamb. "Where's the switch for the porch light, Cailin?" he asked. "No, I mean that big overhead thing." He pointed to the oversize spotlight high on the outside wall.

"Right, I don't think Mom ever uses it. I'll get it." The switch was just outside the mudroom.

It helped. Tully could see the pressure marks along the door, the dent from a bar or big screwdriver along the edge. It hadn't taken much to pop open the old deadbolt. Tully frowned.

Ruth had naturally been keeping up with him, having made it down to the beach and back already. Like the rest, she was soaked. One of the searchers had picked up a child's sweater along the creek banks, caught in an acacia tree. It was on the washing machine in the mudroom where the damaged back door was. It had already been identified as Ebee's.

"Got a break-in," Tully mumbled, probably to Ruth but you couldn't really tell, "and some damned sweater." He raised his voice and called for Hugh Pike, who was outside toward the back of the property.

Hugh came in and saw the soaked sweater on the dryer and Tully said the whole thing was a "bunch of hogwash and by God what do you think of it, Miss M?" Pike, frantic, was silent.

Ruth said the sweater didn't make much sense, as if it had been left there on purpose. "Yep," said Tully.

"Which means," said Chu, coming downstairs from checking upstairs rooms, "they were kidnapped and aren't anywhere in the area. It means they didn't just wander off." Pike still said nothing, but he felt a brief moment of relief because if the children hadn't wandered off, if they'd been taken, the chances they'd drowned in the swollen river grew slimmer. Yet the relief was only good in the short term.

Tully nodded sadly. Under the current circumstances, he decided, for once in his career, he'd follow the rules. He notified the FBI at 8:30 a.m. on Betty Pike's birthday, at which point it officially became a federal inquiry. He was instructed to continue the current search but to otherwise stand back and wait for the federal agents to arrive. He was not to investigate further.

Tully walked around to the front of the house in time to see the first of the news vans arrive for what was supposed to be a festive birthday bash. They'd be in for more than a celebrity party, he thought. By the time the fifth media van arrived, Tully, inside the freshly strung crime-scene tape, was almost happy not to be in charge.

The FBI Takes Over

FBI agents had arrived by ten, helicoptered in from the San Francisco office. Convinced of a kidnapping despite the lack of a ransom request, the agency, under the direction of a veteran agent named Akio Mikatsu, set in motion several areas of inquiry: The official and unofficial background of the senator was probed in an effort to find a reason for the crime, and a listing of local residents who might somehow be involved was compiled. Three agents combed the house, and a fourth had cornered Hugh Pike and was questioning him intently, and quickly.

Sunday brought no relief to the Pike family or to Whitesboro. It was a day of organization marked by the beginnings of the inquiries. It wasn't until the next day, Monday, that the bureau unearthed the names of two Whitesboro men who were unaccounted for: Paul Grassi and Michael Franzetta.

Grassi, they had discovered, had just been fired by Global Resources, and Franzetta, furious at Global for a multitude of reasons, had quit without notice. The motive for the kidnapping? It was seen as revenge for the collapse of an industry, and the collapse was blamed on Senator Hugh Pike, who had plans for pulling the West's most productive timber acreage out of production and into parkland.

Special Agent Mikatsu, however, didn't expect a ransom note. To him, this was simply revenge, and it was something he'd seen more than once. He took the reasonable approach and released the suspects' names to the press. Statistics backed him up: The longer an incident remained unsolved, the chances of survival declined in a converse relationship. By Monday morning, more than twenty-four hours had already passed. The effect of releasing the names and the explosive reaction that followed, however, might be a backwater comparison to what occurred at a more historic incident in East Amwell, New Jersey, on the first of March, 1932: Whitesboro became a wall-to-wall news event.

Whitesboro's capacity to generate electricity was barely enough to supply the demands of more than fifty news organizations, half of them involved in televised broadcasts. The winding roads to the coastal town — the east and south entries — were a plague of white vans with dish antennas on top. The result in Whitesboro was a five-hour brownout.

The difference between the Pike kidnapping and the Lindbergh kidnapping, however, as far as Mikatsu was concerned, was that this time the FBI would find the children.

Mikatsu's discussion with Paul Grassi's wife, Meg, did not go well for either of them. While the once-sleepy town exploded onto the world's stage, Meg's meticulously engineered life imploded in an equal and opposite reaction.

Mikatsu, dodging the video crews that were, of course, of his own making, and ducking under the yellow crime-scene tape that cordoned off the Grassi property, strode across the front loop driveway to the house and knocked on the door. He was a thick block of a man, five-nine or so but easily three hundred pounds ... and not fat. His head was square and was mortared to his shoulders without a neck in between. His arms and legs were thick and muscled beneath his suit. He knew that Mrs. Grassi and her two children, Mark and Jessie, were inside. By now, he knew quite a bit about all of them. From his position at the front door, he could hear her voice and those of the children, Mark being the loudest but all of them in an argumentative state caused by the tension. He knocked, but no one answered the door. He knocked again, waited, and signaled one of the bureau's white Chevy SUVs in off the road. It slowly took the circle drive, the gravel crunching under the tires, the grinding sound mixing with the rain, which had lightened but threatened to pour again any minute.

He knocked a third time, this time louder. Two more agents walked from the SUV to the front door. One was checking his shoulder holster. The door cracked open. A boy looked out, wide-eyed, but was yanked back by his collar by a woman's manicured hand. Seconds later, having sent the boy to the kitchen, Meg Grassi appeared, the half-opened door hiding half her body.

"Mrs. Grassi? Yes? I'm Special Agent Akio Mikatsu. I'm from the FBI's San Francisco Division. May we speak for a moment about your husband, Paul?"

Her face was stern, showing a hardness she didn't know she had. "Why? You think he's involved in the Pike thing. You have no idea. I haven't slept in over twenty-four hours."

"Yes, of course. I think it would be much easier for everyone, your children included, if we could go over a few things. It would be for the best."

She held the door.

"We've already obtained a search warrant, Mrs. Grassi. I would be pleased if we could do this the easy way."

"Fine." She opened the door and walked back to the kitchen, letting Special Agent Mikatsu find his own way into her home. He watched her from the back. She was wearing fitted slacks.

He pushed the door open, allowing his wide, neckless body through. He moved gracefully, even liquidly through the front foyer, then the living room and walked silently into the kitchen. Mrs. Grassi studied the block man as he approached. He absolutely looked like FBI, whatever that was; all he needed was a machine gun. She wondered, briefly, how he managed to walk across the kitchen without making a sound. Behind Mikatsu were two other FBI agents; he introduced them ceremoniously — Special Agents Rogerio Hernandez (he pronounced it appropriately as roherio) and Andrew Milan. Meg Grassi forgot their names as soon as he'd uttered them.

Three more agents left the nearest van and entered the Grassi's open front door, closing it softly, even respectfully. Two of the agents sat with the children in front of the television in the living room while Mikatsu quietly and, with a cordiality that Meg Grassi found irritating, interrogated her. The remaining three agents began a very orderly investigation of the house, ignoring the heirlooms of generations of Grassis while analyzing the contents of drawers and cabinets, desktops and dresser tops as they strategically worked their way into the basement.

Mrs. Grassi sat in a wide, stuffed chair and Mikatsu sat in a matching chair a few feet away. From her position, she could see the children but not the television. Yes, she said, the agents could talk with the children, but only in her presence. So they waited.

"I understand your husband has not been home for several days," he said. His look seemed sincere, but as she peered deep into his small brown eyes, she saw no emotion at all. "Is that normal for him?" Mikatsu asked.

"No."

"Do you know where he is?"

"Yes. Fine. He's out fishing with Mike Franzetta, they're up on the Klamath ..."

"Thank you. Where on the Klamath?"

"I don't know."

"Have you called him?"

"There's no phone reception up there. He won't call until Wednesday. Maybe Tuesday. He said if he hasn't called by Thursday, then I could worry."

"We have to go and look for him. Do you think, Mrs. Grassi, that Paul might have ... expressed his anger over the elimination of his job, of his entire department as I understand it, by getting back at the company, at the environmental situation, by taking Senator Pike's children?"

"Not in a million years."

"Thank you, Mrs. Grassi. Tell me, does Mr. Grassi carry, for example, a rifle or pistol when he goes fishing?"

"No. You don't shoot fish. Maybe you do, but most people don't."

Mikatsu, silently watching Mrs. Grassi's eyes as thoughts coursed through her head, went to a small table near the wall to his right, opened the drawer, observed the pack of cigarettes, and then slid the drawer closed again. He sat down and resituated himself.

She watched. Mikatsu had, effortlessly, already discovered her only secret.

One of the three agents who had been searching the house arrived at the open doorway to the living room where Mikatsu and Mrs. Grassi had been talking. He motioned to Mikatsu, who excused himself momentarily and walked over to the other agent, who spoke in a hushed voice into the thick-fleshed ear of Mikatsu. Then Mikatsu nodded and walked back to his chair and sat down again.

"I am sorry about the interruption. Tell me, do you have guns in the house?"

What was that about, Meg thought? Clearly, they'd gotten down into the basement where Paul kept his firearms in a locked safety case. "Of course," she said, not knowing what direction the questions were taking. There was no reason not to be honest about this — and everything else.

"A number of guns then."

"Yes," she said. Paul liked his guns — everyone in the county, everyone in the North Country, liked their guns, she thought. People hunted and fished, they target-shot and careened through the forests and hills, the riversides and rivers on ATVs. This was their life. "This isn't L.A., Mr. Mikatsu," she continued. "Paul's been the head forester for Northern Timber for decades. That covers more than 300,000 acres of forestland. People who work for Northern use the forests here, they are granted access. They hunt, they fish. Every mill worker, I mean when the mill was running, every logger, every Northern employee had access to hundreds of thousands of acres of recreation, and that includes hunting and shooting."

"Northern?"

"Global. Northern. Whatever," said Meg.

"Yes. Thank you, I will take note of that. How many guns are owned by Mr. Grassi?"

She thought for a moment. "Seven."

"Could you please list them for me?"

"You're going to take notes?"

"I have been taking notes, Mrs. Grassi."

A sick feeling shot through her, leaving as quickly as it came. He disgusted her. No wonder she could read nothing in that face.

"Okay. Let's see then. It's a quiz. If I win, you leave me alone, okay? Okay. He has a twelve-gauge shotgun that he uses for hunting duck and turkey, and he uses two kinds of shells for it; a four-ten that he recently bought for Mark, our son — they've been out shooting three times together and they have had a very nice time thank you; two deer rifles, which he inherited from his father, a thirty-aught-six and a thirty-thirty; a three-eighty pistol that was a gift from his father to me, personally, and Paul calls it a lady's gun and I take it out at least once a month to stay in practice; a forty-four double-action revolver that he takes deer hunting as backup; and a twenty-two pistol for 'plinking.' I'm done now, thanks a lot. I'll show you to the door."

"Yes, thank you." But Mikatsu didn't rise from the chair. He stroked his square chin with his thumb as if feeling for beard stubble. There was none, of course: his face was smooth, as if he'd shaved only minutes before. "Tell me, Mrs. Grassi, to your knowledge are all seven guns in the locker downstairs?"

"Of course."

"He has reloading equipment."

"Of course. Paul has reloading equipment. For goodness sake. He spends many evenings relaxing down there as the kids play ping pong, and he reloads spent casings for the handguns. That's what he does. He buys powder and brass and primers and it's perfectly normal and legal, Mr. Mikatsu, it's just what we do! You're crazy!" She was near tears.

"Agent Hernandez has indicated that there are five guns downstairs, Mrs. Grassi. Therefore, two guns are missing. He observed ammunition for a three-eighty ACP, which would be the 'lady's' pistol that you mentioned, and a forty-four magnum, which would then be the revolver. Yet he could find no guns downstairs to fit the ammunition. Therefore those two pistols are missing. Do you have any idea how long they've been gone?"

Mrs. Grassi rose and went directly to the master bedroom where she took a small key that had been in the drawer of one of two matching bedside tables. She went downstairs where she found one of the three agents pushing in a drawer of table tennis paddles. He turned and looked as she entered. She went directly to the gun case. They had opened it; she didn't need the key. She found that the two handguns were missing, and this confused her. Why would Paul take the guns? He should have taken the twenty-two, if anything. She looked around the room. Everything had been disturbed in one way or another by the agents, so there was no indication of anything out of the ordinary. But the guns were gone. She went back upstairs and sat down again across from Mikatsu, who hadn't left his chair.

"Have you had a break-in in the recent past, Mrs. Grassi?"

"No," she said. There wasn't a chance. She would have known. Wouldn't any mother know, intuitively, if their security had been compromised?

"Thank you."

The interrogation, disguised as it was by formality and even a chilly friendliness, lasted more than three hours. Mikatsu delved into the Grassis' past, their likes and dislikes, their vocations and avocations, even their religion. He learned about their lives, their parents, their impressions of Whitesboro. He unearthed their tendencies, their pleasures and the little things that disgusted them. He focused for nearly an hour on Mr. Grassi's relationship with Mark and Jessie, and Mrs. Grassi found herself saying things she could hardly believe she'd mention to a priest. It was nothing sordid, just personal. It was no one's business but hers. In the end, she felt thoroughly violated, in a place black without hope, and without clothing.

Finally, though, Mrs. Grassi watched the heavy man leave. His back was as wide as the door. There was nothing she could do now. He disgusted her.

The result was formulaic: Heavily armed FBI agents and personnel from the National Security Agency, which had been alerted to the loss of a senator's children, numbering nearly two hundred, were transported to the California-Oregon bor-

der where the Klamath, that ancient river, runs wild with steelhead a month or so two times during the year.

A Delicate Arrangement

On Tuesday, as hope for a rescue had drained like the salt in a cheap hourglass, Ruth said, "Sheriff Tully, I've been reading a lot about your family." She had. She'd hauled the old Ledger folios upstairs and all of us pored through them, marking the pages to be copied for Hugh Pike — if, that is, he was at all interested in them anymore. Why did we go through the effort? Because Ruth had a feeling.

I hoped her premonition was as strong as the one she'd had at two the morning the children were taken.

"Prying? A nasty lot, the Tully's," said the sheriff. He was exhausted from two days in the field — and had nothing to show for it. At this point, he wondered if he should have so quickly called in the feds, who were now concentrating on finding Paul Grassi and Mike Franzetta on the Klamath River. Yet, given both the nature of the crime — kidnapping — and the family involved, a U.S. senator's, there wasn't really much choice.

"So how many generations removed was Stanton Tully, the sheriff when Ben and Emma died?"

Tully reflected on the little skulls that had been cast up into the light of the twenty-first century, only a few days before their distant relatives may have suffered a similar fate. It's as if it were a heralding, he thought, a warning that no one could really miss, and yet had been missed. But Tully didn't want to think about that. Still in his memory, where they would probably be forever, were the shadows of leaves etched onto the thin, melancholy bones of a child.

"Well, let's get the count right, at least," he said, almost enjoying the distraction. "Starting with me, I guess, sheriff since around 2000. Then my father Jed and uncle Jem, who held the office since, say, 1950. Jem first … his given name was Gerald but he never went by anything but Jem, not Gerry or anything like that, and no one tried for anything different, at least not in his presence. He passed of a heart attack, a smoker, and Dad got elected. Before them, then, was Joshua Aaron Tully and he held it for something like twenty years. He'd be my grandfather. And before him was Jeremiah Edward Tully, sheriff since 1910 to about 1930. And then old Stanton Paul Thomas Tully, be the great-great-grandfather of me."

"When did you guys start getting tall?"

Peculiar question, he thought.

"The Ledger indicates that Mr. Stanton Tully was short and wiry," said Ruth.

"Yep, he was. I got a tintype of him upstairs with the rest of the troublemakers. He was the last short Tully, but he made up for it here and there."

"So I gather. They say he was a mean one."

"Even for a Tully." He laughed half-heartedly. He looked over at Ruth with cold gray eyes. They were tired. He had dark circles under them, gray on black like the great-great-grandfather of him. She was sitting in an overstuffed chair with wings that in the old days would have kept the warmth from the fireplace from dissipating in a drafty house. She was dressed in jeans, shirt and sweater, and hiking boots, ready to go out and hike in the wood. Except for the rain.

"Well," said Tully, "you didn't come over here just to talk about my family, Miss M. What is it the White County sheriff can do for you on a bright rainy morning?" Of course, he was right. Ruth had risen at dawn, put the books aside, showered, and walked out of Muriel's house, headed for the sheriff's home on the east side of the small town. She walked in the rain; it was less than a mile. She had reached the only possible conclusion she could, though she was upset that it had taken her so long to figure out. She'd been in denial.

Mrs. Tully brought in a large plate of cookies and asked what Ruth wanted to drink, and Ruth said just water would be fine.

"How about mineral water?" asked Mrs. Tully. She was a tall, slender woman in her early forties, good looking in an outdated, country way, with long dark-blond hair softly curled, and she wore two Bakelite bracelets on her left wrist. One was burnt orange, the other chartreuse. Besides the bracelets, she wore a simple, flower-patterned mid-calf dress as if defying the onset of the winter rain with the hope of spring.

Ruth knew Bakelite when she saw it, and the design of these two bracelets dated them to the mid-1950s. She commented on them, her compliments graciously received by Mrs. Tully, who said they were a gift from John's mother, one for each of their two children.

Their children were undoubtedly tall and thin, Ruth thought.

"I hardly take them off," Mrs. Tully said. "I'm superstitious, I guess."

"If there was ever a time to feel superstitious," said Ruth, "now is appropriate." She took the glass of mineral water from Mrs. Tully and picked up one of the cookies. It all seemed so relaxed, she thought, considering that what little time they had was dwindling quickly.

The sheriff was still waiting for Ruth's response. What did she want? He looked at her and raised his eyebrows expectantly. His long legs were stretched out in front of him, but he was anything but relaxed. Those gray eyes, ignoring for the moment their nervous intensity, betrayed both sentiment and, for lack of words, Ruth decided, justice. The dichotomy was for some reason hugely appealing. It was no wonder Mrs. Tully had fallen for him.

"Senator Pike was threatened," said Ruth.

Tully didn't answer immediately. After a silent few moments, he said, "Yes."

"The kidnapping."

"Yes," said Tully again. "He could have his children back if he let loose of the wood …"

"But he could have notified the FBI days ago."

"Hugh's a little concerned with all that," said Tully. "What he told me was he didn't want the feds involved, you see. The whole thing goes deep into Washington politics. Hugh doesn't know who he can trust."

"Trusts you."

"Yep. Trusts you, too. Hugh said you might be around, said you might know pretty much what was going on. Said you quizzed him pretty good there at Muriel's house that morning."

"He must have a plan," she said.

"He's made a few calls. Even called up Blain Cooper … for advice. Blain always did get things done. But that wood is worth millions. And the ground below it's worth even more. He's already trying to quell the interest he's spent years generating. But he's having a hell of a time coming up with a guarantee strong enough to get those kids back. Hell, Ruth, he can't contact them. Waits for them to contact him. Just waits. It's killing him."

"Who is it?" she asked bluntly.

"That would make it too easy."

"That's for sure," she admitted.

"They'll get what they want, Miss M. The only question is whether Hugh and Aisha can get Ebee and Nina back alive."

After a few seconds of silence, "The children are in Wailing Wood," said Ruth succinctly. "It's two days since they were taken; I feel horrible. I just refused to connect it."

After his initial surprise, John Tully pawed his chin with a hand the size of a basketball player's, quiet now, running theories very quickly through his mind. "Two days," he said. "Gone Saturday night late, or early Sunday." Surprisingly, he didn't ask Ruth the reasons behind her supposition.

After some time, he said, "That's problematic, getting there to the wood, Miss M, because of the flooding. Overland Road, you know, where we all met when this damn thing got started, is flooded out. The North Fork's turned into a lake, and the water's moving fast. I know more than one's drowned, thinking he could wade it. It doesn't look that fast from the bank. Or that strong. But it is."

"We could try the south side and go through Bear Breach, with access from the other road? Old Lake County Road?"

"We?" said the sheriff. "Well, the South Fork's over the banks, too, but a person can still drive Lake County Road, at least for now. The thing is, Northern clear-cut part of the steep south slope, I don't know, it was after the war ..."

Mrs. Tully said, "In the early fifties."

The sheriff nodded. "You're pretty sure they're in the wood." It was a question and a statement. He waited, half expecting the woman to place a twenty on his coffee table just as she had placed her bet with Thom and Eaglejohn in Wailing Wood.

"I spent it on pizza, Sheriff," she said.

Her comment surprised him. "I'm glad," Tully said. "No sense in me losing a couple of bills like the rest of them, especially in light of having to figure out how the hell to get to the wood in this rain. You know, if it was me, I wouldn't particularly want to go. But, the way things are, it's more like it's about old Hugh Pike than me ... makes a difference. The kids.

"Anyway, the steepness of that ridge caused the land to slump after it was logged and it'd be too sheer to get past now. A huge landslide, for these parts. It claimed the lives of four loggers, if memory serves. It's a barrier ... a lot of rubble, lot of rain, lot of sheer, exposed rock, and it's been impassable since then. That was the last they logged there, and probably why the rest of the wood's still around. Anyway, it's not like it was back in 1890, when those other kids of yours went from Bear Breach over the ridge to Wailing Wood. It's only a couple of miles, maybe two at the most, but you can't do it today because of the landslide. Have to cross way to the east ... and I mean it would be miles. And take forever in these conditions."

Ruth didn't miss a beat and said, "Then we need a helicopter."

He was slow in his reply. "Well, here's the thing, Miss M. I think it would be best if you all sort of stayed in town. I mean, I can get us an ad hoc deputy, seeing that Agent Mikatsu took all my men for his shindig up north, but, you know, I'd just hear no end of it if I involved a civilian."

"I've been called a lot of things before, Mr. Tully, but no one's ever called me a civilian."

"Yep. Well, I'm sorry, but you can see my point." Tully scratched his neck. "Might could get a helicopter. Take some conniving, though, these days. The FBI's in charge of the investigation, and they've taken over the search and we won't get a helicopter out of them. Not a chance." He thought for a moment, and then said, "Maybe I could get a Forestry Department helicopter, CDF. That's the usual route for me anyway. But we need a better excuse than to save the lives of a U.S. senator's two young children when the feds are already saving them somewhere else." He didn't disguise the disgust in his voice. "It'll take five or six hours between request and delivery. But I can get one."

Ruth was unhappy with the amount of time that would be lost in making such a request. "We can do this ..." she said, realizing that six hours at this point might be deadly. "... I'll go up there with, for example, Muriel Stanley. ... We could drive up Lake County Road, get out across from Bear Breach — Muriel would know where — and try to get through that old logging tunnel to Wailing Wood ... we'd go under the old landslide area and come out on the other side, right where we met before, the day of the dig."

Paul Grassi had briefly described the tunnel during Ruth's initial foray in Wailing Wood to unearth the bones. It dated from the turn of the century and was a narrow tube through the ridge at its narrowest point, about a quarter-mile in length. It was dug using Chinese labor, and Chinese workers had laid the rails for the timber company trains, which hauled the mammoth logs to the mill. It hadn't been used since World War II.

The tunnel's end was near the parking area, Grassi had said, though trees hid it from view that day they entered the wood. She'd never seen the other opening, which was visible from Old Lake County Road.

Tully started to object but Ruth raised her hand for him to be quiet. He obeyed, and wondered why.

"And you call CDF and say you have a pack of nut cases out on a rescue and you think they're lost, they could even be in the tunnel. And blah, blah, blah."

He smiled.

"Do they have a medically equipped helicopter, Forestry?" Ruth asked.

"Yeah, they do."

"Well, if the children are alive, which I believe them to be, you'll need some help with hypothermia, dehydration, and they haven't eaten for a while. It'll be tough."

"Understood. You're really thinking they're alive. Why?"

"Because Ben and Emma were. I think we're okay, but time's really running out."

He sighed. "They were dead. We have their bones."

"They were alive for days before they lay down together."

Tully didn't want to hear that, and pretended he didn't. Time, people, events: None of them repeated themselves, not in real life.

"Detective Chu would like to accompany us. I already talked with him. He's getting ready."

He could use that kind of organization in his own department. "Gonna wear his good slacks again?"

"Probably. I think they look nice. Muriel likes them too."

"Well, I'll tell you, that's a reasoned approach — have some personnel on the ground, with Detective Chu, and then me, a helicopter and a pilot coming in as quickly as we can. Under the circumstances, not bad."

"There might be some trouble," Ruth said. Tully sat, dead-pan. "The kidnappers. And I don't mean Mr. Franzetta and Mr. Grassi."

Tully took a breath. "Trouble's Italian for Tully, loosely translated," he said, his gray eyes seeming even grayer to Ruth.

"Here," she said, "look at this." She took an old photograph from her bag. It was about two inches wide and three tall, a black-and-white paper contact print, brown with age and faded. But you could easily make out the man in the photo.

Tully held it up to the light. The right edge was cracked. "That Mendez guy from Global, right down to the smirk," he said. "There's that old photo studio up on the way to Yosemite, like he stopped there and had his photo taken for the Old West or something. That tourist thing. They take your picture after you get into costume."

"Look at the back."

Pasted there on yellowed newsprint were the date, 1890, and the name, Black Peterson, taken two years before his death at the hands of Hypolite Dupree.

Tully stared at it for a minute, and then sighed. He didn't say anything. But his back was chilled. He looked at Ruth but said nothing.

She handed him the second photo.

He studied it, sighed again, and turned it over. Hypolite Dupree, 1894, very well dressed.

"I guess I better be getting along, then." If he didn't talk about it, if he didn't acknowledge it, maybe it didn't happen. "I suppose you know exactly where Ebee and Nina is," he ventured.

"Are. Yes."

"Well, I guess you better tell me. Time's not on our side anymore."

After their discussion, Mrs. Tully walked Ruth to the door. "You all be careful," she said, "And don't get some crazy idea to plow through that tunnel with the Stanley girl. You just wait for John. I like Muriel too much and I'm starting to like you, Miss M. John'll take care of things. Don't worry. He's calling for the helicopter right now."

"I worry," she said.

"Promise me, Ruth."

"Trust me. And one other thing, Mrs. Tully …"

"What's that, dear?"

"Tell Mr. Tully not to do anything stupid. It won't be worth it in the long run."

Mrs. Tully furrowed her brow. She had no idea what Miss M was talking about. But, she decided, she'd tell her husband anyway: It was good advice, overall.

Back to Wailing Wood

We took two cars up Lake County Road in heavy, pelting rain and pulled off near the visible logging tunnel that bored its way beneath the ridge, under the ruins of Bear Breach. Chu drove, and Muriel and Ruth rode with him. I rode with Mr. Kasparov.

A pool of brackish water lay in front of the tunnel mouth, its surface smacked and broken by the uneven, constant rain. Water was everywhere; below us, above us and flowing in torrents off the arched cement reinforcement of the tunnel mouth. An acacia tree leaned over the right side and would have created a shadow had the pool not been so black and the sky so dark. Above, very precisely inset into the cement that lined the upper tunnel entrance, five-inch letters spelled out "P.T. Johnson Timber Co. 1894." Ruth studied the printing quickly, nodded to herself, and then started wading through the pool into the black hole in front of us.

"Peter Johnson," said Ruth, not looking back toward me. "He took over the property the year before, after he'd seen to it the rightful heirs, Ben and Emma Johnson, were dead. He didn't know about Howard Pike, and that's probably why Howard managed to live to maturity."

Ruth carried a six-volt lantern and the police-band radio she'd gotten from the sheriff before we all set out, and I had a heavy three-battery metal thing that was almost as bright. Chu wore his fishing waders and had a light on his vest. He carried a second, larger flashlight in his right hand. Muriel Stanley and Mr. Kasparov had two-battery flashlights, and all our batteries were new.

I heaved one of two backpacks onto my shoulders. Mr. Kasparov had the other one. We carried dry clothing for ourselves, clothes for the children, and thermoses of hot, sweet juice to help fight potential hypothermia in Ebee and Nina … if we were lucky.

We started into the tunnel, and the only hopeful feeling I had as we left the world of so-called light was that the pathway under the ridge was only 410 yards long, according to the old map. Thirty yards shy of a quarter-mile. When Johnson had the thing carved out of the native stone a century ago, he properly chose the narrowest neck of the Wailing Wood ridge; the rest of the ridge at this elevation was more than a mile wide.

Dark and close as it was, the tunnel also provided shelter from the unrelenting rain.

Once we were in the tunnel, we could feel the iron rails under our feet. I thought about old photos I'd seen of the small trains hauling redwood logs that dwarfed the powerful steam engines. Parts of the rail had rusted into scales like the back of a reptile, and other parts were slick with deposited clay. We moved slowly, trying to detect the direction of the rails but not slip or cut ourselves on them. Within a few yards, one of the rails jutted up like a broken crocodile jaw, just under the surface, and caught my boot, ripping the side of it and sending a small river of frigid, fouled water around my foot.

Ruth was three or four feet ahead of me, guiding herself along the other steel rail. She tried to avoid the twisted tendrils that dangled, dripping, from the ceiling for the first twenty yards, but the old roots vanished as we went deeper — there was too much ground now between the surface plants and tunnel ceiling. The thick earth created a silence that felt like increased pressure in my ears, and the only sound interrupting that numbness was the echo of liquid dripping from the stone ceiling.

The junk of ages began to pile up before us. We could see sections of tree trunks, some cut by two-man saws probably seventy years ago or more. They were jammed up against the rough stone sides of the hole, rising only partway out of three feet of water. I couldn't imagine the strength of the floodwaters that tossed them into this tube, carrying them so deep into the interior. I realized it would be miraculous if we could get through to the other end — the tunnel wasn't more than a claustrophobic fifteen feet wide, and a few old trunks and a limb would be all it would take to end our journey.

The old redwoods had hardly decayed, but other huge chunks of pine and fir had decomposed into demonic shapes that crawled out of the shadows created by our lights. It smelled; things were rotting, decaying. Caught on the old trunks were masses of gnarled, bark-stripped limbs, stones, bricks and wads of turf. Rusted nests of flat barbed wire and the remains of bent, broken iron rods and posts — the waste of man meshed with the decay of nature — hid in the half-submerged mass, waiting to cut or pierce any invader into this dark realm.

We were forced to carefully climb over and around these deposits, our work hampered by keeping one hand on our battery-operated torches while the other tried to find a safe hand-hold for balance. I tried to shine the light far ahead, but the wreckage appeared to continue forever. The going, I realized, could be so slow as to be useless.

"If you think it would be faster on the surface," Ruth said, looking back at me after seemingly reading my thoughts, "you'd be wrong. We just have to get through this without breaking a bone, or getting a nice sharp piece of rebar through our thighs." Great, I thought. Such an optimist. "Another thing: I'll bet the FBI is gumming up the works up there on the surface anyway," she said. "Up on the Klamath. I don't have a good feeling about it. We just have to wriggle through this and to heck with them. Right? Right?"

She shouted back to Muriel to see if she was doing okay. Ruth wasn't really worried because Detective Chu was beside Muriel, and Mr. Kasparov was right beside Ruth.

Mr. Kasparov smiled, teeth strikingly white in the peripheral glow of my flashlight, and said, "This is a very unclean environment."

I kept going, admiring Ruth's ability to climb, step, even vault, to get through it. She pulled herself up or forward using the sides of the tunnel, took steps on cracked, fanged chunks of wood and steel that, as she raised her foot to seek a new toehold, moved as if trying to bite into her. I slogged slowly along behind, able to keep up by sheer strength, not by agility, trying to skirt the famished wreckage as I sought open water.

With the first hundred yards behind us, the sharp stench of ammonia hit my nose. Ruth scanned the walls and water and the stone ten feet above with her top-handled flashlight. Huge, black cracks ripped through the stone over her head, their edges laced with calcium deposits that looked like deathly white lipstick smattered on black jack-o'-lantern smiles. Anchored firmly in the gaping, laughing cracks was a living, breathing, excreting organism — hundreds if not thousands of bats hanging shoulder to shoulder, leather wings enwrapping inverted bodies. They were the source of the stinging odor. Scores could be seen hanging from the remains of timber beams that spread across the ceiling, and where the timbers had fallen, the bats simply hung at angles, attached to stone.

I tried to remind myself how important the creatures were to the environment. It didn't help.

We carefully navigated another fifty yards, living on shallow, ammonia-tainted breaths, until we came approximately to the halfway point. Here, the bats and the pungent stench of their waste disappeared as if they refused to cross a boundary that only they could see or, more accurately, hear with their biological sonar.

The tunnel widened slightly. The flotsam, like the bats, disappeared, and at the edge of the gnarled mass were the floating remains of bloated wood rats brought in and deposited by recent rains. Muriel and Detective Chu approached from behind, and we were now all together somewhere in the middle. Yet Ruth was hardly anxious to leave the absurd safety of the known — the bats, rat corpses and mountains of debris. In front of us lay emptiness — the barren sides of the hole, the naked stone above and the black-glass glare of the still water in front of us.

There was no dripping, no sound, no light, and no longer any smell; our olfactory systems had shut down. We couldn't see the end of it, squint as we might as we shined our lights into the dark.

Ruth began moving through the mirror-like lake. Her thighs were heavy. Her feet weighed many pounds because her boots had filled with water. It was cold and the chill rose from her feet to her sweat-covered back. One arm hung loose at her side now, and the other ached under the weight of the lantern and its big battery. Muriel didn't speak, though I could hear her breathing hard. In my light, she appeared weak and sick. I cast it onto Mr. Kasparov, careful not to let the glare hit his eyes. He was in water up to his hips, but still stood quite solidly.

Ruth's balance remained good, yet the shifting of hidden debris beneath the water and the slickness of the now-chaotic sections of steel rail did everything they could to throw her into the cold blackness. Her thoughts thickened. Where were the bats? She tried to turn around to check on me, but she was unable to rotate from her hips.

Slowly, over a few seconds, I thought I could hear what sounded like hammers striking steel. The ringing of steel on stone came in small, tight waves, globs of sound that carried clipped bits of words, shreds of human voices like an audio tape running backward. I could hear stone falling on stone, giving up its hold on the edges of the universe and crashing down like meteors. The rock was whispering.

The sound of Chinese laborers grew closer. I knew this was impossible. Beside me, Ruth kept moving, trying to ignore it, trying to re-establish her presence in the twenty-first century, not the nineteenth. Muriel was holding onto Chu's arm. I don't know what Chu heard. Ruth pushed one foot out into the void, tested, then set it down. She picked up the other one, moved, checked, settled it without slipping. Over and over. But the sound of the Johnson company foremen driving the Chinese laborers on, shouting and cursing, stung our ears like the bats had stung our noses. But the bats were from the world of the living.

I was having trouble. Thoughts were scattered and sight was uncertain. A fierce pain crackled along the right side of my head, above the eye. I felt sick.

An odd new light appeared from the torch flames of the tunnel foremen, and I could finally see the laborers' thin backs as they bent over, their knobby spines protruding, the sweaty skin glimmering in the artificial light of kerosene torches. Many wore their hair in long queues and a few, though only a few, wore tight dark caps common to their tradition. I told myself this did not exist, but knew I was a liar. I peered deeper into the unmoving air and made out the forms of men hauling great crates of stone on steel wheels and iron rails, and I could make out the wraith-like shapes of sweat-glazed men splitting the rock with thick steel chisels and heavy-headed hammers and heaving pickaxes above their heads and slamming them down on the floors and walls. Century-old torches lit up modern-day black water. I could even see metal mirrors positioned one after another to catch the outside light and reflect it into the tunnel's gut where the workers gnawed their way through the earth to the other side. The smell of kerosene-soaked rags that burned on the ends of wood poles overwhelmed me. Muriel stumbled, falling forward, her arm reaching out the break the fall but in the process finding the knife-sharp edge of steel beneath the water. She'd forgotten the lake that surrounded her.

Detective Chu quickly picked her up and gracefully got her back onto her feet. Muriel, now standing, wavered like a grass blade tossed by the wind.

I pushed myself slowly, laboriously forward. I finally realized we'd reached a part of the tunnel where the deep cracks had released poison gases that fill the untouched depths of the earth. It was hard to think. My head was throbbing; I felt like there was a huge crack in my head on the left side. I looked from side to side, and on my right, standing on timber scaffolding, were half a dozen men, naked from the waist up, securing timbers to reinforce the ceiling. They were Chinese men, and I wondered, absurd as it was, what they were doing so far from the light of day. The one furthest left noticed my gaze and returned it. I was chilled by the uncontestable connection our eyes made.

A man came up to Chu. His queue had been cut off. He simply stood there, unmoving. Chu put his hand on the man's bony, damp shoulder, and the man then returned to his pickaxe and resumed his labor.

The shouts of construction foremen woke me from the spectral scene, and the man whose eyes met mine drifted into the dark. I was once again standing in frigid, stagnant water, still holding onto the flashlight, panning the light on front of me as I searched for the exit. Ruth was in front and to the right of me.

I heard a crack in the ceiling above, and a big, ragged chunk of stone fell into the water just inches from where I stood. I jumped back, losing my balance, and fell into the water. My head was barely above the surface as I sat flat against the stone floor. I struggled to regain my footing, but the thickness and throbbing of my head forced me to double my effort. When I was once again standing, I panned the light again.

I found Mr. Kasparov beside me, holding me up. I wondered how he could do it; our sizes were so different. He urged me forward with the rest, and we ignored the grasping debris at our feet, allowed ankles to be bashed against hidden steel, and we traded deep cuts for speed. I checked behind, and Chu was holding Muriel up, pulling her forward. One of the laborers tried to follow her, but Chu, so slowly, held his hand up and pressed the wraith's shoulder, as if to say, "turn, friend, and you may follow later." Yet Chu said not a word.

The world began to pass quickly alongside us. The laborers and foremen, the kerosene torches and pounding steel fell distantly behind us. We moved our legs; that was all we could do.

Miraculously, the bats returned. We'd made it through the dead zone. I was euphoric — the bats were like beautiful songbirds. There was life, but there was still darkness. I had regained enough coherence to realize that Global, a company that the locals referred to as a mining company, must know that gas, and therefore oil, lay beneath their land. I saw clearly their plans to clear-cut the forest and then begin the oil exploration process.

We moved on as quickly as we could, though the water had little interest in freeing its prisoners. We were exhausted. Luckily, we couldn't tell how much we were bleeding.

Finally, we found ourselves in a dim, gray light. The sides of the tunnel, too, were visible now. A few more steps, a few more yards, a dozen yards, then two dozen, and we could see the end of the tunnel. It was distant and small. Another ten yards and then another, and trees became visible at the mouth of the hole. By the time we reached the light we could hardly move our legs, we could barely suck in enough air, and we were so chilled we chattered in unison. But we finally stood in the dim afternoon light on the north side of the ridge. It was still raining, lightly and steadily. I looked at my watch. Ruth was right: The tunnel was faster. She smiled softly at me, aware of what I was thinking, and then lurched a few yards to the right to vomit. The route might have been faster, I thought, but it was deadly.

The parking area we'd used only days before — it seemed like years — was upslope about twenty yards away. I remembered the voice of Paul Grassi, when he pointed out the tunnel opening to us as we gathered to head into the wood.

From the parking area, we would take the same path we'd taken before, two miles to the ancient groves of Wailing Wood.

We all changed shirts, socks, and shoes from the packs that Mr. Kasparov and I carried. We were careful with the thermoses, which we would need later. We started walking, and, fortunately, movement began to warm us. The rain-painted world on the edges of Wailing Wood was vivid green.

The mud and rain-pooled parking area came clearly into view in just a few minutes, and we saw that the gate had been opened. It seemed odd, and the most likely reason was that someone from Global had been checking the newly cut roads or that the state forest service had gained access to begin work on the archaeological site before the flooding of the last few days.

We had a long walk ahead of us, heads still throbbing from the petroleum gases in the deep. But no sooner had we passed through the yellow, iron-bar gate than we found ourselves at a bloody scene — a black Lincoln Town Car with rear doors and trunk agape, and the body of a large man on the ground near the trunk, in the mud, in the rain. He was dead.

Mr. Kasparov quickly checked him. It was Salvador Mendez of Global.

Lost in the Wood

William Chu checked out Mendez's body. There was nothing to be done at this point. Chu said nothing, but it appeared to me that the man had been stabbed or otherwise wounded in a manner to draw a lot of blood. The sight put us all on edge. Well, perhaps not Chu, but the rest of us.

We began the trek into the forest. After a hard forty minutes, we approached the grove of old trees where we'd unearthed the bones of Ben and Emma Johnson. Despite our mission and the feeling of trepidation and immediacy that accompanied it, Ruth was overcast with melancholy because of the way the world was a hundred years ago ... because of the children lost then, so long ago, which nothing could ever change. I could tell that feelings were flowing through her like gentle but insistent ocean waves. I don't know whether she shrugged them off, set them aside or simply swam with the current, floating along because she was lighter than the emotional sea.

We heard the distant call of an owl, probably the same one that appeared to frequent this part of the wood when we first

302

encountered the children's skulls. It probably had a nest some-where near.

There were places along the trail where I thought I could make out the footprints of the Pike children, but the impres-sions were vague and may have been nothing at all — or per-haps they were tracks of a deer or coyote that had expanded, their shapes altered by the rain. There were larger tracks as well, but because they were old and rain-damaged, they were equally undecipherable.

"Mendez," Chu informed me, "did not do his dirty work alone. Actually, we have been following the trail of a second man. We must remain alert for this man, because he is or was undoubtedly in the vicinity."

"He's pursuing the children," Ruth said matter-of-factly. "But he's not used to running, and from what I can see, he's slipping all over the place in his street shoes."

"You mean the kids ran from the car up into the wood?" asked Muriel.

"Right, after Mr. Mendez and his partner had it out," said Ruth.

"Stabbed," said Chu. "At least a day ago, maybe two days ago. Possibly shortly after the kidnapping."

"They must have driven here before the flooding," I said, "maybe even the night of the kidnapping. Early, early Sunday morning ..."

Ruth nodded.

Yet something about all this was on the other side of what, to me, was believable. Muriel was the one to voice it, though, when she said, "This is exactly what happened in 1892. After Ruth found the story that my old Robert wrote down in 1906, I went back and read it for myself. When they go around saying that Whitesboro has unsettled spirits, they don't know the half of it."

Chu, keeping us aware of our current situation, said, "All I know is that there's some nutter on the loose out here, so keep on your toes. We know he has a knife."

We turned our attention to the big trees in the distance and to the archaeological dig that was now practically at our feet. The patch of disinterred ground had grown wider because of Jim Miller's recent archaeological foray, and, though I couldn't yet tell, the hole was deeper, although it had been filled in and a layer of leaves covered most of it.

"It's all an echo," Ruth said, looking back at Mr. Kasparov and me. There was a softness in her eyes that I wasn't used to, but it faded quickly as she refocused on her strange mission. "Twisted, twisted, like the flotsam in the tunnel. I mean, what happened a hundred and twenty years ago … things are mixed up. Chopped up."

She was looking around, I'm not sure for what. Mr. Kasparov was clearly waiting for her to make a decision.

"But the major movements are holding true," she said. "Muriel's right. I knew Black Peterson would be dead — Salvador Mendez is a dead ringer. Literally. But as for Hypolite Dupree … I don't know."

I asked, "Who's Dupree?"

Ruth knew, and Muriel knew. They were the only ones besides Sheriff Tully to have seen the old photographs from the drawers of Arnold Stanley in the morgue of the Ledger. And so they knew who was pursing the children. It took me a minute to put it together; I was embarrassed to have asked. "Are the children still alive?" I said.

"Yes, because they were still alive at this point in 1892," said Ruth.

I asked how she knew Ben and Emma Johnson were still alive at this point in their mortal trials.

"Because of the position of the bodies," she said. "They'd escaped Black Peterson, and they'd run away from Hypolite Dupree, stumbling and scurrying madly into Wailing Wood. They were lost. They were left. There was no help. They wandered for hours, and then a day, maybe two, maybe more. They finally lay down together, exhausted, hypothermic, and they died." Then she added, rather ominously, "But they were not supposed to die."

I wondered why she'd said that. How could she know they weren't supposed to die?

"Because we're going through it all again," she continued thoughtfully as if in answer to my unvoiced question.

I tried to think about it …

"The same families are involved," she noted, "removed only by a couple of generations. I mean, the Stanleys, the Pikes,

the Johnsons, even Jim Miller. He's a Gitaine. And the men behind the crime? Why do the men in the old photographs look so
similar to the men we're dealing with today? I can't claim to
know, or to understand. But I do know that events are repeating themselves, and because we know what did happen, we can
know what will happen."

Yet Ruth was troubled. Where were the children? They
had to be here.

She held her hand up to silence us. We hadn't said a word.
She sat down, hand still up, silencing, I suppose, the universe.

Hadn't she thought this out? We'd waded through that
filthy, deadly tunnel and she hadn't even finished thinking this
thing through? She looked at me, glaring.

Then she stood up. We were surrounded by second-
growth redwood and a carpet of ferns, behind which loomed
the ancient trees of Wailing Wood. We could see them, feel their
shadows. There must have been a wind high overhead, because
a few of the trees had begun to creak. Once again, I heard the
hooting of the owl off to the east from the deepest part of the
old grove. Large drops of water condensed and dropped here
and there, hitting the ground hard. It was cold, and, in spite of
the change of clothes, we were wet and chilled. An image of my
father smoking his pipe came to my mind, and I would have
liked, at that moment, to hold that warm briarwood in my
hands.

There was a flutter and some falling needles to our right,
and a robin flew over us from behind and perched in one of the
young trees. It caught Ruth's attention — her eyes if not her
mind, which was clearly elsewhere. A few seconds later, a second robin flew in from the same direction. It had a twig or piece
of straw in its beak and landed a few yards past the first bird.

"I always wondered where robins went in the winter," I
said quietly.

Ruth turned and looked at me. Just then a third bird fluttered past us, this one with a small leaf in its mouth. I decided it
was nesting season.

Moaning eerily, as if the truth had somehow drilled its
way into her brain, Ruth stood bolt upright. It seemed as if the
birds had told her what she needed to know. Certainty showed
in her eyes as surely as if those birds, from their vantage point

305

fifty feet above us, had told her everything they had seen. She looked at the dig a dozen yards in front of us. The birds flew down and perched some distance beyond that, and the first two had already left, as though they were shy of humans. The third remained in a branch on the other side of the dig and to our left.

Ruth dashed to the hole where the midden was, where the children's bones had been found, and started digging through what the forest had deposited since the university crew had left — leaves and redwood fronds, twigs, bits of bark, the duff that, a century before, had created the acid environment that had preserved Ben Johnson's woolen vest. I ran up to her as quickly as I could. I finally had gotten it.

First, she pulled out Nina Pike. Holding her to her chest, she put her ear to the girl's mouth, listening and feeling for breath. Shallow as they were, the girl's signs of life were unmistakable. Ruth rose and handed her to me. Mr. Kasparov had thrown off his pack and was opening the thermos of hot, sweet juice.

She found Elmore, Ebee, next, a few feet away but invisible because of the soggy mass of leaves and duff that covered him. She pulled him out, repeating the test for life. "He's alive," she said, elated to the point that tears were streaming down her face. "Okay, okay . . . look, they're in trouble. We've got to get them warm. Okay . . ." she was thinking as fast as she could.

"Get them under our coats," I said, "next to us." I knew as well as she did that there were only two ways to introduce warmth to a body suffering from hypothermia: Heat it from the inside, using tea or some other warm drink, or from the outside, such as being next to another warm body.

"Yeah, yeah," she said.

"I'll take Ebee," Chu said, not adding that the boy was heavier.

"Good." She started stripping off her raincoat and the wool sweater she'd put on at the other end of the trail. She was down to a T-shirt or camisole, and then those were off. Then she grabbed Nina, tore off the child's soaking pajamas, and I helped her wrap the girl's legs around her waist, tried to place her arms over Ruth's shoulders, so that Ruth carried her face to face. Or face to chest. Mr. Kasparov repeated the same actions as he helped Chu wrap the boy around Chu's torso. I re-dressed

Ruth, pulling over the sweaters, which stretched to cover them both, while Mr. Kasparov rewrapped and rebuttoned Chu's absurdly stylish wool jackets.

This was the best we could do.

"Now we've got to walk out, not wait for the rescue crew from the helicopter," Ruth said. "Maybe we'll meet them partway. There's the logging trail. We have to stay together. Mr. Kasparov and Muriel can go first and I'll follow. In case I slip, they can stop me from sliding too far. Then you, and Detective Chu'll follow you."

We concentrated on walking. Ruth was strong, but that amazing strength had been compromised by the tunnel. After half a mile or so, Mr. Kasparov took Nina, holding her close, under his coat, as Ruth pulled her sweater back down and led the way. And I relieved Detective Chu of the boy. The advantage of size was mine, and the going was smooth. The children had already begun to warm up. Every few minutes we had them drink the warm juice.

The rain had washed out most of the road and we stumbled a few times, but none of us hit the ground. We made fairly good time, all things considered. At the end of a mile and a half, we could see a crew of emergency personnel. The helicopter had set down in the parking area on the other side of the gate.

Mr. Kasparov and I, carrying the Pike children, headed straight for the emergency workers. But Ruth and Chu did not. They veered to the east. Muriel followed them, uncertain of what they were doing.

The Capture of Hypolite Dupree

LOCALS: A vagabond was arrested Monday night by Sheriff Tully for furiously careering through the Business District of Whitesboro in a carriage, in a state of obvious inebriation. He was released at morning after paying the county a considerable $100 bail and promptly left town in a southerly direction.
— *The Whitesboro Ledger, April 21, 1892*

The sheriff, having brought Rene Gitaine back from the wreckage of the Great Earthquake of 1906, orchestrated the manhunt and capture of Hypolite Dupree. The criminal, unable to escape on foot or by carriage because of the condition of the roads, was taken alive but not without a fight. Tully watched the men haul the cart carrying a thoroughly beaten Hypolite Dupree to a makeshift headquarters near what remained of the hospital.

Tully pulled on Dupree, sat him up, and the murderer's consciousness returned. Dupree was quite bruised, but one couldn't tell if it was from the collapse of the courthouse and jail or the fists of Tully's ad hoc posse. All the men had attended the trial, and most of them had to be physically restrained during their violent apprehension of the man.

Dupree scanned his surroundings through swollen eyes. He knew he was unable to move with any surety or speed, so he sat, studying his foes, his gaze narrowed like a snake's, and like a snake, crippled up though he was, he still appeared ready to strike. All the men surrounding him sensed this and maintained their distance. Two rifles were trained on him.

"By order of the court," said Tully, "we'll proceed with the sentence. You got any last words, Hypolite Dupree?"

He looked up at Tully, his eyelids thick and drooping over flaming irises. Dupree was still a very dangerous man. He did indeed have his last words, and with them he began to crush the breath out of those in his presence.

"I come back from the wood," he began. "I come back from the wood those many year ago." He was surrounded now by not less than thirty of Whitesboro's strongest men, and another dozen of the city's hardest working wives and women. They took a collective breath of trepidation and pulled back a step. No one knew what he would say. But they did know it would be devastating in its cruelty.

"I led them childrens into that wood. Sent them to hell. I know they starved. I know they died with the dread of hell on them." His brown, broken teeth showed in a gnashing smile. "But Sheriff, you could of stopped it all, you could of stopped it all fourteen year ago … But you was blind. You 'rested me for plowin' through your sad little town, drunk in that carriage, fined me a hunnerd dollars. You let me go, Sheriff. You gave me my freedom for a coin of gold. Only an hour before, I had left them childrens up in the wood. Left 'em for dead. But they wasn't dead. Not yet. Said I'd be back."

Tully stared at the man. Neither man moved.

Dupree continued. "I come out from the wood, right in that same carriage we took from Peter Johnson's, and I drove it back into town. Drove it with a fury, Sheriff."

Tully remembered, and the images came back despite the years that had elapsed. He remembered the carriage, the horses as they fumed and tore through the dirt Main Street of Whitesboro. People leaped and sprinted to get out of the way, diving from the onslaught of the horses.

Sheriff Tully managed to stop the carriage at the north edge of town. He arrested the driver, who reeked of liquor, and hauled him back to the jail. That was when he first saw the small silver cross. A twinge went through the sheriff's head as he looked at Dupree propped up on the cart: That's why the little icon seemed so familiar when he held it up during the trial. The memory had been so close.

But there had been no injuries from Dupree's drunken fury in 1892. There was no reason to keep the man more than a day, until he sobered up. Sheriff Tully had released Dupree while the Johnson children, though lost in the wood, were still alive.

"You remember?" Dupree said, his voice hissing. "You called me a drunken bastard, to get out of your town. Fined me a stiff fine cause you seen I had some kinda money on me. What I'm saying, is I was feeling this bit of remorse there, and I would of told you about them childrens. Just might of, Sheriff. They could be good solid citizens today. Some good man might of gone back and got them after I told them where they was. I would of said where." Dupree laughed, his breath wheezing, his nose running from the powdered stone that still clogged his nostrils and lungs.

Sheriff Tully sat unmoving, looking at Dupree. No one moved. The first second went by in devastating silence. The second moment drifted mutely past.

Then, in the third second, "Got an earthquake here," Tully snapped, matter-of-factly. He stood up. There was work to do.

"Can't spare the rope to hang the likes of you, might need it," he said. He pulled the Colt Thunder from its holster and shot Hypolite Dupree in the heart. Dupree slumped forward and was dead in a matter of seconds. Tully stood up and walked slowly away from the onlookers, heading west toward the sea. After about ten paces, he turned, walked back, and said, "Let's get this cleaned up. We got a town to get back on its feet here."

The Sheriff's Déjà vu

There's a clearing not far from the parking area where the helicopter had set down. A hundred yards east, maybe two hundred. Whatever the distance, and despite the rain and settling fog, the image was clear. Sheriff John Tully, with his green rain poncho swept over his shoulders, was seated on a stump about fifteen feet from the mud-coated form of the Global Resources bookkeeper, whose bulbous head was bare and glistening from the rainwater. His rain jacket had a hood, but the hood was back. The footprints we'd seen along the trail were his. Tully had trapped him like a rat; he'd known all along who he was looking for and where he'd find him. They faced each other in silence. One of the bookkeeper's hands enwrapped a folding knife; from the other dangled a little silver cross, the one Nina'd been wearing. Her father had given it to her only days before, after it had been found in Betty Pike's attic with the vest pattern and a few old photos.

The bookkeeper was seated on the end of a log, the short trunk of a tree felled and broken and mossed by time. He sat,

311

and seemed to embody that time, all that time, the count of days and years, and his eyes were shallow, his skin waxier now that it was so wet. A sardonic smile coated his face, smeared there. He sat, silent and waiting, his mind coiled like a snake.

Tully had his service revolver in his hand. The hammer on the double action Smith & Wesson was cocked. He, too, waited, as he stared into the eyes of a would-be killer of children. He waited for the man to move, but the man didn't. It was a stalemate of mythic proportions, but whispered so as not to draw down the gods. It felt to Tully as if he'd done this before, a century ago, lost in time. He stood there, facing a laughing, belittling little man. It was everything he could do not to put a bullet where the man's heart should have been. What if there was no heart? For some reason, that created a thread of confusion in Sheriff John Tully's mind.

By the time Tully noticed William Chu, the detective had already sat down quietly beside him a few inches from Tully's right arm. Chu was humming a tune his mother used to sing when he was a child; it was very old, traditional and rather haunting, like a river; it lacked only the whining of a Chinese turtle-shell violin.

Chu said nothing. He just sat there. It was raining. His thick hair had started to plaster itself in odd clumps, fighting the weight of the water. Rain dripped off his nose. He could hear a helicopter not too far in the distance and realized the FBI had gotten wind of the sheriff's excursion to Wailing Wood.

Soon, Chu could hear the men from the chopper coming up behind them. It wasn't what he wanted. From the corner of his eye he could see the wide form of Agent Mikatsu and behind him two, maybe three, other agents. Guns were drawn. How unfortunate, he thought. But that was the FBI for you. They'd apparently dealt with the perceived threat posed by Paul Grassi and Mike Franzetta, both armed, and found no children, no prisoners. There had been no kidnapping by the pair.

Chu looked up and over at the stern face of the gray-eyed sheriff, and moved his head to study the white-skinned bookkeeper, whose face, now smiling, showed what could have been a century of malice. The bookkeeper tossed his knife out in front of him. Anyone could see he was now unarmed. The man's smile was hard to describe. He slowly licked his thin, colorless lips.

The FBI men were now twenty feet off. Chu reached out and put his hand on the sheriff's. He pushed down gently, and the gun was lowered. He put his thumb on the hammer and eased it slowly into the firing pin. Chu slid the big pistol back into Tully's holster, so easily and quickly it would have been impossible to tell if the sheriff had ever drawn it. For all intents, he had not. That made Chu happy. This was a very good day.

Chu waved the agents in. They led the bookkeeper away about the same time that two of the emergency workers carried Sal Mendez's body to the helicopter.

The Mystery of the Leaves

"You were correct, Miss M. May I call you Ruth these days?"

"Of course, Thomas. I hope you didn't have to dig too far, or do too much heavy lifting. There is a lot of heavy reading in your library." Ruth smiled. Father Percy smiled.

"My library is my gym, especially the way I keep it up," said Father Percy.

"Muriel said you've returned some of your books ..."

"I told the sheriff, young Johnny Tully, to keep the leg-breakers off my back!"

"He put the word out?"

"The book mafia was on my tail!" He was joking.

"I assume you eluded them."

"I am sure Johnny's the reason I am alive today, bless him."

"So did you have the old folklore volumes in that mountain of literature, the ones I mentioned?"

314

"I did indeed. I hadn't returned them, and have profited by my lack of morals. Imagine spending eternity for a borrowed book, unreturned! The good one's from England, quite an old chapbook. I would like to buy one, I suppose. Then, of course, the Shakespeare, and the Welsh books. I have them all, and own none anymore!"

"You mentioned the birds' role in the church … I wasn't aware of much of that. I mean, other than the obvious. Well, Thomas, if you have a few minutes, may we talk about … robin redbreasts?"

The rain had broken, if only briefly, and though it was now officially winter, it was more like a spring day — wet, sunny, a breeze, and cold unless you were directly in the sun. And they were comfortably under its rays as they sat on a bench in the church's rose garden, just the two of them, and a tailless orange cat. All the bushes had been pruned, the centers cleared, shallow trenches dug around them. You could still see the little mounds of bone meal at the bases of the trunks. Roses like sacrifice: blood and bone. Father Percy told Ruth that roses are like the Church in that regard, smiling as he said it.

And as they sat, the old priest and Ruth, the roses waited, as they always did, silent witnesses to the seasons.

"I am fond of roses, Ruth. Are you?"

"As I matured."

"Ah. You were a fruit and vegetable person when younger?"

"For the most part. I stole raspberries and strawberries by trade."

"But that was a long time ago."

"Not that long … come on, Thomas. Give a girl a break here. But now I see a sort of need for flowers."

"The rose, like the robin, played many roles through the ages of the Church."

"I'm sure. The robins buried the children in leaves, Thomas. It was the part I couldn't figure out. And John Tully couldn't get it either. We both thought someone had buried the Johnson children, even though it made no sense. But I dimly remembered the old folktales. I'm glad you found them."

Father Percy had a package of Oreos, which he placed invitingly on the bench between them, opened, and he proceeded to eat one after the other until he'd consumed seven.

"You must always buy the value pack, Ruth. That is my best advice. There is a reason that the value pack was placed on this planet. The savings are considerable."

"I know, Thomas."

"You get one-third extra, free, Ruth." But Father Percy didn't smile afterward, knowing that his yellowed teeth were now dark brown from the cookies. "Please," he mumbled and gestured to the value pack.

Ruth took four or five and ate one, then another, and another and another, then stopped.

Father Percy said, "Cymbeline, you know," referring to the Shakespeare play. "'The ruddock would, with charitable bill,' and all that, my dear. Remember? Little Robin spread leaves over the body of Imogen, for she had died. Robins cover the dead with leaves, as if the little birds were actors in a vast and beautiful plan."

"I remember reading it in school, university."

"And they, the robins, would use moss to cover the dead when leaves and flowers were scarce," he said. "So say the old stories."

"Yes. What's the etymology of 'ruddock?' The name was used by Shakespeare. Ruddock?"

"Middle to old English But it always meant robin," he said, "and no other bird."

"Yes. One and the same."

"They had such a vital place in the lives of men, robins," said Father Percy. "It's said a Little Robin followed Mary out of Egypt, and his breast became red from the blood from the soles of her poor, traveling feet."

"I didn't know that story."

"Red from pulling the thorn from the Savior's crown upon the cross?"

"Yes, I've heard that."

"Red from blushing when he touched the baby Jesus in the manger?" he asked.

"I didn't know that one."

"Red from being burned by an ember from the manger as Little Robin fanned a warming fire to keep the child warm?"

"I had heard that one, Thomas, I think. I read it somewhere or other. Is it another case of robin caring for children?"

"It would be such, even outside of religious context."

"A pattern is developing," she said. Ruth ate another cookie. Father Percy helped himself to three.

He said, "And Little Robin carries a mere drop of water to serve the frightened children who've been abandoned. That's Welsh. And then, of course, there's the tale you sent me after, the old English tale, the sixteenth century tale."

Father Percy handed her one of his old volumes.

"He has always taken care of children ..." said Ruth.

"Time and again, tale after tale, myth after lore," interrupted Father Percy.

"And he has always strewn leaves over the dead."

"Yes. Always. You'll find the passage there," he said, pointing to the book whose page was appropriately marked with a leaf.

"Well," she said, "they must have a thing for strawberry leaves? Robins?"

"Oh, yes!" said the old priest, animated. "I see them gather them all the time. Dry leaves for their nests, green leaves for ... well, I don't know. The children in the wood, I suppose."

"I suppose. It was the only thing we didn't understand, Mr. Tully and I. We decided that someone had buried them, the children, but why on earth would they carry in sacks or baskets of leaves from far outside the wood when there was plenty of duff and deadfall around? But then, after he went up there after the Pike children, and they were covered in the same leaves — oak, tanoak, strawberry — it was ... just too ... something."

"But you never reckoned on Little Robin," said Father Percy. "Industrious fellow. Why, Ruth, do you suppose they do that? Strew leaves upon the dead? Whether in Shakespeare, or Welsh folktales or English history from the fifteen hundreds, why have the little fellows such a proclivity?"

"You're asking me?" said Ruth. "I do textiles. I think I will knit you a scarf, so you can switch off with that one," she said, lifting the scarf from his shoulder. It was the same one he'd

317

worn when they met. "A person can't have too many scarves, you know.

"Anyway, the tendencies of robins would be your department, not mine."

"How thoughtful. Well, there's one of them now," he said, pointing to a robin that had lit on a bare rose branch. "Tell me, Ruth, what do you see?"

Ruth turned toward the priest. "I see a cookie freak who sees in colors, as we all do. It's just that they're arranged differently, apparently depending on one's sugar intake."

"Arranged from the inside out, Ruth. That, I think, is the point."

She took another cookie. So did Father Percy. Soon, all the cookies were gone. "I have another package," he said, "two for one." And he went to get it. The sun had passed its zenith, but was still warm. She sighed. Mooncat, who had been listening to the discussion as he sunbathed on the bench beside the old priest, hopped up on Father Percy's lap when he returned. The cat noticed the robins in the roses, but didn't particularly care. Then he walked over and curled up on Ruth. Father Percy opened up the other package of cookies.

Settled spirits

I left Whitesboro the day after the arrest of Global's bookkeeper, and had not seen Ruth for several weeks; she stayed on as the very honored guest of Muriel Stanley, with whom she'd grown close, and Senator and Mrs. Pike and the senator's mother and Mrs. Cooper and … have I forgotten anyone? Yes: the Tullys. Mrs. Tully adored Ruth, and, by the time Mrs. Tully had heard the full story about the apprehension of the Global bookkeeper at the forest's edge, and how close her husband had come to killing the unarmed man, she had also placed her "dear Detective Chu" on a pedestal of equal height as Ruth's.

Ruth felt a hint of melancholy and even loss when she finally returned to the city, though she had been ferried back in the magnificence of Mr. Kasparov's Silver Cloud.

Upon her return home, Ruth returned also to the work she had interrupted in pursuit of the mystery of the children in the wood, and soon there was little time or room for remorse. She would see them all again, she knew, and sooner than later.

The mordanting of the wool yarn a seeming eternity ago had not been finished when Ruth left for Whitesboro. Mr. Kasparov, Ruth's friend Julie, and the cat, Methuselah, had looked after her yarn. Great care had been taken to let it sit, just sit, for whatever period of time Ruth had suggested, and then the skeins were hung from a wooden drying rack. I decided that one could not have better friends than those who would look after what was most important to your heart.

I found Miss M on a chilly morning ensconced in the kitchen of the Avaluxe Theater. A sense of relief flooded through me when I saw her after those very long weeks. I had worried that I might never see her again — she seemed to have very little of either foot in the world as I had always known it. Maybe her toe had touched it, creating a few ripples, little concentric circles that quickly disappear, but when they were gone I feared that she would be, too. Her feet are small.

I was wrong, of course, about Ruth having no feet in the world. I realize now that the world is much larger than I had suspected, and that there are things and events that lurked at its edges, waiting, that I had known nothing about.

There had been a light, cold rain all night, and, as I walked along the front alleyway that led to the Avaluxe, I could see that the damp sidewalk was stained by tree leaves. The leaves were gone; the stains remained. The sun had not yet risen. There were no fallen redwood fronds on the sidewalk, however, and I found that I missed them.

The lobby door had been propped open. But there was no one in the lobby except Methuselah, who had stationed himself near the door as if waiting for me. He was perched regally next to a plant on a small serving table, the old kind of table you see in movies from the 1940s that are used to serve beautiful women with perfect hair in finely furnished rooms, glamourous females in flowing white satin nightclothes. It suited Methuselah. He was washing his hind leg.

Ruth had opened the door in the rear of the theater's kitchen, blocked open the serving door between the kitchen and the small theater lobby, and counted on the cross-draft from the alley to pull the vapor off the just-below-simmering dye vat. Moist air was sent out through the front glass doors and two very horizontal, louvered, stained-glass windows on the lobby's north and south sides. The system worked moderately well, but the air inside remained somewhat muggy, and it loitered in the lobby as if waiting for the ticket vender to open his semicircle window, perhaps hoping to catch a matinee.

Ruth had already chopped and mashed her very valuable madder root, the stuff she'd gotten from the family in Tennessee, the same family that had supplied Mrs. Reynolds with her madder for her dyeing when Ruth was a child. I realized there were multiple generations on both ends of this trade route, and it seemed to be an incredibly comfortable relationship.

Ruth saw me peeking through the lobby door to the kitchen, Methuselah now at my feet, and she carefully walked, barefooted, from the stove to the door and greeted me with her traditional hug. She was warm from tending her steaming dye vat. Ruth said she'd missed me, but, as if catching herself in too human a statement, added, "not that much, because of the madder." I accepted that, and the hug.

Ruth said she'd worked up the red-tinged, sticklike root, and I'm sure it was very well prepared and perfectly weighed on her old brass balance before it hit the water.

She had two big steel vats on the vintage 1930s gas range; one was heating and the other had clear water at room temperature. She wore a sleeveless, shapeless muslin shirt and loose muslin pants that tied at the waist. I realized this was her dyeing garb, and I suppose it was about as comfortable as one could hope for under such circumstances. Ruth's feet were bare because, as she had said to me during the mordanting phase weeks ago, feet were easier to dry than shoes and socks — and far easier to wash. Her hair was up, well pinned with knitting needles.

After finally stabilizing the heat under the vat, she covered it with a big steel lid with a handle. It would have to stay at 175 degrees for a couple of hours.

"Don't worry," said Ruth, "Methuselah will watch the temperature." I wasn't sure if she was serious or not. Nothing she said surprised me anymore. Methuselah stared at me, his eyes seeming to say, "One hundred and seventy-five, Nat."

Her bare feet ached from tending the yarn all morning. She'd finally ordered cushioned rubber commercial kitchen mats, but they wouldn't arrive for another few weeks. "And rubber-soled chef's clogs," she added. "They were supposed to be here weeks ago. A month ago, I ordered them. I haven't told Mr. Kasparov yet, so don't say anything. He loves getting involved in people's mail-order traumas."

"Why is that?" I asked.

She looked up and smiled. "Because he likes to talk. He talks them to death. I think he learned it from the Soviet police during all the trouble. Once, somebody offered to personally deliver whatever Mr. Kasparov had ordered by driving it something like three hundred miles just to shut him up. Drive it themselves. I think it's a gift, actually. I don't talk that much, myself."

"Really?" I said.

"Nope. Not that much. Well, look, I have to go up and change. You could make some coffee or tea. I'll be right back."

Soon, Miss M returned down the north staircase, in silk. I think it was silk. Her face was still flushed from the heat of the stove, which emphasized her freckles and the vibrancy of her complexion.

She settled into one of the chairs on the south side of the lobby so she could keep an eye on the dye in the kitchen. Methuselah had relinquished his responsibilities and joined us. "You just can't get good help these days," she said, kicking off her slippers. Coffee was served to the best of my meager abilities.

"Muriel's coming down," Ruth said, coffee cup in her hand, legs crossed, very casually, as if we'd been talking for hours. Her cat seemed unhappy he didn't have a coffee cup as well. "She could be here any time. Mr. Kasparov has fixed up No. 9 for her — I think she'll stay for a week, and then Arney will come down and pick her up. She hasn't had a vacation for years, I hear. I'm trying to talk Arney and Lou into staying a couple of days with us when they come down to get Muriel. No. 4 is ready just in case. Maybe we could make a big dinner or something like that." Ruth looked directly at me, waiting for a commitment, and I nodded. Definitely.

Detective Chu had already told me that Muriel Stanley was going to visit. He planned on adjusting his schedule as necessity dictated to show Muriel the city, for me not to worry about it, and that he didn't mind. It was the smile that gave him away.

Ruth's and my conversation that morning veered toward the inexplicable incidents that had taken place in Whitesboro ... inexplicable to me, but not to her. For Ruth, the settling of the spirits of Whitesboro was as everyday as dyeing yarn. I wondered if one had to hang old spirits out to drip and dry, like wool. I wondered if they left colored pools of dye beneath them after they had paid up their karma and went on to the world of the dead. Now, whenever I see pools under dripping wool, I think of spirits.

I asked Ruth what had happened to Paul Grassi and the operations manager, Michael Franzetta. I said I hadn't heard, and knew only that Agent Mikatsu sent hundreds of men after them on that ill-timed fishing trip on the Klamath River north of Whitesboro, near the Oregon border. I knew little about their fate.

"Well, Paul Grassi and old Mike Franzetta," she began, "knowing they'd been fired by Global after years and years of loyal work, were at a bar in town, the Pony. The sign says it's a pub, but, really, it's just a bar. They met there to talk about Desmond Blake and the future of the company and their own futures as well. I understand that all the mill workers used to go there, to the Pony, (when there *were* mill workers, according to Muriel). So, I think, there were a number of old mill and timber workers there with them, and everyone was commiserating about one thing or another. Everyone hates Global. Mr. Grassi and Mr. Franzetta decided amongst themselves that there were a lot of steelhead that needed catching this year, and they really didn't have time to work, anyway. They were heartily encouraged by the others at the bar to take a grand fishing trip to the Klamath, and to heck with the company. The other men, you see, had been fired several years before, right after Global bought the company. Bought Northern."

"I don't think Bill Chu caught anything," I noted, interrupting the story when I thought of the detective's rather fortuitous trip up to Whitesboro. He had, after all, set everything in motion by recommending Ruth to the sheriff after the discovery of the bones and the remains of the old wool vest.

"Nope, you're wrong. He caught two, and one was quite large, to hear Mr. Chu tell it."

"Really? He didn't tell me. I've seen him twice since he got back. Mrs. Morton would have said something ..."

"It's supposed to be a secret. A big surprise. He froze both of them at the motel, and they've been in his freezer since he got back to the city. He's going to cook you a fish dinner. Or his mom is, actually. I'm invited. I'm not supposed to tell you." Ruth can't keep a secret.

"Should I act surprised?"

"Why?" she asked, as if I were crazy.

I nodded. There is never room for subterfuge. "So," I began again, "about Paul and Mike?"

"Mr. Grassi and Mr. Franzetta," she said, "were so upset with being fired that they didn't tell their wives exactly where they were going or precisely when they'd be back. All they said was they would be on the Klamath River for a few days, and I suppose everyone just knows where that was supposed to be. Mr. Grassi said he'd call in a day or two, and he was really 'in a mood,' according to Mrs. Grassi, the Obedient Wife. Akio Mikatsu, the FBI agent — did you meet him? What did you think of him? — started singing 'Stand by Your Man,' the Tammy Wynette song, when he was telling me this. He has a really nice voice, by the way ... he said he grew up in Texas ... and he has a very odd sense of humor, for what it's worth.

"I don't think he likes Mrs. Grassi, though," she said, her voice low and serious. "Meg Grassi. I don't know what Mrs. Franzetta told Agent Mikatsu about *her* husband, but Muriel told me that Mrs. Franzetta was probably glad to get rid of 'the old codger' for a couple of days as long as he wasn't going to Tijuana."

I didn't reply for several minutes. I was stuck on her inexplicable ability to talk with people and get so much insider information — what people in my trade call the backstory. Ruth has a knack of getting people to open up, people who would normally be notoriously closed-mouthed. Especially cops. And very especially FBI agents. That ability seems out of character for her, from my point of view, because Ruth is practically a recluse by nature. If I had that ability, well, there's no telling ...

"People still go there? To Tijuana?" I asked.

"I don't think it's a safe party town anymore."

"You have an inside line on all this," I said. I couldn't get over the fact that Special Agent Mikatsu would speak to anyone outside his own department, let alone sing a country song for a civilian. Maybe he knew Ruth, or knew of the Yarn Woman from her previous investigations with the department. Or, more likely, maybe he'd been simply taken by her.

"Unfortunately, they brought their guns with them on the fishing trip," continued Ruth. "If only they'd known what was going on in Whitesboro, but they left before the town erupted and all the film and news crews arrived.

"In any case, on one unfortunate day when the fishing was particularly bad, they decided to do some target shooting at tin cans. It was the same day that we found Ebee and Nina in Wailing Wood.

"But after hearing the gunshots, something like two hundred federal agents stormed the river valley. It was early in the morning and they had just taken their positions in deep forest surrounding Mr. Grass and Mr. Franzetta."

"Oh my God," I said. "That's the incident the TV reports billed as a firefight, fraught with danger from two desperate kidnappers who didn't have a thing to do with it?" I'd followed the wall-to-wall reporting on cable, and had received the early media releases from the FBI. But I still didn't know, after reading them, what had really happened. What I had access to was clearly a cover-up.

"Exactly."

"The bloodshed ..." I said.

"Mr. Grassi was wounded in the shoulder by a rifle shot, and Mr. Franzetta was shot in the thigh at closer range. Poor men. And four agents were hit with friendly fire. Why on earth do they call it that? Sheriff Tully told us, Muriel and me, they were all in Santa Rosa General because of the trauma facility there."

"This is a tragedy."

"Very much so. And these are the agents who protect people like Senator Pike? It makes me worry, Nat. I like Senator Pike."

"How is Paul Grassi recovering? Have you heard?" I asked.

"They say he'll have permanent damage to his arm, and to his whole right side. I'm not going to get into the ballistics, but Detective Chu has all the facts if you really want to know. But I do understand that a nerve was severed, which resulted in a partial paralysis on that side. I suppose he is fortunate to be alive, but I feel badly about his situation.

"I was told that Mr. Franzetta will be okay; the bullet didn't hit his femur or the femoral artery. But he's not recovering quickly. It's a terrible way to start one's retirement." Ruth paused long enough to drink some of her coffee. "Muriel and I went and saw both of them in the hospital."

"You're kidding," I said.

"No, I'm not kidding."

"But I thought Muriel and Paul were barely on speaking terms. I thought they were longtime enemies ..."

"Yes. They are."

"Well, then why would Muriel go see him?"

"Nat, it's just the way it is. You don't get it."

"Oh." I nodded, but didn't understand.

Having emptied her cup, Ruth warmed up the coffee.

"Do you have any better stories? Something happier?" I asked.

"Yes," she said, "the one about turning Wailing Wood into a state park." She smiled broadly, her slightly skewed smile as endearing as ever.

"That would be good," I said. "I would like to hear about that. Publicly, everyone's being very closed-mouth about it. It's still very political in Sacramento."

"Hugh Pike said his mom wanted Wailing Wood to be a state park instead of trying to make it into a national park. That's what he told Muriel and me. I asked him why. Mr. Pike said that Betty Pike, his mom, didn't want the huge changes that a national park would bring to the local communities. And Hugh wants to establish what he calls an outdoor museum for children, so that will be part of it, part of the new state park."

"What kind of museum?"

"It will center on the natural history of the area. There will be science programs, scholarships, that sort of thing, for grade school and high school students. He, the senator, said it would highlight the Native American culture that had been there for centuries. He's been working it out for a few years, he said."

"What about clear title to the land?"

"That's in the works. Cailin Pike has all the paperwork. They have a lot of clout, so it will probably be finalized within six months. That's what they're saying."

"And Pritchard Clay? The senior senator? The master-mind?"

"Pritchard Clay is a Johnson, Nat. And, as you mentioned, he was a major shareholder in Northern and even now is on the board of Global. He is an evil man, and I hope to never meet him."

"We found that out, but ..."

"It's pretty clear to me that he was behind the fires at the church and library in 1986: He wanted to eliminate any evidence contrary to his purported ownership of the land."

"I'm sure he's squeaky clean ..."

"He was behind the kidnapping. I don't know if he would have allowed the children to live. I doubt it. Ebee and Nina."

"So, you're saying he threatened Pike with the lives of Ebee and Nina if Pike pursued park status for Wailing Wood?"

"Yes. Sheriff Tully knew, but I don't think Hugh Pike told anyone else. I guess he told Blain Cooper."

"For goodness sake, why didn't he go to the police?"

"Mr. Tully said he couldn't trust the federal agencies; I think maybe he knew it was Clay, and he knows Senator Clay is a dangerous and powerful man ... a man with friends in the highest places."

"Well," I said, "how did Clay contact Pike, to threaten him?"

"I don't have all the finer points, Nat. But I'm pretty sure it would have been though Mr. Mendez and the other man, the bookkeeper."

"Makes sense," I said.

"Clay's very much in the clear. And I don't think that whatever-his-name, the bookkeeper, is going to implicate him ... I mean, if he were, say, to live long enough."

"Live long enough? That's a grim prediction." Had Ruth actually said that?

"It stands to reason that the man will die in prison. We are talking about two critical things here, Nat: a considerable amount of money, and the political future of California's powerful senior senator. One man's life isn't a high price. Mr. Clay-Johnson is all business. He's already lost millions of dollars, huge millions ... all that land he thought was his, and all the timber and all the oil or whatever might be found beneath the surface. And I think that's where he's set the bar. He will not lose anything more. He's still an enormously powerful man. And he's home free, because there is not a shred of evidence against him once the bookkeeper is gone."

We were silent for a few minutes.

"God, the Pike kids are cute," she said, staring off. "And Ebee has a pretty good sense of humor."

"Senator Clay had a press conference after I got back to the city," I said. "He announced his full support of a state or federal purchase of Wailing Wood to establish a park ... the very thing he's been fighting for ten years. And he said he would lobby for more physical protection for senators and congressmen and their families, after the Pike kidnapping. He said something about introducing a bill on that."

Ruth looked at me. "Of course. What else would you expect?"

I couldn't argue with that. Politicians are very much the survivors.

"He's a scoundrel," she said, and shrugged, like it would never matter. "Hugh Pike is going to give the land to the state or the federal government, free if he has to. But if they actually do get federal backing, he said all the money would go into a fund for trails and infrastructure, and to build and maintain the outdoor museum and the visitor center. They're arranging for the baskets that Jim Miller and his crew dug up to be a major display. Actually, most of the artifacts from the midden will be there. It's an amazing collection with all the tribal history. Either way, he's giving it all away. And he's not rich. Did you see his shoes?"

"He probably has trouble getting shoes that large."

"Hugh Pike isn't rich, and he could have been. That says volumes about him, I mean, if you'd never met him.

"I'm not rich, either, Nat," she said happily. "But I've got a lot of yarn ..." She paused. "Tons." Ruth looked up at me as we sat in the quiet of the Avaluxe lobby. "I have some great merino from last year's dyeing; it's a silvery green from mugwort and fig leaves. I've been saving it. And I've got Mary Wayland's old pattern. It's a real treasure. Such a traditional design, and at the same time so unique. So," her voice soft, "do you want a sweater?"

I didn't know what to say. My heart caught in my throat. I tried to put my cup down without dropping it.

I think I said, "Yes," or something like that.

WAILING WOOD

CPSIA information can be obtained at www.ICGtesting.com
Printed in the USA
LVOW08s0507110716

495800LV00003B/169/P